the Passage Waglisla

A novel by
Gaye Burton-Coe

To purchase the author's book: gayeburtoncoe@gmail.com

Web Site: https://canambooks.com/store
Author's email: gayeburtoncoe@gmail.com

Book cover design and page layout: Kate McDonnell
Cover art: Captain Richard Carpenter (Du'klwayella), Heiltsuk, Waglisla, circa 1860.
Seattle Art Museum, photographed by Joe Mabel, Wikimedia Commons.

Editing: Sharon Lax

ISBN : 978-1-9992412-0-9 the Passage Waglisla

CanAmBooks.com

Dedication

For my parents,
the late Clayton Lawrence Burton & Elizabeth Catherine Burton
& for the Cast and Crew of the 1984 Features Project
and the 1985 Bella Bella Project.

Note to the Reader

Waglisla (IR #1) (Bella Bella) is the remaining village of the Indigenous Heiltsuk peoples who, before contact, lived on the islands of the Canadian archipelago, as well as on the mainland of the Central Coast of British Columbia. This novel takes place in 1981-82 and is meant to represent only a window into the vibrant community history of Waglisla. The English translation of Waglisla is: 'Stream Emptying onto a Sandy Beach.' It is called by many, 'Bella Bella.' 'The Passage' is not a frequently used term, but is the one closest to my heart, and the one I use most often in this novel. Some facts around Waglisla have been altered to fit the timeline of the novel. So, for example, the high school was not completed in 1983, but rather the Bella Bella K-12 Community School was completed in 1977.

Most of the archaeological sites are real, and for some, facts have been changed to suit the narrative of the story. The location of the sites is intentionally vague to ensure that they will not be disturbed. The actual events and characters depicted in the novel are purely fictitious. Franz Boas's life, as documented here, is based on evidence presented by many biographers. His conversations with the main protagonist are purely fictional.

The inspiration for this story is the result of archival research in 1984, and archaeological fieldwork that I conducted in Heiltsuk territories in 1985.

Prologue

I spoke to Franz Boas in a dream last night. We were walking all about Xvnis, which is north and east of the Passage. In the dream, the houses were still standing, and many, many people were there. They were cooking, and carving, and gathering shellfish by the low tide pools, and visiting in groups of three or four. The children were laughing on the beach and playing hide and seek, running swiftly through the deep greens of the forest. I could hear the cry of a raven, and it echoed along the beach, up the mountains, and finally towards the sky.

Franz Boas did not speak, but bided his time, and we walked together along the path to the springs that lie near the rock bluff on the eastern side of the village. It is these springs that give the village its name Franz Boas told me —'Xvnis,' which means 'Springwater.' The sweet smell of the springs, and the cedar, and the Douglas fir, and the rich growth of ferns filled me with a deep sense of peace.

We stopped by a pool and he gazed into it, and then said, "Look back." Following his eyes, I looked into the crystal-clear water, and I saw pieces of my life in random memories. In the vivid images of the pool, it is morning, and I am poring over topographical maps with Jack. Evening, and I am running down a dark road with Nadine. Afternoon, and I am in Maggie's living room, holding the strands of cedar as she weaves them into a basket. It is evening again, and I am taking a bath in the old tub on Daniel's front porch. Through the mist from the hot water, I can see across the Passage to the islands of the Canadian Archipelago. Beyond this, to the east, the coastal mountain ranges are navy blue against the evening sky.

In the dream, I looked back into the eyes of Franz Boas, and his eyes were twinkling, and the hint of a smile lightened his face. I smiled back at him and I knew that my eyes were filled with the joy with which one greets an old, dear friend. He gestured for me to continue looking back. I did, and my eyes settled on the fine sand at the bottom of the pool, and on the rocks and pebbles there, which I know are sacred. And then my memories landed, without fear, on Hecate Strait, and then those memories started at the beginning...

Chapter 1

The waters of Hecate Strait are among the most dangerous in the world. The strait separates the Queen Charlotte Islands, which the Indigenous people call Haida Gwaii, from the mainland of British Columbia. At the southern end of Haida Gwaii, Hecate Strait is one hundred and forty kilometers wide and stretches to the north for two hundred and sixty kilometers, at which point it narrows for forty-eight kilometers, until it merges with Dixon Entrance. From here, fifty kilometers to the north, is the tip of Prince of Wales Island, Alaska, where the marine A–B Line, the international boundary that separates the United States from Canada, remains under dispute.

The strait, called, 'Seegaay,' after a powerful chief of the Haida Gwaii, has the strongest winds in Canada. This, along with the shallow waters of the strait, leads to violent and unpredictable storms. In the winter months, north and northwesterly winds of over two hundred kilometers per hour have been recorded. In the summer and fall, intense and volatile storms, driven by southerly and southwesterly fronts, pound through the strait.

The Northwest Coast Canadian Archipelago contains some of the richest marine life in the world and is home to halibut, herring, shellfish and salmon. In mid-September, in 1982, seiners in the North Canadian Fishing Fleet set out to fish an opening some sixty kilometers west of the northern tip of Haida Gwaii. Sockeye, the most valued of the five salmon species, were running, and a good catch meant payments could be made on boats and houses and money could be set aside for the following year.

On a sunny day, with only a trifling breeze moving across the water and a forecast for good weather for three days, seiners in the fleet arrived at the location on the day before the opening.

The captain and five crewmembers of the seine boat, *Caelum*, like all the seasoned members of the Northern Fleet, were cynical about the unpredictable forecasts and hoped to catch their quota of sockeye on the first day. The *Caelum* set out immediately after the opening was announced by the Department of Fisheries and headed north from the North Central Coast village of Waglisla, called 'the Passage' by some of the locals, and 'Bella Bella' by others and by white people. The crewmember, Grimm, always convinced that each trip out would be their last, said to Matt, the skipper, and Daniel, the first mate and co-owner of the boat, "Hecate Strait? We're doomed."

At first light on the day of the opening, the fifty-sixty-foot long seine boats were scattered throughout the area of the opening, and nets were fed out from the sterns of the boats. These nets were attached to a skiff, which traveled a short distance from the seiners. The seine boats ran large circles around the schools of fish and then returned to the skiffs, joining the two ends of the nets. A line, called the purse line, strung through with large metal rings on the bottom of the nets, drew the net together and trapped the fish, which were pulled in by power blocks. The blocks were mechanized winches, powered by hydraulic pumps, which were, in turn, run by the powerful main engines of the seiners.

By early afternoon, the hold of the *Caelum* was three-quarters full, and one more round would mean a full load. Many of the other seiners were fully loaded and heading back to the mainland.

Sailors often speak with gestures and eyes. Matt and Daniel exchanged looks with the other crewmembers when a barely perceptible shift in the wind occurred from a southwesterly direction. This wind quickly picked up, and the always shifting waters of Hecate Strait moved faster and higher. Cumulus clouds, touched to pure white by sunlight, moved quickly across the blue sky, driven by the front coming in from the southwest. Beyond this, chaotically rolling clouds tumbled over each other in grays and blacks and rose over the southern horizon of Haida Gwaii. In minutes, this horizon disappeared, hidden by what looked like delicate wisps hanging down from the clouds but which were driving rain coming in with the storm.

Grimm, whose doom and gloom personality was balanced by his reputation for being one of the most skilled pursers on the Coast, was in place for the final sweep. He was clearly visible because of the bright orange, state of the art, life jacket that he wore; this, along with the three life buoys he kept in the skiff, made him the object of constant derision by other fishermen, to which he would sometimes respond, "You're laughing now, but when they pry your cold dead fingers from the little piece of what's left of your boat, you won't be laughing, and I'll be drinking shooters in Vancouver."

His words would become part of the often-macabre legends of the entire coastal fleet.

The incoming storm moved so quickly that it seemed, even to the men who had fished on the Coast for most of their lives, like a series of rapid and disjointed picture frames from a surreal movie. The *Caelum* began to visibly pitch from side to side, and with each roll the fish in the hold shifted, adding to the rocking motion of the boat. Matt brought the stern of the seiner into the direction of the oncoming waves, stabilizing the boat. The weight of the no longer shifting cargo added to this stability.

Despite the often-unpredictable forecasts, every vessel that travels the Pacific Northwest Coast is tuned into the Coast Guard Weather Watch. Matt and Daniel heard what was, now, an unnecessary gale force storm warning for the northern Hecate Strait. Matt relayed this information to Grimm via a handheld portable radio and told him to release the net—they were winching up and getting out. Grimm replied through a lens of static, "You tell those friggin' freaks at the Weather Watch, 'Thanks tips.'"

The chatter on the radio between the seiners, which earlier in the day had been light-hearted, brimming with bragging and generally bad jokes, changed to controlled, terse commentary as the seiners kept watch on themselves, and on the others.

Daniel and the other crewmembers picked up gear from the deck and shoved it into lockers, while at the same time pulling out and struggling into life jackets. The powerful block of the *Caelum* was pulling in the net, but it came in slower than it should—Grimm had not released the net. Matt radioed again to Grimm to let the line go. Grimm told him that the line was tangled around the skiff. Daniel, monitoring the incoming net, understood what was happening from Grimm's struggles and in an exaggerated gesture pulled his arm across his neck, signaling Grimm to cut the line. As it was pulled onto the power block, the net was growing tighter and tighter, straining against the winch. Daniel signaled to Ray, a nineteen-year-old Indigenous man, from Prince Rupert, who had been with the crew for three years, to turn off the winch. Grimm finally managed to cut the line, and Ray turned the winch back on and began to guide the incoming net. Gaff, whose stock name fitted his weathered fifty-year-old face, helped Ray.

On the radio, the skipper of the *Echo Cove* asked Matt what the hell was going on. In a tone that had moved up a pitch but was still controlled, Matt replied that the net was tangled and they were pulling it in now.

"Hurry, Matt. Hurry, Daniel, hurry all of you" was the simple reply.

What happened next happened very quickly. The waves, now five meters high, became increasingly steeper. Then the rain came, not gradually, but instantly, cutting sideways across the strait. With the nets cut, the *Caelum* was almost on top of the skiff, and Gaff threw and then threw again a line to Grimm.

On the radio, Matt heard the skipper of the *Echo Cove* coming in again, and this time he was shouting, "The *Regulus* is swamped—Jesus, she's going down!" For a moment after that, his words were inaudible because he had turned sideways to tell his first mate to get the coordinates.

Daniel struggled on to the helm with a life jacket for Matt. Then the *Caelum* moved down swiftly and steeply off the crest of a wave. Daniel and Matt staggered and slid forward into each other. The wheel spun out of control, and the boat swung sideways in a 180-degree turn. There was no time for a Mayday. The *Caelum* rolled violently. In a few seconds, the port side was perpendicular to a trough, with the deck almost touching the water. Like pieces in a game of pick-up sticks, the crew on the deck slid in all directions and over and on top of each other in a downwards motion, before they fell into the water. For a few seconds, Gaff held onto a steel pole that supported the railing on the deck, and then he too went overboard. The seine boat righted one more time. Matt and Daniel knew the next pitch would be the last. They struggled down the stairs from the helm, then jumped just ahead of the wave that swamped the boat, Matt holding his life jacket under his right arm. Daniel lost his footing in the last pitch and twisted sideways as he jumped, hitting his head against the deck of the boat.

The freezing water prevented immediate unconsciousness. Daniel could barely swim, and even if he could, it would be of little value in fighting the storm-driven water. Each time he rose from a trough, he could see the skiff—and more than one crewmember was in it—but who? Grimm was throwing him a lifebuoy, and once he did manage to catch it before he slid down from another wave that pulled it from his grasp.

His life did not flash before his eyes, only a series of pictures that slowly faded into one another. On a beach far up Roscoe Inlet, there was Charlie, much younger, but still with many fine wrinkles around his eyes, telling Daniel a story and then making him carefully repeat it. Across the Inlet, the sun rose over the mountains, spilling soft violets and oranges across a cerulean sky. There was an image of Rose and Laney, whispering and laughing in the kitchen, while they jarred fish. There was Maggie, looking old and fragile, and Daniel himself, fourteen and frightened, but Maggie telling him that it was time to come home. There was Laura, looking defiant at the airstrip at the Passage that first time, and then an image of her sitting with him on the beach, where a fire alternately illuminated and shadowed her face. Laura again, turning to look up at him with her half-smile. Would she write about him? Would she tell his story—would she get the bits and pieces, right? She was a collector of stories and was becoming a teller—and a human being wants their story to be known. Then there was an orca whale jumping in the near distance, creating its own surf in a calm ocean. In front of the orca was a transparent pole on which the Whale was carved in bas relief. The images began to fade into darkness, but there was one more—one that was sharply defined. It was Jenny, her long dark hair blowing about, looking at him with huge dark eyes that looked much older than her nine-year-old face. Behind her was a solid, carved pole crested with the Raven. Her huge dark eyes were angry, almost accusing. She raised her hand into a flat palm which spoke to the connectedness and line of ancestors that stood behind her, and behind him. Defiantly, she spoke to him in Heiltsuk, in a voice heard only in his head: "You cannot come this way."

He renewed his struggle.

Somehow all the crew had managed to make it to the skiff, except for Daniel. Grimm frantically struggled out of his rubber boots and rubber overalls, pulled a buoy over his head and jumped into the freezing water. He worked desperately to reach the unstable point of orange that was Daniel's life jacket, visible for seconds…and then invisible.

By early evening, the storm moved into Dixon Entrance and died out as it moved east over the coastal mountain ranges. At dawn the next day, the Canadian Coast Guard out of Prince Rupert dispatched a plane and two helicopters to search the area where not two, but three seiners in the North Canadian Fishing Fleet had gone down. At 8 a.m., their American cousins from the United States Coast Guard in Kodiak, Alaska joined the search. The two countries often aided each other in dealing with disasters at sea. There was no fog that morning; the sea was serene, and a brilliant sun climbed from behind the coastal mountain ranges of the mainland. Visibility across Hecate Strait was unlimited, aiding in the search for the three missing seiners. By 9 a.m., pieces of wreckage in the area were spotted. But no rafts, no evidence of anyone in the water.

Early in the day, the Coast Guard issued a release that the *Aldebaran*, out of Masset, in the Queen Charlottes; the *Regulus*, out of Prince Rupert, and the *Caelum*, out of Waglisla, had gone down in the waters of Hecate Strait, and the combined Coast Guards of Prince Rupert and Kodiak were searching the area for survivors.

The announcement was unnecessary to the people in the villages and towns of the Coast, most of whom were speaking in whispers. Seine boats, like many vessels, are named after stars. *Aldebaran*, from the Arabic, is the name of the most brilliant star in the constellation, Taurus. *Regulus* is the Latin name for another bright star in the constellation, Leo. *Caelum* is the Latin name for a constellation visible in the Southern Hemisphere. Three stars had gone down in Hecate Strait.

Chapter 2

When I was still quite young, I came to live on the Heiltsuk Indian Reserve, Waglisla, located on the Central Coast of British Columbia. I came to this place as the result of a series of coincidences. It was my first year working on a master's degree in Archaeology, at Simon Fraser University, and my undergraduate specialty was in the area of excavating, identifying, cataloguing and analyzing faunal remains. In my first summer of graduate school, I worked at a Plains Indians' bison bone kill site in Alberta. The endless faunal remains left me feeling bored, almost apathetic. I realized I was in the wrong area of research and found myself without anything to say when my fellow graduate students talked enthusiastically about the bones.

That summer, while most of the department was conducting research in the field, an unknown person accidentally, or by design, unplugged six large freezers that contained the remains of animals that were to have been rendered to bone to enhance our comparative faunal collection. Most of these were road kills, collected by enthusiastic undergraduates and astute workers in the Ministry of Forests. The unplugged freezers had been left propped open and were discovered in July, when the stench filled the faunal lab and began to infiltrate into the corridor until it came to the to the attention of a security guard. For a long time, students and faculty discussed how the freezers had become not only unplugged but had been left wide open; this was a topic of considerable speculation and gossip. Stories became increasingly unbelievable with each passing week, but the event was eventually relegated to myth, and the mystery remained forever unsolved.

In September, the beer in the Student Union Pub flowed freely, as students competed to relate some exaggerated and some not exaggerated stories of field adventures and romances that could only have occurred under field conditions. We were joined by several faculty members, and discussions around romance quickly transitioned to more academic topics. I admitted to Dr. George Clements, who sat next to me, that I had lost my enthusiasm for bones, adding that my apathy was greatly affected by the thought of spending hours doing analysis in the windowless faunal lab, where huge amounts of disinfectants and other chemical agents had barely made a dent in the smell of decomposing meat.

George responded to my comment with "Well, I've never felt an affinity for bison bones, although I do find fish bones quite interesting."

I had taken several undergraduate courses with George and felt very comfortable with him; I rolled my eyes at his remark about fish bones.

Dr. George Clements was brilliant, eccentric and perhaps knew more about the prehistoric Indigenous cultures of the Pacific Northwest Coast than anyone in the world. The advances he had made in techniques for excavating coastal sites were revolutionary, and for this he was renowned. He was close to sixty and refused to join the current trend in Archaeology for identifying laws of culture. His theoretical orientation was that of the turn-of-the-century anthropologist Franz Boas, whose theory of relativity stated that the only way to understand a culture was from within the context of that culture. George's students, who favored the current archaeological paradigm that all cultures could be explained in terms of functional laws, forgave him for his out-of-date theoretical stance because his humility and contacts had paved the way for two generations of research on the Coast.

"Why don't you come by my office tomorrow, Laura? I have some work that might interest you very much."

That night, I went for a long walk through the streets of Deep Cove and reflected on my lack of interest in my graduate research work. I had done fine in my undergraduate faunal courses but had really been interested in human osteology—the study of human bones. My chances of working on sites with human bones was nil. Understandably, First Nations people took umbrage at having their ancestors dug up and analyzed. Currently, there was talk of repatriating human remains from the labs at Simon Fraser University. I felt depressed and wondered what George Clements had to say about something that "might interest me." And even though I was twenty-six years old, which is very young when I look back now, I felt back then that I was too old to change careers.

When I got home, I called my friend Joanna to tell her of my worries. I was friends with most of the graduate students in the Department of Archaeology, but no one was as close to me as Jo. We'd been roommates for most of our undergraduate years and agreed on many theories in Archaeology. Jo had landed on her feet with primate studies and spent her research time in exotic places, studying primates. When I called her and told her my concerns, she agreed with me. "I just never figured you for a bone person." She went on to say that the human osteology was the only one I shined in, and, as she pointed out, the general feeling was that if you found any human remains, the solution was to instantly cover them up.

"Laura, see what George has up his sleeve. He thinks you're the cat's meow, and I am sure he has something that will interest you. It must be something about the Pacific Northwest Coast, and you got an A+ in that course, as well as in his course on Indigenous Cultures of British Columbia. He thinks you're bright and interesting, so keep an open mind and see what he has to say."

I was encouraged by Joanna's advice and spent half an hour wandering about the house, thinking about a change in research directions, listening to Neil Young. My house was a great comfort to me. I had bought it the year before, a purchase made possible by an advance on my inheritance from my Grandfather Fitzgerald. The house was on the beach in Deep Cove, a suburb of North Vancouver, and was all windows and light. The rooms facing the beach had large windows, and the dining and living room had glass balcony doors. There was a family room, a dining room, a front room, a kitchen, a bathroom and a laundry room on the main floor. The kitchen and laundry room were at the back of the house. The four bedrooms were upstairs, two with en-suites. When I'd bought the house, I'd also bought most of the contents, minus some valuable antiques and artwork. It was an estate sale, and the sellers had little need of furniture. The lady who'd owned the home had mostly casual taste in furniture. So, to make it my own, I added a few pieces, put prints on the walls and rearranged some of the furniture. I looked at my collection of Pacific Northwest Coast art and then poured myself a glass of wine and sat in the family room, looking out at what was now a nearly dark beach.

The next day, George told me of amazing sites on the West Coast, many of these in the area of Waglisla, the main village of the Heiltsuk peoples, whose traditional territories occupied much of the mainland Central Coast. He had done extensive ethnographic and archaeological work in this area and had established a network of friends and connections amongst the Heiltsuk. The sites he showed me contained architectural remains that hadn't been fully documented, and he suggested that I finish the work he started many years before but hadn't been able to return to because of other commitments. I could use the sites as a basis for my thesis and come up with a method to ameliorate against the loss of the artifacts.

He showed me old navigational charts. The sites were marked in red ink. But it was the photographs that intrigued me. George's skill as a photographer was widely known; he'd captured in black and white a dramatic record of the past. He showed me 8 x 10 photographs of fallen house beams, lying in perfect linear progression on the forest floor. On a few of the beams, bits of moss had been removed to expose perfectly adzed surfaces. Some of the house posts were still standing. Others were leaning at a precarious angle, held up by the surrounding forest. The carving, done in bas relief, showed the motifs of the raven, grizzly, bear and raven. The moss, growing in the linear cracks in the cedar gave a haunting dignity to the sculptures. I was mesmerized by what seemed like a tragic record of the past.

"Sadly," said George, "archaeologists have paid little attention to this class of artifacts, termed, 'wooden features.' The interest has always been in the sites below the features and has focused on excavation. Now these sites are disappearing, and your research goal would be to mitigate this loss, mainly by coming up with proper documenting procedures."

Although fascinated by this research topic, I had some questions. "George, would I fit in up there? Would I be accepted?"

"As long as a person has some humility, I have found, they can fit in anywhere. Listen, Laura. I would never send you up there blind. I have a friend and contact, Chief Charlie Hunt, who will take you under his wing. Most of the informants and guides I had are long gone, but Charlie Hunt will be able to set you up with others. And all of you graduate students have been trained since Day 1 to have respect for First Nations cultures; this will serve you well. You might be an oddity at first, but you will soon fit in because you have the right personality. As well, in the grant I'll be applying for, you will have two young Heiltsuk people to be your assistants; this will help you to be part of the village as well."

George assigned several courses I would need to take in the next two semesters, and he applied for funding for me from a government heritage foundation, to conduct research in Waglisla.

This turn in direction meant that I had a lot of work to do. Although I'd excavated at several coastal sites, it was in the capacity of a laborer, not as project head. There were a lot of gaps in my knowledge of the cultures of the Northwest Coast. In the next two semesters, I took a graduate seminar course from George and another course in the Anthropology Department. When not in class, I found that my mind was constantly occupied, as I tried to understand and integrate complex kinship, economic, artistic and other aspects of the Northwest Coast.

I sometimes felt overwhelmed by the work but kept my perspective, mainly with Joanna's support. When I told her about my new direction, she replied, "I know, George told me about it, and I told him to make sure you get a decent wage. You know my motto: you pay—I go."

Her clever and saucy remarks, aimed, without prejudice, at both professors and fellow students, were too much a part of her sparkling personality to ever get her into trouble.

In March, the funding came through, and George arranged the trip to Waglisla. The project would last for three months in the field. My crew would consist of two young Heiltsuk people from Waglisla: students who had just completed high school on Vancouver Island. We would resurvey the sites my supervisor had located some fifteen years before, look for others and talk to Elders in the village of Waglisla about the history of the sites.

I left for Waglisla in mid-June 1981. Preparations for the trip had kept me busy, but on the flight from Vancouver to Waglisla, I had time to think. I felt nervous, but also tired, and drifted off into a half-dream about my childhood.

Victoria and Toronto, 1960s

Michael was my older brother, and he was my hero. He was my safety net, protecting me from the rages and inconsistencies of my father. I was five years younger than my brother. Maybe our age difference was the reason we rarely fought. Michael played with me if none of his friends were around. I was a hostage to be rescued or an enemy to be done away with, but usually the former because I was too small to present a real challenge. He frequently teased me but never allowed his friends to do so. When I was seven, we made a formal pact that we would never rat out on each other.

I loved Michael very much, and because he took it upon himself to shelter me from my father, I also needed him. Father mainly ignored me, although on occasion he'd beat me with a belt, striking my legs with swift, hard strokes. The crimes I remember were scraping the paint on his car with my bicycle, telling a teacher I really was just plain stupid and not minding the rigorous manners demanded at the dinner table. Sometimes he struck me hard across the head. One instance stood out the most. I had used the expression, "eh?" Father said that only very low-class people used this term.

But it was mainly my brother who was the constant object of Father's anger, and on many occasions, Michael would take responsibility for our joint ventures and save me from physical rebuke.

There was a time when I tried to figure out why my father was who he was. But by the time I was in my early twenties, I had stopped trying to understand and was long past caring.

My brother became an expert at avoiding Father; in fact, both of us avoided him, eased by the fact that we lived in a very large house in the Uplands area of Victoria, at the back of which was a small, untended area with a stand of Western red cedar, huckleberry bushes and a tree house built by a former owner. Here, Michael and I retreated and played for hours, undisturbed. In the winter, we could play in the basement, which was old and musty and huge.

It was from our grandfather that Michael and I received unconditional love and enduring values. My grandfather was not demonstrative, but he showed his love for us by giving us his absolute attention whenever we visited. Towards the end of the school year, we marked off the days on a calendar until we could go to his house in Toronto for a month every summer.

Grandpa took considerable interest in the complex negotiations we worked out for the various games we played. Not only did he not disapprove but encouraged what we thought of as raucous behavior. We could go pretty much anywhere we wished in his house, the only rule being that we must leave each room as we found it.

We always had an excursion on Sundays, perhaps to a baseball game, or a drive in the country and, after that, dinner at McDonald's. Grandfather was concerned that we be knowledgeable and independent thinkers. In the evenings, we read the Globe and Mail, *and he'd quiz us. If we were able to answer eight out of ten questions, which we always did because of the hints he provided, we could watch our favorite TV shows. When he was thirteen, Michael, in imitation of Grandpa, graduated to reading* The Economist, *leaving me scornfully behind.*

Deep in my thoughts of the past, I barely noticed the passenger sitting next to me, but her remark brought me back to the present. I said something in reply and noticed that she was looking at my hand. I had been unconsciously picking at the cuticle of my thumb, which was now bleeding slightly: an old habit. My seatmate was maybe in her early thirties and both witty and down to earth. Her name was Sue Mitchell, and she worked as a nurse at the Passage. Seeing the puzzled look on my face, she said that many people referred to Waglisla as 'The Passage' and that some of the First Nations people there called the village 'Bella Bella.' To me, it would always be 'the Passage.'

Engaged in conversation, I'd barely noted that we were descending. On the roughly four-hundred-kilometer flight from Vancouver, we had flown north-northwest above cloud cover. I would learn flights were often cancelled because of heavy fog. As we descended below the cloud cover, I couldn't see the Reserve but only a rush of islands and the high, sharp mountains of the mainland to the east. The pilot flew towards these mountains and then banked sharply back towards the islands, where I saw thick forest cover and a small lake. We landed on a gravel airstrip, with a bungalow-type structure off to one side.

Various people came to meet the passengers. A misty rain was falling, and I was wondering where my ride was, when an old pick-up drove up to the cargo-hold on the plane. What I assumed was a Heiltsuk man got out and chatted with the pilot; both looked at me and simultaneously nodded. They started to unload my gear into the pick-up, and I went over and added my hand luggage to the growing pile. When they were finished, the pilot and the man talked for a while, laughed about something and then shook hands. I thought they were pretty much leaving me out and was working up some pique, when the Indigenous man looked at me and quietly said my name as a question: "Laura Fitzgerald?"

I nodded, and he motioned for me to get into the truck. We drove along a gravel road through dense stands of Douglas fir and Western red cedar. I asked him if it was far to the village. "No," he answered. That was all. Following his cue, I lapsed into silence, feeling very uncomfortable. I glanced sideways. He didn't look uncomfortable. Must be cultural, I thought, drawing on everything I'd learned from my course work, from novels and from TV. As we traveled towards the village, curiosity replaced my unease at the silence.

The Passage lies on the northeast side of Campbell Island, in the heart of the West Coast Canadian Archipelago. The large island is about eighteen kilometers from the mainland. In all directions, there are islands of varying sizes. The islands stand in low relief against the imposing Coastal Mountain Ranges and are made up of rolling hills and steep bluffs. They often contain both sandy and rocky beaches. East of the Reserve are the narrow waters of the Passage, and directly across from Waglisla is Denny Island. The waterways in this area form part of what is referred to as the Inside Passage, which is the route used by large vessels, notably the BC ferry that travels from Port Hardy to Prince Rupert.

Coming around a curve, the forest thinned out on my left, and a large area of tall beach grass ran up from the beach along what seemed like dunes. Beyond this, were the waters of the Passage; a fog obscured Denny Island, east along the Passage, beyond a narrow stretch of ocean that separated the two islands. A single small bungalow was located on a hillock in the beach grass at the. Smoke drifted in no particular pattern from the tin chimney.

After passing this area, about a kilometer up, the forest enclosed the road again, then thinned out. Houses were scattered intermittently on either side. Soon, the distances between the houses became smaller. The road widened and ran parallel to the beach that fronted the village. Houses on the ocean side of the road were set back some distance from the beach, and on the other side of the road, where the ground sloped upward, the houses were built on four and five terraces that paralleled the beach. The community was larger than I'd expected, perhaps because the houses stretched along these terraces and along the beach for some distance. We came to a store with a large sign on the front, 'Waglisla Band Store.' Next to it was a wharf, with a large, adjacent building.

From here, we turned uphill and drove about two hundred meters, passing more houses, then turned left. On the corner of this road, on the left, was a large white-paneled United Church. Across the road from the Church, we turned into a narrow dirt lane; at the end was the United Church Manse: my home for the summer. The last minister had been transferred in May, and the new one was not expected until October.

It was a large, gabled house, painted white like the church, and looked out of place among the houses I'd seen so far. George had arranged everything for me. I was beginning to realize how little I'd really done for 'my' project.

"You'll want your boxes and gear in the basement?" my companion asked.

"Yes, please."

He reversed the truck, and we unloaded my gear through a basement door around the side of the house. We carried my luggage up to the front door, which was unlocked. I thanked him. Nodding, he said, "Charlie Hunt says you should come for supper at 6:00."

"Who is Charlie Hunt?"

"The Chief Councilor," he said, grinning. "You had better come."

I was not expecting that smile. It extended from his beautiful white teeth to his dark eyes, which glinted with humor. For the first time, I noticed he was very tall; then, remembering who Charlie Hunt was, I stammered, "How will I get there?"

"Someone will pick you up."

"Thank you for the help." I reached out to shake his hand. He hesitated. Now it was my turn to smile. I knew he was aware that I was perhaps being too formal, that maybe he found me ignorant. Maybe he hadn't met many professionals. I did consider myself a 'professional.' But he returned the handshake with a strong grip and squarely met my look of amusement.

He nodded again…and was gone. And so, I'd met Daniel, although after he left, it occurred to me that he hadn't told me his name.

Chapter 3

The house that would be my base for the summer was large and resembled the type that dates to the Victorian era, wherever the British have been. The front entrance opened onto a landing, to the right of which was a small living room. A set of French doors off this room led to a large, formal dining room. From here, a pair of outdated half height doors led to an equally large kitchen. Expensive but well-worn rugs covered the wooden floors in the living and dining areas. There were several other rooms on the main floor: a study, a small bedroom and a bathroom. On the second floor there were more bedrooms and another bathroom.

Heavy fabric curtains covered most of the windows. The manse was completely furnished and included dishes, cutlery, pots and pans. It was an odd assortment of furniture, with a worn, contemporary recliner and sofa mixed in with what looked like valuable antique coffee tables and lamps.

I went through the kitchen to a steep set of stairs that led to the basement, where my books, charts, maps and office supplies had been unloaded. The basement contained an assortment of junk, mostly old furniture. It also contained what looked like a brand-new washer and dryer, a lawn mower and vacuum cleaner. Stacked in one corner was a fair supply of firewood and kindling. The smell of must was strong, and I propped open the basement door with an old chair. In back, a white fence surrounded the overgrown backyard.

The house was clean, but even houses that have been shut up accumulate dust, especially in places with gravel roads. After dragging up my supplies from the basement, I opened all the curtains and windows on the main floor, put my books and maps in the study and my suitcases in the main floor bedroom, realizing as I did so that this room had originally been intended for a servant.

The mist had cleared, but it was still cool, and I put my anorak back on and headed outside. On that first walk, heading downhill in the direction of the store and the wharf, I passed several people, all of whom nodded to me with a greeting that sounded to my untrained ears like "Mmph." I would come to understand that this had many meanings, including: "Hello," "Goodbye," "How are you?" or "Is everything okay?"

The air smelled salty, damp and clean, even though it was mingled with smoke from woodstoves. I could hear the constant screech of seagulls, occasionally interspersed with a raven's call.

The Waglisla Band Store contained a basic selection of foods, clothes, household goods and hardware. The meat and produce selection were scanty. Later I learned that most of the residents at the Passage depended on a staple of salmon and deer. Moose was highly sought after, and the residents of the village hunted or traded for moose in the Interior.

I had a purchase order for the Band Store and was directed to an office at the back. The middle-aged woman there seemed to me to be very much a clerk, an observation I made based on the interesting relationship she had with her adding machine, which she continued to punch figures into as she talked to me. She started a ledger card for my purchase order. I told her that I had quite a few things to buy and asked if it would be all right to take the shopping cart home.

She looked puzzled. "Sure," she said. "But we do have home delivery. It's only two dollars."

"That's good. I'm living in the United Church Manse. Thank you," I stuttered, feeling embarrassed.

"I know, and you're welcome." She grinned, and once again, I was overwhelmed by a brilliant white smile and dark-eyed humor.

At the manse, I started to unpack my gear. Soon, a white, obviously new van, with "Dodd's Delivery" printed on the side, delivered my groceries. I put these away. The house was warmer, the rain and fog burned away by the hot sun. Changing into shorts and a t-shirt, I went out again, this time to explore the village.

My walk took me down to the wharf next to the Band Store. Across the road from the store and the road that led to the wharf, was the large two-story structure that I'd seen on my way that morning. I turned around, looking at the somewhat dilapidated building. Across the beachside, a large sign, painted in red, stated that this was the "Waglisla Hotel, Restaurant and Pub."

Along the western side of the wharf, a set of stairs led to orderly, marine walkways, where seine boats and trollers were moored. On the other side of the wharf were differently sized cabin cruisers and punts, large metal, flat-bottomed boats used to haul herring.

The wharf stretched out into the Passage for maybe seventy-five meters; it was wide, and could accommodate a large vehicle and, maybe, with a bit of crowding, two-way traffic. It ended in a thirty-meter T shape. On the south side was a marine and gas station, and on the other side of the T, an aluminum rectangular structure. There were no railings at this end of the wharf, a point that puzzled me for a bit before I realized this was where cargo was unloaded.

I sat on the lip of the dock, with my legs dangling over the edge. Men came and went from the gas station. I knew they were looking at me and maybe talking about me amongst themselves, but I didn't care because my senses were drawn into the landscape.

Across the Passage, thick stands of Douglas fir and Western red cedar grew in tiers on Denny Island. Like the village, the gentle slope was probably much steeper than it looked. In front of the island, a rock face dropped steeply into the sea; at high tide, the water came almost to the tree line. The distance separating Campbell and Denny Islands seemed very narrow, and I wondered how the huge ferry that ran from Port Hardy to Prince Rupert navigated through the Passage. To the south, where the Passage opened, groups of islands stretched out toward the open sea. A salt-and-pepper beach fronted this side of the island. The same beach continued north from where I sat. Together, the north and south views formed a bay, with the wharf at the bottom of the U. To the north, in the distance, were the beach grass and small house on the dune-like rise. Beyond this, the Passage opened again, and a huge formation of steep and erratic rocks crept out to sea. On the other side of the outcropping, a red and white lighthouse stood guard—like an old picture postcard.

Past the lighthouse, low lying islands lay scattered across the blue-gray sea. Beyond this, to the south and east, the coastal mountain ranges took up half the sky, row after row, seemingly endless and almost fluid against the horizon. Mist and clouds covered the tree line, and above the clouds, the gray and violet and light blues of the peaks were covered with snow on sharp crests and crevices. I sat for a long time, aware but not thinking. Eventually, I got up to return to the manse. I looked at my watch. It was 5 o'clock. At 6, I had an appointment with a chief.

George Clements had made a point of telling me that I must be careful not to offend Chief Charlie Hunt. His position in the community was one of Hereditary Chief, as he was the highest-ranking heir of his mother's lineage. As well, he was the elected Band Chief. George had explained that, in holding these two titles, Charlie Hunt set an interesting example because it remained the goal of the Canadian government to discredit and divide traditional systems of allegiance and social structure that were more difficult to manipulate. Chief Charlie Hunt had retained his elected position for eight years and was highly respected throughout the Indigenous communities of the Coast.

I washed my sun-reddened face and dressed in a longish, mute-colored printed skirt and an olive- colored sweater that drew out the green in my eyes. My hair was just past shoulder length. Aiming for a mature, professorial look, I pulled it back and added combs to keep it from falling out. Just as I finished dressing, I heard a knock on the front door.

A girl of maybe eight or nine stood, curiously appraising me.

"Hello," I said.

"I've come to bring you to Grandpa's."

"Your Grandpa must be Chief Charlie?"

She nodded.

"Great," I told her, "I'm ready to go."

She continued standing at the entrance, then said, "You gonna wear those shoes?"

"I was, but you don't think I should?"

"Grandpa lives a ways from here."

Dammit, I thought, and changed into a pair of sneakers, thus losing two inches of height and the total overall effect of the look I had attempted to achieve.

The Chief's home was about a kilometer north along the same gravel road I'd been driven down earlier that day. The young girl walked beside me quietly until I asked her name and what grade she was in. Then she kept up a steady stream of chatter Her name was Jenn. "Spelled with two n's," she said, as if admonishing me. She was going into Grade 3 in September and was glad she wasn't in Grade 9. In Grade 9, they had to go to school on Vancouver Island and live in boarding homes. I asked her how she liked school.

"Depends on the teacher," she said, shrugging, and then abruptly changed the subject with an excited discussion of how she got most of her clothes through the Sears catalogue. "Did you get your skirt from the catalogue?" she asked.

"No." I smiled, thinking that the lady who sold me the skirt would be scandalized.

"I didn't think so," said Jenn. "I haven't seen it in the catalogue. Did you know the fall one is out? I could show it to you if you haven't seen it."

"I'd like that," I told her, and we continued to discuss the fashions in the Sears catalogue, as we walked.

I told her that there didn't seem to be very many vehicles in the Passage.

"Well, that's because it's on an island. You can't drive here because there aren't any bridges, and the ferry doesn't stop here. Grandpa says we might freak out the tourists on that ferry if it docked here. Anyway, there's no way we're ever going to get a dock for that because it would cost about a billion dollars, and the Feds won't even pave the roads on a reserve."

I burst out laughing at this long discourse, then quickly covered my mouth. But Jenn didn't seem to take offense, as she continued to educate me on transportation in the Passage.

"Hardly anyone has a car, but you can pretty much walk everywhere around here, and Dodd's Delivery has a van, so it's easy to get a ride if you want one. It costs two dollars to go pretty much anywhere, except the airport—that's three dollars. Uncle Daniel has a truck, but he says it actually belongs to about a hundred people, even though he's the one who owns it."

"A hundred people?"

"Well, I guess he's lying about that," she replied conversationally.

I smiled down at her dark head of hair, wondering who Uncle Daniel was.

We continued to walk and chat companionably.

I don't know why some bits of imagery stand out. But I recall on that day, a soft, intermittent breeze blew long wisps of hair across Jenn's face and that each time this happened, she absentmindedly pulled the strands back into place. Looking back now, I realize that, somewhere on that walk, I started on a journey that would tie me to Jenny Hunt as strongly as the knot that holds a vessel to its mooring.

Chief Charlie Hunt lived on the beach side of the main street of the Passage, in a single-story house, sided with faded blue plywood. It looked as if several additions had been made over the years; on the side facing us, there was a large painted mural. I recognized the motifs of the raven and the whale. The yard facing the street was oddly distinguished by a large standing tombstone. I couldn't make out the inscription and didn't recall this as being a local burial custom. I was very curious and wondered if I could casually ask about it over dinner, then found this ridiculous, realizing that my political skills were probably nowhere near good enough.

Jenn brought me around to the front door that faced the beach. There were four or five children playing in front of the house. "Bye," she said and disappeared.

Several people were sitting in the living room, and Chief Charlie stood up, shook my hand and introduced me to what I quickly counted as six people. I automatically noted some distinguishing feature on each one, and then substituted a symbol and a letter, so that I'd remember their names. This was a mnemonic device my mother had taught me when I was very young, although I'd actually found it most useful as a way of memorizing facts for multiple-choice exams.

Laney, an attractive, petite Heiltsuk woman, maybe a few years older than I, was introduced as Chief Charlie's daughter. A baby lay on her lap, and she gently rubbed the child's tiny back. A Nordic-looking man was introduced as Matt Pederson, Laney's husband.

The men and younger people were casually dressed in t-shirts and jeans. I was overdressed, except for the sneakers. Chief Charlie's sister, Edith, her husband, Gordon, and Charlie's wife, Rose, were introduced. I thought Rose looked older than her husband, perhaps because she was quite slight and seemed frail in some way.

"And this, of course, is my nephew, Daniel, who you've already met," said Chief Charlie.

So, this was Daniel. He nodded and said, "Mmph," and a chair was vacated for me next to Chief Charlie.

"My nephew got you to the house then," he said.

"Yes, thank you."

"I was going to pick you up myself but couldn't. How do you like the manse?"

"It's quite the house," I said.

"The minister lives well, eh?"

"It would appear so." There was an edge of humor to my remark. Chief Charlie grinned, and his face lit up. I began to think that there was some gene running through the population of the Passage that gave the residents this amazing smile.

Chief Charlie Hunt could have been anywhere from fifty to sixty. He was a very handsome man, with dark, sharp eyes and an even sharper mind. Around his eyes were deep laugh lines, and I learned that he had a wonderful sense of humor, tempered by an air of authority. In time, when I got to know him well, he told me about his younger years, when he worked as a fisherman and a logger, and then got lost, first in the Passage, and then in the streets of Vancouver. While he eventually assumed the responsibilities he was born to take on, there was a weathered look about him.

I had the honor of being seated next to Chief Charlie at dinner, during which he learned a great deal about me. My answers to his questions were provided in a daze of panic, as I tried to get through the main course of the meal of deer roast and baked potatoes, topped with eulachon grease and dried seaweed. The deer meat I could swallow by not breathing while chewing. Its consistency was that of roast beef but had a very gamey taste. The potatoes were more difficult, and after the first taste of eulachon grease, it took everything I had not to gag. Made from pressed herring, the grease is pungent and fishy.

I glanced up to see if anyone noticed my reaction, but I only saw Daniel across the table, his eyes filled with amusement. I noticed, at some level, that he called Chief Charlie's sister, Edith, by her first name: meaning, I supposed, that she wasn't his mother. Determined, I finished the meal but declined seconds. I was grateful for chocolate cake and ice cream for dessert and happily took seconds. Jenn asked me how come I'd had extra cake if I wasn't hungry. Thinking quickly, I told her I was addicted to chocolate, a remark that was met with an outburst of laughter from everyone.

The easy chatter, smiles, teasing and animated faces of the people around the table made me realize that the stereotyped image I had of Indigenous people as being stoic with carefully controlled faces and gestures was based mainly on television and movies. I don't think the children understood exactly what all the banter was about, but they giggled, seemingly in response to the laughter of the adults. Sometimes, both the children and adults would lapse into a dialect of the Heiltsuk language.

After supper, Chief Charlie and I discussed politics. Looking back, I realize that he was carrying on the dinner conversation while skillfully assessing my character. He didn't seem to hold my father against me. At that time, my father was a high-profile federal cabinet minister and no friend to First Nations people. I lightly told Chief Charlie that I had no influence over my father and so couldn't be used as a lobbyist. He laughed at this remark. I didn't tell him that I hadn't spoken to my father in years.

Chief Charlie said he wanted to introduce my crew to me "before I met them." By now, the table had been cleared, and everyone was sitting in the adjoining living room. In the exchange that followed, I noticed Daniel looking at me several times. Later, I'd find out he'd been looking at me whenever we were together at Chief Charlie's. After this first time, however, I didn't notice, which meant, I guess, that he'd grown better at hiding it.

When the others went into the living room, Chief Charlie left the room and returned with a briefcase which he opened on the table. He pulled out a manila file. Quietly, he said, "Your first crewmember is Jack Campbell. He has been employed by the Band for the past three years every summer, mostly with helping with Elders; for example, doing odd jobs, getting groceries and arranging appointments. Your second crew member is Kristy Mack; she also spent the last three summers working with Elders. Here are some reference letters from their supervisors."

The letters were well written and very positive. Both Jack and Kristy were punctual, had the ability to anticipate and solve problems and had, so the report stated, a positive attitude. Further, Jack was especially kind, and Kristy had an excellent sense of humor. Chief Charlie gave me copies of their final Grade 12 transcripts. Both had stellar grades. Jack had 92% and 95% in Calculus 11 and 12; Kristy had 89%

and 92% in the same subjects. Their marks in Social Studies and English were somewhat lower, but still high. Chief Charlie, with obvious pride, said that First Nations students excelled in Math but sometimes struggled with English, and the fact that "these kids were A, across the board" meant that I had a great crew lined up.

I thanked Chief Charlie for the information on the crew, and we drifted into the living room.

The discussion turned to the boat that would be used for the project. Like the budget and most other aspects of this project, arrangements for a research boat had been made by George. I learned that the boat belonged to Daniel.

"When are you going fishing?" Chief Charlie asked Daniel.

"Monday afternoon, I guess."

"Any idea when you'll be back?"

"Hard to say."

"Well, I guess you'd better familiarize Laura with that boat before then," Chief Charlie suggested.

"Sure," Daniel replied. "Monday morning." He looked at me. "8:30, at the wharf?"

There was a lull in the conversation, and Jenn, with news on the Fall Simpsons-Sears catalogue, interrupted our conversation.

"It's late, Jenny. Our friend must be tired," said Chief Charlie.

"Oh, come on, Grandpa..."

"Jenn, why don't you come by my house tomorrow afternoon, and we can look at the catalogue?" I said spontaneously.

Jenn turned pleading eyes to her grandfather, and they spoke briefly in Heiltsuk.

"Sure, that'll be fine, and now Daniel will take Laura home to the minister's house," Chief Charlie said.

On the ride home, Daniel didn't talk. A loud, booming sound cut through the village, startling me. In answer to my question, Daniel told me it was the foghorn, to let the children know it was time to stop playing and head home.

Joanna, my friend from Simon Fraser University, had told me a few years prior that when it came to flirting I was basically inept. She had taken it upon herself to teach me the ins and outs of this social grace, and I was becoming quite good at it. Both curiously and flirtatiously and based on what I had learned in my courses at school, I asked

Daniel if his mother was Chief Charlie's sister. He glanced at me out of the corner of his eye. "Yeah."

"And your family takes titles based on your mother's side?"

"Mostly."

"Are you the only nephew?…I mean, on your mother's side?"

Knowing where I was heading, he smiled a bit. "Yeah."

"So, that means, you're a chief? Or…you will be a chief?"

He shrugged; his face unreadable. I continued. "So, should I call you Chief Daniel?"

"Well no, you can just call me Daniel." His tone was even, calm.

I burst out laughing, and while he didn't laugh, he grinned; and that was enough.

After Daniel dropped me off, I found myself thinking about him and wished I could talk to Joanna about it. But I couldn't. She was in Borneo, studying chimpanzees.

Chapter 4

At some point back at Chief Charlie's, during dinner, the sky had clouded over, and rain had moved in. The manse was cold. I made a fire and started to read some old field reports of work done in the area. But I was tired and couldn't concentrate. I looked into the flames and thought about the day, at some point, drifting into sleep, with my head resting on the arm of the couch. My dream was of my brother, Michael.

Toronto and Victoria 1960s

I only ever saw Grandpa get angry once. This was when we were driving downtown and Michael saw an old woman dressed in worn, mismatched clothes, staggering slightly as she walked. Michael made a remark about a "rubby." When we got home, Grandfather sat us both down and told us never to use such slurs again.

"You should know, Michael, and you too, Laura, that my grandfather was an immigrant to this country, and when he came here, he had nothing. Everyone looked down on the Irish as being the scum of the Earth. My grandmother used newspapers in her shoes to keep warm, and she did laundry for other people to help pay for food. Two of her children died of tuberculosis, which is to say, they died of poverty. You have never had to worry about food and shelter, and it is an insult to me that you make fun of those who do not have what you do."

We were devastated by what he said and afterwards went upstairs and disappeared into our respective bedrooms. At dinner, Michael said he was sorry. I echoed the apology.

Unlike our father, Grandfather carried no grudges. He was well off and had retired from a successful law firm that he had started with two fellow lawyers. He was honest, knowledgeable and had invested wisely. My mother told me his greatest life expense was the stately home he built for my grandmother in the Toronto suburb of Etobicoke. But he lived thriftily. In the summer, on cool days, Michael turned the heat up in the house. Grandpa would turn it down, saying it was July, and no one turned the heat on in July. And so, it went. The day after the incident with the homeless woman, he told Michael that his heating bill every July was as much as the bill for the whole year. Michael sarcastically replied, "Okay, you can have my allowance."

He looked over at me and said, "Hers, too."

I jumped in with, "Hell can freeze over before anyone gets my allowance."

Grandpa laughed uproariously and said to both of us, "Well done."

We never talked about home when we were in Toronto, and my grandfather never spoke about our father, but somehow both Michael and I knew there were bad feelings between Grandfather and Father.

When he entered his teens, Michael started to rebel. He experimented with drugs. I knew him well enough to recognize it when he smoked pot. I thought that he was experimenting with other drugs as well. I worried constantly and, being well educated at school about the dangers of drugs, told Michael he was risking his life. He laughed at my fears and didn't even bother to tell me to keep my mouth shut because he knew I wouldn't tell on him.

When the police brought him home one night in possession of a small amount of marijuana, my father's anger was the worst I'd ever seen. He screamed at Michael that "no little twit" was going to ruin his career. Michael was a loser, a disgrace. He began to hit him. My mother, in a rare show of strength, intervened. She stood between my father and my brother and told Michael to go to his room. I had never seen her so strong and thought that part of that strength came from the fact that she was eight months pregnant. I sensed some changes relating to this unexpected pregnancy; it seemed as if she was daring my father to strike her. Still, my father's solution to dealing with Michael prevailed.

The solution was to send my brother to an out-of-town boarding school that had strict rules and strict consequences. It was late in the school year, but my father sent Michael out within the week. The school was in a wilderness setting, some distance up Island from Victoria. A week after Michael left, the police came again to our door.

All manner of physical activity at the school was encouraged. Michael was water skiing, and the ski flipped up, hit him on the head and knocked him unconscious. He would have been going fast, I thought. The life jacket did not prevent his head from falling forward, and by the time they got to him, he had stopped breathing. He couldn't be revived.

I remember my brother's funeral very clearly. In the open coffin, his carefully composed features looked peaceful—but not Michael—some other stranger, my dead brother.

It was a rainy, humid day, and the flowers, so many flowers, made me feel like throwing up. My father, a significant figure in provincial politics at that time and a wealthy businessman, played the stricken parent for the many people at the funeral. My mother simply looked ill. I was grateful for Grandfather Fitzgerald, who held my hand during the funeral.

Often, my dreams of these events turned into a recurring nightmare about Michael's death, and I felt a familiar terror grip me when the dream began to shift into nightmare, but then I heard a soft voice calling me by name. Turning around, I saw an elderly man standing some distance away. He was dressed in the clothing typical of an early 20th-century professional gentleman. The dream I was having now was in black and white, with a peripheral haze of ambient golden light. Slowly, I made my way towards the man who now softly repeated my name. And then I recognized him from photographs in the books I had studied. It was Franz Boas. With some wonder, I regarded the man who founded and forever shaped the study of Anthropology in Canada and the United States.

Franz Boas took my arm and linked it through his, and we walked together along a beach where there were the ruins of what I somehow knew were the remains of a traditional Heiltsuk village.

"This place," he said softly, "is Oo-niece."

"Oo-niece," he said again. "It means 'Springwater.'"

The ruins begin to transform into living long houses; everything slowly took on color; the forests surrounding the village slipping from gray to deep shades of green

"History," said Franz Boas, looking into my eyes, "can be misplaced, but in our thoughts and actions, it is not forgotten."

I heard children laughing in the distance, then the sharp call of a raven. It was this sound that woke me up.

Bemused by the ending of the dream, it was no longer Michael who occupied my thoughts. I dug through my files until I came across the thick one titled, "Franz Boas."

Boas, a native of Germany, with a doctoral graduate in Physics and an interest in Geography, came to North America in 1883 to study the landscape of Baffin Island. In order to survive, he relied upon the local Inuit people and soon began to develop a deep admiration and respect for them. He concluded that their way of life, which had at first seemed crude and appalling to him, was a unique and awe-inspiring adaptation to the Arctic world in which they lived.

He abandoned the field of Geography and began to study the Inuit in depth. His training as a scientist led him to keep detailed notes on all aspects of their lives: their hunting and movement patterns, clothing, language and religion. From a philosophical perspective, he came upon the notion that the Inuit could only be understood from the unique history, ecology, adaptation and perspective of their culture.

For the remainder of his life, he studied many cultures, often relying on precarious funding but eventually setting himself up as a respected American anthropologist at a time when the scientific study of humankind was in its infancy. In the course of his research, he spent many years studying the Indigenous cultures and peoples of the Pacific Northwest Coast of North America. He visited and studied the Heiltsuk people in 1887 and, again, in 1923.

Over the course of his life, he further developed the theory of cultural relativity and argued repeatedly that people could not be judged based on the norms of other cultures—specifically, based on the values and ways of life of dominant Western cultures.

I continued to think about Franz Boas. He was Jewish and had lived and trained in Germany during a period that was barely tolerant of Jews in that country. Still, he remained strongly patriotic to Germany, long after he immigrated to the United States. His parents did not practice religion, and while he vocally opposed anti-Semitism, he did not identify himself as Jewish. Still, I wondered if the essentially never-ending prejudice of some for both the culture and religion of those who are Jewish had a deep influence on his beliefs and writings about the necessity for tolerance between all cultures and on his critical view of the waste that was spent on assumptions of superiority over others. The words he had spoken in my dream echoed in my mind: "History can be misplaced, but in our thoughts and actions, it is not forgotten."

Now I paced between the living room and dining room and thought about other parts of his life. He sold artifacts and carved poles, mainly to Germany, to help support himself. He also sold skulls to what I would call fringe scientists, who spent years measuring craniums in fruitless attempts to establish intelligence measures between races. Perhaps it was not so wrong in the context of his world; the British, French and Americans were renowned thieves of cultural artifacts and human remains. Today, they were no longer welcome in Egypt or Mexico.

Still, while Franz Boas was collecting information on the traditional lives of Indigenous peoples, their way of life was being destroyed by the Canadian government, their children being taken away to the ghost halls of residential schools. Boas spoke as a champion of human rights in his later years. But what about being a voice for the living people he studied at the time he was studying them?

Was I any different in this regard? I had come here to study the past, but what good would this be for those in the here and now? I was a cultural relativist both intellectually and idealistically, but if there were no laws of culture, was there any real universal right or wrong? Was there any room for building bridges between people?

My inner voice answered the question, at least partly. Despite being an outsider, Boas did take down such a great deal on Heiltsuk culture that he'd left these people with a valuable record of the past. My own work would do the same thing, on a much smaller scale.

The loud chatter of two ravens released me from my thoughts; it was a different call than the one which had woken me up from my dream. I was becoming familiar with the pair of ravens who spent a great deal of time in my front yard. It was still light out. After I washed my face, I studied my tired reflection in the mirror. And why shouldn't I be tired? I was in a place I'd never been in before, had met an array of new people and had relived the darkest times of my life. My tired face broke into a smile, and I whispered out loud, "And you searched the depths of the soul of the great anthropologist, Franz Boas."

I went to bed, fell asleep immediately…and did not dream.

Chapter 5

I slept in the next morning, and when I opened the curtains, I saw that the sun had already burned off most of the morning mist. Over breakfast, I listened to the CBC news. The forecast called for sun all week along the North and Central coasts, which may or may not actually come to pass. Along the Northwest Coast, sun is as precious as gold.

Sipping a cup of coffee, I wandered around the manse, finding towels and bedding neatly stored in a closet on the main floor. I washed some towels and bedding in the washing machine downstairs, thinking it would be nice to have real sheets and a comforter on the bed, instead of my mummy bag.

I organized books, cameras, field documents and office supplies and covered the walls in the study with topographical survey maps and aerial photographs. This was partly decorative; I needed to bolster my self-image as an archaeologist.

I was thinking about what to have for lunch when I heard a quiet knock on the front door. It was Jenn, holding in her arms not one but two catalogues. We went into the kitchen, and she was quiet and shy again. I asked her if she'd had lunch.

"Yeah," she replied.

"I haven't. Do you want to have lunch again with me?"

"Sure." She grinned. "What are you having?"

"Let's search the cupboards and see what I have."

Over peanut butter sandwiches and cookies, the open, chatty girl emerged. To my surprise, I found that I was quite interested in the Simpsons-Sears catalogue and noted several items I could use. Jenn explained to me that I could place an order from 9 to 12 in the morning, Monday to Saturday, and we could walk down to the wharf and she'd show me the Sears outlet.

I asked her if we could walk along the south part of the village first, which I hadn't seen yet. She looked perplexed and stuck up two opposing thumbs pointing roughly east and west and said, "You mean that way, or that way?"

I pointed south, and she swung one of her thumbs to mimic my direction. I burst out laughing at, what to me, were comical gestures. She grinned and replied, "Sure, I can show you the Band Office, the hospital, and the cop shop and that stuff. Maybe, if you don't get too tired, I can show you the school."

There was an area of dense forest next to the Hotel, and I couldn't see the ocean from the road. Next to that was a house similar to my own, which was adjacent to a modern style building, built in brick and glass, with a sign over the front entrance that read, "Waglisla Hospital," and under that, a split cedar plank, with "the Passage" deeply carved into the plank.

"That's Dr. Chris's house there, and that's the hospital next to that. Dr. Chris is nice; he fixed my friend Stephanie's arm, when she busted it, and she had a cool cast, and I drew a big heart, and wrote 'Jenn Hunt' on that."

Across from the hospital was what looked like a compound, consisting of mobile homes and a small brick structure. On the front of the building was a small cut lawn with a Canadian flag and a sign, "Royal Canadian Mounted Police, Gendarmerie royal du Canada."

I guessed that the mobile home compound must be the residences of the hospital staff and police officers. There were flower baskets and pots on the decks that had later been built onto the mobile homes.

"Now that's where the nurses live, and those people who do other stuff, like taking pictures of Stephanie's arm. The police live there and that building; that's the cop shop, the one with the police car in front of it."

Jenn spoke in an authoritative voice, using hand gestures but not pointing at the buildings. She had assumed the role of a serious guide.

Beyond the hospital and compound, the gravel road began to thin out; here, the forest also blocked the view to the beach. As the road narrowed, the houses across from the beach side were spaced more widely apart. Along the beach side, dirt lanes ran into the forest. As we passed these, Jenn told me the names of the families who lived down each lane. Near the end of a road that narrowed and almost disappeared, she pointed down a lane which curved sharply towards the beach, and remarked, "That's where Uncle Daniel lives; maybe we could go and visit him for a while, but he might not be home. He's probably down at the wharf, fixing up his boat."

I let this comment slide, and we continued our walk. A trail, obviously well-used, carried on from where the gravel road ended.

"At the end of that trail is the cemetery, and before that is another trail, which leads to Grandpa's and those guys' secret sweat lodge."

"If it's a secret, how come it isn't actually a secret?" I asked.

"Well, it's a secret because no one is supposed to know where it is, but, of course, everyone does. We never go there, the kids and the girls; we're not allowed to. Grandpa says that's a sacred place. But we could walk to the cemetery."

I didn't want to inadvertently run into some men returning from the sweat lodge, so I suggested we walk back up to the terraces that fronted the village.

We retraced our steps back to a steep road, intersected by crossroads. These roads divided the terraced section of the village, where most of the houses were located.

"We can go to the last road up there," Jenn said. "And then walk back along that road, and then you'll be able to see the school."

The road got increasingly steeper. I was glad that over the past two years, back at Simon Fraser, I'd worked out with Joanna at the gym. Fitness was Joanna's latest kick, and she'd dragged me into it. At first, I didn't feel comfortable at the gym, but Jo was convincing and insistent, so I went along for the ride and soon began to like it, making it part of my routine. It felt good to build back the muscles that I'd had before, when I was still dancing.

On our second or third time at the gym, a very well-built jock had suggested condescendingly to Joanna and me that if we wanted to build muscle, we needed to use more weight. Joanna, always fast with comebacks, had snapped back at him, "Have you heard about the fight or flight response? You should because I am about to throw a pitchfork through your lungs."

The guy turned out to be quite witty, although clearly obsessed with his body. Both Jo and I flirted with him at the gym. A few weeks later, over lunch, I admitted to her that I had a crush on this obvious egoist.

"You have a crush on him?" she asked, her voice rising a pitch.

"Well, so do I."

"You mean you have a crush on my crush?" I asked incredulously.

"Well, it's a mild crush." She grinned.

"Same with me."

We laughed outrageously, causing most of the restaurant to look our way. In an unspoken pact, neither of us went out with him. The memory made me laugh, and Jenn asked what was so funny.

"Just something I remembered from university."

"What's university like, Laura?"

"It is a lot of hard work but tons of fun, Jenn. Are you thinking you might go there sometime?"

"Well, maybe. Grandpa's already bothering me about that. I'm a good writer. Maybe I could tell stories. But I don't know; maybe I'll own my own boat. I could be rich. Some seiners have women working on them, you know. I guess maybe I'll go to university and own a boat."

I told her it was a neat idea, and I thought that it was.

The houses of the Passage spoke to the poverty on the Reserve and to the sense of order, defined differently here than in my culture. Houses in the Passage were small and weathered, with plywood siding, faded paint and tin chimneys. There were old mobile homes, with haphazard additions. Some of the homes were newer and recently built. These were larger, with basement windows at ground level, balconies on the main floor that faced the ocean and planks made of cedar. Sheets and blankets covered most of the windows of these newer houses. Along the street were several roughly hewn cedar shacks, obviously used for smoking fish.

There were no lawns or flower beds, and old fridges, stoves and furniture sat along the sides of many houses. Toys and bikes were strewn about in front. There were a lot of children absorbed in games, and some had toys. Several of the children seemed to be chasing each other on bikes, maybe playing tag. Some of the bikes were newer, and some were in various states of disrepair.

A raven passed overhead. Somewhere in the tall Douglas firs along the road, other ravens were chattering in many different voices.

A girl about Jenn's age ran up to us and said "Hi" to Jenn, who gravely introduced me as "Grandpa's friend, the archaeologist." The girl looked at me curiously, then asked Jenn if she was going to be around to play.

"Maybe later on, I guess," she replied.

We continued walking, and I noted, with some interest, a small, but very nice log home, with a big deck. Seeing that I was obviously admiring it, Jenn said, "That's where Not-Doctor Sinclair, the biologist, lives. She shoots bears with a sleeping gun and then figures out where they go after that."

I knew she was referring to a researcher who was studying bears and asked why the biologist's name was Not-Doctor Sinclair. Was it because she was not a people doctor?"

"Maybe. That's just what people call her."

We continued and eventually came to the school. It was single-story, freshly painted and seemed to be a good size. Adjacent to it were well kept bungalows.

"That's where the teachers live," said Jenn, "They come up at the beginning of the school year and stay until the end, and then go back to Vancouver, I guess." She pointed to a trail that veered off into the forest from the edge of the schoolyard, "The water reservoir is up that trail. Do you want to go there?"

"Maybe I'll explore that later," I replied.

We headed back down to the main road. Two streets down were the manse and, across the street, the church. Looking now with a different eye, I felt discomfort—two or three of the village houses could fit into the manse.

From here, we headed down to the aluminum structure at the end of the dock. So, this was the Simpson-Sears outlet.

I asked Jenn why they put the Sears here. She explained that this was where the weekly supply boat unloaded, and the stuff from Sears could be loaded right from the wharf into the outlet.

A raven, grasping a stick in his claws, flew off from the dock. He flew about, while other ravens seemed to scold him, trying to wrest the stick away. I noticed there were no children playing on the beach and asked Jenn why.

"Well, hardly anyone can swim around here." In a clear mimic of an adult's voice, she added, "We're not allowed to play on the beach. That surf's dangerous, you know." She paused. "Sometimes people burn food on the beach to remember dead people, and sometimes they have fires and visit each other on the beach. And sometimes we go to places with really big beaches and go clam digging. If we had a swimming pool, we could learn to swim. But that'd cost about a million dollars, and as you know, the Feds won't even pave a road on the Reserve."

From this, I intuited that the gravel roads on the Reserve were a source of contention for Chief Charlie. And why not? Even a village half this size in a Euro-Canadian community would have paved roads.

"I've got a dollar," Jenn said. "We can get an ice cream at the Hotel, just one scoop each."

She warned me that people drove their trucks along the wharf to get gas and supplies, so I'd have to be careful. I thanked her for the advice. We got our ice cream, with Jenn ordering chocolate for me, and then headed back to the manse. She carefully explained to me exactly what I had to write down for the things I was going to order and said I could keep the Sears catalogues for a few days. Then she said, "I have to go do some homework now. It's really stupid homework, and this should be a fun week because there's only five days left of school, but Grandpa watches me like a bird."

I wondered where Mom was, and replied, "I know what you mean, Jenn. When I was your age, my grandfather also insisted that I do a lot of really dumb homework."

The walk with Jenn had not tired me out at all. I had a need to know the landscape and late in the afternoon headed up to the trail that led to the water reservoir. It was a slow, easy, windy kind of narrow walk through a forest that seemed very still. I could not hear any ravens, only the muffled sound of sea gulls from the beach. The path wound upwards for about a kilometer and ended with the small lake that I'd seen on my flight in. The water was very still and clear, and there was a sign with a "No Swimming Allowed in the Waglisla Water Reservoir." I wondered if that actually stopped anyone. I took deep gulps of the icy cold water and followed a game trail around the lake. It became apparent that the Reservoir was nearly at the top of the island and that the elevation meant that the Reservoir must be spring fed.

I was suddenly very hungry and decided to go to the Waglisla Hotel for dinner. The deep-fried halibut and chips were excellent. After dinner, I took my coffee to go, walked out to the end of the wharf and sat down, with my back leaning against the warm aluminum siding of the Sears outlet.

The sky was changing. Cloud and trailing mists covered the

mountains. I vaguely heard seagulls and, intermittently, ravens along with the chatter from other birds. Chief Charlie's voice interrupted my thoughts.

"I noticed you walking down this way. Can I join you?"

"Of course."

He sat down alongside me and pulled out a package of Cigarillos. He asked if I minded if he had a smoke.

I smiled and shook my head.

"It's a beautiful view," I said.

"Yes," he answered. "You can't see much from the minister's house: the church blocks the view."

"Too bad," I answered. He grinned. I went on. "I take it you're not a church-going man, Chief Charlie."

"No," he said. "You?"

"Well, I was brought up to be sort of Catholic by my grandfather and Episcopalian by my father."

I didn't explain this odd combination. Grandpa had occasionally taken Michael and me to a Roman Catholic Church, but he was never strong for the Church. My father was Episcopalian because it suited his political aspirations. Only my mother was a devout Catholic, but she mainly attended the Episcopalian Church with Father when I was growing up.

"I guess I'm agnostic," I offered.

He found humor in this remark and laughed. "Church can be related to a belief in God for many but isn't always so."

For some reason, I had no inhibitions about discussing God with Chief Charlie and asked him if he believed in God.

"Sure," he answered.

"So, who is this God of yours, Chief Charlie?"

He didn't answer me right away but looked out to the Passage. I intuitively knew that he was trying to frame a simple answer to a complex question.

"In some ways, the same as yours, Laura," he replied.

"You mean, like the Great Spirit?" Too late, I heard a slight edge of humor in my voice and felt ashamed. But, he laughed; after a moment I joined in.

"Sure, that would be okay, although possibly you've been watching too many cowboy and Indian shows on TV." Then in a more serious voice, he said, "Here, many people call God, 'the Creator.'"

"Should I put that in the ethnography section of my field report?" There was still an edge of humor in my voice; not what I'd meant, not at all.

He was quiet, and I was worried I'd offended him. "I'm very sorry, Chief Charlie. I shouldn't joke about such things."

"Laura, I take no offense. I was actually just wondering if you should put that in your ethnography section," he said seriously.

"Right now, it's not a problem. I don't have an ethnography section."

I was rewarded by his rich laughter. "Maybe you should save the Creator for your PhD."

I laughed with him, feeling relieved that I had not offended him.

He continued, "But, you should have some idea about our connection to our ancestors."

My confusion showed in my face, and he looked once again as if he was trying to frame simple answers to complex issues.

"When I pray…when a traditional Heiltsuk, no, I guess, most Indian people, when they pray, they pray to their ancestors. That is why knowing my ancestors and their stories is so important. You need to know their clans, their crests, their personalities. You need to know this because they are born again in children, and you have to know who they are."

I think some understanding showed in my eyes. I had read about the idea that children were reborn as the incarnation of an ancestor—I had read of this in the works of Franz Boas. A half-smile crossed my face, and Chief Charlie questioned me with his eyes.

"I was thinking," I said. "I was thinking that I like the idea of praying to one's ancestors. I guess…it's real. I guess it is like something real…" I was repeating myself and struggling to formulate the response that was not as garbled in my head as it came out. "But, I don't know my ancestors, only my grandfather—my father's father, the other grandparents—they were gone for a long time before I was born, and I only know a little bit about them."

"What do you know?" asked Chief Charlie softly.

"On both sides, they were Irish. Poor Irish. Starving in a famine in the 1880s—in Ireland, before they came first to New York and then to Canada. My grandfather sometimes talked about his mother, and with respect, but I think he had a hard life growing up. Lots of his relatives died from illness. He said what they really died from was poverty, and I guess some drank themselves to death; my great-grandfather would be one of those. But I guess I don't really know my ancestors."

Chief Charlie was quiet for a moment. "There's been hard times for people everywhere, all the time, I guess. But, you could, you know… you could speak to your grandfather. I think he would hear you."

"Yes, he would hear me," I mused. "Maybe I do talk to him, without even thinking about it."

There was an amiable silence between us, and when I spoke again, it was on another topic. "Chief Charlie, do you know what the Heiltsuk word, 'On-niece,' means?"

"You mean 'Oo-niece'?"

The way he pronounced it was very melodious and sounded exactly as Franz Boas had pronounced it in my dream. I nodded.

"Well sure," he said. "That would be one of the old winter villages." He paused and added, "Laura, Oo-niece is one of the villages you wrote down that you were going to study in your research that you outlined to the Band."

I was mystified. "It is?"

He looked puzzled for a moment…then, "Ah," he said, nodding. "Now I understand; it's the language and spelling that's confusing you. Oo-niece is spelled X-v-n-i-s. It has very minor difference in the various dialects of the Heiltsuk. It means, 'cold fountain from the rocks' or 'cold spring' or, simply, 'Springwater,' in Heiltsuk."

I was very quiet, and Chief Charlie asked if I'd seen a ghost.

"Yes," I answered seriously. I didn't elaborate, and he didn't press me. We sat companionably, for a while, until he left, wishing me good luck with the boat.

For a while, I lingered, then headed home.

Chapter 6

When I woke up and opened the curtains, my eyes were met by brilliant sunshine, and I was filled with a sense of well-being. It was 8 a.m. I'd forgotten to set the alarm.

After two days of sun, my nose was peeling. *Great*, I thought. I put on an old t-shirt that said, 'Property of SFU' in faded letters across the front, and slipped into khaki shorts. On the way out, I grabbed the baseball cap that I generally wore in the field for sun protection. It was stained and faded, but I had an emotional attachment to it.

Daniel was waiting for me at the Esso station and nodded when I walked up to him. Feeling slightly irritated, I wondered if he was ever going to talk to me.

We walked back up the wharf, down a ramp and along a narrow dock to his boat. It looked new, and I thought the white color, with the deep blue trim, was very nice.

Daniel showed me the boat. It slept four, had a small stove, fridge and a head. There would be lots of room for me to stow our gear. I tried to look intelligent as he explained various features of the engine to me. In the helm, Daniel explained the operation of the gears. I guess, at this point, the blank look on my face was obvious.

"Do you have much experience with cabin cruisers?" he asked.

"No… none actually," I painfully admitted and then added, "But I have done a fair bit of sailing. Would that be of on any use?"

Daniel looked at me, looked at his boat and seemed to think for a few moments before saying, "Maybe."

He maneuvered the boat out of the marina, and we took off at what seemed like breathtaking speed, northwards, up the Passage. I wondered, and hoped, that he was showing off. After a while, I took over the steering, and under Daniel's directions, thought I was doing quite well. We switched seats, and he headed to Denny Island. He slowed down as we entered the Edgewater Dock. From the dock, I saw a large, cedar-planked building and several outbuildings. I asked Daniel what this place was. "A fishing resort," he replied.

Later, I learned that the Edgewater Resort catered to wealthy American, Canadian and even European sports fisherman. Carefully explaining his maneuvers, he expertly came to a stop next to the dock. Steering back out into the water, he told me it was my turn to try.

The results were disastrous. My attempts to maneuver, even against the light ocean swell, were sloppy. I hit the dock with a resounding bump. Daniel told me to cut the engine. I fumbled with the key, unable to turn it to the off position. Daniel reached over me and cut the ignition.

It took a while for me to look at him. I asked if I'd damaged the boat.

"Probably not," he answered.

"I guess this isn't one of my talents, Daniel."

"Well, maybe it's just experience you need. But I don't think I have the time to teach you before your project starts," he said in an almost inaudible voice.

My shoulders slumped.

"Laura?" He said my name as a question.

I looked up.

"Jack Campbell is one of your crew, isn't he?"

"Yes," I answered.

"Jack is an ace at operating this kind of boat. You could let him be in charge of the boat. That could make it work."

"Yes," I replied. "That could work."

When we returned to the Passage, I asked Daniel if I could take him for lunch or coffee.

"Coffee would be good."

We walked up the wharf to the Hotel. The café was plain, with kitchen-type formica tables and chairs and plastic checkered table-cloths. The coffee was excellent. Daniel alternated between sips of coffee and chewing on a toothpick, which in no way struck me as rude. My previously confident, flirtatious presentation was ruined, and I found it difficult to think of what to say to my companion. I started to talk about the beautiful day and then asked if he thought it was going to rain. He glanced out the window at the crystal blue sky, looked at me and said, "Maybe."

But his dark eyes glinted with humor, and I burst out laughing at my ineptitude. He responded to my laughter with his remarkable smile.

I asked if he felt comfortable about us using his boat: Was the rent the project was paying enough?

"Sure, as long as Jack Campbell doesn't broadside the ferry." He smiled when he said this, and I laughed again.

Then more seriously, I ventured a question: "It's a pretty expensive boat, isn't it?"

He shrugged. "That project you're doing is important. Don't worry about the boat."

I smiled and nodded as a way of thanking him. He asked me to tell him about some of the other field projects I'd worked on. Now I was in my element, and we chatted for half an hour about work that I'd done.

On the way back to the manse, I decided that Daniel was quite personable when he wanted to be.

I spent the rest of the day going through my files and reports looking for information on Xvnis. The results were scant. George had drawn a rough sketch that showed beams and posts, indicating that there were several decayed houses at the site. But his photographs of this site were only of a few rapidly excavated test units. In his notes, George indicated that the site was quite old, its age determined by the stratigraphy of the test units. A research team from the University of Pennsylvania did research in Bella Coola in the 1960s and made a brief foray west, digging test units at various sites, including at Xvnis. The observations of this team were similar to George's and noted that a test unit yielded artifacts that demonstrated the site was indeed thousands of years old.

It seemed as if the archaeologists who stopped by Xvnis and other Heiltsuk sites were not interested in house remains but in the middens beneath them, perhaps because they did not attach a value to house remains that dated back more recently in time. At least George had taken photographs at many other sites, and years later he remained impressed by Xvnis. Although he did not photograph the beams or perhaps had misplaced these photographs, he recalled quite clearly in the notes he gave me and which I used to put together my research proposal that the site was large, that the house beams were very large and that there would have been many houses there at the time and before contact with Europeans.

Frustrated with the lack of information on the site of Xvnis, which I now pronounced, even though it remained not quite right, "OO-niece," I cleaned up the files I'd been going through and lay down for a nap, trying to rest my mind. But my thoughts did not rest, only changed direction.

There is something about new places and new situations that draws me into old memories and events. Perhaps, in dreams and thoughts, it is something that my mind uses to create a frame of reference for new experiences and unfamiliar places.

Toronto and Victoria, 1965-66

After Michael's funeral, my grandfather took me back with him to Toronto. A few weeks later, Grandpa told me that I had a new brother, John Robert Fitzgerald. I barely registered this information and simply asked my grandfather if I could take dancing lessons. We had been to a ballet a few days before: hence, the source of my idea.

And so, when I was ten years old, I began to dance. I may have had little grace, but I had a terrible desire to escape, which gave me the boundless energy that every teacher loves.

I stayed with Grandfather Fitzgerald until the Christmas after Michael's death. Although my journey with my mother would soon take a new turn, it was under the care of my grandfather that I began to heal from the death of my brother.

I went to a school in Etobicoke, which was not much different than the one in Victoria. I did my homework without being told. I resisted any attempts that the other girls made to befriend me. After a while, they left me alone.

In taking up dance, I worked hard to escape my grief and shock. Every day after school, I worked for two hours with an instructor whom grandfather had found by polling the wives of his friends. Sophia was as much a therapist as a dance instructor. She taught me the basic elements of the art form and pushed me hard to exercise, to breathe and to extend myself. "Come on, Laura, you're just relearning what your body has forgotten. You must become like a baby that can bite her toes."

I would smile at her interesting metaphors, but one day I proudly sat on the floor, my back as straight as a rod, and, bringing my right leg up to my mouth, I bit my toe.

Sophia was also my artistic instructor. She taught me to listen for what she called the subtext of the music: the beat, the feeling, the story that a composer was trying to tell. "Listen to the subtext; it is here," she said pointing. "In your heart."

My dance training was unorthodox because, at first, I didn't work with other girls; working alone with a dance instructor, as a way of starting, was unusual.

This unusual training method was the result of my grandfather's realization that my desire to dance must allow me not simply an escape but the ability to feel. Although I was not conscious of it, I was dancing for Michael. I danced out my anger, my grief, my frustration and my love.

After dance class, my grandfather picked me up. I often fell asleep in the car. One night, I woke up and went to the kitchen to find something to drink. A light was spilling out from beneath the door of Grandpa's study. I heard sobbing from inside and knew that he was crying over Michael. I wanted comfort and wanted to give comfort. When I went in to see, I found Grandpa hunched in a chair, in front of a dying fire, hands covering his face.

He looked up. He did not try to hide his tears, and I ran to him, knelt, threw my arms around his waist and put my head in his lap. I began to sob, crying not just with my body but my soul. The whole world was shaking. It was the first time I had cried since Michael's death.

Grandpa wiped my face with his white linen handkerchief. "I hate him, Grandpa, and I hate God."

He knew the 'him' I was referring to was my father, but he didn't speak of this. He said, "Try not to hate God, Laura. Maybe someday you'll forgive Him, and maybe someday you'll need Him."

"I don't even think there is a God, like some old man ruling heaven, like they say in church. Do you believe that, Grandpa?"

"No, I don't think it's that simple. I think that God is far too large to fit inside a church. But, yes, I do believe, and I believe there's more than just this life."

A few weeks after Christmas, he told me it was time for me to go back to Victoria. I pleaded with him to let me stay, sobbing and telling *him that I never, ever, wanted to go back there. He sat down next to me on the couch, held my hand and said I needed to get to know my new little brother, that my mother would have great need of me now. There was no mention of my father. Grandpa told me that I could call him collect anytime I wanted to and that I'd be coming back next summer. And Sophia was arranging for me to continue my dancing in Victoria. "Laura," he said, as his face softened. "We both know that you have to go back."*

Of those sharply defined and uncluttered memories of my past, one is of my grandfather holding my hand as we walked down the long lane to the departure gate at the airport, past shops and cafés, all lit up for Christmas. He left me in the care of a flight attendant. I turned around to say goodbye and patted my carry-on bag. It contained my first pair of toe shoes.

A change to a far more consistent and safe life began with the change in my mother. My father started to spend a lot of time away from home, and the house was calmer in his absences. My mother took a huge interest in my dancing. She drove me to lessons every day and took me to recitals on the Island and, by ferry, into Vancouver. She started to have coffee with the other mothers. Years later, I realized this was a politically calculated move on her part. Being a successful dancer meant being the progeny of a mother who, along with the other mothers, were part of an unspoken club.

At first, I was suspicious of this, but as my father spent an increasing amount of time away from home, a part of her I'd rarely ever seen emerged.

I fell in love with my new brother the moment I saw him and again when I carefully held him in my arms. Constantly frightened that something was going to happen to this baby, I often sat next to his crib and held my own breath to hear him breathing. One afternoon, my mother came in and watched us. A look passed between us, and all those years dropped away. I was looking at a strong woman and knew, at that moment, that between my father and this baby, there would be two strong women.

His name was John Robert, named after the Kennedy brothers. I don't know why, but I started to call him Jake and sometimes Jakes. Except for my mother, who almost always called him John, this is what most people call him, even today: Jake.

My father's strong disapproval of the social status of my mother's family meant we spent little time with her family in North Vancouver—maybe just ten days in the summer. All three of her brothers were blue collar workers: two worked at the Burrard Dry Docks, and the other for the city, in maintenance. They had eight kids between them and wives who nagged them about their drinking too much, which they did. They went to the Catholic Church on Sunday and had heated arguments at Sunday dinner about whether the priest was an idiot. And they cursed the English.

On those short vacations with my cousins, Michael and I were accepted as if we'd lived there all the time. We left the house in the morning, went almost every day to Lynn Canyon, where we swam in a pool called "30 foot." We argued, teased and dared each other to jump from the cliffs into the waters below. We begged quarters off Mom and our aunties and ate salt and vinegar chips and popsicles. At lunch, we ate wherever we happened to be at our cousin's houses or at the houses of their friends. We stayed out until dusk, and when the first star came out, we headed home.

After Michael died, my mother turned to her family for comfort, and we spent more and more time with them in North Vancouver.

One weekend, she went with Jake to North Vancouver. I was to stay at a friend's, and her mother was going to take us to a weekend dance workshop. I realized I'd forgotten my tights and stopped by the house to pick them up. I heard someone rustling around and went into the sunroom off the kitchen. My father was sitting there with a woman, who was dressed in a scanty housecoat. He had his arm around her. They heard me and looked up. They didn't look shocked or ashamed. The only look they threw my way was one of disdain.

I returned to the car, where my friend and her mother were waiting and said I needed to call my mom. I told Mom what I'd seen. My friend's mother dropped me off at the ferry, and I went on my way to North Vancouver.

I never went back to that house in Victoria.

My mother told me when I was older that she was glad the affair gave her the courage she needed to leave my father. She also told me other things—about who she was as a young girl, and her motivations for marrying my father. This added to my insight, but not to the fact that I had long forgiven her for her inaction, when we were children, in protecting Michael and myself.

With the settlement she got, she bought an old house in North Vancouver, and we worked at fixing it up over the next few years. This teamwork, during which my input was taken very seriously, became the final series of events that cemented our relationship. I refused to see my father, and he didn't want to see me anyway. I continued to spend a month each summer in Toronto, and soon Grandpa came to spend every Christmas with Mom and me and Jake. I don't think I ever heard him laugh so much as when he jumped into the constant arguments with my Irish uncles. Those years were full of halcyon days.

The sound of the foghorn brought me back to the present, and looking out the living room curtains, I saw a thick mist moving slowly about the streets and, above, in the sky of the Passage.

I put on sweatpants, a t-shirt and moisturizer for the sunburn on my face. Before me were memories of happiness, as well as of sadness, that had never really gone away. Not feeling very hungry, I only had a bit of an egg, half a toast and tea. I went to bed early. The word "OO-niece" played about in my thoughts, but my mind was quiet, and I was drawn into sleep by the steady sound of the foghorn.

Chapter 7

The next few days went by quickly. I transferred site data onto high resolution topographical maps and again studied George's notes and photographs. I decided that the location we would investigate first would be the remains of an old village site known as Boston's Retreat, on nearby Denny Island.

I moved the maps on the wall in the study, as well as other supplies, into the dining room, realizing this room was larger and better to work in.

My crew, having finished school that Tuesday, showed up at 9 a.m. on Thursday morning. We went into the dining room, and I offered them coffee, which they politely refused. I explained what our goals were and told them that, in the next few days, I'd be teaching them about taking photographs and making maps.

Jack was stocky; he looked older than eighteen. Kristy was nineteen. She'd missed her first attempt to live in a boarding home but then had landed on her feet and succeeded at the second attempt. During the day, they went to school and then returned to eat, sleep and study at what were generally white family homes. Very few were able to escape homesickness, and the quality of these boarding homes was not consistent. Some people treated the Heiltsuk with respect, but others were more ambivalent.

Jack wore his long hair tied back and had thick-framed glasses. I quickly learned that he had the characteristic of moving slowly but getting to his destination very quickly. He had a strong Heiltsuk accent.

Kristy was tall, and lithe, her dark eyes expertly made-up. She held her head high and moved very gracefully. In terms of personal dynamics, it was clear that she and Jack were not friends. In body language, they were aloof, keeping their distance from one another. In the societal-class arrangement of teenage sociology, Kristy was ultra-cool, and Jack was a geek.

I presented them with a discussion of the importance of the project, reiterating several times that we'd be exploring their heritage. Jack avoided eye contact and was instead fixated on the kitchen wall. Kristy's dark eyes were amused, and I felt irritated, thinking she wasn't taking me seriously. Jack perked up when I said he'd be in charge of the boat for the project and that it was Daniel Hunt's boat. Kristy continued to look amused. I decided to start with the photography end of things and to go over the workings of the cameras.

Kristy became interested, especially when we went out into the backyard to take some pictures, but Jack lacked any expression during the lesson. He did roll his eyes when Kristy insisted that he pose as a carved house post so that she could photograph him. At this point, I burst out laughing, as did Kristy. I had, I thought, made one friend…but possibly one enemy.

I explained they would keep a field journal, where they'd write down facts, observations and information that could be backed up by facts or would be "just intuitive thoughts." Both looked skeptical.

"Think of it as a cross between a novel and a textbook," I said.

By the time they'd left, I had a headache and felt anxious. I looked in their journals. Kristy had written, "It was a dark and stormy night. Nevertheless, Gwendolyn ignored the weather and worked on the questions in her Calculus 12 textbook."

Jack hadn't written anything.

Going over the day, again and again, I wondered what I could have done better. I had some doubts about the crew, even though Chief Charlie had recommended these young people to George Clements. After dinner, I sat at the kitchen table, staring out into the backyard and picked at the cuticle of my thumb. I desperately wanted my project to succeed. But then some insight and clarity came to me. How could they possibly know how to record findings in a journal, without the methodology to do this? I needed to do more teaching. Kristy had done exactly what I'd asked; she'd made an entry halfway between a novel and a textbook. With this new insight, a sense of lightness kicked in, and I laughed, especially at the name, "Gwendolyn."

If I hadn't been so naïve about so much then, I would have realized that the fact that Kristy and Jack had completed high school was a tribute to their perseverance and dedication. Only one out of five Indigenous students in British Columbia graduated at that time. Thinking about it now, I realize as well how condescending it was to suggest that I was going to teach them about their own culture. I came to know, as well, that my doubts about Jack and Kristy were self-doubts around my competency and ability to succeed. I had never been in a supervisory role, and it would take some time to begin to acquire leadership skills.

When I went to bed, not even the rhythmic sound of the foghorn could lull me to sleep. I should have known by then how true the adage was: our worst fears rarely come to pass, and it is the unforeseen that changes the direction of our lives.

We worked on mapping for most of the next day. Teaching Kristy and Jack how to make a chain and compass map, once again using the backyard of the manse as a test site, was easy. We quickly moved on to making more accurate maps, using a transit. Neither of my companions displayed any interest in learning how to use this surveying instrument. I thought Jack had trouble focusing because of his eyesight. However, when I showed them how to convert the raw numbers from the transit and stadia rod readings into an actual map, he became fascinated. Kristy wandered off to experiment with the cameras.

The day before, I noticed they both brought Pepsi back from lunch, so I stocked up on these. As the day drew to a close, we sat at the dining room table drinking the soft drink. While I worked with Jack on constructing a map of the backyard, Kristy fiddled alternately with the three cameras I brought for the project. I went into the kitchen to the bathroom, and just as I was about to come back into the dining room, the pencil behind my ear fell to the floor. As I reached down to retrieve the pencil, Jack came through the swinging dining room doors with the grace of an elephant. He knocked me halfway across the kitchen. I lay flat on my back for a moment, then slowly sat up, probably not a good idea, as my peripheral vision began to go black and I began seeing stars. By that time, the two were sitting next to me, supporting my back.

There was a confusion of, "Are you okay?" "Laura, I'm sorry, I'm sorry."

"Laura, your nose is bleeding."

"I'm all right," I said. "Maybe you could just get a wet tea towel and help me to sit on the couch."

In the living room, I sat on the couch, holding the tea towel to my nose.

"Laura, I'm so sorry," Jack said in a tortured voice.

"Jack, it's not your fault. It was an accident."

"Does it hurt?" Kristy asked.

"Yes."

"Let me see," Kristy said, moving her hand in my direction.

I removed the tea towel, and Kristy diagnosed the injury. "I think your nose is broken. Jack, do you think her nose is broken?"

"Yeah," he said. "You'd better go to the hospital."

"No thanks. What are they going to do there? If it's broken, I'll get some plastic surgeon in Vancouver to fix it up later, when the summer's over."

They stared at me, uncomprehending.

Breaking the silence, I said, "I know what we're going to do. We're going to get rid of those doors. I hate those friggin' doors."

They were taken aback by my use of the sort of swear word. I added, "Don't you guys ever swear?"

"Sure," said Jack.

I asked Jack if the Band Store sold electric drills. He said, "No" and asked me skeptically if I had a multi-bit screwdriver.

"Yes, in the blue box, in the study…maybe the not blue box. Somewhere in there."

"Do you know how to use a drill, Laura?" Jack asked.

"Yes, and I can also fix a diesel generator, use a chainsaw and map the entire world between breakfast and lunch. I learned all of this in Archaeology field school, although I did fail 'Shooting a Rifle to Kill a Bear Who is Charging, or Otherwise Harassing You.' That was an advanced course, 'Archaeology 401.'"

This comment finally elicited some laughter, and Kristy got some frozen peas from the fridge to place on my rapidly swelling nose.

Jack skillfully removed the screws that held the swinging doors. When he was finished, I somehow found it in me to stand up and open the back door, then asked him to bring the swinging doors out onto the porch. I said we would count to three, and then Jack could toss the doors into the backyard, which he did. As he threw them out, I said, "Goodbye, doors."

I told them the day was over and that we'd meet here on Monday at 8 a.m. sharp. Kristy again told me I should go to the hospital, but I reassured her I'd be fine.

When they left, I went into the bathroom and examined my face in the mirror. My nose was swollen, but it didn't look crooked to me. I noticed that my forehead was red and starting to bruise and that bruises were also forming around the bridge of my nose and under my eyes. However, my main concern was that I was going to have to walk around the Passage looking like an abused woman. Sighing, I took the pillow from my bed and lay down on the couch with the frozen peas covering my face.

Chapter 8

Less than an hour later, there was knock on the front door, but before I could answer it, Chief Charlie and Daniel came into the living room. I sat up, feeling embarrassed, stupid and, for some reason, guilty. I read the concern in Chief Charlie's eyes. He let out a short whistle and, turning to Daniel, said, "What do you think?"

Daniel, chewing on a toothpick, appraised my face. He removed the toothpick, came closer, looked again and said, "Broken."

"Laura," said Chief Charlie, "I think we're going to take you to the hospital."

As if on cue, blood began to trickle from my nose, and I went to get the bloodied tea towel from the kitchen. Returning to the living room, I said, "Those kids told you, and I know they were worried, but you can't do anything for a broken nose—I mean isn't that what plastic surgeons do, like you know, later?"

"Laura, how many people do you know that have broken their nose?" asked Chief Charlie.

"I…I…don't, I…don't know anyone."

"Well, I know quite a few people, like Daniel, for example," said Chief Charlie, glancing at his nephew. "And they need to set it, so then maybe you won't need a plastic surgeon later."

I looked at Daniel's nose, which I thought looked pretty good. His expression, for about the tenth time since I'd met him, was one of amusement. Irritated, I gave him a dirty look but said, "I guess you're right. I'll go to the hospital." I glanced down at my now bloody white shirt. "I'll just change my shirt, and then if you'll take me, I could…" my voice trailed off.

"You don't need to change your shirt," Chief Charlie said gently. "Maybe just get a jacket."

"Yes," I replied, feeling more stupid and idiotic. "My jacket is… it's…you know, I don't remember where my jacket is."

Daniel, his forehead knit in concern, said quietly, "I'll find it while Charlie takes you out to the truck."

Carrying my anorak, Daniel caught up with us, as Chief Charlie was helping me into the truck. Daniel draped my anorak around my shoulders before sitting next to me on the passenger side. Chief Charlie drove in the direction of the hospital. On the way, Daniel remarked that it was hard to believe that I'd gotten all those bruises from a door.

"A 'friggin' door," clarified Chief Charlie.

The remark, coming from him, seemed absurd and made me laugh. Daniel and Charlie grinned, their faces displaying the usual lighting-up expression.

There was no one else waiting at the hospital; a nurse quickly took down the information about the accident and all the kinds of things hospitals need to know. I entered a room with two stretchers and various medical paraphernalia. A few minutes later, a man, who I thought might be in his early thirties, introduced himself as Chris Sutherland. He shone a light into my eyes; I followed his finger back and forth, while he asked me a lot of questions. I knew my name, birth date, day of the week and who the Prime Minister of Canada was but stumbled over the current date. I was easily able to grip his hands. Although he was very gentle when he examined my nose, it hurt like hell, and, I suppose, to distract me, he asked me about my work. I told him what I was doing. He said there was a biologist working out of the Reserve and that she was from the University of British Columbia. Did I know her? I told him I'd only been here about a week; he said he'd let her know I was living at the manse…if I wanted her to drop by. I said that'd be great. He explained what he was going to do to fix my nose and called Chief Charlie and Daniel in.

"I'm just going to give your nose a tweak and put it back in place," he said.

"A tweak?" I asked suspiciously.

"Daniel, you hold her right arm, and Charlie, this arm, and Laura, you take some deep breaths."

I shut my eyes tightly and took some deep breaths, although my whole body tensed. Dr. Sutherland gave my nose a tweak, and I heard a crunch.

I did not scream, but tears ran down my face. Chief Charlie patted me on the shoulder and whispered something. I think it was in Heiltsuk.

Dr. Sutherland did not say, "Now that wasn't so bad, was it?" He said, "Sorry about that, Laura. I'm going to get the nurse to give you a shot for the pain now."

Why not earlier? I wondered but didn't say out loud.

Dr. Sutherland directed his next remarks at Chief Charlie and Daniel.

"What I'm concerned about is that Laura may have a mild concussion. She got a good whack to the head, and she might be a bit confused." He turned to me. "I'd like you to stay the night here."

"No," I said, "I don't…I don't like hospitals. They make me sick."

Amazingly, he took me seriously. "Well, we are kind of overcrowded." Turning to Chief Charlie, he took a different tactic. "Can someone stay with her tonight and wake her up every two hours to make sure she is all right? If she doesn't respond or if she becomes confused and is difficult to wake up, she needs to come right back."

"That won't be a problem," Chief Charlie said, his voice warm and consoling.

"Thank you," I said. "And the thing is, I'm not confused. This is, maybe…like you know, my normal personality."

"Laura, you are as sharp as a knife and may be just a little confused right now. Your speech is a bit different, *you know,*" he added.

"Oh, well, okay." I started to say something more but decided to be quiet.

Just then a nurse came in and asked Chief Charlie if he would move his truck because it was blocking the Emergency Room door. After a few moments, Daniel asked if I was in much pain. I shrugged, and he added, "You should be more careful."

His comment sounded condescending, and my quick temper cut in. I whispered to him with an edge of sarcasm. "I know that. Aren't you supposed to be fishing?"

He didn't react to my tone but said quietly, "I went and came back, and I'm leaving again the day after tomorrow."

"I know that," I whispered, although I didn't. Taking a deep breath, I continued. "I'm sorry Daniel. It's been a lousy day."

In response, he simply nodded.

Dr. Sutherland spoke again to Daniel and Chief Charlie. Then they took me home.

I guess, at some point, it had been decided that Daniel would stay because, when we reached the manse, Chief Charlie left with the pickup and said he'd be back with some plates of food.

I invited Daniel to help himself to anything, then went to take a bath. I stood before the mirror, stunned at my appearance. The bruises under my eyes and on my forehead had deepened, and the bandage on my nose, held in place by white tape, seemed to take up most of my face. The gauze stuffing, packed into my nose, was very uncomfortable, but the hot bath was soothing. I managed to get out of the bath and put some sweatpants and a t-shirt on, thinking, first, that I looked horrible. The second thought I had was that I'd like to sleep forever.

Taking my mummy bag into the living room, I laid it down on the couch. Daniel had lit a fire. Wandering into the kitchen, I told him I didn't use the upstairs, hadn't cleaned it, I said. I could fit on the couch much more easily than he could, and maybe, I added, he could use the downstairs bedroom. He nodded and said that he'd just finished brewing some coffee; did I want some? Yes! Despite my earlier desire to sleep, I found that coffee was exactly what I wanted…also, some fresh air. So, I took my warm cup out onto the back porch. I must have looked comical, trying to sip the coffee with most of my face bandaged. Daniel followed me and, looking at the doors that were lying on the back lawn, asked if it were "those doors."

"Yes."

"So, you said goodbye to a door?" He grinned.

I noticed he was chewing on a toothpick again. "How did you ever get around to saving me, considering you had to listen to…like, you know… my whole life story before you got around to coming over?"

He laughed. I asked if he carried around toothpicks all over the world.

"No," he said, smiling. "I got them from, *like you know*, your cupboard."

I abruptly changed the subject and asked Daniel how tall he was.

"About 6'2, I guess. Why?"

"Well, that confirms my hypothesis that I probably can't beat you in hand-to-hand combat. Guess I'll have to rely on my wits."

Our laughter filled the small porch but made my face hurt; I quickly covered it with my hands. He put a tentative hand on my shoulder and said in a soft voice, "Are you all right?"

I looked up at him. "Yeah, but don't make me laugh."

As soon as I'd said this, I started to laugh, and so did he. I quickly covered my face with my hands again. Taking a deep breath and reaching out to grab the sleeve of his jean jacket, I said, "Daniel, I'm not the strong, silent type. It really hurts, and I want to go out into the backyard and scream now."

"Why don't you just lie down now for a while, Laura?" His voice was filled with quiet sympathy.

I laid on the couch and wrapped myself up in my mummy bag. Daniel asked me if the light bothered me.

"No."

He sat on the recliner and took up a newspaper I had lying around, reading it, while I dozed off. At some point, I thought I heard Chief Charlie talking with Daniel, but when I woke up, it was to the sound of the foghorn, and Chief Charlie was nowhere in sight. Daniel was still there, reading the paper. I sat up. He asked if I was hungry because Chief Charlie had dropped off some food. I could feel the wariness overcome me, probably showing in my eyes because he said it was chili, and I was thinking of the wild game we had for dinner only a few days ago. The chili was made with beef, he added, although I knew he was lying. I couldn't taste anything anyway, and I wasn't very hungry but ate a bit and washed it down with some chocolate ice cream that Chief Charlie had also brought over. The shot of morphine from the hospital was wearing off, and I shifted several times on the couch, trying to get comfortable. Daniel reached into his pocket and took out a little brown envelope. He handed me a white pill. "Take this now, for the pain."

"I'll take two," I said, and he handed me a second one. He made coffee for himself and tea for me, while I asked him about seine fishing.

I learned that Daniel owned a half share in a seine boat with Laney and Matt. Laney was his cousin. He was leaving on Sunday for an opening in Milbanke Sound. The Department of Fisheries controlled the industry, and it was their decision as to when and where fishing could take place. His Indian status made no difference in seining, and because the fishing was done Off-Reserve, he paid income tax, a fact that many white people didn't understand. Fishing usually started in March, with the herring runs, and concluded in late September, with the sockeye salmon run.

Daniel's features did not reveal much about his feelings, but in his eyes, I could see that he loved fishing. He tried to steer the conversation to me, but I was elusive. I instinctively felt that he could be put off by his perceptions about me.

After a while, he told me my eyes were drooping and that I should rest. I snuggled into my sleeping bag.

"Daniel?"

"Yes?"

"Thank you for all you did today. You've been a great help to me."

He nodded, and after a few minutes, I fell asleep to the comforting sound of the foghorn.

I did recall Daniel waking me up during the night and in the early morning, and I was a bit irritated at being woken up. He would make me sit up, which caused the blood to rush to my face, which really hurt. I recall that once, after sitting up, I told him that my name was Dracula and that I lived at 1313 Mockingbird Lane, right next to the blood bank. This was an address Michael had given to a charity of some sort who had called the house one day when we were children, and Father was not at home. Daniel laughed when I asked if he wanted to donate.

"I think that your concussion has healed."

I drifted off again, thinking what nice shoulders he had.

The next time I woke up, it was morning. Daniel was sleeping at an odd angle in the recliner, and I studied his face and met his eyes with a smile when he opened them. Not saying anything, he brought me a glass of water and gave me another pill.

"I'm starving," I said. "Would you like some bacon and eggs?"

"Sure," he replied.

I grinned. "Um…could you make them?"

It looked like it was going to be a rainy day, and before he left, Daniel stacked a load of wood in the box next to the fireplace. As well, he told me that Chris Sutherland wanted to see me on Monday morning before I left for wherever I was going.

Chapter 9

Later that afternoon, Jenn and Chief Charlie came by. Chief Charlie asked me how I felt. I told him the painkillers had made me so sleepy that I was going without them for a while and actually felt fine.

"And your work?" He looked skeptical.

"I guess I look a lot worse than I feel—I'll be off on Monday to the first site we're going to investigate. It's on Denny Island, so if I find it really difficult, we can come home early."

"That would be Boston's Retreat," said Charlie. There was a far-away look about him.

"Boston's Retreat," echoed Jenny, but I didn't pursue her comment.

Jenn was very quiet and stood close to her grandfather, shifting her weight from side to side, clearly upset by my appearance.

"I guess I look kind of scary," I said in a soft voice.

"Well, yes, Laura," Jenn answered honestly. "You do kind of look like a Halloween costume."

I smiled, although perhaps the effect was more like a grimace.

"Is your nose going to be like it was before? That nose you had was very nice, you know."

"Yes, it will be. Dr. Chris fixed it up nicely."

She looked as if she didn't believe me and abruptly changed the subject with a question on whether I had any of the red nail polish left, the polish on my toes, which she thought looked very nice. I told her that I did and that, if she liked, I'd paint her toes.

"And my fingernails too?" Her question was directed at Chief Charlie.

"Sure, but don't stay too long, Jenny. Laura needs some rest."

Chief Charlie and Daniel, I learned later, were the only two people Jenn ever allowed to call her Jenny, having clearly established her personal identity as Jenn.

Before he left, Chief Charlie issued an invitation. "You should come for dinner tomorrow, Laura, but I'll pick you up; that's a bit too long of a walk."

Jenn chattered, while I painted her toenails red; she admired the results at length. I gravely told her that bright red nails were good for toenails because the red indicated a passionate person, but red finger-nails were for downtown women, and we were country girls.

"What does passionate mean?" she asked.

"It means…like, you know, spirited."

She nodded, although I don't think she understood me. "Why don't you have any nail polish on your fingernails, Laura?"

"I don't wear nail polish when I'm working, but I do have some really nice, pink polish we can use for your fingernails."

While I polished Jenn's fingernails with the pink color, she sat very still; she barely spoke until her nails were dry. I asked her why she was so quiet; hadn't she ever had her nails polished before?

"Sure," she grinned. "But not by a professional."

The foghorn started up, and I could see a thick mist was moving in. "I'd like to go for a walk," I said. "I think that would clear my head. Jenn, would you like to go to the Hotel for ice cream?"

"Sure" was her reply.

On the way to the Hotel, we passed several people. Some chuck-led when they greeted me with the usual "Mmph."

"Jenn, I know I look odd, but why are those people laughing at me?" I asked indignantly.

Jenn giggled. "Well, that's quite the story around here: you busting your nose on a door…they aren't actually laughing at you, you know…just the story."

"And how does everyone know about it?"

"Probably, mainly, Kristy Mack. Not Grandpa or Uncle Daniel or Jack Campbell. The Campbells pretty much keep quiet about things." She added as an afterthought, "Also, I did tell some of my friends."

I was in no way upset with Kristy; she had assuaged my false pride in believing that the residents of the Passage would speculate in a negative way about my appearance.

On that walk, I saw that some people did not grin or chuckle. They gave the usual "Mmph" but shifted their head down and eyes downward and, in a clearly perceptible way, shifted their shoulders away from me and shuffled as they passed.

The walk felt good, but by the time I returned to the manse, pain had set in, and my head was pounding. After Jenny left, I took a painkiller and lay down on the couch. As the medicine took effect, my thoughts drifted. I thought about when it was that I started on the journey of trying to understand my own life and the lives of others. There were moments of epiphany when knowledge and experience simply fell into place. Often, this was in the company of others, especially my grandfather, who, as I grew older, guided me in my journey with the same insight, humor and sensitivity with which he had guided me as a child.

As I grew older, I sometimes accompanied my grandfather to social occasions. I found the conversations of law and politics fascinating and thought-provoking. Other occasions were duty-bound, and these courtesy occasions were generally tedious. At one such event, an elderly lady commented on the accident that had ended my career as a dancer. Her comment was: "No pain, no gain, dear."

It was as if someone had slapped me. Grandpa and I left shortly after, his hand covering mine as we drove home. He did not say anything but left me to work it through. I twisted my thoughts around in my head for a while. "I have never really understood that saying," I said. "It makes it sound as if pain is good for its own sake. Isn't happiness just as important? What about happiness, Grandpa? Is it possible to recover from pain if there is no happiness, nothing to measure it by?"

"No. Laura. I don't think so," he replied softly.

"And what about strength, Grandpa? Some people can hurt and hurt and still be okay, but others can't. I guess, Grandpa, I just always knew that I was stronger than Michael. I think I was aware of how much he hurt, but it wasn't just about circumstances; it was how we were born."

"I think it is true that many people have an innate strength—that, like you say, we are born that way, Laura, but people are not predictable; maybe you'd have to live many lives to know that. What do you think?"

"What I think right now is this: that it is not true that age automatically means a person is wise. That woman was horrible."

"Now that I am sure of," Grandpa replied dryly. "The idea that age

is tantamount to one's degree of wisdom is a lie our society perpetuates."

If I had moments of epiphany, most of my growth was slow and cumulative. Perhaps the journey of becoming more than simply a mindless observer was through the vicarious learning of being a dancer. As part of my senior training in dance, I took theatre courses where I studied and practiced how human personality and circumstance are reflected in movement. It was a new dimension of subtext, beyond what Sophia had taught me about so many years before. It was about the subtext of the spirit.

There is the boundless movement of an unfettered child, the straight posture and firm footing of a confident adult, the intense focus, with complete indifference to their surroundings, of people who are in love. There is the shuffle of those who are broken, who avert their eyes and whose lives are interwoven with the lives of others in an almost invisible way. There is the child whose eyes are never seen, whose limp posture shifts but who no longer flinches, even in the face of physical attack.

I played these roles in theatre classes. I had probably been surrounded by them my entire life. But, today, on that walk with Jenn, I thought of what my instructors taught me. Taking up my thoughts were the averted gazes, the turning away from the wounds on my face by the people I'd encountered. I wondered why they'd seemed to wish to make me and themselves invisible. In the months to come, I would begin to understand why.

My reflections were interrupted by a light knock on the door. Opening it, I was greeted by a tall, stunning-looking woman, who smiled and introduced herself as Nadine Sinclair. I invited her in, and she accepted my offer for coffee. Her anorak was soaked. I draped it over the recliner, then tried to get a fire going. She said she'd do that, while I made the coffee.

Over coffee, she told me she was a biologist and gave me a synopsis of the work she was doing in the area. Nadine had been based in the Passage for two years. Together with two young First Nations people, she'd been tracking the movements of grizzly bears by attaching radio collars to them. This would be her last field season, and she hoped that her PhD dissertation would be completed in the next year or so. "That is," she said, "if I don't crash and burn."

Although this last remark had been accompanied with a smile, there was something serious in the way she said it. As she talked, I studied her. She was slim and graceful, with fine features, playful dark eyes and long, curly dark hair. When she spoke, Nadine used her hands to add emphasis. I could tell that she had a good working relationship with her crew. I told her that I was afraid of bears and didn't think I could do what she did: tranquilizing grizzlies, moving rapidly to put collars on them, taking various measurements and then leaving quickly.

"Hey," she said. "I have to tell you that I don't actually love bears. But I'm very fascinated by them and have an enormous amount of respect for them. I recognize and would fight for their right to live on the planet. However, they are not self-actualized and have no idea what my motives are. I've never had an urge to take home any fuzzy bears."

She'd made her statement in a deadly serious voice and then, at the end, presented me with a huge grin. I burst out laughing.

I asked her if she was the Not-Doctor Sinclair that Jenn Hunt had referred to.

"Actually," she replied in a humorous tone, "my crew and probably half the village call me Not-Not Doctor Sinclair."

I raised my eyebrows.

"I can't remember exactly how the name evolved. First, someone started calling me, 'Not-Doctor Sinclair' because I don't have my PhD yet, and then somehow the other 'Not' was added because I'm not a medical doctor—so there you have it: I am Not-Not Doctor Sinclair."

Once again, we burst into laughter, and I was grateful for the painkiller I'd taken earlier, which allowed me to laugh without restraint. Nadine asked me about my work. I explained what the project was all about. She listened quietly and, then, looking pointedly at my face, asked what the other guy looked like.

"Didn't Dr. Sutherland tell you what happened?"

"No. Chris Sutherland wouldn't reveal patient information to the Pope. He just suggested that I might want to visit you."

I told her about the door and the events that followed, and it became funnier and funnier as I went through the story. When I'd finished, she said that the white female scientists at the Passage were going to become a legend. I questioned her with my eyes; she responded by telling me that her foot had accidentally been sliced with an axe by one of her crew.

"How could that happen?"

"We never really figured it out, exactly. We were building a tree platform, and the axe slipped. It happened." She shrugged. "But that was nothing. My foot got infected, and I picked up blood poisoning. They were going to fly me out, but the fog rolled in, and they couldn't bring my fever down, so I had to sit in an ice-bath in front of Chris. Sue, the best nurse around here, was there as well, so it wasn't as personal as it sounds. But the thing is, I'm crazy about Chris Sutherland. And every time I think about sitting naked in the tub, I turn red, even if I'm by myself."

I grinned and told Nadine that Chief Charlie thought Dr. Sutherland was the best doctor that had ever been at the Passage.

"He is a good doctor," she said and then added with a grin, "And good-looking too."

We continued to chat until Nadine asked me if there was anything I needed.

I told her "no," that my main concern was that I had no idea how I was going to wash my hair.

"Does it hurt more when you put your face forward or back?" she asked.

"Both."

"Can I check out the place and see if we can figure something out?"

"Sure." We examined the kitchen sink, looked at each other and shook our heads. She carefully assessed the big, old, claw-footed tub in the bathroom.

"Got it," she said. "We'll put a chair next to the bath, and you can lean forward as far as you can, while I wash your hair. If we get the floor wet, so what? I can wipe it up."

We had a hilarious time; water did get all over the floor. Later, sitting in the living room again, I asked her, "What about Dr. Sutherland?" Is he crazy about you?"

"Maybe. I asked him out. I'm going to make dinner for him next Saturday."

"You asked him out?"

"I did. He said no and gave me this line about I'm his patient etc., etc. This was on my follow-up visit, after I was out of the hospital. I told him he was fired, and then he just shut up and said, 'Yes.' So, there you have it."

70

She was going to be out in the field all week, but we planned to get together the following Friday night. I was looking forward to seeing her at the end of the week.

The sky was beginning to clear, and the sun was just setting when I went to bed. I lay awake, thinking about Nadine's and Chris Sutherland's interesting romance, which led me to thoughts about Daniel Hunt. I replayed every moment of the time we'd spent together, replayed it more than once. If, at the time, I'd begun to think about what it is that makes people work, my level of maturity meant that I didn't give any thought to the realities of being with Daniel, of the obstacles of any future we might have, of the different worlds that we lived in. I was here now, and he was here now; there was something between us. Romance was the extent of my reflection.

What I'm certain I did not think about at the time was that standing between us was the here and now of my life, his far greater maturity and the differences that separated our worlds. Later, Daniel told me what had been running through his head.

On the deck of his trailer, he drank black coffee as dusk settled over the Passage. Daniel was thinking about Laura Fitzgerald on that first night at Charlie's. She was ridiculously overdressed, and it was difficult not to laugh at her unmatched sneakers. It seemed she wore herself lightly. If she was embarrassed, she didn't show it. She was respectful but at ease with Charlie and the others. He smiled at the thought of the horrified look on her face when she bumped his boat on the Edgewater Dock. She was witty, and there was a strong edge of sarcasm in her quick comebacks; but she was not unkind. Her laughter was spontaneous and catchy…and made her endearing somehow.

Even in an old t-shirt and shorts, she looked graceful. There was something about the way she moved—not designed to impress, something she was clearly unaware of. She could flirt but seemed equally oblivious of the effect of the half-smile that often played across her face, a smile that made him want to touch her.

She was very young. It was not just intuition but practicality that gave him made him cautious. She was vulnerable; a casual affair could hurt her very much. A serious entanglement would be just that—an entanglement. There was no place for her in his world; there was nothing in his past or in his present that could provide him with what he'd need to meet her on even ground.

But other thoughts were tugging at his mind, thoughts about who she was, what was deeply hidden. She had neatly steered the subject of herself towards his work as a fisherman. And there were the scars on either side of her right ankle—scars that were common among fisherman who had broken a leg after slipping on greasy decks. Grimm, who had gone into great technical and non-stop detail about his broken tibia and fibula, made him aware of the type of injury Laura had. Was this what her comment to Chris had been about? Did this have something to do with her dislike of hospitals and related somehow to that comment, "Hospitals make me sick."

Through the open balcony doors of the trailer, he listened to the surf; the rhythm worked its way into his thoughts. He had no idea that someday he would tell Laura about what had gone through his mind that night.

Chapter 10

It turned out that my broken nose was the single most important factor in my acceptance into the community of Waglisla. Widely discussed, it was an event free of scandal and the topic of considerable humor. When that door hit my face, I became a person.

Dinner at Chief Charlie's the following evening consisted of a good-sized salmon that was smoked and then barbecued. Rose fussed over me and patted me on the shoulder; each time she said, "Have more of this good salmon, Laura. I can see you like it. No, don't eat the potatoes. You don't like them."

Besides Chief Charlie and Rose, Laney, her three children and Jenn were the only people at dinner that night. Several times, Laney told her oldest son, who was maybe five, not to stare at me, although, clearly, she herself was trying not to grin at probably both my appearance and at the circumstances that led to my appearance. I took a painkiller before dinner, which I'm sure loosened up my presentation, and I finally said to Laney's son, "It's okay, Eric, you can look at my face; my self-confidence lately has been dangerously high."

Laney's laughter was the beginning of our friendship.

In the living room after dinner, I talked to Chief Charlie about the project and told him that I had read all of the work of the anthropologist Franz Boas, who had studied the Heiltsuk in the 1880s and 1920s and wondered if any of the Elders would remember him. Also, I wanted to ask the Elders about their recollections of the sites we'd be researching, but I had no idea how to begin a relationship with these members of the community.

"Margaret Brown, she's my aunt. She'd remember," Chief Charlie said. "And she'll tell you the truth. Sometimes people just tell you what they think you want to hear. In fact, I think that sometimes was the case with Boas. Maggie would know something about that too. I'll talk to her; I'm sure she'll be very curious to meet you. Start with her."

Jenn, who had been listening to us without interrupting, saw a lull in the conversation and asked, "Laura, how long until have your regular nose back?"

"Only a few weeks. You know, I completely smashed my ankle once, and it works just great, except that I can't dance on the tables anymore at parties."

Chief Charlie took my remark literally and asked quite seriously, "You're a dancer?"

"I did dance for a long time—when I was growing up."

"Laura," piped in Jenn enthusiastically. "Grandpa is a dancer; you should see him in his regalia. It is so beautiful. Do you have regalia? Do you own your dances?"

I smiled at her. "I did have regalia of a sort, and I suppose I did own some of my dances but not like your grandpa. If someone used my dances, it would be a compliment, but if someone used your grandpa's, it'd be stealing, and he'd have to kill them."

Chief Charlie laughed that deep, wonderful laugh and said, "I guess you read about our dances in that work of Franz Boas."

"I did."

"Well, he would be right, eh, Jenny?"

"Right, Grandpa."

"You have probably also read the stories of the Heiltsuk that Boas wrote down?" Chief Charlie asked me.

"I have."

"Well, Jenny knows some stories. Why don't you tell Laura a story before she goes, Jenny?"

"Okay, which one?"

"Tell her the story that belongs to you," he answered.

"But, how can Laura understand? She can't speak our language."

"Well, translate it into English—just do the best you can. Let's sit in the living room while you tell your story."

"Okay." Jenn sat cross-legged on the living room floor, and we arranged ourselves around her. A look of concentration crossed her face. Then she began her story.

"This is my story," she said. "It belongs to me, as I am born to the Raven, and it was given to me with my Heiltsuk name, Gigaxstalis,

74

which means 'Sunshine' in English. It is a story about Raven Stealing the Sun."

In the beginning, it was only the moon that gave light to the people. The sun was kept by a Chief as his own property—he guarded the sun in a box that was tied up with strong ropes made of woven cedar. Raven saw that the people needed the sun, and he decided to steal the sun from this Chief. Raven went to the village where the sun was, and he transformed himself into a cedar needle and placed himself in a spring, where the people in the village got their water. The Chief's daughter went to drink from the spring, and the cedar needle landed in her cup, but she knew it was Raven, and she threw it away. Next, Raven transformed himself into a salmon berry, but just as the Chief's daughter was about to eat the berry, she knew that the berry was Raven in disguise, and she threw the berry away. Then Raven transformed himself into a spot of eulachon grease, and the Chief's daughter ate the grease, and she became pregnant, and when her time came, she gave birth to Raven. All the time, Raven cried because he wanted to play with the sun-box, and finally the Chief let Raven play with it. At first, Raven played with the box in the house, then just outside of the house, and then every day, he played with the box further and further away from the house and so tricked the Chief, who stopped noticing the box that held the sun. Finally, Raven flew away with the sun to a village in Rivers Inlet. Here, he met a group of people who had canoes full of eulachon and asked for some of the eulachon in return for freeing the sun. The people refused to grant his request, except for one Chief and his family. Raven told the Chief and his family to hide behind the canoe and to hide their eyes because he was going to open the box and change the world. The Chief and his family did this, and Raven opened the box, and the sun came out. The people who refused to give eulachon to Raven were turned into frogs, but the Chief and his family, who had given eulachon to Raven, were saved. And that is how Raven stole the sun and gave it to the people.

I had read a story like the one Jenn told, one that was recorded by Franz Boas. But in the telling, the inflections and the details, it was truly Jenn's story, and all of us acknowledged this respectfully in the silence that followed the telling. Even Laney's children had listened carefully. I saw pride in Rose's face, and Chief Charlie told Jenn she had done a good job and that the translation was good. I thanked Jenn for telling me her story, but I think it was the look of admiration on my face that she read. She beamed. I wanted to ask her about her Heiltsuk name, "Sunshine," but did not wish to break the story's spell and so let it go for the time being.

Rose packed up some salmon and the remainder of the chocolate cake we had for dinner, and Chief Charlie and Jenn drove me back to the manse. Chief Charlie sternly told me that I shouldn't go out the next day if Dr. Sutherland hadn't given it the okay. I said that I'd take the doctor's advice. As I was about to close the door of the pickup he said, "Don't worry, Laura; you'll do just fine."

I already liked and respected Chief Charlie and realized that he was fully aware I lacked some confidence in myself. I was glad he believed in me...or so it seemed.

It was still early when I arrived at the manse. I did a careful checklist of the field equipment for loading onto the boat the next day and made up backpacks for Kristy and Jack that contained trowels, paintbrushes, forms, their field journals and other paraphernalia used by archaeologists. I checked my own backpack. I checked the wooden supply boxes—machetes, axes, variously sized root clippers. The equipment suddenly seemed endless. I checked the large metal supply container—cameras, transit, compasses, 1:50,000 maps, George's photos, and field documents about Boston's Retreat. On the top of each box was neatly stenciled, "Property of SFU—Department of Archaeology."

In the study was a pile of archaeological reports, documents and books relating to the Heiltsuk. I needed to reread the reports of early European explorers, traders, Hudson's Bay fur traders and the published documents of the Heiltsuk and of other Coastal Indigenous groups, anything that could shed light on the Heiltsuk. In Vancouver, the material was more abstract, but now that I was in the territory of the Heiltsuk, there were more specific and significant meanings to be found.

I took a stack of documents and set them on the coffee table. One-by-one, I read each, underlining and taking notes. The project was taking on ominous proportions. I felt overwhelmed and discouraged. Vaguely, I noticed I was picking at the cuticle of my thumb.

The sound of the phone ringing in the kitchen startled me, but then I remembered the phone company said it would be hooked up sometime on Friday. It was my sixteen-year-old brother, Jake. Recognizing his voice, I found that my anxiety evaporated.

"How did you find me? I told you never to call me here." I laughed.

"I got your number from Directory Assistance, you idiot. How are you? Why didn't you call? Do you miss me?"

"I didn't know the phone was hooked up yet, and I'm fine, but I only miss the fact that you aren't here to help me get some sleep."

We both laughed. At Sunday dinner several months before, I'd had several glasses of wine and decided to spend the night rather than drive home. I couldn't sleep and got out of bed and joined Mom and Jake in the living room, where they were watching the late news. Jake was commenting on the stories being reported on CBC. During any newscast, my brother would offer non-stop commentary that was cynical, hilarious and aimed at no one in particular. I remember that on that night, during a commercial break, he parodied a character in the newscast. It was a lawyer who had told a group of reporters that his client was the victim of injustice and was innocent.

"Yes, my client is not even slightly guilty, ladies and gentlemen," mimicked Jake. "The fact that the body was found in my client's Whistler chalet and was shot fourteen times with my client's gun, *and* with a note written in blood on the wall saying that my client did it, is purely coincidental."

My mother and I laughed and laughed at Jake's sharp remarks. On that night, I finished my herbal tea and headed back to bed.

"I thought you couldn't sleep," my mother said.

"I couldn't, but Jake's analysis has exhausted me. I think we could make a lot of money from this. We could start up a "Dial-A-Jakes" for those with insomnia."

I truly believed this kind of joke would last a lifetime.

"I need to ask you a favor, Laura."

On the other end of the receiver, Jake went into great detail, providing a lengthy explanation on why he needed a car. I always listened to him carefully when he was serious.

I hesitated after he spoke. "You don't even have a driver's license yet."

"I know, but I'm starting lessons this week. I could get my license in a month or so."

"Why don't you run this past the firm of Messrs. O'Donnell, Fitzgerald, Murphy…and the token LaChapelle?" I asked.

"You've got to be kidding. First, Fitzgerald; that would be Grandpa, is dead, and so is O'Donnell. LaChapelle is in an advanced stage of dementia, and Judge Murphy thinks you're Miss Perfect Manners and that I'm a possible copy of Richard Murphy."

My grandfather's law firm were the trustees of his estate. He'd divided his estate equally between Jake and me; we'd not inherit the proceeds until we were thirty. It was not a large fortune, but if we invested as wisely as Grandpa had, the money trusted to us gave us a financial advantage that few people had.

"That's outright misrepresentation, Jake. Richard was a rebellious teenager but is now a respectable lawyer, and none of those charges was ever proven. Plus, I was with him that time he was falsely accused of drunk and disorderly conduct and assaulting a peace officer."

"Okay, Okay, I know all that. But, could you ask them to advance me the money for the car?"

"No way. You must prove you're capable. It took me two months of research and getting advice from Richard to talk them into getting the money to buy my place in Deep Cove. They do not want to hear from me for a while. Listen, Jakes, it's not that hard. Write down all the reasons you need a car and how responsible and wonderful you are. And don't even think about a new car. The judge will never give you the money for that. Send all the information to Richard—he'll look it over and then call you, and the two of you can figure out what vehicle is the safest. Then, you rewrite the letter. Of course, the judge will know Richard was involved but will give you the money based on the soundness of Richard's presentation. He knows his son is a good lawyer, and he has forgiven him for his crimes."

"The safest vehicle? That would be a ten-ton truck."

"Who cares? A truck is safer. And you're a new driver."

"Come on, Laura, I don't want to look like a redneck…and anyway, wasn't that you who rear-ended some guy in the McDonald's drive-thru last month and embarrassed me in front of all my friends?"

I burst out laughing. "True, but you were distracting me."

"All right—but could you go over my letter? Maybe on the phone. I could start on it tomorrow. And…what's wrong with your voice?"

"I have a cold…and, yes, I will go over the letter with you."

"So, how's it up there in Waglosla, eh?" asked Jake in a generic Indigenous accent.

"It's the Passage, Wag-lis-la, to the Natives," I replied crisply, adding, "I see some evidence of racial intolerance on your part."

"Just trying to uphold our father's political position, Laura," he joked.

"I like it up here, and the Natives are friendly."

"Any guys?"

"Well sure. I sort of like this guy. He's tall, dark and handsome… and he might be a chief."

"Great, I'll phone Father and tell him you're making a huge contribution to the Indian problem," said Jake. I think that Jake's best parodies were of our father.

"Is it serious?"

"Jakes, I've only been here a week and anyway, I doubt he's interested in a serious relationship."

"That's a new concept, Laura. Man, you sure do need a shrink."

In a recent fit of psychoanalysis, Jake explained to me that my failure to have been in a long-term relationship related to issues around our father.

"Sure, and blah, blah, blah to you too."

"'Sure'? Where does that come from? Please, don't tell me you're picking up a local dialect?"

"Sure," I answered and laughed. "Anyway, what's new with you? How is everything with your girlfriend?"

"Man, she is something else, Laura. We went to the movies on Friday and Saturday night this week, and I'm going over to her place for dinner tonight."

"So, it's getting serious. What does her father do?"

"What are you, my parents?"

I laughed again. "No, just curious."

"I don't know what the guy does, and I don't care. And…oh, yeah, Mom's here and wants to talk to you, and I love you, and blah, blah, blah."

My mother immediately asked what was wrong, said my voice sounded strange. I gave her the story about the cold. We chatted for a while about her garden and about Bruce's daughters. Bruce was a retired fireman and had been a widow for many years. Mom had been seeing him for almost two years.

"What do you think about the car idea, Mom?"

"Well, he's growing up. He's a good kid, Laura, but it wouldn't kill him to wait either."

I heard Jake in the background. "Thanks, Mom. I love you too."

I did not discuss my nose but told her about the Passage and that I had a lot of support from the Chief Band Councilor and had been to dinner with his family twice. She sensed my uncertainty about my work.

"Forge on, Laura. You're really interested in this. I haven't seen such level of excitement from any other field work you've done. You'll do fine."

Her words were comforting and restored my perspective.

After I hung up, I returned to the document I'd been studying. My anxiety, I found, had vanished.

That night I dreamed of Raven stealing the sun, rushing upwards towards the sky with a huge, beautifully carved bentwood box from which brilliant rays of light were escaping. Franz Boas was standing next to me and was trying to tell me something, in a language that I recognized was German, and I could not understand him. I vaguely recall that I woke up, thought about the dream for a few minutes, and then fell quickly back to sleep.

Chapter 11

On Monday morning, Jack arrived ten minutes early, and Kristy just after that. A bright sun was rapidly cutting through the morning fog. We loaded most of the gear into Dodd's taxi for the first trip to the wharf. I asked Jack and Kristy to get the rest of the gear and stow it on the boat, while I went to see Dr. Sutherland.

Dr. Sutherland examined my face and said that my nose was healing nicely. I told him that I was heading out into the field. Smiling, and looking pointedly at my steel-toed boots, he said, "That would be my best guess."

I asked if he could take the bandage off my nose. Not until the end of the week, he said, and proceeded to change the bandage. After my nose was wrapped up once again, he said I ought to "take it easy out there."

Most of the equipment was already loaded neatly in the boat when I got back to the wharf. Jack was carefully examining every part of the cabin cruiser and pronounced it "a pretty good boat." We heard a helicopter. I saw it was heading for the mainland.

"That's the biologist's helicopter—that is, Not-Not Doctor Sinclair's helicopter," remarked Kristy in a conspiratorial voice.

"I know. I've met her; she told me about her nickname, but she didn't mention a helicopter. She has her own helicopter?" I asked.

"Yeah, well, sort of. It belongs to some Vancouver logging company, but they take her and her crew up the mountains at the beginning of the week and then pick them up on Friday. All those loggers and hot shots are in love with that biologist and would probably fly her to Vancouver to go shopping," said Kristy, adding, "My cousin is on her crew. He thinks she's pretty cool."

"How come they're going up to the mountains?" I asked.

"Because it's summer, and the bears go up there for food," answered Jack, somewhat scornfully.

"Well, excuse me; sorry for not being a wildlife expert. Anyways, that means we don't have to worry about bears."

"You always have to worry about bears, Laura. That's why I'm bringing my rifle." He was admonishing me.

"That gives me a lot of confidence. Just don't aim that gun at me." But I was smiling as I handed him the key to Daniel's boat.

It occurred to me that Jack's and Kristy's easygoing tones were a positive change in our relationship. Once again, I was reminded that my nose served as an ice breaker.

Jack was, as Daniel said, an expert at handling power boats. It seemed to take only a few minutes to reach Boston's Retreat, which was on the northern side of Denny Island, not far from Edgewater Resort.

George had visited the site in 1965, made some notes and taken photographs. He noted that the site was located on top of a shallow midden that was a few meters back from a small beach. The remains of Indigenous houses at the site probably dated back to 1833, or thereabouts, when the Hudson's Bay Company built a fur-trading post near the current village of Waglisla. Boston's Retreat would be in a strategic spot to control trade, ensuring that the Heiltsuk could act as middlemen and intercept Natives from Bella Coola and the Interior who might try to directly trade at the Fort. George's notes indicated four houses at the site, a very small encampment for a winter village. Still, building a winter house was an enormous investment in labor, so if the reason was mainly to control the fur trade, doing so must have been highly profitable.

Jack moored the boat on a shallow rock outcropping, and we walked around the site. It was overgrown, but the house posts were easy to spot, as were the remains of large fallen house beams. Both Douglas fir and hemlock were rooted in the beams; deteriorating cedar created a perfect environment for these species to grow. The trees were younger than those of the surrounding forest, indicating the relatively recent occupation of the site.

The brush on the site was heavy. Salal, huckleberry bushes and ferns covered the forest floor, as well as aspen, typical of disturbed forest habitat. Jack and I walked about the site, while Kristy explored the beach.

The outlines of the houses were easy to find because of the hemlock and fir rooted in the cedar floor sills and floor supports. The site seemed flat, but it would take a lot of work to clear the brush in the area in order to map and investigate the architecture.

"Looks like we have a lot of clearing to do."

Kristy had reappeared. "We have to clear the bushes out of here?"

"Not all of it," I answered. Just enough to map and photograph the site."

"How are we going to clear it?"

"Machetes and axes," I replied, "We'd better unload the equipment."

"Could I just photograph you guys doing that?" asked Kristy.

Both Jack and I rolled our eyes.

I was anxious to see the carving on the house posts; we started cutting away the growth. I knew immediately that something was not right. Beneath the overgrowth, the entire front of the first post was gouged out.

I was stunned. Kristy and Jack seemed equally shocked.

Jack looked closely at the edges of the cut and ran his fingers along the edges. "Chainsaw," he said.

It took us very little time to remove the growth from the remaining standing house posts. On all of these, the carving on the front of the posts had been cut away.

At mid-morning, I went to the boat and got out George's file.

Together, the three of us sat on the shallow beach and looked at the 1965 photographs of the posts, the carvings clearly visible and in beautiful condition.

"Who would do this?" I asked.

"Not us," said Jack. And by 'us,' I knew he was speaking not only about Heiltsuk people but about Indigenous people in general. "Wouldn't be of any use, and even if it was, would stir up too many ghosts."

I looked at him. "Souvenirs, white people souvenirs?"

He nodded.

"When could it have happened? You know this place, Jack. Chief Charlie knows it; even Jenn Hunt knows of it. When were you here last?"

"A long time ago—I guess when I was a kid. The carvings were there then."

"We never come here," said Kristy. "To Denny Island, I mean."

I looked at Jack, who nodded.

"Why not?" I asked.

"Well, duh. Edgewater owns this place," Kristy said.

Jack nodded his head in agreement.

With an edge of anger, I countered with, "Edgewater only owns part of this island."

It took the rest of the day to clear the site and to determine where the transit could be set up to produce an accurate map. Setting up a transit would take a long time, and the fewer times we had to move it to map the site, the quicker we could complete our work. The houses appeared to be almost fifteen meters square and the cedar house posts one meter in width. The beams were covered in moss. Carefully removing bits of moss revealed the beautifully adzed surfaces I had seen in George's pictures of traditional villages. The defaced house posts were about 3 meters high and between half a meter and a meter in width. The top of the house posts was concave and would have supported the huge beams that now lay below, on the forest floor.

At the end of the day, we sat on the edge of the tree line, just beyond the rock beach, and wrote in our field journals. It took Kristy about three minutes to make her entry.

"Exactly, what did you write, Kristy?" I asked.

"I wrote that it was a nice day, that we worked very hard, that some jerk stole the carvings and that the road to perdition leads to hell."

"Why did you write that? And anyway, it's 'The road to hell is paved with good intentions.'"

"I know that, but I was thinking of whoever stole those carvings and cursing them with the idea that the road to hell leads to hell."

I tried to wrap my thoughts around that, wondering where her religious background came from, then just burst out laughing. Jack just shook his head.

That night, I phoned George to give him an update of what I was doing and to report, without containing my anger, on the carvings cut out from the house beams. He listened quietly, then said, "Don't be surprised if you run into that again, Laura. It's happened at many coastal sites."

"Do you think it was people from Edgewater Resort?"

George paused, obviously thinking and replied, "That doesn't make sense. The house posts would have been part of their overall tourist package. Defacing them would take away from that. I guess it is possible that a tourist hired someone to make a return visit." George went on to say he recalled that some of the house posts had fallen over at Boston's Retreat and that he'd noticed this when he was there, and that these may not have been identified as house posts. Maybe I could get some information if these posts hadn't been defaced.

That night I pored over documents, jotted down notes and read and thought, often pacing back and forth. For me, the long-abandoned houses at Boston's Retreat were something tangible, something immediately recognizable as being created by human hands. I wondered at the work and skill of constructing the houses and about the families who lived in them. This evening also marked the beginning of the routine I slipped into that summer: working during the day and, at night, reading and writing down thoughts and speculations in a personal journal. A copy of the formal field journal would go to the Band Council and the Heritage Conservation Branch, where better written and more formal hypotheses would be recorded. My personal journal ended up being halfway between a textbook and a novel.

We did find two toppled over house posts, but the carved side was face down on the forest floor. In this position, it was doubtful that decay would have made the carvings legible. And, in any case, it would have taken a crane to turn them over.

Jack had taken his field journal home every night, and finally on Thursday, at lunchtime, I asked if I could check it out. In the journal were carefully kept notes where Jack had written down objective information about the site. At the back of the journal were the trigonometry formulas for cosines and tangents that I'd shown him when we'd mapped the backyard of the manse, formulas that would be used to construct the highly detailed counter map and architecture of the site when we finished field research at Boston's Retreat.

I looked up and for the first time saw some anxiety in his eyes.

"Thanks, Jack." I said. But it was the shine and admiration in my own eyes that really thanked him, and he knew that.

As I was handing it back, I noticed that on the cover page of the journal were my name and Kristy's, followed by a series of checkmarks.

"What's this?" I asked, and Kristy leaned over to look.

"That's a record of the number of times that you and Kristy swear."

"That's quite a lot. I'm ahead of you, Laura," Kristy said; then, accusingly, "Why exactly are you keeping this record?"

He grinned. "I'm keeping a record to be used as evidence for the Band Council if I get fired. There are several really religious people on the Council."

"Oh, for God's sake, you're such an asshole, Jack," Kristy retorted.

He neatly put another check next to her name, and we laughed all the way back to the Passage.

By Friday, we'd mapped about a quarter of the site. At the rate we were going, it really seemed we'd be at Boston's Retreat for the rest of the season, but I had a lot to learn about how to approach the documentation of the sites. I was encouraged by the fact that Jack and Kristy were hard working, and I imagined we'd speed up as the project continued.

On the way home from Boston's Retreat on Friday, Kristy, shy for once, told me that it was her 20th birthday the next day and that she was going to have a big party with her friends at the Hotel pub. Would I like to come? I told her I'd be there for sure…except I wish I'd known sooner because I could've gotten her a present.

"I don't need a present, you goof," she said.

Her term of endearment meant a lot to me. Leaning over towards Kristy, I asked if Jack was going to go. I didn't think he'd hear me over the roar of the engine, but he did.

"No way," said Jack. "Her friends are all a bunch of crazy Indians."

Chapter 12

The phone rang a few minutes after I arrived home. It was Nadine, who'd seen our boat come "flying across the Passage."

Laughing, I told her I'd seen her on Monday, "flying over the Passage in her own personal helicopter."

We decided we'd have dinner at the Hotel and then go to her place for a few drinks. I met her at 5:30, and over hamburgers and beer, she told me hilarious stories of her work in the Passage. This included accounts of complete and near misses with the tranquilizer gun, bears that appeared to be asleep but were awake, and ongoing dares between herself and her crew to go moonlight swimming in the glacial lakes high up the mountain passes. It was clear that she was close to the young Heiltsuk woman and man that made up her crew.

I asked her if she had many friends among the white people who lived in the village.

"A few. Most of the white people here are elementary school teachers, or work at the hospital, or at the RCMP Detachment, and except for a few who have married into the community, they don't stay very long. There is even a kind of physical segregation. Have you noticed what sort of looks like a compound across the street from the hospital?" she asked.

"I think so," I told her. "Is it an area that contains several small houses and a bunch of mobile homes?"

"Yes. That's where all the nurses, hospital technicians and RCMP live. Most of the teachers live in a group of houses right next to the elementary school." She paused. "There isn't often any outright tension."

Nadine took a sip of her beer, and a troubled look passed over her features. "When I first came here, I did go to some of the parties that the white contingent held. But there were a lot of slurs against the

Natives. I understand that white people feel isolated here and that the housing separation is not their design. I know the RCMP must get involved in some ugly situations—usually ones relating to drinking. Still, I think I tried to give another point of view about the Heiltsuk, but it's like there just isn't any concept that these people have a real culture, that they aren't all freeloaders and drunks. Especially as I got closer to my crew—that would be Allie and Jason," Nadine clarified, "I felt like I was banging my head against a wall of ignorance. So, I jumped sides."

She smiled at this last remark, then continued in a serious tone. "When I first came here, there were some bad feelings against the RCMP, at one point, even allegations of mistreatment to several Indigenous people who were in lock-up. For a couple of weeks, there was some vandalism. All the windows in the teacherages were broken."

I asked Nadine where things stood now.

"It's a lot better. They sent in a veteran sergeant about a year and a half ago, and he came, not as punishment for screwing up somewhere else but because he's very good at cleaning up other people's messes. His name is Brian MacCallum, and he runs a tight ship. There won't be any misconduct on his watch. I've had dinner a few times with him and a nurse named Sue Mitchell that he's paired up with. They're both nice people. And MacCallum seems to have attracted more mature members to the Detachment here."

I asked Nadine if this was the same Sue who'd stood watch with Chris while Nadine sat in an ice-bath.

"It is."

I told her I thought I'd met Sue on my flight in and then asked her how Chris fit in.

"He's been here about the same amount of time as I have, but I never met him at any of those parties. I think he's very busy, and my sense is that he has a broader perspective. He's in charge of running the hospital. People don't care for the other doctor that works here, but Chris is well respected in the community. To tell you the truth, I really don't know that much about him, except that I feel this strong attraction. I hope my intuitions are right." She smiled.

After dinner we walked to Nadine's house. On the way past the hospital, she pointed out Chris's white house. Jenn had showed me the house the week before. Like the manse, it came with the position he'd been hired to fill. The house Nadine lived in belonged to a Heiltsuk couple who'd gone to visit their daughter on the Island and had decided to stay to help care for their grandchildren while the daughter went to university. The small, log home was very open and had lots of light. It contained a huge rock fireplace and an incredible view of the Passage.

We sat on the balcony off her living room, drank wine, and talked about ourselves. After each sip of wine, Nadine's use of her hands to emphasize a point became more exaggerated. For some reason, I found this endearing. She had a younger sister and brother and parents who'd been married forever. Her father was a lawyer, specializing in corporate tax, and her mother, a teacher. They lived in Vancouver.

I told her that her family sounded perfect and asked her about any skeletons in the closet.

She contemplated this for a moment and, grinning, replied, "Well what with the mental illness and all, there's me."

"You have a mental illness?"

"Yes, I do. Bipolar disorder."

In response to the quizzical look on my face, Nadine nodded. "I know," she said, her tone serious. "I don't look like I have a mental illness, and most of the time I guess I don't notice it myself. But it took three breakdowns and hospitalizations before they got it right. The medication I'm on works very well, and usually I don't think about it, but sometimes I do worry I'll get sick again. But then, I just get caught up in the fear, and that feeds it, so mostly I just don't think about it."

I guessed she'd told me all she wanted to about it for now. I did tell her I knew something about the disorder because I'd done some reading on mental illnesses and disorders. She wondered why.

"I was trying to understand my father. He's a cruel man, a hard man." I said his name out loud, which was strange for me. How long had it been since I'd heard that name spoken?

"He's your father?" she asked.

"Yes."

"It's so hard to believe he's your father—he's so far to the right…" Her voice trailed off. I finished her sentence. "…that he's one step from being a Nazi."

This comment broke the serious tone of our conversation, and we burst out laughing.

"Did you find a diagnosis for your father—in your reading, I mean?"

"I think he might be a psychopath; for sure he's an asshole."

Perhaps buoyed by the wine, my remark caused us to laugh, almost hysterically.

"Well, if we are going to share skeletons, I have another one that ups yours," said Nadine.

"You do?"

Leaning closer and in a quiet, conspiratorial voice, Nadine said, "My Dad's an alcoholic. I guess that could be a skeleton."

I stopped laughing; my expression turned sympathetic.

"He's been sober for twenty-six years. In fact, I spent most of my quality time with Dad when I was a kid going to AA meetings. I still think I might eventually die of secondhand smoke. Also, I learned probably every swear word there is at those meetings."

Our conversation turned to Nadine's upcoming date with Chris, which she was very nervous about. I couldn't imagine why he wouldn't be crazy about her and told her that, by this time tomorrow night, she'd be wrapped up in his arms.

"Hey, don't think I wouldn't. But I think he's cautious, you know, a slow mover." As an afterthought, she added, "Also, I don't have any birth control."

"The guy's a doctor, Nadine. He should be able to come up with something."

"True," she speculated. "But do you think I should play hard to get?"

"Well, I think you might've already blown that idea, so my short answer would be no."

I left just after midnight, taking Mack's taxi back to the manse and paying the standard two dollars. Perhaps because of the wine, I didn't sleep well and tossed and turned all night. Sometime before dawn, I had a vivid dream.

In the dream, I was alone in Nadine's house. There was a terrible storm and the wind was sending curios smashing to the floor. I closed all the windows and then heard more crashing.

A raven was trapped in the house and was flying about in a crazed, haphazard panic around the living room, crashing into walls and knocking down lamps. I cowered in the corner, not knowing what to do. Then, through the glass balcony doors I saw Franz Boas, surrounded by that ambient light. He motioned for me to open the door, and I did. He drew me gently outside onto the balcony. Inside the house, the raven calmed and flew out the door. It seemed to give a cry of relief as it disappeared into the dark night.

Chapter 13

I woke up early with a slight headache, but a cup of coffee cleared my head. I did the laundry and cleaned up the manse. The question of removing my bandage was solved when it fell off while I was scrubbing out the tub. My eyes were still bruised, but the reds and purples were edged with greens and yellows. The swelling had gone way down.

Mid-morning, I walked down to the Hotel, had breakfast and then checked the Sears outlet to see if my order had come in. I bought Kristy a Sears gift certificate, went grocery shopping and returned to the manse. Unpacking my Sears order, I admired the cotton sheet set and comforter I'd bought for my bed.

Just after lunch, Chief Charlie and Jenn came by in Daniel's pickup, and Chief Charlie asked if I wanted to go to Margaret Brown's. I did.

We drove north for some distance, past the last house on the main street, then continued until we came to a dirt track leading to the lighthouse, where the tall beach grasses gave way to forest and rock. Margaret Brown lived along this dirt lane on the edge of the beach grass, in a small, weathered house. It was the same bungalow I'd seen on the way in from the airstrip and from the wharf. About thirty meters from the house was a very large post and beam structure for smoking fish; noticing that I was staring at it, Chief Charlie said that most of the family smoked their fish here.

Margaret Brown looked like she was about ninety years old. She was very slight, and perhaps because her back was hunched over from osteoporosis, she was less than five feet tall. Her hair was gray, shot through with streaks of white, and although she wore thick glasses, she had sharp eyes.

"Sit down, over there," she told me, pointing to an old chair covered with a colorful afghan. "I'll make some coffee."

Her accent was pronounced, but I had no trouble understanding her. The space consisted of a kitchen, dining and living room, which was dominated by a black iron stove against one wall that was giving off a slow, even heat. I admired some beautiful baskets that were stacked in the corner. With obvious pride, Chief Charlie praised Maggie as the best weaver on the Coast.

Mrs. Brown brought us coffee, then sat down in a faded recliner close to the stove. I noticed there was a cane, resting against its arm that looked far too big for her.

When we arrived, Jenn hugged Mrs. Brown and offered a greeting in Heiltsuk. She went into the kitchen, opened a drawer and got out a pad of paper and some crayons. Then lying on her stomach near the stove, she arranged the paper and crayons in a neat row in front of her.

Chief Charlie told Mrs. Brown that I was the woman he'd spoken about and that maybe she could tell me about some of the sites in the area. She nodded, with a "Mmph."

I asked Mrs. Brown if I could take some notes while she talked, and she nodded again. So, I asked for her full name and place of birth.

"Margaret Brown, but I was always called Maggie. I was born in Rivers Inlet, but I don't know exactly when. Before the 1900s."

"We actually think it might have been 1895," Chief Charlie said.

"Now, Charlie." Mrs. Brown spoke as if she were ordering around a small child. "If you're going to interrupt me every few seconds, this young girl is going to be here forever. Why don't you just come back later?"

Chief Charlie grinned good-naturedly and, on his way out the door, told me to phone when I was ready to go home. I told him I'd like to walk back, if that was alright with Jenn.

"Call if you change your mind," he called out.

Feeling very nervous, I began the interview. "Mrs. Brown, I was wondering if you talked to, or if you recall the American anthropologist, Franz Boas."

"Well, I remember seeing him. He was a proper English kind of man, but not, you know, not uppity like a lot of those English were. I guess I saw him a few times, and I heard he was collecting information about the old ways. Mostly he talked to Willy Gladstone. I think that would be in the 20s. There isn't anyone alive today that I know of who spoke to Franz Boas."

"Do you think that Gladstone was honest with Boas?" I asked her.

"Yes, I do. They had a close relationship."

I changed the subject. "Mrs. Brown, we've been working at a site called Boston's Retreat on Denny Island. I'd like to start there and ask you to tell me what you might know about that site."

She settled into her chair, which was almost identical to mine, took off her thick- lensed glasses, rubbed her eyes and then seemed to be looking at some point in the far distance.

"Boston's Retreat. Well, yes. My great-grandfather lived there for a while when he was a boy. Boston and some of those other Heiltsuk chiefs built the village when the Hudson's Bay set up a fort at the Passage. Those chiefs, they built that village to keep the mainland tribes from trading at the Fort. The Heiltsuk got those furs from those Indians and then turned around and traded them to the Fort for more than what they paid. Made the traders mad." She chuckled.

"Many people didn't want to live in the old villages anyway. The souls of too many dead people were there. My grandfather said that was another reason why that village was built. Because the people were coming apart. Mainly it was because of the smallpox. Before that, there were hundreds of people in the villages but, after…only a handful. There was trouble among the Heiltsuk tribes and clans. Starting a new village was a way for Boston and the other chiefs to bring together survivors and to claim the rights of their ancestors. You know, only a Chief could build a house—oh, I mean, not build it himself but lay claim to owning it. My grandfather said Boston was one of the few left who could really claim to be a Chief through his ancestors."

She paused, then continued, "Boston wasn't his real name. He was called that by those white traders, who, of course, could not say the Heiltsuk words and so made up names for the people. Boston did make a lot of money from that trade, but after a while, the white people left that fort."

"The people continued, as they had always done. In the spring, herring eggs and seaweed were gathered and traded to the Interior tribes. In the summer, the winter village broke up into families, and they gathered plants and material for weaving. In the fall, they moved again for the salmon runs and then back to the winter village."

Mrs. Brown stopped talking and, looking at me with her sharp eyes, asked, "What did you find out there at Boston's Village?'

"We've just started, but it looks like the remains of four houses. There are large beams and several house posts that seem to be from one of the houses. Most of the carving is gone." I hesitated but decided to continue. "Someone has taken a chainsaw and cut away the carvings from the posts that are still standing."

She didn't comment on the defacement, saying only, "That's too bad. I remember some of those posts." Settling deeper into her chair, she said, "There were two ways among the Heiltsuk. Some of them got their ancestors through the mother. Some took their ancestors from both sides. Boston got his claim to be Chief from his mother's side. He would have taken that side because she was the higher-ranked at that time—born to the Raven."

"Do you recall that house?"

"Well, yes. Boston's house followed two ways. The front posts were different than the back ones. The front posts would be built for the Raven, and the back ones were for his wife. She was powerful in her own right, not Heiltsuk but from another tribe, one on Vancouver Island. She brought a rich dowry with her, and that added to Boston's influence as well as clan rights."

Four families lived in each house. This was the old way. But before that, in those old days, there would have been many more houses at a winter village. Families were in an order, you know. Because of his potlatching, Boston always kept that number-one position.

Mrs. Brown stopped and got out of her chair, using her cane for leverage. Once she was standing, she dropped the cane back into the chair and held out her hand for my coffee cup. She came back with more coffee and then went and got a plate of Oreo cookies.

"After the fur traders left and the missionaries came, many of the chiefs, in what was left of the winter villages, moved to Waglisla. By then, there had been more smallpox, and you know, those other diseases that killed so many. The people were so few in number that they looked to the missionaries for order. Boston held out.

"One of Boston's granddaughters got mixed up with a white man—maybe a trader, maybe a fisherman, and she got pregnant. Boston was angry, and the girl ran off and lived in that Christian Church Mission. But she didn't feel right there, and Boston sent word that she could come home. She did, but she'd gone strange. Well, that girl died giving birth to that child. In those last hours, she was half crazy with pain. She thought she was going to hell, they said."

Jenn had been very quiet and seemed absorbed in her coloring during our conversation. But, when Maggie started to tell the story of Boston's granddaughter, she stopped her coloring and paid close attention to what Mrs. Brown was saying.

Mrs. Brown paused, sipped on her coffee and continued.

"The name of the older sister of the girl that died was Wikash, and she was furious with the missionary. Wikash snuck into the village one night and waited in the church until the missionary was alone. She had a knife and cut him up pretty good. But, then, when she was running away, someone shot her. She managed to make it to a canoe being guarded by a boy from Boston's Village. His name was Klayiush. I guess she was thinking those white men would follow her back to her village, so she ordered that boy to take her to Xvnis. This was the old village of Boston's people. Maybe Klayiush was afraid, but she was the daughter of a Chief, and he did what she said. They reached Xvnis just before sunrise.

"Klayiush helped her onto the platform of one of those houses and leaned her up against a house post built for her mother's lineage.

"'Do you think our gods have abandoned us?' she asked the boy.

"He was crying, 'I don't know.'"

Mrs. Brown looked at Jenn, who had been sitting very quietly throughout the narrative. She said something in Heiltsuk to the little girl, and, then, in English. "Jenn, why don't you finish this story?"

Jenn sat very straight. "Just then the sun began to rise," she began.

"'Look there,' said Wikash. And I know this: if Raven and this god of the white man do not meet here together, then everyone will die, both our people and theirs."

"Klayiush, when he told all of this to Boston, said that just then they saw a raven flying against the horizon, and then Wikash reached up her hand to touch the Raven; and, in that instant, she touched the sun."

Jenn finished the story and looked at Maggie, who nodded her approval with obvious pride. I felt as if I'd just lived the story. I'd been mesmerized into silence.

Maggie chuckled, breaking the silence. "Boston did consider killing that missionary, but after careful thoughts about the visions that had been revealed to Wikash, he decided to leave him alone. But those white men, they didn't know she was dead. They went crazy looking for her and never did know what happened to her." Mrs. Brown slowly got up. "That's enough for now. You can come again. You know how to listen."

"Thank you very much, Mrs. Brown," I said, hoping that the tone of my voice communicated the respect I felt for her.

"Well, everyone calls me Maggie, you know. You should call me that."

On the walk home, Jenn and I said very little. I think we were both caught up in thinking about the story. My memory of that walk is of the wind playing through the beach grass and of the rich scent of cedar and Douglas fir, of a raven in the distance, of a woman named Wikash, reaching for the sun, and of a village called Boston's Retreat.

While it was fresh in my mind, I wrote down in detail what Margaret Brown told me. I needed to record her stories on tape, but that seemed too intrusive for my first visit. Perhaps I would try it next time. Then I took out the historic publications and notes that I had brought with me.

Based on data from Franz Boas and on his own interviews with Heiltsuk Elders, George Clements believed that, prior to contact, the Heiltsuk may have consisted of five or more distinct groups or tribes. By the time the Hudson's Bay Company Fort was established, these groups, attempting to cope with population losses were amalgamating into new groups and struggling to maintain their complex social structures.

I found in my studies that it was difficult for me to integrate into understanding the complexity of the kinship systems of the Indigenous peoples of the Northwest Coast, which were very different than my own. The western world has a long tradition of patriarchy. In this system, descent is through the father; power lies with the husband/father, who essentially owns his wife, her property and their children. Over the last century or so, this pattern, in some places, changed to a kind of bilateral system in which the children more equally belong to the family of both the husband and the wife. This was the way things had evolved in the society that I belonged to.

The Heiltsuk terms for kinship suggest bilateral descent, with no distinction between mother and father and aunts and uncles and no distinction between brothers, sisters and cousins. In this system, parents, aunts and uncles are all referred to by the same name. Similarly, all cousins were the same as brothers and sisters.

Other Heiltsuk tribes appeared to lean towards the matrilineal and to trace descent mainly through the mother.

In addition to individual family units, Heiltsuk groups identified themselves as belonging to crest groups, based on descent. Crest groups owned the right to display, represent and depict artistry from the group to which they belonged. This included the right to depict such mythical beings as Raven in carvings and the right to own stories, titles and dances. Family groups owned resources, such as salmon streams and gathering areas; for example, berry patches.

Perhaps the strongest embodiment of the crest group were the huge houses built at the winter villages of the Heiltsuk. In these houses, the four corner house posts depicted the crest of the Chief who built them. If it was a family that was bilateral, the crests of both the mother and father would be represented. If it was matrilineal, the crests would belong to the mother's side and would represent her descent group.

Parents often placed their children in the mother's crest group, but not always. The fact that some of the Heiltsuk leaned towards the mother's family or towards being matrilineal was indicated by the fact that titles were often passed to the eldest sister's son. Women's titles were passed from sister to sister and then to the eldest sister's daughter.

Although the Heiltsuk did not have a true matriarchal society, the tendency to identify with the mother's side or to take titles and rights from both sides meant that women had access to power. They could own land and even hold the title of Chief.

Crest groups had chiefs. A chief was not accepted simply based on ancestral claim but must validate this claim by potlatching. In order to assume and to keep one's rank, it was necessary to hold feasts, at which time huge amounts of goods were distributed.

There were three ranks in Heiltsuk society: nobles, commoners and slaves. But there was fluidity. Those born to a noble position could lose it if they were not able to support their claim, just as commoners could achieve noble status through skill and patience. Slaves were usually war captives. When they married or were freed, they were given the same standing as the families that they married into or who had previously owned them.

I was pacing and lost in thought, but some warning bell went off. If I hurried, I would only be slightly late for Kristy's birthday party.

Chapter 14

I found a card in my things that I thought Kristy would like and, having written my wishes, left to go to her party at about 7:30. I could hear loud music coming from the pub that was across the lobby from the café at the Waglisla Hotel. Walking through the door, I was overwhelmed by the smell of beer and smoke. It was small but seemed like a pub anywhere, with small round tables, an area for dancing and loud, canned music. I spotted Kristy, surrounded by people who were sitting at a group of tables which had been pushed together. Kristy seemed like she was already half drunk.

She got someone to get a chair from somewhere and made room for me next to her. I handed her the card and gift. She gave me a hug and thanked me very much. Then she introduced me to her friends, telling them I was a great boss. With some embellishments, she told the story of how I'd broken my nose. This was met with laughter, but not in an unkind way. Her friends looked at me with some curiosity but quickly settled back into talking. I traded remarks with them and with Kristy, almost shouting to be heard over the loud music. Someone started to dance, and this seemed to set off a chain reaction. I danced with several of Kristy's friends and had a good time because I liked dancing, although after a while, my eyes were stinging from the heavy cigarette smoke.

After about an hour, I was ready to go and didn't think Kristy would mind my leaving, especially as she was caught up in an animated discussion with a very good-looking young man sitting on her other side. Kristy thanked me again for the gift, gave me another hug, and I left.

As I was passing the bar an arm reached out and blocked my way. I looked up. There was Daniel. Taken aback, I asked him when he'd returned home.

"Yesterday. We picked up some supplies; we'll be heading out again tomorrow."

I stumbled, not knowing what to say. "Did you...catch a lot of fish?"

"Sure," he said and grinned. "You know Matt?"

"Hi, Laura." Matt greeted me with friendly blue eyes.

I attempted to chat with them, but it was too loud. Matt was drinking a beer. I noticed Daniel was drinking coffee, which, for some reason, made me glad. I made a gesture to indicate that I couldn't hear and then held up my hand to say goodbye.

The air outside of the Hotel smelled cool and salty, and I contemplated walking out to the wharf but changed my mind and headed home. Just as I was about to cross the main street, I heard someone behind me. It was dark, but I recognized a surly-looking red-haired man who had been in the bar.

"Hey, pretty lady, it's early. Why don't you let me buy you a drink?"

"No, thanks. I have to leave now." I wasn't feeling particularly concerned.

"Hey, what's the matter? You only like the Indian bucks?" His voice was ugly.

"Fuck you," I answered and turned to leave.

He grabbed my arm, roughly swung me around, and then grabbed my shoulders.

"I'm going to scream now!" I shouted at him.

"Scream, little lady, outside a bar on a reserve? Who'll care?"

I did start to scream then and tried to hit him, but he had a strong grip on my shoulders. I think I gave him one good kick. He was trying to kiss me and dragging me at the same time, and I was fighting him as hard as I could. Then someone grabbed him from behind and threw him onto the ground. I saw that it was Daniel and Matt.

"What do you say, Dan?" said Matt. "He slips off the wharf, and they find him tomorrow, drowned by accident."

"Not him; he's not worth the investigation," replied Daniel.

They dragged him up from off the ground, and Daniel said, "Next time you touch a woman around here, Blako, we're going to make sure that you really do drown. Now get the hell out of here."

Blako quickly disappeared. Somewhere outside of myself, I realized I was shivering. Daniel put a hand on my shoulder and then leaned down and looked carefully into my face. "Are you all right?"

I nodded yes, although I meant no.

"I'll walk her home, Matt. See you tomorrow."

"Thanks, Matt," I said.

"Take care, Laura," Matt replied in a gentle voice.

I'd never been frightened like this in my life, and I didn't know what would have happened if Daniel hadn't intervened. We started to walk. I was shivering. Daniel took off his faded blue jean jacket and told me to put it on. I was grateful for that. When we got to the front door, I fumbled in my jeans for my keys. But I was shaking so hard that I couldn't fit the key in the lock, and the keys fell from my hand. I leaned my head against the door and started to cry. Daniel picked up the keys, opened the door and turned on the light. He led me into the living room and told me to sit down. A steady stream of tears was rolling down my face. He sat down alongside me on the couch.

The quiet tears turned into sobs, and covering my face with my hands, I said, "I don't know what's wrong with me."

He said softly, "Laura, to me it looked like a man just tried to rape you. It wouldn't be quite normal if you were jumping for joy."

Then he pulled me into his arms and held me and gently stroked my hair and whispered, "There now. Shh. There now, Laura, it'll be alright."

Eventually, the sobbing stopped, but I remained there with my forehead resting against his chest, gaining comfort from his steady breathing and the feel of his hands touching my hair. After a while he put his hands on my shoulders, and I looked up. He told me to go and take a bath, while he made some tea.

When I had washed the smell of smoke out of my hair and put on a flannel nightgown, I felt better. Daniel had made a fire; we sat next to each other on the couch, while I drank my tea. He said that my face looked much better but that I'd lost weight. I asked him how he could notice someone losing weight within a single week, but he just smiled and shrugged. We talked a bit about my project. There was a period of silence. Then Daniel said, "I never should've let you walk out of that bar alone. But you're independent, and I thought, well it doesn't matter what I thought. I didn't use common sense. We saw him looking at you in the bar and saw him leave after you. Even then, it took me a few minutes to make any connection. I'm sorry."

"You're sorry that I'm stupid?"

He smiled and said, "Not stupid, Laura, maybe just not all that experienced in some things. I mean," he added quickly, "I know you're very experienced in some things, in your world you know, but here some things might be different. If you go to the bar again, maybe you should take the taxi home."

"Yes," I agreed. And then out of the blue I asked him if he drank.

"No," he replied, but his eyes said, "Don't go there."

I didn't and instead asked him if he knew that person, Blako.

"Not really. I've seen him around over the years. He runs a seiner for someone in Prince Rupert."

We sat looking into the fire. For a few minutes, I searched for something to say, but then I realized that it was only me who found the silence uncomfortable.

When I finished my tea, he asked me if I was going to be okay. and I nodded, but I was lying, and he knew it. "Go to bed now. I'll stay up here for a while."

Wrapping my new down comforter tightly around me, I left the bedside light on and fell asleep almost immediately. Hours later, I got up to go the bathroom. I noticed that Daniel had turned out the bedside light, but he'd left the light in the hallway on. Before I fell asleep again, it occurred to me that I was twenty-six years old and, except for my grandfather, when I was a little girl, this was the first time in my life that I had received such comfort from a man.

The rain the next morning was steady, and I knew from the low cloud cover that a front had moved in that would last for a while. It wasn't until after I'd started a fire that realized I hadn't given one thought of Blako or the events of the prior evening. I wondered if my lack of reaction was something that might affect me later, but then reflecting on this, I realized that what had affected me was Daniel. I had an ache to feel those arms around me again. I thought about this over coffee and then reluctantly pulled out my notes on the period of contact along the Central Coast.

The first contact with white people began in 1793, with the almost simultaneous arrival of Alexander Mackenzie by land and Captain George Vancouver by sea. Both these explorers made only brief mention of the local people. Russian and American fur traders soon followed and competed for the valuable furs in Heiltsuk territories. In 1833, the Hudson's Bay Company set up Fort McLoughlin, a fur-trading post, close to the present-day location of Waglisla. The Fort was established to break the monopoly of the American and Russian ocean-going traders and to drive down the cost of furs brought in from the Interior of British Columbia. Keeping the cost higher by acting in a kind of retail capacity was successfully accomplished by Chief Boston.

Some academics argue that the traders had little effect on Indigenous life, saying the traders simply cut into an already well-established economic trading system. Reducing the idea that two economic systems meshed in some way and that contact, for this reason, had little effect on Indigenous peoples seemed insane to me, considering what happened to the Native populations.

The complex social system of the Heiltsuk guaranteed that wealth was distributed throughout the community, that status was given to those who were the most generous and that women had considerable authority. But long before the traders had reached the Northwest Coast, populations had been stricken by smallpox epidemics that had probably originated to the south and maybe from the west. By the time the recurring smallpox epidemics were documented, these had occurred in Heiltsuk territories in 1824, 1836, 1853 and 1862. A vaccine against smallpox was first introduced into Canada in 1798, but many people were suspicious of the vaccine, and outbreaks continued. In 1837, the vaccine was introduced in the Puget Sound area; this had a positive effect on the white population. However, the vaccine was not made available to Indigenous people. Because some white people refused to get the vaccine, infections spread to include the Indigenous people. As well, Indigenous people picked up the disease in Victoria and then unwittingly carried it back to their villages. During this period, malaria, measles and other infectious diseases also swept the area. The last epidemic to be introduced resulted from the trade in alcohol.

Death, caused by epidemic diseases, left the Heiltsuk in chaos. By 1897, the population had diminished to an all-time low of 298, a decrease estimated to be close to ninety percent of the pre-contact population. In short, ninety percent of the Heiltsuk people had been wiped out.

I reread my notes from Maggie again, and then I thought about a Chief named Boston and what it would be like to live and forge on when so many of your people were dead. The loss was even more incomprehensible because Boston's kinship group was not just his family but his complete material, social and spiritual world. It must have taken a lot of courage to gather together those people who were left and to try to start over. It must have been difficult, in all that disarray and betrayal, to know how to dedicate your house, when your soul was born to the Raven, but your descent group was scattered to the wind.

Jenn arrived in mid-afternoon. I was glad to see her, glad not to be lost in thought about smallpox and other epidemic diseases. I gave her a t-shirt and sweatpants and put her wet clothes in the dryer.

"That's what I told Grandpa you'd do," said Jenn. "He says he'll pick us up for dinner if it's still raining."

We played cards for a while. The rules for the various games Jenn wanted to play were pretty much the same as those my grandfather had taught me years before. Jenn was very glad that my face was looking better.

"I was worried about that nose," she said gravely.

Later in the afternoon, we walked down to the Hotel for what was becoming our traditional ice cream snack. The rain seeped into my waterproof anorak and soaked my hair. Jenn was even wetter than I, and I put our wet clothes back into the dryer. She experimented with my makeup, while I cleaned up my books and papers.

When Chief Charlie picked us up for dinner, he raised his eyebrows at Jenny's inexpertly made-up face but didn't say a word. At his house, I realized that I now felt comfortable and relaxed.

I missed not seeing Daniel but chatted comfortably with Laney and Rose. Laney's and Matt's three children ranged from six months to six years old. In their faces were beautifully mixed the Heiltsuk looks of their mother and the Nordic characteristics of their father. Just before dinner, Gordon, Edith and several children arrived. It would take me a long time to figure out the actual connections of Chief Charlie's relatives, and I would come to learn that the lack of discord which was apparent in his home was not the case in many of the other homes in the village.

Chief Charlie drove me home and told me that Maggie liked me and that this was good. I told him that I liked her too. Then I finally got up the nerve to ask a question whose answer I was very curious to know.

"Chief Charlie, do you mind me asking who is buried in your front yard?"

He chuckled and answered, "It was my great-grandfather. He was born into the old ways but over time took some of the missionary teachings. Like a lot of people, he took the Christian ways that suited him and ignored the rest. Anyway, some years before he died, he had an argument with the United Church minister, who had taken it upon himself to pull down some mortuary poles near the village. These poles were erected to commemorate those who drowned at sea. This was an old custom. One of those poles was built for my great-grandfather's brother, who drowned off the point where the lighthouse is located. Anyway, my great-grandfather cut all his connections with the church and arranged to be buried in front of his house, which was built where my house is now. He also arranged to have the most elaborate tombstone in the village constructed for him—he even designed it. He saved up the money for that for years. Such a tombstone was a sign of power and having it outside the cemetery was a sign of defiance."

Chief Charlie hesitated for a minute, then added, "I think that it did make that minister angry."

The following day was not only rainy but very windy, and we decided to work at the manse for the day. Jack and I started a map of Boston's Retreat from the data we had collected so far from the site, while Kristy went to the post office to pick up a package that I thought was probably her first set of photographs.

The subjectivity in my perceptions always amazed me in constructing a map based on objective mathematical principals. As Jack and I converted the measurements to the actual location and elevation of the house beams, I began to see that my ideas of which features corresponded to which house, along with the orientation of the houses, were often wrong.

Jack, who lived, hunted and fished on the Coast and had a far greater intuitive sense of his world than did I, thought the map unfolded pretty much as he thought it would.

The three of us examined the pictures that Kristy had taken. The shots of the manse, of Jack and of me were very good. The black and white ones seemed to have the same magical quality that George seemed to have captured. I couldn't wait to see what the site photos would look like.

"What we need is to develop our pictures here, Kristy," I told her.

"You know how to develop pictures?" she asked.

"Sure, I learned it in…"

"Archaeology field school," finished Jack.

"No, dammit. I took a course in it. We could set up one of those old bedrooms upstairs as a dark room, Kristy. I could teach you to develop the pictures."

Jack continued to work on the map, while Kristy and I checked out the possibilities of one of the smaller bedrooms upstairs. Then we compiled a list of the things we would need to make a darkroom. When we were done, to set up the darkroom, she went to the Band Store to get basins and other stuff we could get in the village. I ordered the rest of the material from Vancouver.

Towards the end of the day, Jack and I stepped back and looked at the map. He had done an excellent job. Suddenly it struck me that two of the beams were completely out of place. I pointed this out to him. These beams were located very close together at one end of the site and were not associated with any remains of a house.

"What the hell are those beams doing there?" I asked.

"I've been wondering about that," he replied.

Looking at each other, we arrived at the same conclusion in the same instant.

"Loggers," I said.

We spent the rest of the week at Boston's Retreat. The days were mostly overcast, and when it did rain, it was only a light drizzle. Routines that had started slowly also started to go more smoothly and quickly, so that by Friday afternoon we'd completed the work at the site. We left Boston's Retreat at 2:30 on Friday. I felt a huge sense of accomplishment.

At the dock, we gassed up for the following week and worked quickly to clean up the boat. Climbing up onto the wharf, I glanced over at the other craft tied up at the dock and saw Daniel hosing off the deck of a seiner. I waved; he grinned. Without stopping to think, I went back down to the dock and walked over to him.

"Catch any fish?"

"Sure," he said, smiling. "Are you finished for the day?"

"Sure."

"You're on Indian time, eh?"

"Eh?" I echoed, smiling.

"I brought you a present."

"A present?"

He disappeared into the cabin and came out a moment later with a package that was wrapped in foil and plastic and handed this to me. I looked up at him, a bit puzzled.

"It's a salmon. You can't keep losing weight. You won't have a figure. This will fill you out."

He was flirting with me, and I flirted back.

"Daniel, why do you care if I have a figure, exactly?"

"Just my general concern for humanity, like you know."

I laughed. "Sure, I know."

Looking down at what was obviously a very large fish, I stumbled a bit. "Do I bake it? Or..."

He made a sound in the back of his throat and shook his head, but he was chuckling.

"How about if you cook it for me?" I asked spontaneously. "Yes, that's it. You should have dinner with me because I have this fish which was given to me by a humanitarian."

He smiled and asked if the minister's house had a fire pit.

"No," I answered.

He made the same sound at the back of his throat. "Okay, I'll cook that fish for you at my place. What time do you want me to pick you up?"

"Anytime is fine. Should I bring anything, besides the fish I mean?"

"No, I'll get you at about 5." He paused and grinned. "You might as well give me that fish."

I think I danced all the way home.

Chapter 15

I didn't want to spend time planning any possible outcomes of dinner with Daniel or overly analyze the fact that it was even happening, so I kept busy for the next few hours. I cleaned my backpack and updated my field journal. The amount of work I'd been doing was a far cry from any of my previous efforts as an archaeologist.

I felt sometimes overwhelmed by this work, but the tactics I learned as a dancer helped me to keep it all in perspective. Even a simple dance is put together in small pieces; by focusing on a single element at a time, the whole came together.

After a bath, I examined my face in the mirror. There was still some bruising around my eyes, but this was less obvious because I had acquired a tan, even though most of the days in the field had been cloudy. I dressed in jeans and a white East Indian style blouse I'd ordered from the Sears catalogue. My jeans were loose. I had lost weight. Twenty minutes before 5, I thought I would also just be myself, and so I put on mascara and eye shadow and a pair of simple opal earrings left to me by my Grandmother Fitzgerald.

Daniel arrived promptly at 5. On the short drive to his house I felt nervous. He told me that I looked nice. I returned an exact replica of the compliment, which I immediately realized must have sounded idiotic. But he gave no indication that he thought this, although he grinned just a bit.

Daniel lived on the beach, off the main road, about half a kilometer south of the hospital, down the lane that Jenn had shown me in our first walk. His house, not visible from the road, was accessed by a narrow dirt track that was overgrown with huckleberries. The house was an old portable that had been used before the elementary school was built, and perhaps because the living area was one space, it seemed quite large. The entrance area led into a hall with shelves and coat hooks and a bathroom at the end. To the left of the front door was a single room that held a combined kitchen, eating area and living room. A large window and a set of balcony doors looked out onto the Passage. Two doors off this main living area led to what I thought were bedrooms. The living room furniture was old and comfortable, and there was a large bookcase against the wall and a cast iron stove against the other.

While Daniel made coffee, I looked over his books. There were some mystery novels, books on fishing, books on car and boat mechanics, and several of the volumes of work by Franz Boas that I was using in my own work. I took a copy of Dee Brown's *Bury My Heart at Wounded Knee* from the shelf and, leafing through it, came across a speech made by Chief Joseph of the Nez Perce. The traditional territories of this group covered most of the present-day state of Idaho. The Americans repeatedly promised the Nez Perce that they would not take away their lands. These promises were broken. Like many people of the Indigenous Americans in the American West, the Nez Perce fought back. An ever-dwindling group of three hundred Nez Perce warriors eluded capture by the entire Northwest American army, who chased them for months. Under Chief Joseph, the warriors decided to flee to Canada but met defeat close to the border. Only a few made it across.

Glancing up, I noticed that Daniel was looking at me, and I read out loud a sentence from Chief Joseph's speech of surrender to the Americans: "'From where the sun now stands, I will fight no more…'"

Daniel finished the sentence with the word, 'forever.'

I smiled at him. He prepared the fish, sprinkling it with brown sugar and soy sauce and covering it with foil. When we went out onto the front deck, I was about to exclaim how fantastic the view was, but my words were cut off in mid-sentence because, to my right, on the deck, was an old, claw-footed, white enameled bathtub. The tub was clearly in working order, and, on a shelf alongside, was shampoo, soap and towels hanging from hooks.

"This old portable didn't come with a shower or bath, and I always meant to build one, but this works for me."

"I like it," I said, and I did.

We walked down a few steps from the deck to the beach. There was a big fire pit close to the house. Next to the fire pit were two weathered gray benches, made from two-by-six-inch boards nailed to cedar stumps. I sat down, looking out at the Passage, while Daniel started the fire for the fish.

It was a beautiful setting. Tall Western red cedar and hemlock surrounded his house. There were no other houses visible from where I sat. The tide was out, but I could see from the driftwood and seaweed that at high tide, the ocean would be close to the deck.

My house in the Lower Mainland was on the shores of Deep Cove, and I realized how much I missed the sound of the ocean in the evenings, especially when I was falling asleep or when I felt troubled.

We sat on the bench drinking coffee, waiting for the flames to die down, so that Daniel could cook the fish. I told him that Jack and I thought maybe loggers had taken the beams from Boston's Retreat.

"Could be," he mused. "But, don't be too careful to lay it all on those white loggers. Could have been some Indians. They would often take beams if they were going to build a house somewhere else. Could even have been some Native loggers."

We ate on the beach, and it was very good. Daniel teased me, saying he had specially gotten some sour cream for my baked potato and that he thought I was very brave that first night at Charlie's. We were quiet for a while; then, in a teasing voice, I asked when he was going to assume his role as Chief. I was surprised when he answered me seriously.

"In a year or two. I still have things to learn from Charlie. He wants a big potlatch to validate that title. I guess I want it to be a big feast, as well. I've been saving for it for a long time."

He changed the subject abruptly with a suggestion. "Let's get another coffee."

We took our second cups back down to the beach and watched the tide coming in. I asked Daniel about how Charlie fit into his life and where his parents were. He'd taken up a piece of driftwood and was whittling it out with a sharp hunting knife. He hesitated for a moment, then began to talk and, then, more and more easily.

"Charlie is my uncle—my mother's brother, but I never knew my parents. My mother was from here. She was seventeen when she met my father. He was a hand on a seine boat out of the Charlottes. He spent some time with her one summer here, and she got pregnant with me. It turned out the guy had a woman and two kids in Skidegate, and when he found out she was pregnant; he just never came back. I guess she loved him and had dreams that they would be together. Our family was not very strong then. They were messed up, and there was lots of drinking. I don't know what was going through her mind. I guess no one did. A month after I was born, she got drunk one night and hung herself."

All this was said this with no apparent emotion in Daniel's voice, but he paused for a while before continuing. "Margaret Brown—she would be my great-aunt—well, Maggie found her. And after that, well—Maggie took care of me. I never met my father. Never looked for him. Guess he never looked for me either, and I don't have any interest in finding him. I really haven't even wanted to explore the Haida side of my culture. I took my ancestry from my mother's clan. Some of the Elders say I look like him. Maggie says it's just my height that I got from the Haida side of the family; she says I look like my mother."

Daniel paused in his story and looked at me. I didn't need to tell him I was sorry. He could read that in my eyes.

"Charlie came back to the Reserve when I was about four. He brought my Aunt Rose with him. She's from the Stolo Nation down there on the Fraser River. He logged and fished when he brought her home and did well, but then he would disappear down to Vancouver for months. One of these times when he was gone, his son, Charlie Jr., who was five, was playing on the dock and fell in and drowned. By the time Charlie got back, that kid had been buried for three weeks. Rose had had enough, and she went back to Chilliwack.

"The drowning hadn't been his fault but to miss the funeral, that was a disgrace. And no one thought too much of him. He loved Rose and Laney and his son, and I guess that was his bottom. He stopped drinking and worked as steadily as he could, sending money down to Rose and letters to try and get her back. She still has those letters. Charlie never did go to school and mostly taught himself how to read and write. For a long time, she wouldn't have anything to do with him, but I guess he convinced her, and he went down to Chilliwack and brought Rose and Laney back with him. He's been sober since then."

Daniel got up and put some more wood on the fire and continued, "Charlie started to learn the old ways. I thought he was very stern in those days, and I think I was a little bit afraid of him, but he started to take me under his wing. Pretty soon I was spending as much time at Rose and Charlie's as I did at Maggie's. Those were good days. I remember that in the house, Laney and I were only allowed to speak our Native language with Charlie. So, from Maggie and Charlie, I kept the language, and I'm grateful for that.

"The government said we had to go to the residential school in when we were seven. But lots of people fought this. Laney and I didn't go until I was eleven and she was nine. Eventually, the authorities figured out we were not down in Stolo, which was the story put out. The Alberni Residential School is not a shining light in my life. It was bad. I remember being hungry a lot. I remember being very quiet and kind of disappearing into myself. You know—it's starting to come out now. We knew who was being abused. It was like they targeted the kids who seemed the least able to stick up for themselves. Pretty much all of us got beaten up. But I was a strong kid. I was always big, and I had a tough look, and they couldn't beat it out of me. It was easier for me, and easier for Laney, because of this. When I was fourteen, this dormitory supervisor beat Laney up. I don't even remember the reason; it was something trivial, I think. I waited for him that night and snuck up on him. I had decided to kill him, and by then, I was almost six feet tall, and I knew I could do it. I almost did.

"They were going to take me to the police and said I'd be thrown into juvenile detention. I got away, found Laney and we took off from that place. Eventually, we hitched a ride to the Passage with a seiner. I couldn't go back, even if I'd wanted to, and Charlie wouldn't send her back. It was a hard time for Charlie. It was a hard time for all the Heiltsuk. You know, they wanted us to be educated, but the residential school was not just destroying our spirit and our culture. Kids were dying there."

The flow of Daniel's conversation stopped then. I didn't say anything, as I waited for him to continue.

"Charlie did some work for a rancher some summers on the Plateau, and this rancher's wife did homeschooling for her two kids up there. Anyway, for several winters after leaving Port Alberni, Laney and I lived in an old cabin on that ranch with Rose and Charlie and took lessons from that white lady. She treated us like real people and taught us to love books. Her name was Pat Peale. She saw through my tough guy act and told me that one day I would be a Chief and that I needed to learn how to be that. She had me reading all about King Arthur. I ate up those stories like crazy."

Daniel put more wood on the fire, and I knew his narrative was over. His tone and manner when he had talked had an edge of sadness; he'd spoken in a quiet voice.

"Don't you feel anger, Daniel? Resentment?" I asked with quiet curiosity.

"I did. For quite a few years. But it was me I was destroying, and then I came back to myself and worked it through and even feel some gratitude that neither I neither I or Laney was touched by the ministers."

I nodded.

"What about, you, Laura?"

"Me, Daniel? There's nothing to tell really."

I had taken off my sandals and was rubbing my feet through the course black and white sand. He reached down and gently traced his finger along the scar on my ankle and said, "Today, down at the wharf, you were limping a bit. What about that?"

I told him that I'd broken my ankle and that sometimes, when I was in the field for the day, it would hurt a bit and swell up. But then I went back further, telling him about Michael. And, then, it was like a floodgate opened. I told him about my mother and father and about Jake and a lot about my grandfather, who had died four years ago and whom I still missed very much. I told him that I still went to Toronto when I could and stayed in my grandfather's house. It was a place of enormous strength for me, and I knew that someday it would have to be sold but that I didn't think about that. I told him about the house in Deep Cove that I had bought with money left to me by Grandpa. I paused and told him the story of my broken ankle.

"When I was a teenager, there were all kinds of new things happening in dance. The place to be was New York, and I got accepted into a Fine Arts school there for my Grade 11 year. On New Year's Eve, I went with a bunch of kids from the school to Times Square. It was snowy and icy. One of the guys was walking me back to my place. It was dark, and I slipped. I guess it was just the way I fell, but I badly fractured my tibia and fibula—my anklebones. The surgeon spent almost three hours putting them all back together."

I was picking at my cuticle, and Daniel took my hand and put it in the pocket of his jean jacket.

"Two days later I asked the doctor what the prognosis was. He was blunt. "Do you have a back-up plan?" he said. I wouldn't accept it. I went to physiotherapists and experts and even psychic healers. I just couldn't believe I wouldn't have that flexibility in my ankle again and kept telling people that other people had bad injuries and they had made a comeback, and I could do that too. When I wasn't trying to make it better, I was feeling anxious and sorry for myself."

"Finally, after about a year, my grandfather told me sit down. He poured a strong drink for me and one for himself, which was odd, because he rarely drank and certainly not with me. Then he told me he was getting tired of my crap and that I could be the world's biggest victim…or that I could just get on with it. I did what he said. I finished high school and then went to university and studied Archaeology."

There was an easy silence between us. Then Daniel, smiling and with a slight edge of sarcasm, said, "So, Waglisla is your back-up?"

"Yes," I replied, laughing.

We sat quietly, looking into the dying fire. He drove me home. We didn't talk, our silence, comfortable. He walked me up to the front door. Spontaneously, I reached up and hugged him. I think he was surprised for a moment, but then he returned the hug and whispered, "Sleep well," and was gone.

It was late, but I made myself some herbal tea and sat sipping it in the dark living room. In sharing so much with Daniel, I'd given a lot of myself. There was a voice of caution—until I remembered that he'd given me a lot of himself as well.

I didn't sleep well because my mind was filled with dreams of love and possibilities, and my body ached with desire.

When I finally did fall asleep, I dreamed I was standing next to Franz Boas on a Canadian prairie border. Behind us were the Sioux, who had fled to Canada, seeking refuge from the battle that had become known as "Custer's Last Stand." On the American side was a worn-out band of Nez Perce. Boas was speaking to me with great urgency, but it was in German, and once again, I couldn't understand what he was saying. Still, I could understand the words of a Sioux warrior, who was mounted on a roan horse and gesturing from the top of a hill. He was shouting to the Nez Perce, who were on the American side, shouting the same words over and over again: "You will find no comfort here."

Chapter 16

I slept in the next morning and when I finally got up, rushed to get ready because I'd arranged to meet Maggie at 11. I decided that I'd walk to the Hotel, get some coffee and donuts and then take the taxi to her house. Halfway to the Hotel, the light drizzle turned into a downpour, and my anorak was soaked through. I took the taxi to Maggie's, then made a dash for the front door. I heard her "Come in" before I knocked. Her tiny figure was hunched in a chair next to the stove. She was making a basket.

Appraising me, she chuckled and said, "Go into my room there down the hall and get some dry clothes, and then you can hang yours over that line behind the stove."

I went down the short hall and into a room on the left. There were heavy curtains covering the windows, the room quite dark. I found the light switch next to the door and turned it on. The room contained a double bed, set close to the floor, probably to make it easier for her to get in and out of. There was an old dresser against the wall. Inside, I found a pair of pants and a sweater; I gratefully put these on. Looking around at the plain room, with the mismatched bedcover and curtains, I felt a deep pang in my heart.

I hung my wet clothes on the line behind the stove.

"Is that Hotel coffee you brought? They make good coffee there," Maggie said.

We drank coffee and ate donuts in companionable silence. Then I took out a tape recorder from my backpack and showed Maggie how it worked. I was trepidatious, but Maggie seemed quite interested in the device and asked me to play back her voice several times. Each time, she chuckled and finally said, "Sure, you can use that."

I rewound the recorder and, speaking into the microphone, gave the date, my name and Maggie's name. I paused to compose a question, but before I could do this, Maggie said, "I heard you were out with Daniel last night."

I nearly spilled my coffee, then quickly turned off the recorder. "How did you hear that?"

"Agnes Campbell phoned me this morning and said she saw you and Daniel driving up to the minister's house about 12 o'clock. But she's pretty much of a busybody."

Feeling my face growing red-hot, I said, "It was nothing, really. He cooked a big fish up for me at his house."

"Sure, but Daniel never takes women to his place."

"Oh" was my brilliant reply.

There were a few moments of silence before Maggie continued. "You've got it pretty bad for him, eh?"

I nodded. "Does it show?"

"Maybe only to an old woman. Maybe it's because you're young. Your face shows everything."

"Well, I'm not sure the feelings are returned."

"Sure they are."

"Maggie, how do you know that?" I asked.

"I know Daniel, and anyway, Laney and Rose say he looks at you all the time over there at Charlie's."

This was a surprise to me. I paused and asked, "Is the whole village talking about it?"

"Well, yeah sure. But they're talking about a lot of things. Daniel would know they're talking. If he doesn't care, why should you?"

"I guess I shouldn't." I paused. "Maggie, Daniel seems careful about women." I searched for the words to express myself but could only come up with "Is he cautious?"

"Mmph, sure he's careful. He lost the two main women in his life, and he needs to feel he's in control. I'm guessing you'd hold your own, and maybe that scares him."

"Who did he lose?"

"Well, there was his mother. And then there was a girl from here. Everyone thought they'd stay together, but she ended up on the streets in Vancouver. She died down there. Drugs, I think. Mmph." She paused. "It would be more than ten years now."

I reflected on this information. Daniel hadn't told me about this. I asked Maggie, "Isn't all this time long enough to heal and move on?"

"For some. He always felt strongly about his Mom. When he was growing up, Daniel used to drive me crazy, asking questions about her. And Dorothy, well, I think in a way she reminded Daniel of this picture he had in his head of his mother. It nearly drove him crazy watching her throw her life away."

Maggie offered no further details, and even though I was curious, I didn't pursue it. She asked me to hold the three separate strands of cedar as she wove these into a simple, beautiful basket, and now, more at ease, I turned the recorder back on. Sitting on the floor next to her, as I carefully kept the strands of cedar separated, I told her we were finished at Boston's Retreat and had mapped the houses. After I had turned the recorder back on, I told her the size of the houses.

"Well, that information wouldn't be wrong. You know, building a house was a big project. It took a long time."

"Maggie, there are several beams missing. Do you think loggers took them?"

"Could be. Maybe white people, maybe Indians moved those beams. But, you know, other houses have been built since then. At one time, there was some of the old houses right here at the Passage. They might have taken the beams to build those houses."

I told her about the defacement of the carved poles and asked her if anyone had done anything about it. "What is there to do? Although this new sergeant encourages people to report crimes, the distance between the RCMP and the Heiltsuk has traditionally been one of distrust."

Eventually, I changed the subject and told her about the hemlock growing in the cedar house remains.

"Well sure. When I was younger and gathered berries at the old village sites, I remember how the hemlock grew out of the fallen cedar."

There was a pause in the conversation. I told Maggie we were going to map a burial site on Denny Island that was almost directly across from the Passage.

"That would be Campbell's Pole," she replied. Then she chuckled and said, "You might not feel too comfortable there."

"Why?"

"Well, there's a small log grave house there, overgrown with moss. In the old days, one kind of burial was to build a little house and place the dead people inside. The other burial house at that place was copied from the English type of house—it's like a little white-man house, complete with a glass window. Daniel told me, oh, more than twenty years ago, that the glass had been broken and that a body was lying halfway out of the coffins. It really spooked him." She chuckled when she said this. "He felt very strongly that someone should put those bodies back in the right place, but he wasn't going to do it. And I don't think anyone ever did."

"It seems odd to think that even kids would do something like that," I mused.

"It wasn't kids. It was some white fishermen. There's a mortuary pole there. It's not that old, carved in the 1940s, for two brothers who drowned nearby and whose bodies were never recovered. Those white people, they tried to steal the pole. Attached a rope to it and tried to drag it off the bluff where the burials are. They managed to pull it over, but it's cedar and heavy, and I guess they were having problems. Some Indian people came by and scared them off."

"I don't think I feel really comfortable about going there." I said.

"You should take some tobacco. Before you get to the burial houses, sprinkle it around and say a prayer and explain what you're doing...and that you mean no disrespect."

"Who should I pray to?"

"To the spirits of the people that are buried there. This is an ancient thing, Laura. The Elders here always leave offerings when they fish or even gather berries or collect cedar for weaving. A lot of the younger people are starting to do that again."

Maggie had nearly completed the basket. She put it aside and asked if I was hungry.

I realized I was very hungry. She said I could help her with lunch. I made salmon sandwiches, while she brewed coffee, and we ate this simple lunch at the kitchen table

After lunch, I admired the baskets stacked in the corner. They were, to tourists, purely decorative, but I could see that many were also functional. There were various sizes and shapes, made from cedar, grasses and other materials I couldn't identify. Most were interwoven with dark, brown-dyed strands to create beautiful patterns. The grass ones would be waterproof, used traditionally for cooking.

I asked Maggie where she sold her baskets.

"By commission. In a Native craft shop in Victoria. They sell pretty well. Helps with groceries and presents. Have you seen Daniel's jewelry?"

"Daniel makes jewelry?"

"Sure, he's been fooling around with it since he was a teenager. Practices whittling in wood and then carves in silver and gold. He's starting to make a name for himself. Commissions his stuff in Victoria and Vancouver."

I thought of Daniel's hands, big and scarred from seining, and couldn't imagine him carving the delicate Native designs into gold and silver. It was a new element that made him even more intriguing.

"Maggie," I said. "One thing I'm confused about is the relationship between you and Chief Charlie and all the kids that are at Charlie's for Sunday dinner. Why don't you go over there for dinner?"

"Well, I do sometimes. But I have arthritis, and that bouncing truck of Daniel's is painful. For the relationships, it would be hard for a white person to understand how it all fits together. Many of the young people don't. There is too much intermarriage these days. It was forbidden to marry even up to the level of fourth cousin in the old days, as well as frowned on to marry within a clan."

"How was it enforced?" I asked.

"Well, marriages were arranged. The main reason was…" Maggie stopped and seemed to be struggling for the right words. "To create ties."

"To create alliances?"

"Yes, that would be it. Clans owned property. If there was a food shortage, those obligations made it possible to winter with your husband's or wife's clan. Children were brought up from the start to understand that their place among the people would be dependent on marrying who their parents chose. And cousins were the same as brothers and sisters, so that marrying even a distant cousin would be like a brother and sister marrying in the white people way."

"Was your marriage arranged?"

"Sure it was. I married my sister's husband. She died of the lung disease. She had three small children before that. It was common to marry your sister's husband if she died. Some even took that sister as a second wife in the old days."

"Did you love your husband?"

"Not at first. He was fifteen years older than me. But I loved those kids and brought them up, and after a while, I came to love him. He didn't drink and was a good provider and treated me well. He was good in bed."

She made this last statement with no fluctuation in her voice, but her eyes were sparkling. I burst out laughing, and she chuckled. "I never had any children of my own. Something wrong with my insides."

"Does that make you sad?" I asked softly.

"No, I had so many other kids to bring up. I guess God just thought that would be enough."

"Tell me about your family. I can put it on the tape recorder, and maybe this way I can understand it. The people and the crest groups—the clans."

She settled back into her chair. "I was born through my mother to the Orca whale. I had nine brothers and sisters. Two of my sisters died just after they were born. A few years later, one of my brothers and one of my sisters died from the cough at the Alberni Residential School. They call it whooping cough today. My older brother died in that Great War. That left just the four of us. Me and my two sisters and one brother that was younger than me. My one sister died from the black lung disease, and it was her husband that I married. My brother married into the Nuxhalk and had a big family. My one remaining sister lived here on the Reserve. I was close to her. She had six children, but she died twenty years ago from cancer. Her name was Rose, same name as Charlie's wife. One of her children is Charlie. Two of her younger children, a boy and a girl, died at residential school in Port Alberni. I don't know why. We never found out. We do know that they beat a lot of those children to death. The second youngest girl married into the Stolo, down there on the Coast. Rose's youngest girl was Daniel's mother."

Maggie paused, lost in thought. "And the second eldest girl married here, on the Reserve. That would be Edith, who you met at Charlie's, I guess. It would be a lot of her grandchildren that you see at Charlie's. Gordon is the Hereditary Chief of the Raven, and he and Charlie think a lot alike, even though they compete to hold ranking. Charlie is the Hereditary Chief of the Orca. He had two children, Laney, who you know, and a boy, who drowned. And Daniel would be the other Hereditary Chief of the Orca—through his mother, Charlie's sister. He is my great-nephew. He'll be a Chief when he has that big potlatch. He would be expected to have a wife and children to be really considered a man, but I don't think that will stop him. He's still waiting for Pocahontas."

With this remark, Maggie chuckled, and I burst out laughing.

"What about Jenn?'" I asked. "Where does she fit in?"

"Jenny is a great-niece of Rose's. Her mother died in a car accident. She's been with Rose and Charlie since she was two. Her mother put her in Jenn's father's clan, so Jenn is born to the Raven, and Gordon's family makes sure she is learning about the Raven clan. On her seventh birthday last year, she was given a name of a Raven ancestor and collected her first story. She's a cute little thing, smart too—I think she will maybe be a storyteller. Rose and Charlie are pretty attached to her, and she's taken the Hunt name. In terms of relationship to Daniel, she would be a second cousin, but she has always seen him as, and called him 'Uncle.'"

"Did you go to Residential School, Maggie?"

"No. I guess I was lucky with that. I think it was 1880 that there was a Methodist missionary who came here, and his wife offered day classes to the children of Waglisla. A few years later, a full-time instructor was hired to teach the children. I went to the classes offered by these instructors, but I don't remember their names. They were very frustrated because the Heiltsuk left Waglisla seasonally to hunt, fish and gather. Eventually, it was decided that the solution to seasonal attendance was to send the children to residential schools. So, the children went to Alert Bay, Chilliwack, Port Simpson, and Port Alberni. They called these places industrial schools. The students spent half the day learning English and basic skills-for the girls, things like sewing and cooking and for the boys sometimes half-days and sometimes all day doing agricultural labor to feed the students. Those were horrible places. So many children died, and the authorities would not even bother to tell the parents. The children were almost always hungry, and they were beaten for the slightest reason. If they spoke their own language, they could be whipped. Their sex was abused, and you know, when you do that, it affects a person for their whole life. They could come back to the reserve for six weeks every summer, but even so, this was not long enough for most of them to hold on to their language and customs. They wanted to make Indians into white people, but at the end, the children came home and had nowhere to fit in."

Maggie took a deep breath and continued. "It was not normal here for most of the year, because there were no children playing and laughing like they had in the old days. It seemed to me as if the village was empty, and I suppose in many ways, it was."

"What about Chief Charlie and Daniel?" I asked her quietly.

"Well, Charlie went for one year to Alert Bay and after that he just stayed here, always hiding, always escaping the Indian Agent. People would not say where he was, and they sheltered him. He would also go up to the Interior and stay with cousins, the same for Bella Coola." She chuckled and said, "He became a sort of legend. Daniel went to Alberni and Laney too, but they escaped and schooled with a white family in the Interior. Charlie paid them back by working on their ranch, doing chores and such."

I watched quietly while she tied the ends of the basket she'd picked up again. After a while, thinking, I said in a hesitant voice, "Maggie, how do you stand it, the way you were treated, and all the deaths in your family?"

She paused, until at length, she said, "You just do. Because if you don't, you'll go crazy or drink yourself to death or take your own life. Some do."

She was quiet then, looking off into some distant landscape. I sensed that it was time for me to go and gathered up my things, then changed into my clothes, which were stiff and dry from the heat of the stove. We arranged to meet the following Saturday.

On the way home, I went shopping and added a package of *Export A* tobacco to my groceries. Sitting at the kitchen table, I listened to the recording I had made at Maggie's that day. I stopped and started it, drawing up a genealogical chart as I did so. When it was finished, I had a clearer understanding of Maggie's family. Taking a pen, I traced the descent of the Raven and the Orca.

Then I circled the number of people who had died for that part of the family that I'd been able to chart. Margaret Brown had lost seven brothers and sisters, three nieces and nephews and one great-nephew.

Thinking about Michael, I tried to comprehend this. I couldn't.

I made a fire and lay down on the couch, with the intention of just resting for a few minutes. Instead, I fell into a restless sleep. It seemed like only seconds later that I began to dream, the kind of dream that was like the others, except that this time I was aware that I was dreaming.

In the dream, a huge antiquated map of the New World was spread out in front of me. Place names were written in carefully inscribed letters of black ink against a bronze background. Franz Boas was stand-

ing next to me, but he didn't speak, only nodded his head in the direction of the map. A fog gently swirled and created a mist that protected this world. Out of the fog came a ship. It was the Spanish landing in the Caribbean. Several men scrambled ashore, one holding up a torch against the mist. He tripped and the torch hit the map. A flame was ignited on the map and grew into a raging fire that engulfed South America; the flames moved northward, and, now, the entire New World was in flames.

I woke myself up from the dream, sweating and feeling a sense of the unreal.

Sipping on a glass of ice water as I lay in a scalding hot bath, I tried to make sense of the dreams I'd been having. I never had put much weight on dreams and had certainly never seen them as prophetic…or at least I didn't then. Looking for a scientific explanation was not difficult. My dreams must be metaphors for the real feelings and events I was experiencing. The key word was 'felt' because before I came to the Passage, I had only an academic understanding of the impact of contact. But the people that I was living with now were not 'Native' or 'Indigenous' or 'Aboriginal' or 'Indian.' They were just people. I felt a deep sense of sadness at the loss that had begun when Spain tripped upon what would become known as the New World.

Satisfied by my understanding of my dreams, I relaxed into the bath. Then I sat up, startled by my recollection of the words of Franz Boas: "This is Oo-niece—it means 'Springwater.'"

There is no way that I could have known this pronunciation, or the meaning of the word.

Then I remembered what he said to me, "History can be misplaced, but in our thoughts and actions, it is not forgotten." These words were nowhere in any of the work I had studied about Franz Boas.

Jake called after dinner, describing a car he'd found that was safe and all over 'cool.' He was very excited, and I could barely make sense of what he was saying. He read the letter that he'd written to Grandpa's law firm. I made a few suggestions but told him it was just fine, although I admitted I wasn't sure if what he was describing was a car or a spaceship.

"God, Laura, how could a guy like me have a ditz like you for a sister? Mom's right here. Do you want to talk to her?"

"Sure," I said, discarding my quick come back.

During our conversation, I wished I could share my growing attraction to Daniel Hunt, but it wasn't the right time. I did tell my mother about my new friend, Nadine, and about Maggie and Jenn. After talking to Jake and Mom, I realized that I felt very homesick and would like to go down to Vancouver that very weekend. But for the time being, I had too much work to do.

I pulled out all the data on Campbell's Pole and went over it. Later, I went down to the Hotel and got a coffee and walked out onto the wharf. I noticed there were a lot of docked seiners. I was beginning to understand the rhythm of the village; there must be an opening for fishing coming up.

The sky had cleared, but there was a brisk wind coming in from the West, and it was cold. I looked out at the Passage, at the islands and the mountains, but I didn't really see these because I was thinking about Maggie and wondering how she could have stood so much.

Chapter 17

The next morning, I was up early and drank my coffee on the back porch, enjoying the sun and listening to the CBC. I thought about the information that George had collected at Campbell's Pole. It was sketchy, but the photographs he'd taken were stunning. In one of these, he had captured a setting sun that slanted in such a way as to create sharp edges and shadows on the two burial houses. This stream of sunlight played through the trees before becoming part of a greater body of light in the dark ocean far below.

George had investigated the site before it was vandalized. His photographs showed the carved pole still standing in front of the European-style burial house. The pole had carvings that protruded from the main body, and was dominated by a feature representing an eagle. It was very different than the carving I'd seen in other photographs of the region. I would have to ask Maggie about this.

George had also made a quick sketch of the site and noted that there were large numbers of grave offerings, including enamel pots and pans, cups, bowls and even part of an old treadle sewing machine. In the ethnographic category, George noted that people in the Passage still burned food on the beach in memory of the two brothers who had drowned and for whom the pole was commissioned.

I wondered who these two brothers were and what the story was behind the pole. Looking at the photographs, I imagined Daniel as a young boy, feeling outrage at the desecration of the graves but too frightened to touch the disturbed burial house. Would I be afraid? Maybe not. But then these were not my ancestors.

Jenn arrived for our weekly Sunday get-together. I made some lunch and listened to her chat about her friends. She was upset with a boy who had been in her class that year and who was always bugging her. The teacher, she explained, was rude and hadn't done anything about it.

"What does this boy do?" I asked her.

"Mostly bugs me, calls me names." She hesitated, then added, "On Friday, he saw me walking to the store and called me a 'horrendous hoe.'"

Jenn was clearly mortified, and I had to use all my willpower not to burst out laughing at this term.

"Do you know what a hoe is, Laura?'"

"I think so."

"Well, how can I be a horrendous hoe when I haven't even had sex yet?"

This was too much, and I did burst out laughing. Jenn's perfect little face was crestfallen, and I wanted to kick myself but instead did some quick talking.

"Jenn, I'm sorry. The reason I laughed is that it is just more stupid than I can imagine that some idiot would call you that name. But, I mean, the thing is, did you ever stop to think why he might be talking to you like that?"

"Because he hates me or maybe someone in my family. But I asked Grandpa, and he says he has nothing against that kid's family, which means they have nothing against us."

"I think it might be because he actually has a crush on you. Kids that age, when they have feelings like that, often don't know how to express them. So, he's getting your attention by being mean to you because it works. It does work, doesn't it?"

"I guess so. When no one is looking, except my friends, I call him names like 'dickbrain.'"

"Why don't you try to ignore him? Maybe try just looking at him like he's less than a slug when he's mean. You could also say, 'Look, I'm just not interested in you. Why do you keep on trying to get my attention?'"

Jenn looked skeptical but said she'd give it a try. Then she paused and asked, "Laura, did the other kids bug you when you were little?"

"Not too much. I had an older brother who would threaten death to anyone that bugged me," I laughed.

"Where is he now?" she asked

"He died in a boating accident when we were still kids."

"I'm sorry, Laura."

"It's okay, honey; it was a long time ago."

I changed the subject and asked if anyone ever went swimming at the lake I'd hiked up to.

"Oh, you mean the Reservoir. Not too many people go swimming up there. Most of the people on the Reserve don't know how to swim anyway."

"Can you swim?"

"A bit. I learned some down there visiting my cousins at Stolo."

"Would you like to go up to the Reservoir and go swimming with me? I'm a good swimmer, and I'd keep a close eye on you."

Jenn's eyes started to twinkle, but her face fell, as she admitted, "I don't have a bathing suit."

"Would the Co-Op have one, or maybe we could get you some shorts and a top, and you could swim in those?"

"Well, yeah, sure."

I collected my suit and towel, and we went to the Co-Op. The selection of swimsuits was pitiful, so we got some shorts and a tank top for Jenn, loaded up on pop and chips and headed for the Reservoir. It was a beautiful, hot, sunny day. The air smelt like cedar, with a trace of salt that drifted in from the ocean. Birds and unseen small creatures filled the air with chatter. Jenny was not a competent swimmer, but she could float and do the dog paddle marginally well. We worked for some time on these elements of swimming. Then I introduced her to the front crawl. At first awkward, she did make some strides forward with this technique.

Afterwards, we drank Pepsi and ate salt n'vinegar potato chips. "I'm usually not allowed to eat chips and drink pop, but this is a special occasion," she confided to me.

"As long as it's only once in a while, I think Grandpa would understand," I replied, realizing how carefully Chief Charlie and Rose guarded Jenn.

Those few hours spent with Jenny Hunt at the Reservoir left me with a memory of crystal-clear clarity: a memory of laughter and sunshine, of cold, clear, blue water and of teaching an eager student how to swim. I have often returned in my thoughts to that day and found solace in the simple joy that it brought me.

It was late in the afternoon when we walked down the trail to the village. I wasn't having dinner at Chief Charlie's that night because Rose had the flu. I told Jenn to tell her grandmother that I hoped she felt better soon. Jenn shyly asked me what she should do with the top and shorts. She should keep them, I told her. Just then, Daniel pulled up and parked on the wrong side of the road, facing us.

Jenn launched into a stream of excited chatter. "Uncle Daniel, we went swimming at the Reservoir, and Laura taught me some cool ways to swim and you should see her swim. She's so good—she can stay under the water forever."

Daniel looked at us with amusement. "Well, I guess I'm going to have to tell the cops on you. It's illegal to swim up there. And you two have sunburn. You'll be sorry for that tomorrow. But at least it looks as if Laura is putting on some weight, eh, Jenny?"

"I don't think she's putting on any weight. That's kind of like an insult, Uncle Daniel. Laura told me that if a boy insults you, it must mean he's interested in you. Are you interested in Laura?"

Jenn's words were said in a chatty, taunting voice. I laughed and quizzically raised an eyebrow. "Well, that wasn't real serious insulting." His tone was light, and, for some reason, set Jenn and I off into a fit of laughter. When we finally stopped, Daniel asked us if we wanted a ride home. We did.

For once, I welcomed the cool draft of air that greeted me when I entered the manse. There was work to do, but I decided today would be a day of no work, and I lay down on the couch, dozing off. The ringing of the phone woke me. It was Nadine. "I am," she paused for effect, "in love."

"So, your date was a success?'

"Hey, I'm not analyzing it—it's just this feeling. Like he's the one."

She asked if I wanted to have dinner. I did. She said she thought that we could get some food to go from the Hotel and take my boat to some springs she knew about on Denny Island. I hesitated.

Nadine said, "Hello?"

"Is it hard to get to? The thing is Nadine; I can't operate that boat. One of my crewmembers does it."

My remark was met by laughter. "Laura, you're supposed to be a research scientist working on the Coast, and you can't operate an outboard?"

"I'm planning on learning," I laughed back.

"Hey Laura, I'll drive your boat."

We met at the Hotel and loaded up on food and coffee. Nadine guided me in piloting the boat for part of the way there.

The springs she was talking about were on the western edge of Denny Island. Water from these springs trickled down a steep rock face into the ocean; it was a ten-minute uphill hike to get to the source. There was no name, at least no white name for these springs, which consisted of a series of shallow pools. Nadine quickly stripped off her clothes and let out a loud scream when she splashed water from the springs all around her and then sat down in the middle of the largest pool. as she splashed in the water from the springs. She sat down, with a 'splat!' in the middle of the largest pool. I followed her lead, also letting out a scream because the water was ice-cold. Nadine passed me a bottle of shampoo and some soap, and I very quickly washed up before vigorously toweling myself dry. It was the coldest water I'd ever been in, but left my skin and hair feeling soft and clean.

We ate our fish and chips on a rock outcropping where we'd tied up the boat, sitting there, chatting and enjoying the continued warmth, even though the sun was moving quickly towards the west. I asked her about her date with Chris.

"No, you first. How was Friday night?"

I had whispered to her at the Hotel, while we were waiting for our food, that I'd had dinner at Daniel's. Looking out at the near evening water, I sighed. I was kind of scared, I told her, because I was falling for him in a big way and didn't want to get hurt. Other than that, there wasn't much to say.

"Laura, you're nice and witty and great looking. If he's not interested, he's loony."

I grinned and thanked her for the support.

She then went into minute and often hilarious detail about her date. Her account ended with the two of them going for a walk after dinner.

"Nadine don't leave me hanging. I want all the dirt. What happened when you got back?"

She responded with her light, infectious laugh, but I wouldn't let up.

"Talk, Nadine. Did you sleep with him?"

"Well, no, but we necked and…you know…fooled around for a while."

"You necked? Nadine, you're twenty-eight years old. So, you were playing hard to get?"

"No. The thing is, we didn't have any birth control. Besides, waiting makes it even more romantic and exciting, don't you think, Laura?"

"Well, yeah, sure. So, when are you going to go all the way?"

"Two weeks from yesterday," she replied with a saucy shake of her head.

"Let me get this straight. You've cold-bloodedly planned when you're going to do it?"

"That's right. Next week, I'm working about a kilometer from Bella Coola. I'll just go to the hospital and get a prescription for some birth control pills and grab some condoms. Chris has to work next weekend, but he's free the Saturday after that. He's going to come to my place for dinner again, and, well, that's when we're going to do it."

"Before, or after dinner?" I laughed.

"Maybe both."

By this time, I was laughing hysterically; Nadine soon joined me.

"I know you think this is kind of cold-blooded, but, hey, Chris and I are scientists, and you know sex is a biological, scientific thing."

My stomach hurt from all the laughter, but eventually we stopped and admired the rapidly disappearing sun.

Nadine piloted the boat back, and I invited her over for a glass of wine. Back at the manse, outside, she expertly started a fire, and we sipped the wine in companionable silence.

Sometime later Nadine called out my name as a question: "Laura?"

I looked at her. Her usually up-tilted mouth was now a grim line.

"What is it, Nadine?"

"Something happened on Friday night."

"Well, what was it? Talk to me."

"Around midnight, Allie…Alysa Owens, a First Nations girl that's been working with me for the past three years, showed up at my door. She was very drunk. She said she was pregnant. I made her some tea and got her sobered up a little bit and got her to talk."

Nadine put her head in her hands and seemed unable to continue. Several questions crossed my mind, but I kept silent and poured her another glass of wine. Then I sat next to her on the couch and took her hand; she gripped mine tightly. After a while, she continued.

"I asked her some questions about the pregnancy. I don't know exactly what—how far along she was, had she been to the doctor, did she want the baby, did the father want the baby? She told me this baby was a joke from God, that the father didn't want it but that, for some strange reason, maybe she did. I said, then if that's what she wanted, she'd better see a doctor and start taking care of the baby. Then I asked why it was that the baby was a joke from God.'"

Nadine paused, then continued with more agitation in her voice. "Allie hesitated and said that the father of the baby is her uncle."

"What?" I asked, stunned.

Nadine repeated what she'd said: "The father of the baby is her uncle. She'd been to a party and gotten drunk. Everyone was passed out, and she was just coming around and getting ready to leave. He called her into the kitchen on some pretext and then raped her. There, on the kitchen floor."

Nadine hesitated a moment. "She tried to fight him. When it was over, he offered her money, but she just ran home in hysterics and told her mother. Laura, her mother, told her that she'd asked for it, that her uncle, Lyle Dodd, is a powerful man in the community, and she should just shut up."

I listened in stunned silence as Nadine reflected for a moment. "Allie's mother is at the bar in the Hotel a lot of the time. There are three younger kids, all from different fathers, I think. Allie spends most of her pay cheque keeping them clothed and making sure they have enough food. And those kids aren't normal; they're like scared rabbits. Starting last year, and especially this year, I've developed a strong tie to Allie. She's kind of like a little sister to me, but instead of a little sister, she sometimes seems like an old, wise woman. She's been responsible for those younger brothers and sisters since she was five, and she shared with me that telling her mother about Lyle Dodd was her last-ditch at-tempt to get her mother to support her."

Nadine stopped her narrative and took a deep breath.

"Who is this Lyle Dodd person?" I asked.

"He is a kind of Passage hotshot, or at least he acts that way. He owns the taxi and part of the Hotel. You know, Laura, he gives me the creeps; he is the type that looks at you as if he can see through your clothes." Nadine paused, swallowed a fair measure of wine and then, in a cold, calm voice, said, "I want to kill him."

"What is Allie going to do?"

"I told Allie that I didn't think God was playing any cruel tricks. I told her she hadn't done anything wrong and that she needed some counseling. She had choices, I told her, and I couldn't make those choices for her, but I'd support her no matter what she did. I told her to see Chris right away. Finally, I offered her the spare room and stayed with her until she fell asleep. Before she fell asleep, though, she told me she was going to see Chris about an abortion. Yesterday morning, when I got up, she was gone. She left a note saying she'd be away from work Monday morning and would hitch a ride to Bella Coola and meet me there on Monday night or Tuesday."

"Did you tell Chris about this?"

"No, I don't think that would be right. Allie trusts me—she would never assume that I'd tell Chris and working out the details is between them…at least, I think it is. If she wanted me to tell him, she would have said so, wouldn't she have?"

"I guess so. I mean, of course. The thing is, Nadine, it's out of your hands."

Nadine had easily drunk twice as much wine as I, but she was stone cold sober. She looked exhausted. I suggested that she take the taxi home. When she left, I hugged her tightly and told her to call me from Bella Coola.

I studied the dying fire after Nadine left. There was a very dark side to the Passage. It occurred to me that alcohol fed this darkness, and I vowed that I would never drink in the Hotel again, although as it turned out, I did. I thought of Daniel and of Nadine and Chris and of a Native girl named Allie, whom I'd never met. I could not possibly know then how the inclinations of Lyle Dodd would lead to a path of death and division in the Passage.

I blocked out thoughts of Nadine's story and returned instead to the earlier, happy part of the day I'd spent with Jenny. When I fell asleep, it was to thoughts of swimming through crystal-clear waters with a delightful little girl named Jenny Hunt. Although I couldn't see them, I knew that Chief Charlie, Daniel, Maggie and a host of relatives watched over us from the shoreline.

Chapter 18

"Because miracles do happen, you are here before me," I said to Jack and Kristy when I arrived at the boat the next morning. "What are you guys doing here?"

"We quit," said Kristy. "Our boss is a nut case who tortures us."

"Well, that's my job. I'm a white man," I retorted. "You have to rise up and overthrow me."

"Yeah sure," replied Kristy sarcastically and then in a serious voice said, "Laura, do we have to go to this site? Like, there's dead people up there; it gives me the creeps."

I glanced at Jack, who immediately looked the other way; I sensed that he was also uncomfortable. Taking a deep breath, I thought of what to say. "The thing is we're not going there to dishonor or disturb those spirits. We're just going to record some information about your culture—information that can give back some of that culture that was stolen from you."

The discussion about their culture that had been met with indifference only three weeks earlier had an impact this time, perhaps because I was speaking from my heart. Jack nodded an "Mmph," and we climbed into the boat.

Campbell's Pole is located on Denny Island, about two kilometers from the Passage. The site is on the edge of a ten-meter, sheer bluff that overlooks the waters of the Passage. The view from the edge of this bluff is spectacular. There is a small cove at the base of the bluff and a path that is rarely used leads from here up to the site. We anchored the boat, unloaded our equipment and headed up the path. As we approached the top, I saw the first grave offering—an enamel bowl, half buried in the dirt. We continued to the top of the bluff, walking silently.

The grave offerings—mostly old dishes—increased in number

as we walked upwards. The top of the bluff was flat, and the two grave houses were immediately apparent, even though the entire site was overgrown with huckleberry and other foliage. I stopped on the edge of the flat spot on the bluff and signaled for Kristy and Jack to stop as well. Pulling off my backpack, I reached inside and took out the pouch of *Export A* tobacco. I told Kristy and Jack I was going to sprinkle some around the ground where we stood, as an offering to the dead; did they want to do the same?

Kristy looked at me like I was crazy, but Jack simply nodded and took a small amount of the tobacco. We both turned to Kristy, who shook her head and mumbled something under her breath but then came forward and took a pinch of the tobacco.

Looking at Jack, I said, "I think we say a prayer."

Jack gave a tiny nod. Taking a deep breath, I began. "To the spirits that dwell in this place, we offer this gift to show our respect. We have come to learn from you, and we ask that you teach us and protect us from harm."

I then sprinkled the tobacco around the ground; then, Jack and Kristy did the same. I don't know what I expected from this ceremony. I sensed no change in the forest around me, but I did feel a sense of calm and, looking at Kristy, saw that she did as well. In Jack's face, I saw a new sense of respect.

We spent four days at Campbell's Pole; no bad luck visited us there. The whole week was hot and sunny, but it was cool under the thick boughs of fragrant cedar on the rock bluff, and we worked quietly and efficiently. Just as Maggie had said, there was one miniature, square log-house structure and another miniature, European-style house. The more recent house faced the ocean and was built with milled lumber and a square window. The contents of this grave house were macabre. Inside were several coffins, stacked haphazardly, ranging in size from ones constructed for small children to those for older children, to those for adults. The lid on one of the European-style coffins had been removed and the skeletal remains, dressed in a turn-of-the-century man's suit, had been pulled halfway out of the coffin. The window of the grave house was broken. I supposed it was possible some animal had dragged the corpse out, but the haphazard stacking of the coffins suggested human intervention.

Jack and I mapped the grave houses, as well as six tombstones that dated from 1886 to 1929. The names on the tombstones suggested that this had been a family burial ground. I thought that we could raise the pole that had once stood directly in front of the European-style grave house, but it was waterlogged and made of cedar; it would have required heavy equipment to move.

Kristy worked hard at clearing the site and mapping in the grave goods. These were mostly cooking and eating utensils, such as plates, cups and pots. Maggie later told me that food contained in these artifacts was intended as an offering for the deceased and that this food was simply set down and left in the containers in which it was brought.

After mapping the grave goods, Kristy took photographs of the site and, although nothing was ever said, pictures of every angle of the European-style grave house, except any that would show the coffins and skeletal remains inside.

On Thursday afternoon we collected our gear and carried it down to the boat. Taking a pair of work gloves that I'd never used out of my backpack, I told Jack and Kristy I was going to go up there and put that skeleton back into its coffin; I raised my eyebrows, questioning if they were going to help.

"No way," responded Kristy.

Jack's response was "I'm not touching those bones. And besides, you could cut yourself climbing in that window."

"Okay, just pass me the axe. I'll get rid of the glass—there's hardly any left anyway."

"I'll get rid of the glass," said Jack reluctantly. "But I'm not going in that grave house." He knocked out what was left in the windowpane of the grave house and carefully checked to make sure there were no sharp edges remaining. He then moved away to the top of the path where Kristy was waiting. She was eyeing me nervously. I put on the leather work gloves and climbed through the window. This was easy. I was small, and the bottom of the window was at the height of my waist. As carefully as possible, I placed the skeleton back into the coffin. There were clothes lying about, which I placed in the coffin as well. One of these pieces of clothing, which probably dated to the 1880s, was a white cotton child's dress, edged with lace. It filled me with a feeling of sadness.

The lid of the coffin was half on, with the other half wedged against another coffin. It was heavy, but I managed to place the lid back on top. Using my hip as a lever, I pushed the coffins into an order that I thought approximated the way they were originally placed. As I climbed back out the window, I realized I'd thought about this moment with some trepidation but that in accomplishing it, I had felt no unease.

I walked over to Jack and Kristy, and a moment of craziness came over me. I looked at their very serious faces and in a loud voice said, "BOO!"

Kristy jumped about a foot into the air, and Jack stepped back abruptly.

"You scared the shit out of me," admonished Kristy, and stomped off down the path.

"Christ, Laura, that's not funny," said Jack.

"Jack, I don't know what came over me. I'm sorry." But then I started to laugh. "Did you see the look on Kristy's face?"

Then Jack started to laugh. This was such a rare event that I started to laugh uncontrollably. From the direction of the boat came Kristy's voice: "You guys are sicko nutcases."

This only fueled our laughter. When we finally calmed down, I looked at Jack, reached into my back pocket and pulled out some loose tobacco. The look that passed between us then was serious and, letting the tobacco fall slowly through my fingers, I whispered, "Thank you."

It seemed to me in that moment as if there was a sudden lightness in the air about Campbell's Pole, but perhaps it was only my imagination.

When we returned to the Passage, I took Kristy and Jack to the Hotel for an early dinner. We discussed our plans for the next few days. The photo lab equipment had arrived from Vancouver, and Kristy and I would work the next day setting it up. Jack would finish off the map of Boston's Retreat and start on the one for Campbell's Pole. Kristy had forgiven me for scaring her and, over the course of the summer, would exact revenge by sneaking up on me constantly and shouting, "Boo," until it finally had no effect.

The evening we'd returned, I had an appointment after dinner with Agnes Campbell, who had grown up a Campbell and married a distant cousin who was a Campbell, so should be a mine of information on the Campbell site. I was a bit leery of meeting with her, as she was the women who had called Maggie to let her know that Daniel had been seen with me late at night.

Over the last few days, I had come to a decision to somehow mitigate against the defacement of artifacts at Boston's Retreat, and Campbell's Pole. I phoned the Detachment and asked to speak to the CO, Sergeant MacCallum. I was put through to his office immediately and explained my concerns. He told me he was free, and could I come right in and discuss the issue? I could. Not bothering to change out of my field clothes, I went to the Detachment right away.

I told Sergeant MacCallum about the desecration of the sites. His initial response was non-committal, saying there was a huge territory to police. I responded, "You have to understand, Sergeant, that disturbance of archaeological sites is an indictable offense, in the province of British Columbia, punishable by a $50,000 fine and two years in jail. As well, there are federal statutes that apply to disturbance of sites."

This caught his attention, and he said he would pass on this information to the members of the Detachment. "I think, as well," he said, "that I can encourage locals to report archaeological site disturbances, both to myself and other members of the Detachment."

I felt a sense of ease that I had done something to mitigate against the lawless and immoral desecration of the sites I had visited. But the day was passing, and I had only a few minutes to change and make my appointment with Agnes Campbell for the evening.

Agnes Campbell lived only two blocks from me and did prove to be an excellent source of information, although I was cautious at the start. She made an excellent cup of coffee for me and then started with several references to Daniel, but I didn't take the bait. She told me to make sure that I didn't take everything Margaret Brown said as being necessarily true. I took a deep breath and refrained from asking her if I should make sure that I didn't take what she said too seriously.

Finally, however, Agnes Campbell did give me some interesting information about the site. The pole had been carved to commemorate the death of her uncles: two brothers, Lawrence and Edward Campbell, who had had got caught in a storm off Hunter's Point and were lost at sea. The pole was erected in 1939, a year after their death, at the family burial ground. It was placed there so as not to anger the missionaries at the Passage.

"This was the old way. If someone drowned and no body was found, a pole would be carved and raised close to where that person died. I remember there was a feast for those men as well, held a year after their death. I was fourteen years old at the time. It was a secret and hurried affair because potlatches were outlawed," she said.

I said, "My supervisor at the university has photographs of the pole before it was pulled over. The style is not like what we call the bas relief technique of poles we have found around here. Do you know anything about that, Mrs. Campbell?"

"I think I can help you with that," Mrs. Campbell replied. "The pole was commissioned by the family to a carver on Vancouver Island, not to a local carver. I don't know if there was no one here who still had the skills to carve, but that skill was easy to hide, although not when the children were away at residential school. Usually, they were allowed home for part of the summer. The older ones taught those young kids how to whittle and carve, so they would learn that the carving is just slightly above the surface, what you call bas relief. I think for the pole for those brothers who died, maybe, the carver was held to be the best, so maybe that is why they chose him. And, of course, he would do the crest designs with what he was familiar with."

Although she was very curious, Mrs. Campbell was very helpful, but when I got home, I didn't do paperwork on the Campbell site. Instead, I gathered the papers that I had written for my courses on the history of European colonization.

Chapter 19

The next few weeks went by quickly. Kristy and I set up a photo lab in one of the upstairs bedrooms at the manse. She very quickly mastered the processes of developing film. I began to think that her skill as a photographer would rival George Clements's. She had an intuitive sense of angles and light in the photographs she took of the landscape and in those she took of people. One of her pictures, which is very dear to me, is of Jack and me. We are standing with our backs to her, at the end of the wharf. Jack's head is tilted downwards to catch what I am saying I think, and I am looking up at him, telling him something. I never did remember what it was we were discussing, but the expression on our half-visible faces and our closeness suggested that it was a discussion between friends.

We mapped several seasonal fishing camps that Maggie had told me about. At these sites, there were narrow moss-covered poles that had been used for smokehouses and possibly shelters. We also completed work at a site called Grizzly Pass that had been visited by George in the early 1960s. It contained the frame of a single intact traditional house. On one of the carved house posts, the central crest carving had been hacked out with an axe. The hacked-out portion would have been a depiction of a grizzly bear holding a small man. It was believed in the village that an American pleasure craft had done this. No person of Heiltsuk descent would risk the bad magic that could come from doing such a thing.

Maggie said that when the traditional winter villages were abandoned, often one house would be maintained and utilized by a family or several families, for seasonal use. She told me that I should talk to Clifford Martin, an Elder, whose family had used the site.

Clifford Martin told me, when I visited with him, that the house was used for potlatches, both before and after this cultural practice was outlawed in an amendment to the Indian Act in 1884. What he said then about Grizzly Pass would often echo in my thoughts.

"The police and the Indian Agent found it. They came right in there to that house. That was a sacred place too, you know, and they came right in there and said we were going to jail if we potlatched there anymore."

I asked him if they continued to potlatch at Grizzly Pass, and he shook his head and said, "Not there, no." Then he chuckled and added, "But we still had potlatches, and those men were pretty stupid—they never could catch us in the act."

I was working hard and had little time to think of anything except about the jobs at hand. Still, sometimes, I thought about Daniel. I hadn't seen him since the day Jenn and I had run into him after our swim at the Reservoir.

I continued to have dinner every Sunday at Chief Charlie's, but neither Daniel nor Matt were there. I had seen their boat at the dock during the week on two occasions but had not run into Daniel. Occasionally, at Charlie's, Matt and Daniel's names would come up, along with a statement that they were fishing in places whose names I didn't recognize and, so, couldn't remember.

I also saw Maggie every Saturday, and Jenn remained a regular Sunday afternoon fixture. On those days when it was warm, we went swimming at the Reservoir. Jenn was an excellent student.

Nadine and I got together whenever we could, usually for quick meals at the Hotel. We also managed to have long phone conversations. Both of us were busy, and now that she had a man in her life, she had even less time. I had always thought that she was beautiful, but now she had a soft glow about her that made her even more so. Love suited Nadine.

It was almost the end of July, and it seemed to me that we were experienced enough to tackle Xvnis, the largest known winter village of the Heiltsuk and the mystic resting place of Wikash, who had challenged a missionary and who had touched the sun. It was also the site where I walked with Franz Boas in a dream.

Over the past few weeks, we had moved slowly eastward in our investigations. Xvnis is a forty-five-minute commute from the village, even with our boat and its powerful engine. We would camp there for the time that it took to investigate the site. Our chances of finding the remains of a complete village, occupied both before and during contact, were good. On the Friday before the August long weekend, we went out to the site and did some reconnaissance work.

We found Xvnis right away because it was known to most of the residents of the Passage, and Kristy and Jack were no exception. The southern facing site is at the mouth of a fjord that extends deep into the mainland. It is located on a narrow, flat strip of land that backs against the mountains. The location is strategic: the site is protected by high rock bluffs on both sides and a steep islet in the front. Xvnis is neatly divided in half by a stream that cuts through a two-to-three-meter midden, the depth of which suggests that the area had been used for thousands of years. In front of the site is a shallow beach that at low tide extends out for more than a hundred meters from the village. On either side of the stream, on top of the midden, are two distinct rows of houses. Walking along the beach in front of Xvnis, I had a vague sense of the familiar.

Xvnis is in an old-growth forest. The cedars are huge and hundreds of years old. There is scant undergrowth, and the floor of the forest is mossy, soft and heavy. Younger cedar trees and hemlock grow in perfect lines along the sills of the houses and almost fully encased the house posts. The cedar beams on the forest floor were higher than my waist. I could hear a pair of ravens calling to each other. I was almost impervious to the sound of ravens by now, but each cry seemed to cut through what felt like thick air, even though beams of sunlight penetrated through the cedar canopy. I felt as if I was being watched and twice turned around, expecting to see something or someone, but there was nothing.

Jack and I discussed strategies for mapping the site, and I wondered why we were talking in whispers. I exchanged a look with Jack and knew that he felt the same weight I did.

Chris Sutherland had a VHS machine and a good supply of movies that his sister had sent up. Nadine borrowed it, and we arranged to spend Friday night at her house watching movies. I walked over at about

6, and we ate dinner and talked for a few hours. It seemed like Nadine and I never ran out of things to say, whether it was philosophical or just gossip. It was after midnight, and we were near the end of the second movie we'd watched that night. The phone rang.

I didn't hear what the voice on the other end said but heard Nadine listen for a while and answer in a soft voice, "Yes, we have had a lot of good times."

The voice on the other end said something else, and Nadine's voice, still soft, replied, "Well, you don't need my permission to decide to keep the baby. I am not disappointed in that decision. It will work out."

Nadine paused and continued, "Well, sure, I can tell you've been drinking Allie, but what about the baby? That stuff's not good for the baby."

There was another pause. Then Nadine said, "Why doesn't it matter, Allie?"

The look on her face quickly changed to one of panic, and her reply to whatever Allie said was sharp and loud. "Don't even think about it, Allie. You've got your whole life, and tomorrow, you'll feel differently."

Nadine was now pacing as far as the phone cord would permit. Her hand held the receiver tightly, but it was shaking.

"Allie, too many people need you. I need you. I love you, Allie." There was a pause, and Nadine said her name again. "Allie?"

She dropped the phone and raced to the door, scrambled into her rubber boots and put on her anorak.

"Nadine, what's going on?" My voice was a near scream.

"She just lives two blocks from here, says she's going to kill herself." And then she was out the door.

I wasn't far behind but couldn't keep up with Nadine's terror and long legs. Just as she was about to enter the front door of an old dilapidated house, a single shot rang out. I've always remembered the sound of that shot. It seemed to echo around and around the Passage, to bounce off the mountains on the mainland and then to return home. Nadine stopped dead in her tracks, screamed out an anguished, "Nooo!" and then she was up the stairs and in the house.

It must have only been a few seconds later that I entered Allie Owens's house. It was a clear, cold night, with a new moon, and it was very dark out. Still, some light filtered in through the front window, and I could see a living room of some sort and, beyond this, a dimly lit kitchen. A door in the kitchen was wide open, and the light from below framed a steep set of stairs that led to the basement. Instinctively, I knew that this is where Allie Owens was, but my feet were frozen to the floor. I couldn't move. Then I heard a sound on the other side of this door, and it slowly began to close—it was like some scene from a cheap horror thriller. I held my breath before I saw that on that other side of that door were two children, maybe eight and ten years old.

The oldest looked at me fearfully and said, "Allie?"

I pulled myself together. "Do you know Nadine?"

The older child, a boy, nodded.

"I'm Nadine's friend. My name is Laura, and Allie wanted me to take care of you for a while. Right now, I want you to go back to bed, and then I'm going to get you something to eat."

To my ears, this sounded completely unbelievable, but they headed back along the hallway to a bedroom and I followed them and tucked them in.

"Where's your Mom?" I asked.

"Gone out," the boy replied.

"You stay here now for a while, and I'll be back soon."

The older boy nodded, as the younger child looked at me with huge, dark eyes, full of fear.

I went to the top of the basement stairs. Now I could hear sobbing. This time, I went quickly down the stairs and when I got to the bottom, turned in the direction of the sobs.

There were no real walls in the unfinished basement, but an area had been partitioned off with some old drapes. Through a large opening in these drapes, I could see Nadine crouched on the floor, holding someone on her lap. There was blood everywhere: on the walls, on the bed, on the floor and all over Nadine. Walking a few steps closer, I could see what must have been Allie Owens, but most of her face and what seemed like half of her head was missing. Through Nadine's sobs, I could hear the rattling sound of Allie's breathing and Nadine saying, "Get an ambulance. She's still breathing."

I turned and went quickly up the stairs, while some macabre voice in my head kept saying over and over, "But not for long."

The phone was on the kitchen table. When I dialed the operator, some separate part of me realized I had located the phone without looking because I'd come to recognize that all the Indigenous people in the Passage kept the phone on the kitchen table. I'm not sure what I said when I was finally put through to the paramedics, who said they'd call the police. I was having some difficulty explaining where the house was and said I'd wait outside, but please hurry because there were children in the house. The police arrived before the ambulance, and I briefly told them what had happened and then said I thought I'd better go and sit with the children. This was a good idea because, just when I entered their bedroom, the sound of a screaming siren could be heard. It seemed like forever that I sat in that room with those children, telling them a story about how Raven stole the sun, before a police officer came and asked if he could talk to me. I got up and moved into the hallway.

It was Sergeant MacCallum. "You look like you're holding up pretty good here."

I simply nodded, and he said quietly, "Allie Owens is dead. But Nadine is holding onto her as if she'll never let go. Could you talk to her, Laura?"

I nodded again and said, "Someone has to stay with these children."

"Children in the bedroom? Who?" he asked.

"A boy and a girl. I don't know, young, maybe eight and ten."

"There should be a toddler as well. Are you sure there's no baby in there?"

"I don't think so."

The sergeant walked to the end of the hall and into another room, coming out only a few moments later. "The baby's in there, sleeping. You wait here, and I'll send a police officer up to watch these children, and then you come downstairs."

"Sergeant?" I asked.

"Nadine has an illness, and…and," I stuttered. "If that girl is dead, maybe those ambulance people should take Nadine to the hospital."

"Does Dr. Sutherland know about this illness?"

"Yes, he would know what to do."

"Well, I agree with you, Laura, and actually, I think she's in some kind of shock anyway." The sergeant went downstairs, and a few minutes later another RCMP officer came up the stairs. Unlike the sergeant, he was very young, younger than I, and he was clearly shaken up. I nodded to him and headed down the stairs.

The sergeant was kneeling next to Nadine and Allie, speaking quietly to Nadine. Off to one side, two ambulance first responders were standing. The sergeant nodded at one of them, who came over to me, and with his back to Nadine, spoke in a whisper. "Every time we try to get close, she just hugs that dead girl closer. The next step is to pry her away. Do you think you can get her to let go and come with us?"

I glanced at Nadine, who was holding Allie tightly, her head buried in the dead girl's shoulder. "I can try."

The first responder moved away, and I walked towards Nadine. I glanced around the room as I did this and saw cut-outs from magazines of movie and rock stars on the walls. There was also a bookshelf that contained books and photographs, several of these being snapshots of Nadine and Allie and a First Nations boy I assumed was Jason. On the table next to the bed there were perfume and candles. I knew in those few seconds a little bit about who Allie Owens was and knew that she'd been headed somewhere far greater than where she had come from.

When I reached them, I got down on my knees. The stench of alcohol and blood was overwhelming. I hadn't known until then that blood had a smell. "Nadine?" I whispered.

There was no response. I touched Nadine's hair and said her name, but she only hugged the dead body closer. A kind of coldness came over me. I gauged how loud I could raise my voice so that I would get Nadine's attention but not disturb the children up there.

"Nadine, look at me."

She did.

"Listen to me. She's dead, Nadine. Allie is dead. And there are three children up there that need help, and until you let go of her, they aren't going to get it."

Nadine heard me but responded by shaking her head and repeating "No."

In a softer voice, I said, "Nadine, I'll stay right here with Allie, and you go with the paramedics. Give her to me to take care of for a while. You go with them and tell them about Allie's brothers and sisters. They need you to do that. I won't leave her, Nadine."

With this blatant series of lies, I won Nadine's confidence, and she slowly let go of the body, ensuring that the head came carefully to rest on the floor. Without a word, she went with the two first responders.

When she was gone, I stood up, gagged and rushed to a corner of the basement. I vomited until I thought my entire stomach would come up. The sergeant stood behind me, with a hand resting lightly on my shoulder, and said several times, "Good Laura—that's a good way to be done with it."

Chapter 20

The rest of that evening was a collage of images that never fit together very well. Sergeant MacCallum said they'd need a statement right away, while everything was fresh in my mind.

Yes, I could go but needed to clean up. A cruiser would take me to the manse and then pick me up in half an hour. There was blood all over my clothes, on my hands and even on my face. I took a bath: the water was almost hotter than I could stand. I washed my hair and body with strongly scented soap and shampoo, trying to get rid of the smell of blood. Images of those children, of Nadine and of Allie Owens flitted through my head. My half hour was almost up, and I quickly got dressed.

I gave the sergeant a statement at the detachment, telling him everything I knew about the events leading to the late-night phone call and what occurred after that. The other young police officer was there and continued to look nervous. For a moment, I saw the Passage through his eyes, and it seemed like a very dark and foreign place.

Sergeant MacCallum asked me why we hadn't called the police as soon as we got the call. I thought for a few seconds, asking myself the same question, then answered, "I don't know. It didn't occur to me, and I guess it didn't occur to Nadine. I just followed her out the door." I stopped for a second, adding, "I guess it wouldn't have made a difference, anyway."

Then it was my turn to ask questions. I wondered if anything could be done about Lyle Dodd. A look of distaste crossed the sergeant's face. "Probably not at this late date. If she had come to us right away, we could have done something, but most women don't."

After giving my statement, I declined a ride home and went to the hospital to see Nadine. It was only a few steps from the detachment to the hospital, but the young constable walked me to the admitting door. I thanked him and went inside. There was no one at the desk, so I stood, waiting. After a few minutes, a nurse whom I recognized as Sue came walking down the corridor.

"Hello, Laura." She smiled. "You must be here to see Nadine."

"Hi, Sue. Is she alright?"

"She's sleeping now, but you can have a quick peek. It's the third door on the left, down the corridor. Dr. Sutherland is with her."

I walked down the corridor to the doorway, which was ajar. Nadine was lying in the bed, covered with two blankets. She looked as if she was peacefully sleeping. Next to her was Dr. Sutherland, hunched in a chair, leaning forward, with his head resting in his hands.

He must have sensed that I was there because he looked up and, when he saw me, came immediately to the door. "Hello, Laura," he said very softly.

"Hi, Dr. Sutherland."

"Chris," he said absentmindedly.

"Is she going to be all right?"

"I don't know, Laura. I had to give her enough drugs to kill a horse to get her to sleep. You know about her illness?"

"Yes."

"Well, they aren't very pleasant drugs, and she probably won't be very happy with me for giving them to her. But this is a critical time. Her illness can be set off by the seasons, by stress or for reasons no one really knows. The stress factor is huge right now. She needs to sleep. That's my concern."

I asked if I could sit with her for a while. His features softened; I could see why Nadine was so attracted to him.

"That would be good. Maybe I can go and have a quick cup of coffee while you do that."

I pulled the chair close to Nadine's bed and studied her finely structured face. I realized that I had come to have a deep love for this good friend. Thoughts of her playful smile and the way she said "Hey" played through my mind. Slow tears fell down my face, and I wanted to say a prayer—but to whom? I wasn't sure I believed in God, and I had no kinship with Chief Charlie's Creator. Then it came to me—I would pray to Franz Boas and to my grandfather. And, so, I did. I asked them to use what power they had to bestow grace upon Nadine and to protect her from the darkness.

I woke up the next day, confused for a moment as to why I'd

worn my clothes to bed. Then the events of the night before spilled into my waking thoughts, and looking at the clock next to my bed, I saw that it was 1 in the afternoon. My first thought was that I had to see Nadine. As if on cue, the phone rang. Nadine's voice was whispery and hesitant. "Laura, I'm in the hospital. Can you come and see me?"

"Of course, I can. In fact, I was just heading out that way when you called. Can I bring you anything?"

"Well, Chris said I should maybe stay in the hospital for tonight. Could you get me my toothbrush and face cream and, you know, that stuff, from the house?"

"Sure, Nadine. I can do that."

"Could you maybe bring some coffee too? They have me so drugged up, I can hardly think."

I took the taxi to Nadine's and asked Silas Dodd, the driver, to return in half an hour. I brewed a pot of coffee, poured it into Nadine's thermos, collected the things she'd asked for and added some slippers.

I put everything into her backpack and waited on the balcony for the taxi, which came a few minutes later. On the ride to the hospital, I sensed a subtle difference in Silas Dodd's demeanor towards me. Of course, I thought. Allie's death and rumors of some of the circumstances surrounding it would be spreading through the village.

I found Nadine in a chair, gazing out the window of her room. She had circles under her eyes and still looked tired and pale, but she had been up and walking around, I found out.

"There's a deck at the far end of the hospital. Let's take that coffee and go sit out there," she said.

When we were sitting at a table on the small deck, Nadine said, "It's hard for me to stay still. It's the drugs: major tranquilizers and anti-psychotics."

We drank our coffee in silence for a few minutes. Then Nadine said, "I don't really remember what happened last night." She paused and continued. "Do you know if those kids are safe?"

"Yes, the sergeant told me they'd found someone who the children would be able to stay with until things got sorted out."

"Who has the kids?"

"Allie's mother's cousin has the kids, and Allie's mother has no chance of getting them back until she stops drinking…and the Ministry completes an investigation."

This answer seemed to satisfy Nadine, and Chris came out a few minutes later. He touched Nadine's shoulder, kissed the top of her head, then sat down next to her. Taking the hand that wasn't holding the coffee, he asked her how she felt.

"It's hard to keep still. It's these drugs. Couldn't you cut back on them?"

He brought her hand up to his lips and kissed it. "I'm sorry, sweetheart, not today; maybe tomorrow. I couldn't reach your specialist, but I talked to one in Vancouver. You have to get solid sleep and keep your thoughts from racing."

Nadine buried her head in his shoulder, then, looking up at him, said, "It's okay...it'll be okay."

He kissed her on the cheek and was gone.

"Nadine," I said, "I'd kill to have someone look at me the way he looks at you."

"Don't say that word Laura; it gives me the creeps."

It may have given Nadine the creeps, but we laughed anyway, and that laughter felt so good.

I would have bypassed my Saturday shopping, but I really needed groceries. Did I imagine it, or did people seem to notice me whereas they hadn't before? When I got home, I phoned my mother. As soon as I heard her voice, I started to cry and related the events of the last few days. She never once told me to calm down. That was her way—to just listen. She was able to put together the important details, even though the way it came out wasn't linear.

"You wouldn't have taken a black dress up there, I suppose?" she asked softly. "One that would be suitable for the funeral?"

"No, I hadn't even thought of that, Mom. Could you go out to the house and get me a dress and some shoes and stockings? But you'd have to send them up by courier. No, maybe not—I don't even know if courier delivery makes any difference up here."

"I'll drive out to the airport, to that outfit that flies things up there. Now what about your friend? What about clothes for her?"

"Well, she's about your height, tall and slim, and I know her feet are bigger than mine, but I don't know what size. No, wait, I do. She said once she wished she had baby feet like mine, not size nine and still growing."

We both laughed. After the long, serious conversation, it felt good.

"I'll send a dress of mine and some shoes."

I thanked her; she ended our conversation with "Why don't you call again tonight, Laura, before bed? I'll be up."

I told her that I would and, wishing I were there with her, hung up the phone. Then I walked around the manse, vaguely aware that I was picking on the cuticle of my thumb. Someone knocked quietly on the door.

It was Chief Charlie. I was glad to see him. He watched me from the kitchen table, with a kind look in his eyes, as I made a fresh pot of coffee. I told him the story of the night before, but by this time my emotions had been dulled, and I spoke of events in a kind of detached way. He told me that Sergeant MacCallum had said to him that I'd done a good job with Nadine and with those kids.

There was a long silence between us. Then I spontaneously asked, "Why would Lyle Dodd want to have sex with his own niece?"

Chief Charlie did not at all seem shocked by the question. He stared at the table-top, his forehead furrowed in thought. After a while, he looked up at me and said, "I don't know if there is a complete or single answer to that question. He was one of those children that was molested."

"What children?"

"At the Alberni residential school. He was there for a long time. They beat him up and molested him, not just the people who worked there, but. they say, the older kids did that too. And then, when he got to be older, he did the same to the younger ones. Like a cycle. Maybe, that's part of it. A kind of sickness. It goes pretty deep here, Laura."

"But how do you know this—that those things happened to him?"

"I'm not really sure. On the Reserve, people just seem to know what happened to others who went to residential school; maybe not what happened to everyone. No one talks about it, except in whispers."

"Do the police know? Does the government?"

"Well, yeah, sure they know," he answered in a resigned voice.

"Why didn't anyone do anything? Why isn't anyone doing anything?"

"They are now. Stories are starting to come out. A few are speaking out. But there's so much shame. Those kids—they were starved, and raped, and they thought it was their fault that those things happened to us. And then they came back to the Reserve, and they kept quiet because…others knowing? Well, that's shameful to them too."

There were tears in Chief Charlie's eyes. but from somewhere deep inside of me there came another forbidden question. "Why did you send Daniel and Laney there? I know you tried, but couldn't you have stopped them from going?"

"I know it is hard to believe, Laura, but there was not much I could do about it." He wiped his eyes with the back of his hand. I thought my heart would break.

I took his hand in mine and said, "No, don't you cry. You didn't do anything wrong. They didn't get to them, and I don't know Laney, but Daniel's strong. He's so strong, Charlie, strong like you are, strong in a way that I can never be."

He placed his other hand over mine. "You're young," he said. "And you don't know your strength yet. You're stronger than either Daniel or I, and someday you'll know this. Why, you'd tell a whole room of fancy people to go to hell."

I eyed him skeptically. He smiled tentatively. "You know, Laura, hardly any of our children make it to Grade 12. After Grade 8, they go to Port Alberni to boarding homes, and they just don't make it there. But I've been fighting—me and many others on the Reserve, to get a high school at the Passage, and I won't rest as a chief until that's accomplished. It's my dream to bring the children home."

There were no hard feelings between us for my hard questions, and we talked about his plan for a school while he finished his coffee. He told me that the funeral for Allie Owens would be on Thursday. Just before he left, he said, "I don't mean to forgive Lyle Dodd's behavior. What he did was unforgivable."

After Chief Charlie left, I packed my bathing suit, a towel and a thermos of tea in my backpack and hiked up to the Reservoir. I swam lengths until I couldn't possibly take another stroke, then sat on the edge of the lake, drinking tea. It was 7 o'clock when I got back to the manse. A fine drizzle was falling, and I was soaking wet. I had a hot bath and went to the hospital. Nadine was sitting in a chair in her room, picking at a cold supper.

"Stop it, Nadine," I told her. "I'll go to the Hotel and get you a hamburger. Besides, I haven't eaten dinner yet, and I'm starving."

Her eyes were clearer. I was happy to see at least a half-grin.

"I'll take you up on it."

There was still a light rain falling, but part of the deck at the hospital had an aluminum overhang. We ate our dinner out there, listening to the rain, which beat a steady rhythm against the aluminum. Nadine looked pensive and, when we finished eating, said, "What makes me so angry about this illness is that I feel like I can't have those really deep or extreme feelings that God gave us, whether it's happiness or grief. Because if I do have them, I can go crazy. Not crazy like, you know, the way people say all the time, 'I'm going to go crazy.' I mean, I can really lose it. Become certifiable." She paused. "But mostly I don't think about that because what's the point?"

From this statement, I realized the profound effect that Nadine's illness had on her. Still, I didn't know what to say, except a simple, "I'm sorry, Nadine."

She smiled gently. "I know."

Sometime, very late that night, I dreamed of Franz Boas and of Raven stealing the sun. I understood the words that Franz Boas spoke. Looking into my eyes, he said softly, "The grace that is given me." And then he gazed upwards and I followed his look. Under one wing, Raven held the sun, and under the other, he gently enclosed and cradled Allie Owens. It seemed as if Raven looked into my eyes for a moment, before moving swiftly upwards towards the stars.

Chapter 21

The next morning, I could not eat breakfast and started to cry for Allie Owens and for Nadine. I also cried about Lyle Dodd and about what Chief Charlie had said about a residential school near Port Alberni.

My thoughts wandered to thinking about Michael; then a memory of a question I'd asked my dance instructor came to me.

"Sophie, what do you think about when you dance?"

"I don't think. I feel. And when I'm dancing, I don't dance for an audience, whether there is one or not. I am dancing for God because that's where music really comes from."

"Well, Sophie, I'll never dance for God because I don't believe there is any God."

"Great. A ten-year-old atheist. Well, someday, you'll believe in God, but for now it doesn't matter. You don't have to dance for God, Laura. Just dance for the feelings in the music. All of the feelings."

I wondered why I was having these memories, but as soon as the question was asked, I knew the answer. I had witnessed a horrible event. I'd made a good start in dealing with it by talking to my mother and to Chief Charlie, but it was only a start. I needed to let the feelings wash over me and to accept what I'd seen. I needed to accept that the averted eyes I'd encountered when I first came to Passage bore the subtext of spirits that were broken…or near broken. I cried, then, for a long time. Then I remembered my dream, which brought me comfort. I had prayed to Franz Boas; he had answered my prayer by sending a vision of beauty and peace.

Later that afternoon, I visited Nadine.

"I'm going to be alright, Laura. I slept for nine hours last night, and I don't really need to be in the hospital now. Chris and I have decided I'll stay at his house. He'll come over several times a day and check up on me. After the funeral on Thursday, we're going down to Vancouver for several days. When I come back, I guess I'll look for someone to replace Allie and carry on. Or maybe Jason and I can finish up the work."

It sounded like a good plan to me, but there was some hesitancy in her voice, and I asked her about this.

Tears welled up in her eyes. "I'm scared to be alone, Laura, and I'm scared of the memories that are coming back. I know I need to deal with this, but I'm afraid to because I'm afraid my illness will crash in and take over."

"Can you think about it just a little at a time? Maybe say to yourself, 'I'm going to think about this for five minutes, and then I'm not going to think about it for an hour.'"

"I could try."

I thought for a minute, searching for ways that I could help my friend. The answer was instantly obvious. "Listen, Nadine, I can take the next week off work. We can do things together. Go up to the Reservoir and swim, go to the springs…"

Nadine looked excited but then asked, "What about your work, Laura? Your crew?"

"It's a long weekend anyway, and then there will be the funeral, so we'd be missing days anyhow. I can ask them to work through a few Saturdays or on a weekend to make up for it. They'll be glad of the break."

Nadine and I spent the next few days together, swimming and exploring and talking. Each day, she spoke a little more about Allie Owens. Meanwhile, I saw that the seiners were in and hoped I'd run into Daniel at the wharf. I didn't. Every so often, an achy feeling to see him would come over me, but I kept this to myself.

On a hot Wednesday, sitting on a rock at the springs, with our feet playing in the water, Nadine abruptly cut the companionable silence with a question: "She didn't have a face left, did she, Laura?"

I took a deep breath and answered. "No, she didn't. She used a shotgun, Nadine."

Tears were rolling down her cheeks. She started to sob and continued crying for a very long time. When the tears finally stopped, we were quiet and stayed this way for a while. Then I cut the silence. "Nadine, you know this is good, isn't it? I mean you're having these really extreme feelings…and you're not crazy at all."

Her eyes filled with fresh tears, which she wiped away with the back of her hand. "Yeah…I'm not crazy."

There was silence for another long while; then I told Nadine about my dream of Franz Boas and of Raven carrying Allie to the stars. I asked her what she thought about it.

"I think it's beautiful, Laura, and comforting. I'd like to carry that image with me. And the words: 'the grace that is given me.' It sounds like something an angel would say."

I didn't even know what motivated me to decide to walk out to the cemetery on Wednesday evening. I'd learned from Chief Charlie weeks before that the Waglisla cemetery was called, 'Old Town,' because it was in the original location of the Hudson's Bay Fort. The day's heat carried on into the evening, and it was a beautiful walk along the dirt track that started just past Daniel's. The forest was fragrant with cedar and the smell of salt from the sea. The cemetery was large, and although it was not kept up in the manicured way of the colonial European-style cemeteries, it seemed somehow right to me that huckleberry, ferns and other greenery grew between and even over the gravestones. On the earliest stones, wind and salt had washed away the names. There were many that dated back to the 1890s, and a disproportionate number were infants and women. As I strolled through, pushing aside greenery to read the information on the tombstones, I saw that there were more young people than one would expect to find. Suicides, I thought. Some of the tombstones had carvings of clan crests, and some contained both a colonial European and a traditional Native name. I noticed that the newer stones, made from granite, often contained the picture of the deceased. It was a peaceful place, made more so by the soothing sound of the surf on the shallow beach nearby. But I did not linger.

It was foggy on the morning of Allie Owens funeral. I knew the sun would soon burn off the mist. I spent that morning with Nadine; we dressed together for the funeral. The dress and shoes my mother had sent fit her perfectly, and, staring at herself in the mirror, she said, "I think this dress probably cost double my monthly wage."

"It probably did. It dates to BWF, and my mom says you should keep it."

"What's BWF?"

"Before we left Father."

"What's after you left Father?"

"TG—which stands for 'Thank God we left Father.'"

She laughed. We went into the living room, where Chris was waiting for us. He gave me a warm smile. Looking at Nadine, he remarked, "Perhaps it's inappropriate to say…because of the circumstances, but you look lovely."

He then turned to me and asked how I was doing.

"All right. Tired, I guess."

"You look tired, Laura. How much have you been sleeping?"

"Not much these last few nights." I hesitated, then added, "I get nervous at funerals."

"I think you should have something to sleep for a bit. I'll leave a prescription for you at the hospital."

"Thanks, Chris."

Allie Owens's funeral was crowded and the service, long. It was a closed casket, but at the end of the service, most of the people in the church went up and touched the top of the casket and talked amongst each other before moving along.

There was an incident with Nadine in front of the church before the service. I was standing next to Daniel, Chief Charlie, Rose, Matt, Laney and other people whom I didn't know. Nadine and Chris came over. She looked very tense and had a tight grip on his hand. I took a few steps, so that I was standing next to her, and whispered, "It's almost over, Nadine."

Suddenly, she froze. I followed her gaze to where a man who looked to be in his forties was making his way past us. Her facial expression turned to one of disgust, and, dropping Chris's hand, she planted herself squarely in front of this man.

"You have no business here," she said between clenched teeth.

Chris made a move towards Nadine, but without thinking I touched his sleeve and shook my head. Somehow, I knew this was a battle Nadine had to fight.

"What do you mean, lady?" asked the man I knew was Lyle Dodd.

"I mean exactly what I said. You have no business here."

Dodd began to splutter; his face turned red. There was dead silence all around us. At that very moment, Sergeant MacCallum, dressed in a civilian suit, showed up and, taking Dodd by the arm, moved him out of the way.

Nadine turned around and faced us, as well as the other people who had overheard her. There was a challenge in her eyes; feeling uncomfortable, people looked away. The exception was Chief Charlie, who nodded at her and gave a "Mmph" of respect.

At the gym, after the service, I joined the ladies in the kitchen, arranging plates of sandwiches, cake and cookies. It seemed like there was a mountain of food and an endless need for more coffee. I hadn't slept well for almost a week; I was very tired and didn't wish to visit with anyone. After an hour of arranging and setting out the food, I went out the back door of the kitchen, adjoining the gym. It was very quiet and peaceful, and I enjoyed the feeling of the sunshine on my face. Lost in some trance, I didn't hear the back door opening, but I did hear footsteps and then felt a pair of strong hands on my shoulders. I wasn't even startled. I knew it was Daniel and leaned back against him for a few moments before turning around.

He reached down and touched my hair. "You look pretty tired," he said, softly.

"I guess I haven't slept much these past few days. Chris—Dr. Sutherland, left a prescription for me at the hospital."

"Why don't I take you home now? You can rest."

He drove me home and told me to have a hot bath, while he went out and picked up the prescription. When I came into the living room, he had already returned and had made tea. I couldn't get the lid off the container of the prescription. He took it off and read the instructions: "Take one tablet as needed for sleep."

I took the pill and sipped on my tea.

"Charlie said you were a great help to those kids and to your friend."

I didn't say anything for a while, then replied, "It isn't supposed to be like that. It's supposed to be like…like my grandfather, with my brother and me talking to him, even though he maybe couldn't hear us."

We sat quietly, and, then, spontaneously, I looked up at him. "Stay with me, Daniel."

There was a look of surprise and questioning in his eyes, and I knew he was searching for something to say.

"I'm tired of all this death. I want to feel…I want to feel alive," I said.

"Laura, you're all messed up right now. I understand what you're saying, but right now, it would just be an escape."

I was silent for a long time, knowing in my heart that it was more than an escape that I was looking for, but I said, "Well, sure. You're right, Daniel."

"Maybe you can sleep now."

"Okay.…but…could you just maybe lie down with me and hold me for a while?" I stopped. "I'm sorry, I can't believe I'm begging someone to hold me."

Daniel was holding me tightly then and talking gently into my ear. "Stop it. Stop beating yourself up. Of course, I'll stay with you."

So, there was me in my flannel nightgown and Daniel in his dress clothes, minus his shoes, in that double bed that was far too small for the both of us. I cradled myself into his chest, his arm snugly around me.

"Is my arm too heavy?" he whispered.

"No," I replied, reaching down the length of his arm to put my hand in his.

"Is that pill working?"

"Mmm, Daniel?"

"Yeah."

"You know, she hardly had a head left, but she was still breathing. How can that be?"

Daniel buried his head in my hair and kissed the back of my neck and answered, "I don't know, Laura."

"I've been helping Nadine with this, you know, like I'm some kind of expert, or something."

"Well, maybe for a while, you could just think of something else. Think of the Raven."

"Why?"

"Because if you were Heiltsuk, you'd be born to the Raven."

"Why?"

"Because you're so chatty and busy and witty. And think of the ocean, Laura. You can always get comfort there."

And I did. I saw a raven dancing along a pounding shore. And, then there was sweet darkness.

Chapter 22

I slept soundly until sometime before dawn. The first thing I did when I woke up was to reach out to make sure that Daniel was still there. He was. Turning over, I snuggled into his chest. My movement woke him, and he adjusted the covers and gently smoothed my hair. I asked him what time it was. "Time to go back to sleep," he whispered.

The next time I woke up, sunlight was spilling in through the edges of the curtains, and pieces of light danced across Daniel's face. Careful not to wake him, I studied his dark lashes, finely structured bones and aquiline nose, thinking how handsome he was. He looked much younger in sleep, and I realized I didn't know how old Daniel was. In those few minutes before he woke up, I felt an upwelling of emotion. I wanted, at that moment, to just look at him forever, but I suppose he sensed me watching him because he opened his eyes.

I smiled. "Daniel, how old are you?"

He looked at me as if I were crazy. "Why?"

"I don't know. I was just thinking that it's harder to tell how old Indigenous people are compared to white people."

Daniel's response was to laugh. I looked at him, puzzled.

"Now think about that, Laura. That's like saying all Chinese people look alike or all black men are, well, you know..."

I immediately felt stupid. "You're right, Daniel. All these years of training, and I guess I still don't know much after all."

"Sometimes you just don't think things through is all."

"But, of course, you do," I said, with an edge of humor.

"Well, yeah, sure." He grinned.

"Well, yeah, sure," I mocked him back, "So, how old are you?"

"I'm thirty-two. I'll be thirty-three in October. How about you?"

"How old do you think I am?"

"You look like you're about eighteen, but with all that university and knowing that you've traveled and stuff, I guess you must be around twenty-five."

"I'm twenty-six."

He pulled a strand of hair off my face and said, "Well, I have to be careful being seen with you. People will talk. Say I'm robbing the cradle."

I laughed and snuggled into his chest, and he gently stroked my hair. It was a nice moment, and for a second, I thought it might lead somewhere, but he pulled back slightly and asked me what I was going to do with my day.

"We're setting up a camp at Xvnis on Monday. I have a lot of gear in the basement that I need to get down to the boat and would like to get it done today. Jack's uncle has a pickup. I guess I'll try and track him down and see if he'll take our gear down to the boat for me."

"I think that might be Roland Martin. Yesterday, I talked to him at the funeral. He's waiting for a part for his pickup."

"Dammit. What time are you leaving? Could I use your pickup?"

"I'm not leaving. I was fishing in Nootka Sound; it's closed there now…no openings for a while anyway. I can help you move that stuff, Laura, but only if you give me some breakfast. I'm starving."

Daniel made coffee, while I made breakfast. After breakfast, he went home and changed, and I sorted the camping gear into piles. We spent the morning cleaning, organizing and loading up the boat. Daniel said he'd invite me over for lunch but hadn't had time to pick up groceries. I offered to buy him lunch at the Hotel. He accepted.

Over lunch, I told him that since Allie Owens had died, I'd thought some people were looking at me strangely. It seemed as if some people were kind of distant and others, friendlier. It seemed even stranger because I didn't know these people. I asked Daniel what he thought. Was it because I'd been there when it happened?

He hesitated before he answered, as if choosing his words carefully. "Well, no, I don't think you're imagining anything, but it isn't because you were there when she died."

"Well, what is it?"

"Her death has caused a rift in the community."

"Why?"

"Mainly bad feelings towards Lyle Dodd. Some people believe he forced himself on Allie, and others think she made it up."

"But how does anyone even know about it?"

"In a small community, people know stuff. Maybe Allie talked to a friend; maybe a cop talked to his wife, and she talked to someone at the hospital, and so on. And I think a few people heard what your friend said at the funeral."

"So, people are talking about me? And about Nadine?"

Daniel looked uncomfortable; then, as if once again searching for words, he answered. "Well sure, you'd both be part of the gossip. More your friend than you because she spoke up at the funeral, and because she was close to Allie Owens. But you have to understand, Laura, you and Nadine...well...you're strangers here, and you're white, and you're both young and attractive. People would gossip about you, no matter what you did. I don't pay much attention to gossip, and I sure as hell don't put any weight on it. If I did, I'd have to spend my whole life tip-toeing around."

"Did Lyle Dodd go to the funeral? I didn't even notice."

"Yes, he stood at the back."

"What do you believe, Daniel?"

"I believe he had no business at that funeral."

I paused, sipping my coffee and then, changing my voice into one of playful conspiracy, asked if people were gossiping about us.

His eyes filled with humor. Glancing around the café, he answered, "Well, sure they are...as we speak."

I burst out laughing. Daniel didn't look embarrassed at my outburst but just continued to look at me with eyes that were filled with humor.

"I'm sorry. I'm embarrassing you," I said.

"No. I love that, when you laugh like that. It's like, I don't know, just very joyful." He was grinning.

This made me laugh again. After a few moments, I asked Daniel what people were saying.

"I don't know for sure. But you can put two and two together."

We had another cup of coffee and talked about my project. He was a good listener; it was nice to share my ideas with him. When we'd finished our coffee, he asked me if I'd like to come over to his place and "hang out" for the afternoon, before we went over to Charlie's for dinner. Chief Charlie had asked me to come over for dinner, not just because it was becoming a custom but because he knew I wanted to discuss Xvnis and on Saturday, he was going to Vancouver for a few days on Band business. I did want to go to Daniel's for the afternoon but then remembered I'd asked Jenn to come over.

"Put a note on your door and tell her to come down to my place," suggested Daniel.

And, so, I did.

It was a healing and laughter-filled afternoon. We played cards around the kitchen table for quite a while. I caught Jenn cheating more than once. Finally, I gave her a stern lecture. I think it was almost verbatim to the one my grandfather had given to Michael many years before. She listened respectfully to this lecture and then, when I had finished, said, "Laura, all Indians cheat at cards. Isn't that right, Uncle Daniel?"

Thinking of the conversation we'd had earlier that day about generalizing, I laughed, joined by Daniel.

"Is that true, Daniel?" I asked.

"Well yeah, sure," he said, grinning and winking at Jenn.

"Oh, I see. Well, it's a good thing we aren't playing for money. My entire fortune would be gone."

"Maybe we should play for money," laughed Daniel.

"Uncle Daniel, you know I'm not allowed to play for money," Jenn admonished.

This set me into another spurt of laughter. When I'd finally stopped, Daniel said he had to unpack his things, take his laundry to get cleaned and get some groceries, so why didn't we entertain ourselves? Jenn's immediate response to this was to ask if I could teach her some dance steps. I looked skeptically at the small living room and then out the window, where there was a big stretch of beach in front of a low tide.

"We can dance on the beach, Jenn."

Jenny Hunt's dance lesson was a huge success—for both of us. Taking off our shoes, we stood just above the surf line.

"Today, I'm going to show you the first two positions in dance, and then we'll do some steps to make up a simple composition."

"How many positions are there?"

"Five. Now pay attention," I told her sternly.

"Don't we need music, or maybe some drums?"

"Sure, but we can dance to the music in our heads. We can hum it."

Jenn was insistent about the music.

"Okay, we'll dance to a song called, 'The Waltz of the Flowers.'"

I hummed out the bars of the song and after a minute or so, Jenn hummed with me. I made up a very simple dance and could see that Jenn had an inclination and a grace for this art. In our dance, we flirted with the surf, and our jeans got soaked to the knees. After about half an hour, Jenn asked if I would dance, using all the five positions.

"Okay, but you have to sing the notes."

I didn't need to hear Jenn's soft humming. It was a dance I was familiar with; I could hear the music in my head. I modified the space so that I was dancing along the line between the beach and the surf. After the first few steps, I was dancing with all my heart. The song is a joyful one, and there was no sorrow in that dance along the beach. In my mind's eye, I was dancing on a stage, dressed in a filmy white dress and wearing toe shoes. I went faster and faster, outpacing Jenn's humming, until she simply stopped and watched me.

When I was finished, I was completely out of breath and leaned over with my hands on my knees, gasping for air; my physical condition was a longways away from what it was when I was seventeen. Jenn was viewing me with something like awe. "That was beautiful," she said. "Could I learn to dance like that?"

"Yes, you definitely could. But, hon, it might be hard to find a teacher at the Passage."

She beamed and said, "It seemed as if you were dancing with somebody that wasn't there."

"I was. The dance is meant to done with others. But, today, I was dancing with God."

Daniel's voice interrupted our conversation. From the house he called, "Come on you two. We have to get to Charlie's for supper."

Still out of breath I went with Jenn up to the house. My ankle was aching.

"Uncle Daniel! Did you see Laura dance?"

"I did."

"Well, you know," Jenn continued. "Laura was dancing with God and waltzing with the flowers."

There was humor in Daniel's eyes, but beneath was another layer that seemed to be a kind of respect.

I sat next to Chief Charlie at dinner and talked about our plans for documenting Xvnis. After dinner, Daniel, Chief Charlie and I went into the living room, and Chief Charlie brought up Allie. He warned me not to make too much of the gossip and to just ignore it. I asked him what Lyle Dodd would do.

"Hard to say. Right now, he's being very loud about the fact that he was told not to go to the funeral. It'd really be a lot better for him if he just shut up. But his family is pretty strong on the Reserve, and they'll back him."

"Is my affiliation with you causing any problems for your family?"

"No, Laura. What happened had nothing to do with you, except that you happened to be there. If you hadn't been, our views would be the same. I don't say too much, but I don't have to. People know I have no respect for Lyle Dodd. They knew that before Allie killed herself. And as for the rift, well it will go on for God knows how long. There are so many rifts in this village, I couldn't even count them. Daniel, how many feuds are we involved in right now?"

Daniel had been listening quietly, chewing on a toothpick. His eyes filled with humor. "Maybe a hundred or so. But, that's only since 1900."

I burst into one of my crazy laughing spells and noticed that Rose and Laney, who were in the kitchen, rather than disapproving of this outburst, started giggling themselves.

Jenn asked if she could come and visit me at our camp.

"Well, you could Jenn, but I don't know how you'd get there."

"I'd like to go out there myself," said Chief Charlie. "Maybe you could send Jack Campbell out to get us."

"I could do that."

"What's a good day for you, Laura?" asked Chief Charlie.

"Any day would be fine. Maybe Wednesday or Thursday."

"It's settled then. I'll be coming to Xvnis on Thursday."

"And me too," said Laney's three-year-old son.

Daniel and Matt left, saying they had some work to do on the boat, and Laney and the children also left. But I lingered because I wanted to talk to Chief Charlie. I told him about the heavy feeling that I felt at Xvnis—that I thought Jack had felt it too. Chief Charlie thought for a bit, and Rose nodded her head in understanding.

"Well, Laura, a lot of sad things happened at Xvnis. So many died. Before that, it was a very powerful place. It seems to me that some of that power is still there. It would be good to make an offering, like you did at Campbell's Pole."

After a pause, Chief Charlie said, "In the afterlife, there is no division between countries, or tribes or races. And your grandfather, well, he would be there and the rest of your ancestors looking out for you."

Rose nodded in agreement. I felt reassured.

The weekend went by very quickly. I spent Saturday talking to Maggie, holding the strands of cedar, while she skillfully wove these into a basket. We talked about Xvnis.

I told Maggie that Charlie had told me that the name of the site meant 'Springwater.'

"Yes, it does." She thought for a moment and added, "I don't recall any springs out there. But it's been a long time since I was at that village."

Maggie changed the subject. We talked about Allie Owens's funeral and about Lyle Dodd and the way things were unfolding in the village. Maggie told me which families would support Dodd, and which would not. She mentioned so many people that I couldn't keep track of them. It ended up being mainly a day of visiting; I didn't record our conversation.

I spent Saturday evening reviewing the data on Xvnis. I tried over and over to pronounce it in the correct Heiltsuk way, but it came out wrong almost every time.

By the time they got to British Columbia, the Canadian government no longer bothered to sign treaties with local Indigenous groups. The Reserve Commission established reserves in Heiltsuk territory in the 1880s. Xvnis was designated as Number 4 Reserve of the Heiltsuk in 1888, meaning that, at that time, at least some people were probably living there. The total amount of land covered by the twenty-two reserves set aside for the Heiltsuk was 1,369 hectares, or 3,383 acres. I tried to find some meaning as to how much land this was, and I thought back to excavations I had done on the Canadian Prairies. There, the land was divided into sections, each comprised of 640 acres: a square mile. It is not unusual for prairie farms to be two or even three sections, if it is a family operation. The Heiltsuk reserves would translate into 5.3 sections.

The traditional territory claimed by the Heiltsuk consisted of thousands of square kilometers, which included both land and sea. Taking out a piece of paper, I drew a square, divided it into 5 and added .3 of a square. Then I counted the number of miles I would have to walk to make it around the boundaries of Heiltsuk territory, as set out in the government in designating the reserves. I calculated that it would be about ten miles, or sixteen kilometers, an easy day's walk.

Chapter 23

We got groceries and loaded these into the boat. It was mid-morning by the time we left for Xvnis on Monday. It was sunny, and I enjoyed the 45-minute boat ride, with the feel of a cool breeze in my face. Kristy and I shouted at each other, trying to talk over the sound of the engine, but the subject of Allie Owens didn't come up, and I was glad. The loud engine made comfortable conversation difficult, so we focused on the view. The mountains, so spectacular from the Passage, now seemed to loom so close that it was almost as if we were underneath them.

Jack was an expert at camping. I was pretty good at it myself, and it didn't take long to set up the camp. We put our camp on the edge of the eastern midden. It was solid and secure, with a kitchen area covered by tarps, and tarps over the two tents, to protect these from rain. Kristy had decided she was going to sleep on the boat so made up her bed in there, then busied herself with sorting groceries and being of no particular value in setting up the camp. She kept up a constant stream of chatter, some of which was designed to torture me.

"Hey, Laura, do you know Daniel Hunt?"

"Yes."

"Are you going out with him?"

"No."

"I thought you were a classy white chick. You're sleeping with him, but you're not going out with him?" she asked slyly.

"Kristy, we're friends. That's it. Friends."

"So, you sleep with your friends?" she continued.

"What makes you think I'm sleeping with him?"

"Well, like, it's the Passage, Laura, and people know what goes on here and when a guy parks his pickup overnight at your house, people don't think you're just playing, like, cards all night."

"Well, like, maybe I borrowed his pickup." I said, emphasizing the 'like.'

"Laura, you can tell me," she replied.

"Kristy—that would be like giving a live interview on CBC."

"Okay, everyone's saying maybe he's in love with you and you're in love with him and you're sleeping together, but hey, you don't have to talk about it," she told me, with her hands raised in protest.

"Kristy, go grab that machete and start hacking down some bushes," I said sternly.

"Okay, fine. I'll back off. I'm going to go and hack down some bushes now."

After lunch, Jack took a clipboard to make a rough map of the western midden, while Kristy and I went to search for a spring. I had noticed on that first day at the site that there was a small trickle of water working its way down the mountain on the other side of the eastern rock bluff.

We found the springs about twenty minutes later. These springs were larger and just as beautiful as the springs Nadine and I visited. There were two large pools formed by the springs and numerous smaller ones. We rolled up our jeans and waded in the icy, crystal-clear water. The air was sweet with the smell of the springs and the fragrant cedar and ferns.

That evening, Jack, Kristy and I went to the springs and sprinkled tobacco about the edges of the water. I looked at Jack, raised my eyebrows, telling him, without words, that it was his turn to say a prayer. He instantly understood and for a few moments seemed lost in thought. Then he said, "To the spirits that dwell here at Xvnis, and to my ancestors—we do not mean to disturb you. Or to harm you. Please take this offering, and please watch over us."

His pronunciation of Xvnis in the Heiltsuk way was soft and melodious. In that moment, the world seemed very right to me.

I have tried to find words to describe how Xvnis felt, and the only one word I can think of is 'old.' I sometimes felt a sense of this age, often when I was aware of ravens. But the deep heaviness I felt when I first came to Xvnis was gone.

The time went by quickly. I knew that Jack and Kristy felt that they owed me some time because they'd had two days off the previous week. I think they sensed that I was anxious to make up for lost time. Without saying anything, we continued past our regular quitting time and worked until it was time to cook dinner. We easily put in an extra hour and a half on the days we spent at the site.

On Thursday morning, I got up early and went out to the springs and, holding my breath, washed my hair, then bathed in the water. This was partly because I really did want to clean up and partly because I wanted to look good for my guests.

Jack left at mid-morning and returned with Chief Charlie, Daniel, Matt, Jenn and Matt's three-year-old and six-year-old sons. I greeted them and put on a pot of coffee, feeling nervous about Daniel being present and at the site and just generally insecure about what Chief Charlie might think of my work. I glanced at Daniel several times. He was chewing on a toothpick and met my looks with gentle humor.

We looked at the western midden first. All the house posts were completely decomposed there, not even visible beneath the roots of hemlock. The beams were still visible, but these were badly decomposed, as well. I got Jack to explain how we were mapping this part of the site; Chief Charlie appreciated some of the ingenuous methods Jack had come up with to prevent having to move the transit over and over.

The features on the eastern midden were in much better condition, and approximately fifteen house posts were still identifiable, although the carvings on these were almost completely worn away. I had not been able to make out any of the crests on the posts, but Chief Charlie carefully studied these. Through his eyes, I could see there were depictions of the raven, the eagle and the orca. The house beams at Xv-nis were even larger than those at Boston's Retreat. Matt asked me if the difference in the sites was because the western one was older. I told him that I thought it might be older, but probably not a lot older.

Looking at Chief Charlie I said, "I think when smallpox hit, they abandoned the older part of the site and moved to the newer part, and because it was maintained, it's lasted longer. But I think at some time in the past, the two parts of the site were occupied at the same time."

Charlie looked at Jack, Kristy and me and said, "Mmph."

I knew it was a sign of approval.

At some point in my conversation of the work we were doing, I'd forgotten to be nervous. We went back to the campsite and drank coffee and ate cookies.

A frequent topic of conversation over the last weeks had been the annual Salmon Queen Dance, during which a girl from the village would be crowned the Salmon Queen and festivities would be held in the school gym.

"Are you going to the Salmon Queen Dance?" asked Jenn out of nowhere.

Laughing, I said, "I doubt it. I don't have a date and I don't have a thing to wear."

"You don't need a date, you goof," piped up Kristy.

Jenn, obviously thinking, looked as if a light had come on. "Well," she said. "It's too late to order anything from the catalogue, but you could wear your green flowered dress…and," she exclaimed triumphantly, "Uncle Daniel can be your date!"

I guess the pause in the conversation only lasted a second or so, but it seemed forever before Daniel spoke. "Fine with me, although I don't know what I'm going to wear."

Matt laughed. "I'll lend you a shirt."

The conversation turned to Jenn's birthday party; she reminded me not to forget about it.

"How can I forget, Jenn? I'm bringing the cake."

"You know how to make a cake?" asked the usually quiet Jack.

This set off a round of laughter, which only increased when Kristy interjected with, "How hard can a Duncan Hines be?"

We worked hard for the rest of the week. I fell far behind in my paperwork, focusing instead on spending endless hours reading numbers through the transit. I decided I would miss my Saturday visit with Maggie and use that day to catch up on forms and on my field journal. We tied down everything at the camp on Friday and arrived back at the Reserve at about 5:30. At the manse, I took a long, hot soapy bath, and just as I finished toweling off, Nadine phoned. She'd returned from Vancouver on Monday; they'd had a wonderful time. Chris was on-call, and did I want to go out for dinner? I told her I was so tired that I doubted I could walk to the Hotel and asked if instead she wanted to pick up some food and bring it up to my place. She did.

We had a good visit, one that reminded me how much I had come to treasure the time that I spent with Nadine. For once, we did not talk non-stop but spent long periods of silence, looking into the fire

Nadine had made. She had decided that she'd spend two more weeks in the field with Jason and his younger brother to wrap up her field project. After that, she would stay at the Passage with Chris for a week or two, doing paperwork and getting to know him. She was thinking of moving up to the Reserve to live with him, although she would have to go to Vancouver frequently to finish her degree. Both she and Chris hoped that they weren't jumping into things too quickly, but they were in love and wanted to be together.

We talked a bit about Allie, and Nadine's face clouded over. She said she thought she remembered most of that night now, and whatever she had forgotten, she didn't want to remember. Chris had told her to keep a picture of Allie next to the bed—one that showed her happy and smiling. He thought that, in time, the picture would replace the gruesome memory of Allie's face.

Our talk turned to the subject of the village rift over Lyle Dodd; we agreed we wouldn't let it affect us.

"I'm not going to be part of this community if I have to live in fear all of the time over what people say and anyway, it's like Daniel told you, it's natural that people would talk about us," said Nadine.

"Well, at least we're not alone. In fact, we're right in there ourselves, seeing as we're talking about them."

We burst out laughing. Then Nadine said it was time to go because I looked tired and needed to get some rest.

"But before I go, I have to tell you, I came bearing a gift."

I raised my eyebrows quizzically.

Reaching into her jeans pocket, she pulled out a small jewelry box and, with a huge smile, handed it to me.

It was a beautiful gold, carved pendent necklace, with the motifs of the raven and the bear.

"I thought you would be the raven, and, of course, I would be the bear." Smiling, she added, "Look at the inscription on the back."

On the back of the pendant in tiny letters were the initials DH and, beneath it, the words 'Kindred Spirits.'

Tears formed in eyes, "It's beautiful. I've never gotten a gift that meant so much, Nadine."

"Don't go sappy on me, Laura. I had the words 'Kindred Spirits' engraved, and did you notice the initials of the carver?"

Turning the pendant over again, I looked bewildered, and then it finally clicked. "DH. Daniel Hunt? Daniel made this?"

"Yes, he did, and I was lucky to get it. His stuff is in hot demand."

After Nadine left, I admired the necklace. I had told her the truth when I said that I'd never received a gift that had meant so much to me. Not only that, I was in love with the carver.

Chapter 24

Daniel phoned me in the morning to say we were invited to go to dinner at Matt's and Laney's before the dance, and would it be all right if he picked me up at 5:30? It would.

I had asked Kristy about what to wear to the dance; she said anything, even jeans would be fine. But I was tired of wearing jeans. I put on the only dress I'd brought with me, the lightly flowered, gypsy type of dress that Jenn had suggested. I tied my hair back with a green ribbon that matched the dress and put on some makeup. Daniel arrived a few minutes early, and I called to the bathroom for him to come into the house and that I'd be there in a minute. When I entered the living room, he gave me one of those brilliant smiles and said, "You look like a girl."

I laughed and said, "Thanks for the compliment."

Shyly, I showed him my necklace and told him I hadn't known what a hot item he was. He smiled and asked how much Nadine had paid for it. Indignant, I replied, "I didn't ask her."

"Well you know, I just want make sure I'm getting my cut," he said lightly.

I grinned and told him to ask Nadine himself.

Matt and Laney lived in a bungalow facing the ocean, just down from Chief Charlie's. It was small but very comfortable. Matt was barbecuing a fish in the fire pit on the beach when we arrived. Daniel joined him out there. Laney and I talked about the chronic housing shortage on the Reserve. The Band council had entered into a loan arrangement with the Federal Government to start construction of new housing that was due to start up in a few months. But the waiting list was long, and Laney said it could be years before they were in a new house. By that time, their oldest might be ready for high school.

"Dad is working hard to get that high school built here. I guess we'll see what happens," she said.

I asked if Matt wanted to move off the Reserve.

"Well, he talks about it sometimes," said Laney. "But he's out fishing a lot, and I want to be with my family then. Also, his family lives in Vancouver, and neither of us wants to live there. So, I guess we'll just take it as it comes."

Over dinner, Matt asked me if my father was an archaeologist.

"No." I smiled, then added, "My father is an idiot."

This comment was met with laughter.

"What does he do?" asked Matt.

"Mainly he's into politics."

"You're not related to Stephen Fitzgerald?" asked Matt.

"Actually, I am. He's the idiot."

This was met by more laughter; then Matt said, "Can I ask you a personal question?"

Looking at Laney, I said, "Can he?"

"Well, sure. But you don't have to answer him."

"Okay, Matt." I grinned.

"Why is a high society girl doing Archaeology in Waglisla'?"

My normal response would have been to give a sharp, witty reply, but for some reason, I took Matt's question seriously and answered, "It's a long story, Matt, and I'm not even really sure I know the answer to that myself."

Matt smiled and replied, "Well, maybe someday you'll be able to tell us. In the meantime, here's a toast to Laura, who, like the rest of us, has no real idea why she's here."

The Salmon Queen Dance was loud, smoky and crowded. I drank a couple of beers, which Daniel insisted on paying for, even though he was drinking Pepsi. He would, he said, dance the waltzes, but not the quick tunes. So, I danced several slow dances with Daniel and a few of the quicker songs with Kristy's friends. At about 11 o'clock, Daniel asked me what I thought of the dance. I told him it was fine but that it was okay to leave. "Let's go to your place and light a fire on the beach," I suggested.

He quickly agreed to this, and I realized that the loud music and crowded, smoke-filled room were not his element.

We sat on the bench in front of the fire and chatted about Xvnis and about fishing. After a while we were quiet, just staring into the fire. In a light voice, I asked him why he didn't have a girlfriend.

He grinned and said, "Haven't I mentioned my wife and six kids in Rivers Inlet?"

"Maybe, you could tell me about Dorothy."

This remark, which I immediately realized demonstrated a huge lack of tact, was met with silence.

"I'm sorry, Daniel. I guess I'm prying. Maggie mentioned her when she was outlining the family tree. I shouldn't have said anything."

"It's okay. Just took me by surprise is all." He paused, then went on. "People say she looked like my mother. Dorothy was beautiful, the kind of beautiful that white guys like. Small, and delicate features... and kind of frail, I guess. The guys on the Reserve were falling over each other to protect her. And she chose me. She was the first woman I ever knew; it was the first for both of us. I guess we were seventeen. She was very witty and funny. God, she could make me laugh. And she told me I could never fight; said she'd leave me for good if I did. I wanted her so much and wanted to be a man so much. Her and Charlie—that's why I stopped being a punk, I guess. That same year, I started working on the seiners. I wanted us to have a decent life. About a year after I started fishing, she said she wanted to go to Vancouver and take a hairdressing course. I knew she wanted to live in the city, but she knew that, even for her, I wouldn't live there. Anyway, she was going to have that year, and when she came home, we would live at the Passage." He paused. "I kept hoping, but inside I don't think I ever really believed she'd come back. Her head was full of dreams. I wasn't surprised when I got a letter saying she'd met some white guy. Inside, I knew what I had to offer wasn't enough, but I got drunk anyway for a few days and then wrote her back and wished her the best."

Daniel paused again in his story and looked deep into the flames before continuing. "After that, I don't know exactly what happened. I guess that white guy wasn't serious. She started hanging around the bars down there on Hastings Street and got into drugs and booze. I continued to write her, hoping she'd have enough of Vancouver and would come back, and then everything would be like it had been, but that's not what happened. She overdosed on drugs and alcohol."

Daniel paused before finishing the story. "Charlie and I went down there and brought her home...I mean...her body. I could understand her dreams, but she'd been so innocent. On the Reserve she'd been popular and important. I think she thought her looks and importance would carry over into Vancouver. She wanted to be in that magical white-man world."

I told Daniel that I was so sorry about Dorothy.

"She died a long time ago, Laura. I rarely even think about her anymore, and when I do, it's just with a kind of old sadness."

We stared into the flames for a while. Then Daniel went and got a coffee for himself and another cup of tea for me. We sipped the hot drinks for a while. I asked Daniel if he avoided commitments because of Dorothy.

"Maybe," he said. "But not because of Dorothy, at least not now. I haven't been exactly celibate, but I'm not sure about this girlfriend thing. I like being alone, and I get itchy when demands are made."

"Do you think I'd be demanding, Daniel?" I asked softly.

"Well, you're pretty easy to be around. Would you be demanding? I don't know. Maybe. You seem more like if you wanted to do something, well, you'd just go do it."

"Is that good or bad?"

"Could be both."

"Daniel, what you just said is like a non-answer. Maybe I should reframe the question: 'Could I be your girlfriend?'"

He was quiet for a bit, then, very softly, answered. "I guessed you've been thinking about that, and you know, if it could just be a casual thing, maybe we'd be sleeping together. But to you, that's a huge commitment. And I don't want that commitment, so I guess you can't be my girlfriend."

"Daniel, I want you to explain to me why you can't be committed to me. I'm not talking about commitment in general. I mean, why you can't be committed to me?"

He didn't say anything, so I continued. "It seems like you're attracted to me, I mean, on a deeper level than just…like…coming to my rescue, which I know you've done a lot. I mean, is my feeling that you're attracted to me all some big delusion on my part?"

The corners of his mouth turned up a bit. "I am attracted to you, just like you say."

"Well then?"

Daniel stood up. "Come with me for a second, Laura."

I stood up. Daniel took me into the room where I assumed he made his carvings. I'd never been in this room, and the contents barely registered. Against the wall was a full-length mirror. Daniel walked me over to this mirror, so that our images were reflected back to us.

"What do you see?"

Puzzled, I studied the reflection. I saw a tall, handsome man, with beautiful dark eyes and strong, perfectly defined features. And I saw myself. Five feet, three inches tall, dark hair, green eyes and a tanned face, with a flush of sunburn across my nose. Looking up at Daniel, I shook my head, not knowing what I was supposed to see.

"From the minute I saw you," he said. "I knew who you were. The way you carry your head. The way you walk. We belong in different worlds, Laura. Here, in the Passage, this is my world, and this is where I want to live."

"Daniel, you're making assumptions. I could stay at the Passage, and anyway, my world is actually very simple. You could fit into my world just as easily as I've fit in here—and isn't the main thing: that we create our own world?"

"Laura, you're chasing this thing around inside your head, so that it tortures you…and, to be honest, so am I. Let it go."

My shoulders slumped. I looked up at him again, defeated. The look in his eyes was one of anguish, and he moved towards me as if to hold me. I held up my hand. "Don't. Don't comfort me. Don't you dare comfort me."

On the ride home, I could tell that he was searching for something to say, but then he just gave up and was quiet. When he walked me to the door, he said softly, "Good night."

I didn't answer.

The following day seemed almost surreal. I hardly slept, and at 10 a.m., Nadine showed up to help make Jenn's cake. I briefly told her about the night before, but Kristy, complaining of a severe hangover, showed up a few minutes later. We didn't have time to talk. The cake, made by baking and combining four large square pans of cake mix and slathered with a ton of pink icing, was a success.

The party was held in Chief Charlie's yard. It seemed as if all the children and half of the remainder of the village were there. Jenn thanked me over and over again for the pink, frilly dress and asked how

I'd known she wanted it so much. That had been easy. She'd nearly worn out the page of the catalogue that it was on. I just smiled and answered, "Women just understand each other, Jenn."

I avoided looking at Daniel; he didn't try to talk to me. I went home as soon as I possibly could and sat on the couch and cried. Nadine sent Chris home after leaving the party; she came straight to the manse. She told me that Daniel had been watching me throughout the birthday party and had thought he looked as "burnt out" as I did. "He's scared, Laura. I wish I had a solution, but I don't."

Later, I lay on the couch, trying to block out my feelings and imagined myself dancing along the beach at Xvnis.

I fell asleep and had a dream that followed the storyline of a Heiltsuk story that was told to Franz Boas, called "Why the Raven is Black." My dream followed the storyline. I was dressed in a beautiful, light cotton dress and was sitting on a piece of driftwood on the beach at Xvnis. Franz Boas, in the full light of day, sat next to me. We laughed together at the many birds who had gathered on the beach to dance. The birds had decided to paint themselves in beautiful colors. Raven stood aloof, and when he finally decided to paint himself, the only color left was black. That is why the raven is black. Franz Boas changed the subject.

"He is born to the Whale," Franz Boas said, and I knew he was speaking of Daniel.

"Yes," I replied.

"He is quite well-grounded for one born to the Whale. Still, he's afraid to dance." Franz Boas chuckled.

I smiled back and, in a saucy voice, said, "I was laboring under the belief, sir, that the character attributes of the clans are generalizations. Have you changed your mind?"

"Not really. But it means something to him, doesn't it?" He continued smiling.

"It does. But I guess it means, as well, that he doesn't want me."

"Yes," said Franz Boas. linking my arm through his. "He does."

With these words, I opened my eyes and was filled with a sense that the world was, for now, alright again. I was wide awake. Through the window, I could see the stars, but I didn't really see them because I was thinking about Franz Boas.

With the security of a university position, Boas traveled less. He focused on supervising the work of his students, two of whom worked with the Heiltsuk. Boas also compiled into transcript the huge amount of data he had accumulated in the field. This included, eventually, two volumes on the Heiltsuk. His greatest energies, however, were devoted to dispelling the myth of racial superiority. In *The Mind of Primitive Man*, published in 1911 and again in 1928, he spelled out the scientific basis for his hypotheses about race. The first of these was that the concept of race itself was a vague and dangerous idea. There was more variability between individuals in a 'race' than between races. Physical differences were largely a function of environment. Culture was not hereditary but was learned. Culture represented the result of historical events and adaptation to environment. The mind of so-called primitive man was as sophisticated as that of civilized man. European ideas of superiority had no basis in science. And in order to really understand where a person was coming from, it was necessary to get inside the culture that the person lived in.

Boas championed the cause of those who were the victims of racism, including Jews, Blacks and Native Americans. He watched with growing alarm the rise of the Nazi government in Germany. In 1933, Josef Goebbels ordered the burning of books written by Jews and other seditionists: this included the work of Albert Einstein, H.G. Wells, Karl Marx, Helen Keller and Franz Boas.

My mind came back to the present, and I became aware again of the stars outside the window. Deep inside, a voice told me that it wasn't over between Daniel and me. Neither, for that matter, did Franz Boas think so. That made two voices.

Chapter 25

The following week, at Xvnis, we worked hard. There was one day of drizzle, but mostly it was sunny or only partly cloudy. Jack remarked that it was an unusually hot summer. After work, Kristy and I looked forward to the icy baths at the springs. The days were already noticeably shorter, and the imposing mountains that surrounded Xvnis on three sides meant the sun went down early. After our dinner—as usual, a late one—I set the lantern on a folding camp table and caught up with my paperwork.

If I was more quiet than usual, Jack and Kristy kept their own counsel.

We worked late on Friday. As we were packing up our gear, I told Jack that when we got back to the Passage, I was going to go straight to the Hotel for a beer. He eyed me skeptically. "Laura," he said. "Maybe you shouldn't go there by yourself."

"I'll be fine, and in any case, as soon as she gets cleaned up, Kristy will show up." Jack grinned and said that could take hours; he'd go to the bar with me until Kristy arrived.

I realized there was a lot about Jack I didn't know. "Do you drink, Jack?"

"Not too much," he answered.

We arrived at the Passage at 6 on Friday, but by the time we hosed down the boat and carefully stored the expensive equipment, it was 7. I noticed that there were a lot of seiners tied up and assumed this must mean that there was an opening coming up nearby. Still, when Jack and I got to the Hotel, the bar was half empty. I ordered bottled beer and a Pepsi for Jack and hamburgers for both of us. Jack was a good companion. I learned a lot more about his family, and it was obvious to me that they were a close-knit, caring family.

By 8, the bar was full, and by then I'd had several beers. Coming out from the washroom, I noticed Blako sitting at a table with a bunch of people that included Lyle Dodd. They eyed me speculatively. I returned their look with a cold stare and said out loud to no one in particular, "There's a winning combination."

By the time Kristy arrived at 8:30, I thought I'd probably had too much to drink and should be thinking about leaving. Within a few minutes after Kristy sat down, Blako approached the table. He asked me if I wanted to dance. I simply shook my head. To my surprise, he shrugged and walked away. I told Kristy and Jack that he'd tried to kiss me outside the bar a couple of months ago. A few minutes later, I noticed that Jack had disappeared. Kristy and I were talking, when she whispered that Blako and that Dodd creep were looking at me and talking to each other.

"Oh yeah," I replied, and turning in their direction, gave them a dirty look.

"Whoa, Laura," said Kristy. "Now Blako's coming over here."

Blako came straight up to the table and leaning towards me, stuck his face into mine and explained exactly how he was going to take me. Kristy had a full glass of draft beer in front of her. Reaching over, I grabbed it, smiled at Blako and threw the entire contents into his face. He whipped his head back and started to swear; then someone grabbed him from behind.

Of course, it was Daniel. It was fated, I mused; he was destined to always show up and save me. Daniel dragged Blako out of the bar and returned a minute later. "Did you kill him?" I asked.

He was not smiling. "Laura, you're drunk. We are leaving."

"Yes, I've had too much to drink, but I'm not drunk. Thank you for saving me, and…goodbye."

"Laura, believe it or not, that guy has friends, and they'll probably be back in force. Do you want to get me killed?"

"No, Daniel."

"Okay, so we are leaving."

Daniel practically lifted me up into his pickup, but when we drove off, he didn't turn in the direction of the manse. "Where are we going? Aren't you taking me to my house, so I can have a hot bath?" I asked.

"No. We're going to my house."

I vaguely recall sitting on the couch and Daniel saying he was making some coffee…and that was the last thing I remembered.

When I woke up, it was daylight. I smelled bacon and eggs cooking and coffee brewing. I was lying fully clothed in someone's bed—Daniel's. I checked my watch; it was already 10 a.m., and I had a headache. I got out of bed and walked tentatively into the kitchen.

"How are you feeling?" Daniel asked.

"Headache," I answered.

He put a steaming cup of coffee on the table and said, "Come here and sit down and drink this. You'll feel better."

I felt humiliated about drinking too much the night before and for getting Daniel in a fight and said meekly, "I'm sorry, Daniel."

He ignored my apology and asked me what had happened the night before. I told him, my voice stumbling with embarrassment when I repeated what Blako said to me.

Daniel looked angry, but he didn't say anything.

"What did you do to Blako?" I asked.

"Nothing, just dragged him out of there and told him I was headed directly for the cops. He headed off in the direction of his boat."

Daniel placed a plate of bacon, eggs, potatoes and toast in front of me. I was surprised that I was suddenly hungry and how delicious the food tasted. I asked him how he happened to show up at the bar.

"Jack called me," he said.

Daniel cleared the dishes off the table and then put on his jean jacket. "Have a hot bath and try to get some more sleep. You'll feel better."

Suddenly angry, I said, "I know you rescued me again, and you know, you do that really well. But the only time you show up is when I'm in trouble, and then you're just gone again. Is that your solution for my problems? Be a good girl, have a hot bath and I'll see you in the movies?"

"No, Laura, no. Think about that. I haven't just been with you when it's this rescue thing you're talking about."

His voice softened. "I called you last night, but I guess you were at the bar then. I have to talk to you, if you'll let me, but right now I have to do something, and I want you to stay here. That nutcase might still be out there."

There was something in Daniel's eyes that I hadn't seen before, although I've seen it since. It was a look that pleaded understanding. I nodded at him, and he was gone.

It was the most delightful bath I've ever had in my life. It was outside, of course, and on that foggy morning, I couldn't see very far past the beach but also didn't need to worry about anyone seeing me. I used some shampoo for bubble bath and to wash the smell of the bar smoke out of my hair. Afterwards, I searched the dresser in Daniel's room and found a plain white t-shirt that fell almost to my knees. I sat for a long time on the balcony, drinking coffee, speculating as to what Daniel wanted to talk about. After a while I brushed my teeth with Daniel's toothbrush and snuggled into his comfortable bed. I lay there, looking around the small bedroom. Aside from the dresser, there were several pegs with shirts and jeans hanging from them. A beautifully carved bentwood cedar box stood against one wall, and there were two Native prints on the wall. I felt very safe. My eyes were heavy, and in a few moments, I was fast asleep.

When I woke up, Daniel was gently shaking my shoulder.

"Get up and get dressed, sleepy head. Charlie's here," he said.

"Chief Charlie?" I asked, a wave of embarrassment flooding over me.

"Laura, you're going to have to report what happened with Blako. Your professor asked Charlie to look out for you; Charlie wants to come along to the police with us."

"You mean I'm going to go to the cops?"

"That's what we've decided is the best thing."

"Do I have a choice?"

"You'd have to discuss that with Charlie."

Feeling bewildered and embarrassed, I got dressed. I don't know what Chief Charlie thought about my emergence from Daniel's bedroom, or what Daniel had told him, but he had a grim look on his face.

He asked me to describe exactly what had happened with 'that' fisherman. Then looking at Daniel, he said, pointedly, "both times."

So, I told him, flinching with embarrassment about the incident outside the Hotel and at the bar.

"Laura, this is a police matter. Sergeant MacCallum's going to meet us in half an hour at the Detachment and you need to give a statement," he said gently.

I nodded and asked if I could go home and change my clothes first. Chief Charlie said I could, but we'd better hurry.

Chief Charlie and Daniel waited in the pickup outside, while I changed with lightning speed into white painter pants, a navy-blue sweater and white deck shoes. I added a touch of mascara. I was, I realized, looking for some credibility. It simply did not occur to me that I didn't need any.

Brian MacCallum was very kind. I huddled in a stainless-steel chair and, with hesitancy and humiliation, told him about my encounters with Blako.

When I had finished, Sergeant MacCallum said, "Laura, your feelings are completely typical of a person who has been a victim of criminal behavior. You really must work on the fact that what Blako did to you isn't your fault. You didn't do anything wrong when he assaulted you outside of the Hotel: you were just on your way home. And giving someone a dirty look in the bar doesn't mean you're giving them permission to tell you how they are going to rape you. Stop beating yourself up."

The sergeant paused and said, "Now what I'd like to do is press charges against him, but that decision is actually up to the Crown. A circuit judge, the Crown Council and a defense lawyer fly up here every few weeks. They'll be here on Tuesday. I think that Blako will be charged then. I can pick him up and hold him here. In the meantime, I'll get statements from Daniel, Matt Pederson and Kristy Mack."

"Will Daniel and Matt get in trouble for beating on him?"

"He could press charges against them for assault, but the chances are remote that they'd stick. It was an urgent situation, and those two were protecting a citizen. The next woman he picks on might not be lucky enough to get away from him."

"You're right." I told him, "Of course you're right. I want to press charges."

After Daniel gave a statement, Chief Charlie talked for a while with Sergeant MacCallum, and just before we left, the sergeant asked me if I could be reached at the manse.

Daniel piped up, "Until that guy's in jail, she'll be staying at my house."

"Uh yes," I stumbled. "I'll be staying at his house."

It was almost dinner time when we left; we went to Chief Charlie's. Jenn asked if she could come over to my house the next day, and

Chief Charlie said, "Not tomorrow, Jenny."

"Next week, Jenn," I told her.

I felt overwhelmed by the events of the day and was very quiet. I could tell from his stance that Chief Charlie was angry. At first, I felt horrified, thinking he was angry with me. But my perceptions were all wrong. It soon became apparent that it was Daniel he was angry with. If this bothered Daniel, it was not obvious to me.

We left shortly after supper. As we left, Chief Charlie said very gently, "Be careful, eh?"

I smiled at him. "I will."

On the way to the manse to pick up some things, I asked Daniel why Chief Charlie was angry with him; he answered, "Partly because he thinks we should've reported the first incident. And I guess he would be right about that."

"And what's the other part?"

Daniel didn't answer. "Does Chief Charlie think that you're taking advantage of me?"

"No. He thinks very highly of you. I guess he thinks I *should* be taking advantage of you."

"Oh," was the only response I could come up with.

As I packed some things into a duffle bag, I kept thinking that all of this was absurd. I would be staying at Daniel's, who didn't want to be with me. And what was it he wanted to talk about?

At his place, I felt very awkward, but if he felt the same way; it didn't show. I sat on the couch, curling my legs beneath me. There was a long period of silence, during part of which I stared out the front window, enjoying the steady heat of the fire.

"Laura?"

I turned to look at him.

"Do you think that maybe you could still consider being involved with me? I mean, like, more than just friends?"

Just like that he'd asked me into his life. Simple, neat—no lead-ins.

Looking into his dark eyes I was about to say, "Yes." But something held me back. I had been hurt and was looking for something to bolster my trust.

Standing up, I went over to the window. Beyond, were the trees and the beach and the deep, gray waters of the Passage. I could also see my own reflection in the window and, in a very quiet voice, asked, "Why?"

"I guess you're looking for some blood, and I don't blame you for that."

I couldn't think of an answer, and a moment later, behind my reflection, was Daniel's. I felt and saw one hand gently touch my shoulder. I could feel the vibration of his voice behind me. "I thought about what you said, and I have to tell you, I'm afraid. But I love the way you're so funny and so serious, and I love the way you laugh. I love the way you're so strong and so fragile, and the way you care so much. And I can't get you out of my mind, and maybe we can make our own world."

He paused and seemed to be struggling. "I don't know the right words." He said something in Heiltsuk and said that it translated into something like, "I've been waiting for you." Then he added, "And that's the longest speech I've ever made to a woman, Laura."

I felt incredibly light, although tears were welling up in my eyes. Turning around, I said, "Well, I guess that will be enough, Daniel. And I don't know what else to say because you already know that I love you."

He reached down and gently wiped the tears from my face. "Then why are you crying?"

"I don't know. I guess, I mean—this does mean I'm your girlfriend, doesn't it?"

He grinned. "Well, strictly speaking, I guess we have to do certain things…" His voice trailed off.

I suddenly felt very afraid and told Daniel. Then I said that it wasn't that I felt afraid, it was that I felt nervous.

He held me tightly and whispered, "It's okay, and whenever you're ready is fine."

"I'm ready now, Daniel."

Chapter 26

I felt more happy and serene the next morning than at any time I could recall. After we had breakfast, I had a soapy bath. Daniel sat in a chair next to the bath and talked to me, while he whittled with a sharp knife on a piece of cedar.

We talked about Xvnis and my concerns that I get all the work done in the field in the three remaining weeks that were left in the project. He asked me what would happen if I didn't get all the work done.

"Well nothing, really. I'll just say in my thesis that 'Time constraints prevented us from blah, blah, blah.'"

Daniel laughed at this. "Then stop worrying. Do a good job at Xvnis: that's an important site."

He pronounced Xvnis with that melodious inflection that I could never quite reproduce. I agreed with him that Xvnis was important. Then we spoke about fishing. There was an opening coming up, and they'd be heading up towards Prince Rupert. He thought he and Matt would be spending the day working on the boat. Did I have any plans?

"I haven't seen Maggie for a few weeks, except to visit with her at Jenn's party, so maybe I could go out there and talk to her about Xvnis. Are you having dinner at Chief Charlie's?"

"As far as I know. But Laura," he hesitated. "Why do you call him Chief Charlie, and not just Charlie?"

"I guess it's because he never asked me to."

"Well, yeah, sure, feeds his ego I guess," Daniel laughed.

"Maybe someday, I'll be calling you, Chief Daniel."

"Probably not if we're sleeping together." He smiled with—that smile.

I smiled back. "Getting back to the original subject, maybe you could drop me off at Maggie's, and I could walk over to Chief Charlie's…I mean, Charlie's later."

We stopped at the café. I picked up coffees and the sticky donuts that Maggie loved. Before I got out of the pickup, I reached over, gave Daniel a whispery kiss on the lips and said, "That's a down payment for later."

He grinned. "That's not enough of a down payment. Come here."

He kissed me thoroughly, until I said, "Okay, either we have sex on the front seat, or I'd better go."

He laughed. "You'd better go."

I heard Maggie's usual, "Come in," just as I reached the door. She was sitting in her familiar place by the stove, but she wasn't weaving. I asked her why.

"Arthritis is pretty bad today. I took some aspirin; that might help. Maybe that coffee will loosen up my fingers too."

We drank our coffee and talked about events in the village, including the success of Jenn's birthday party. She looked at me speculatively. "So, last week at that party, I see there was a lot of storm clouds between you and Daniel. Now I see you're necking with him in his pickup. Guess you cleared it up, eh?"

Looking at the window, then back to where Maggie was sitting, I asked her how she could have seen Daniel and I necking.

"Well, I was standing by the window, peeking out from behind the curtains."

I burst out laughing, and she chuckled.

"Well, if the word's not out yet, it will be. Daniel Hunt has finally been caught." She chuckled again, almost gleefully.

"I didn't catch him," I protested lightly. "He caught me, or maybe we just caught each other."

"That's not how people are going to say it. They'll be saying you chased him."

"Well, to hell with them. And I want you to phone Agnes Campbell and tell her Daniel Hunt is my boyfriend."

"Well, yeah sure, I'll do that, but boyfriends are for teenagers. I'll tell her he's your man, and that the whole family is pretty much relieved about that."

"Why?"

"Well, ever since you showed up, Daniel's been moody. Laney told me that Matt says he's been a pain in the ass to work with. Matt went over there to Daniel's to talk to him this week, and Laney said Matt straightened him out."

"What did he say?"

"I didn't get the details. You could ask Daniel."

But I never did ask Daniel, and he never did talk about what happened. However, Matt Pederson held a special place in my heart from that time on.

I obtained a lot of information about Xvnis from Maggie that day, although her memories of the site only added to the mystery of its history, rather than clarify it. It was overcast but not raining when I left her place at 5 to walk to Chief Charlie's. I loved the walk from Maggie's into town because of the clear view of the Passage and because of the sound of the wind rippling through the beach grass. I felt overwhelmed with happiness…and that wonderful new feeling of serenity. For a moment, I was curious as to where that feeling came from, but, as soon as the question was framed in my head, I knew the answer. I was secure in my love for Daniel Hunt because I knew that he'd thought long and hard before taking our relationship to the next level. I knew that he was in love with me.

Thorough some unspoken communication, I was seated next to Daniel at dinner. It was a small group that evening: just Rose, Daniel, Matt and Laney and their children. Chief Charlie and Matt did most of the talking, throwing back and forth ideas about salmon fishing rights. Chief Charlie then turned to me and said that the sergeant had dropped by that afternoon to say that Blako had been arrested and was in jail. I said I was glad about that, but that I was unaware that George Clements had asked him to look out for me.

"Well, sure he did, Laura." Chief Charlie smiled. "And right from the time you broke your nose, I knew you needed the protection of the Hunt family."

This statement was greeted with laughter. After a while, Matt said I was very quiet and asked if I was at all offended by my "protectors."

"Not at all," I replied. "I've been wondering how my brother is making out with his new used car."

"Well, what kind of car is it?" asked Chief Charlie.

I paused to think. "I don't remember."

Of course, howling and laughter greeted this response. Daniel made a circular gesture that was maybe universal, a sign I knew meant "loco." Then he smiled and draped his arm over the back of my chair. It was a small gesture, but it validated to the family that we were together.

The conversation turned to Band politics, and after a while, Jenn, who was sitting on the other side of me, tugged at my sleeve. She gestured that she wanted to whisper something, and I leaned over to hear her. Putting her hand over her mouth she whispered, "Is Uncle Daniel your boyfriend now?"

Everyone heard her whisper; there was a moment of awkwardness. Jenn hung her head and said, "Sorry."

I laughed softly. I didn't feel awkward. "It's okay, Jenn. Yes, Uncle Daniel's my boyfriend."

After dinner, alone in the kitchen for a few minutes, Daniel and I made hurried plans for the evening: that I'd be spending the night at his place was an unspoken assumption, but I would be leaving for Xvnis in the morning and hadn't sorted my things or washed my field clothes. After we left Chief Charlie's, Daniel dropped me off at the manse.

I started the laundry and then called Mom and Jake. It seemed like ages since I'd talked to them. Mom said she'd tried to call several times; there was a hint of rebuke in her voice. I apologized and told her I'd been camping in the field. She said she was just relieved that I was doing well.

I filled her in on the events of the last few weeks, including the major events that had led up to my new romance. My mother listened carefully. I think she was able to see the Daniel that I saw: a decent, caring person. I knew that she sensed the happiness in my voice, and this was enough for her to indicate her approval of the relationship. We also talked about Nadine. Mom said she was anxious to meet both of my new friends.

My conversation with Jake was lively and, like it often did, deteriorated into hysterical laughter, when he launched into an analysis of current political situations. Then he talked about how cool his car was and how cool his girlfriend "still" was. Just before he hung up, he said Mom wanted to say something else. My mother got on the phone and told me that that nice boy, Richard, from my legal firm in Toronto, had been trying to get in touch with me and that maybe I should give him a call. I said I would and told her how much I loved her, and could she tell Jake that I loved him as well? She called out, "Laura loves you!"

I heard Jake's reply from a distance. "Ditto!"

I also made a quick call to Nadine, updating my life. She sounded happy that I was "finally with Daniel." We decided we'd get together the following weekend.

Later, when Daniel and I were sleepily wound around each other, I recalled that when I'd arrived at Chief Charlie's for supper, he and Daniel had been deep in conversation, speaking in Heiltsuk. I asked Daniel what it was all about. He hesitated. I added, "It's okay, just curious."

"Well, I should talk about it with you before tomorrow because it could be a while before I see you again."

Sitting up on my elbow and looking down towards him, I said, "Talk to me."

"Chief Charlie wants me to tell you that maybe you shouldn't go to the bar, even if you are with your crew."

"Is it because he's afraid I'll get harassed?"

"Well, that would be one reason."

"And the others?"

"I'm trying to frame the words, Laura. I don't have Charlie's experience as a diplomat."

"Why didn't Chief Charlie just tell me himself?"

"Well, he would have said something, except that..." Daniel's voice trailed off, and I could see that he was frustrated. Finally, he said, "Laura, you're strong and independent, and I don't know how to say this without offending you."

"So far, I'm not offended, Daniel, just dying of curiosity. Why don't you just spit it out?"

"Chief Charlie is old fashioned. Being with me is sort of like being with the whole Hunt family...more than would be the case with most white families. Now that we're together, I'm responsible for you and even for your behavior. Hanging out at the bar is a bad example for those kids that are working for you, and you hanging out at the bar makes me look bad, so it makes the whole family look bad."

"How do you feel about this?"

"Well, I agree with Charlie. Otherwise, I guess that I would've been arguing with him, instead of talking to him. You need to understand; this is not about being patriarchal. If I drank in the bar, it would be embarrassing for you and the entire family."

I think that I was looking puzzled, wondering how I felt about what Daniel had said.

"Laura, you have to understand that it's not about a perception that you're a loose woman. It's mostly about alcohol. You've seen the heartbreak that it causes here, and what you've seen is only the tip of the iceberg."

"Daniel, I understand that. I can understand that, and to be honest, I'd already made the decision that I wouldn't drink at the bar. And then I decided to get drunk *at* you, to…I guess, to pay you back, in a way."

Daniel laughed, obviously relieved, but then I remembered something.

"What about Matt? What about that time when you were in the bar with him?"

Daniel's brow furrowed. "I see your point. Matt and I do occasionally go into the bar, and I hang out with him while he has a few beers. I guess that's a double standard." He paused to consider. "Maybe I could go with you to the bar once in a while."

"Daniel, I don't really want to go anyway. I understand what you mean, and the point is taken." I paused, then added, "Traditionally, this society leans towards the matrilineal. Doesn't that mean that I have a fair bit of power?"

"Well, yeah sure. It goes both ways. I'm obligated to keep your respect and the respect of your family."

I was tired, and the whole conversation was, by this time, not really being absorbed. Finally, I just smiled and said, "So, if you bring shame to me, my brother can kill you?"

"Well, yeah, sure."

I could hardly keep my eyes open, but another question occurred to me. "Daniel, when did you stop drinking?"

"A long time ago," he answered softly. "I did a lot of binge drinking until I was 25, and that was enough."

"Are you ever going to drink again?"

"Not even if you drive me crazy" was the reply.

At the dock on Monday morning, Kristy was excited to talk about the statement she'd given to the police. On the ride out to Xvnis, she shouted the details of what she'd said, and while she did give the facts, her presentation was so melodramatic that even Jack was in stitches.

We worked hard at Xvnis that week. By late Thursday afternoon, we'd finished the onsite work. I'd been working in the evenings, and I'd caught up with my journal and paperwork. Jack, Kristy and I had become a great team, and in my heart of hearts, I knew I'd become a good boss. They took a great deal of initiative when it came to the work but trusted me to give them direction.

I noticed over the course of the three weeks that we were at Xvnis that Jack and Kristy's relationship had changed dramatically. Whereas before they'd tolerated each other, they now accepted each other. While the banter continued, I saw that they had formed a friendship.

The final phase of our project was to survey as much of Roscoe Inlet as we could. George Clements was extremely interested in knowing if there were any differences in the nature of the sites that would make it possible to delineate the Heiltsuk from neighboring tribes. This was also a topic that was of interest to Chief Charlie because, although land claims were in a state of infancy, he was aware that determining tribal boundaries would be a considerable problem.

The official ending date of the project was September 27th, but I had the manse until the 30th. I figured it would take about four days to complete the map, photos and related data on Xvnis. Then we would have a long weekend and return the following Monday to our camp at Xvnis. We'd use the camp as our base for a week, surveying Roscoe Inlet and working right through the weekend. When we got back, we would spend the final two days of the project doing paperwork related to the surveying.

When I returned to the manse, I called Nadine. She suggested we go out to the springs for a couple of hours. We met at the wharf at 6. The weather looked as if it couldn't decide whether to clear up or not, but we didn't care and headed for the springs. After wading around in the icy pools for a while, we went back down to the rock outcropping, where we usually ate our dinner. The western sky had cleared, and a bright orange sun was disappearing below the ocean and outer islands of the archipelago. I noticed again that the days were getting shorter, and that, especially at night it was much cooler. Fall had arrived.

I told Nadine the longer version of how Daniel and I finally got together, and she told me that it was my turn to be glowing.

"Nadine, I think you're right. When I looked at my face in the mirror today, I thought that my eyes seemed brighter, and I can't explain it, but I really do look different."

"Hey, I just told you were glowing, you idiot."

Then she was quiet for a moment. I knew she was thinking about how maybe what had happened with Allie had changed the look on her face.

"All that stuff, Nadine; I'll tell you the truth. It did change the way you look, and I'm not sure I can define it. But it's not bad. It's kind of like…well, there's more depth to your eyes, and sometimes this moment of sadness passes over you. But you don't look tough. If anything, you look softer, and when you talk about Chris, you just look really sparkly."

She smiled and draped her arm around my shoulder.

Chapter 27

By 6:30, Friday morning, I'd cleared off the dining room table and spread out the map of Xvnis that Jack had started in the field. I wondered what it would look like when it was finished. I spent an hour making summative notes on Xvnis and speculated on my perception of the history of the site. I had breakfast at the Hotel, and when I returned to the manse, found Jack at the dining room table, working on the map, and Kristy, upstairs preparing to develop photographs. I called Maggie and asked if I could come over. Just as I was heading out, there was a knock on the door.

It was Sergeant MacCallum. I invited him in for coffee, but he said he was short on time, that he'd come to update me on what was happening. The Crown had charged Blako with assault and uttering threats and had him barred from the Passage. A court date was set for October. I'd need to be there. I told the sergeant that I would be.

Shaken, I sat down on the couch. Kristy had come downstairs when she'd heard voices. She sat down alongside, telling me everything would be alright. Although he didn't say anything, I could sense Jack's quiet sympathy. Pulling myself together, I told them that going out to Maggie's would get my mind off Blako.

Picking up coffee and donuts at the Hotel cafe, I took the taxi out to Maggie's, hoping to glean any information that I could about any sites that might be up Roscoe Inlet. On the way, I mulled again over how Kristy's and Jack's interactions had changed a great deal from the start of the summer. It seemed as if their relationship had changed into one of closeness, beginning at Boston's Retreat, and coming together at Xvnis. I found, as well, that as the summer progressed, especially at Xvnis, Jack and Kristy offered insights into the forms we were devising for documenting the sites.

I knew that I should also ask other Elders about sites in Roscoe Inlet, but I didn't have any time left to do that. Maggie sensed my urgency. As she described the location of each site, I plotted these on the maps that I'd brought with me.

By late afternoon, I had enough information to keep me going for weeks, so I headed home. Walking along the edge of the beach grasses, I realized that I hadn't thought about Blako since that morning

Kristy had developed several rolls of film but had stopped because there was no room left to hang the damp photographs. She was working on sorting field forms in the study when I got back. We went upstairs and I admired the work she'd done. The most beautiful picture was not of the site but of Jenn. Kristy had taken this when Chief Charlie and the others had come out to Xvnis. It was clearly a 'moment,' rather than a composed photograph, and Kristy seemed to have captured the essence of the little girl. In the picture, Jenn's head is inclined towards someone, although I never did figure out who that is. She must have sensed Kristy because her eyes, full of mischief, looked directly into the camera.

Jack was working on the map of Xvnis. He'd plotted in all the house posts, most of the beams and points that represented the Inlet, the rock bluff, the middens and the stream. We had already determined in the field that there were two rows of houses on each of the middens at the site. My perceptions of the cultural features and the landscape were better than they had been when I'd first come to the Passage, but the data emerging on the map indicated that the site was larger and more complex than even Jack had anticipated.

Jack, drawing imaginary lines with his finger on the map, pointed out a total of twenty-three houses on each of the western and eastern middens. Each house in the first row, facing the beach, was separated by about ten meters from the row of houses behind. The back row of houses had been staggered against the first row, to maximize the view of the beach and the Inlet. There was nothing haphazard about the planning of Xvnis. Kristy, taking a break from her work, said, "Wow, it's like the Vancouver of the Heiltsuk."

Her comment seemed to make us feel contemplative, and then we called it a day.

Later, making notes in my field journal, I speculated on Xvnis. The size and monumental architecture suggested that the village had been built before smallpox had devastated the Heiltsuk. In fact, the depth of the midden suggested the site had been occupied for thousands of years. It had taken all my restraint not to take a shovel and do some digging to try and find some diagnostic artifacts that would give some indication of the age of the site. But my Heritage Conservation permit allowed for only shallow test pits.

If four families lived in each of the twenty-three houses, there would have been over five hundred people living on the eastern midden. If the western midden occupation overlapped, this number would be doubled. I wondered if the abandonment of Xvnis had been gradual or swift.

In the end, I remained with only questions about Xvnis. The site must have been named for the springs. This was indicated in the work of Boas and in the work of a later ethnographer in the 1950s, Ronald Olson, whose informants told him that 'Hoones' translated as meaning 'Springwater.' I had located this information in the pile of documents and books I had brought with me.

Maybe Xvnis was the birthplace of the Heiltsuk. I was romanticizing, I suppose, but it seemed to me that Xvnis was also the Springwater from which survivors had endured and carried on what was left of a thousands' year-old cultural tradition.

Daniel said he would call me on Sunday night, if he could. They had a radiophone, but it was generally reserved for emergencies. I fell asleep on the couch to the sound of the fire crackling. At about 9, Daniel called me. It was a hurried conversation because it was a pay phone and there were others waiting to use it.

I told him I was fine and that I missed him and loved him.

"We might be heading home for a few days next weekend. It will cost some extra gas, but all the guys want to."

"Daniel," I said in an exasperated voice. "I'm going to survey up Roscoe Inlet through next weekend."

"Well, that's the way it goes sometimes," he said, but I could tell that he was disappointed.

"I know," I said, with some excitement. "I could send Jack to get you."

There was a pause, and I wondered what Daniel was thinking. Then he answered, "I think I can borrow someone's boat to come out to Xvnis."

"Yes!" I exclaimed into the phone.

For the first five days of our final stint in the field, we worked our way up the northern side of Roscoe Inlet, returning to camp at Xvnis in the afternoon. In addition to Maggie's information, I'd acquired an intuitive sense of where sites would be located, although Jack was even better than I. There was almost always a site at the location of spawning streams. In some cases, it was only possible to say that there had been a fish-processing site because of the presence of depressions in the ground that may have been used for storage or for cooking. On several high rock bluffs, we found gravesites of the crib house variety that we'd seen at Campbell's Pole.

We found three deep midden sites. The surface vegetation suggested that they hadn't been occupied for a long time. On one of the middens there appeared to be the almost completely deteriorated remains of cedar beams. By Friday, we'd gone as far up the Inlet as time had permitted and decided that, the following day, we would turn around and survey the southern side. Because of exposure, we weren't likely to find as many sites on the southern side.

On that survey up the northern side of Roscoe Inlet, I gained a deeper understanding of the land. Maggie had told me of locations where people hunted and collected berries, and as we moved up the Inlet, Jack also pointed out places that people at the Passage still used at different times of the year. I began to realize that the material remains we found were like a whisper of a landscape that had been fully utilized.

The afternoons and evenings were spent filling out site forms and drawing out good copies of chain and compass maps. I had butterflies in my stomach all day Friday, hoping that Daniel would be at Xvnis when we returned from the field that afternoon.

I was not disappointed. As we approached Xvnis, I could see a boat anchored off the camp, but when we tied up our own boat, I felt suddenly shy. Daniel had a fire going, and I could see him up at the camp, sitting on a lawn chair.

He looked relaxed and at home, sipping on a cup of coffee.

"Hope it's okay if I made coffee," he said and smiled.

Because he seemed so at ease, I quickly felt the same way and ignoring the presence of Kristy and Jack, I kissed him lightly on the lips. I could see that there was a foil wrapped fish on the table.

"I thought you might be running out of food," Daniel said, grinning, as he prepared dinner. Jack, Kristy and I took turns cooking. It was good to have a meal that was made by someone else and better tasting than most of the concoctions that we'd come up with. "It's halibut," said Daniel. "I thought you might like a change." It was delicious.

Daniel opted out of surveying with us the next day, saying he wanted to read and catch up on his sleep. He had to leave Sunday morning to return to the Passage to go out fishing again. We slept on the boat he'd borrowed from a friend while he was at Waglisla, and on Saturday night, as we lay underneath the warm covers, he could tell that I was agitated.

"Your mind's going a hundred miles an hour, Laura," he commented.

"Daniel, do you love me?"

His arm tightened around me. "Yes."

I took a deep breath. "Daniel, my project is finished in less than ten days. I might not even see you before then."

I could sense that he'd tensed up, but he answered in a calm voice. "Well, we knew this was coming. What do you want to do?" he asked.

"I just want to be with you."

"But where?"

"Daniel, I know you're against living in the city, or living anywhere, except for the Passage. I understand that. This has been your home all your life. I could live with you here."

"Wouldn't you get a need to go to the city?"

"Probably. But I can fly out for a break any time I want. And maybe you could just try spending some time at my house on the Lower Mainland. It's on the ocean. You could carve there. It might be okay for you."

"That would be fair, I guess. My place is pretty small. Could you do your work there?"

"Yes. It's all books and paper now. I can work on my thesis at your place and do the word processing later."

"Okay, Laura. I hope we don't drive each other crazy. If I'm not here, I'll get Charlie to move your things over. Don't you have a meeting at the end of the month?"

"I have to go to Vancouver and get some articles and books, as well as some clothes. And I must go to Toronto to sort out some financial and legal things. I guess I'll leave the Passage on the 30th. I'll be gone for a couple of weeks."

"It could be a while until I see you," Daniel said and then added softly, "I'll be missing you a lot."

"You will?" I smiled.

"Well, yeah, sure."

I was serious then. "Daniel, I love you. I love the way you laugh, and the way you're so strong and so calm. I love the way you're scared but take the risk anyway. And I love your decency and the way you think things through. I have never felt so certain about anything in my life, as I have about you. I'd wait four years for you—and that's the longest speech I've ever made to a man."

"Why the time limit?'

"It's how long Franz Boas's wife waited for him."

"It will be enough," he replied softly.

Because we were so busy, I had little time to reflect on my relationship with Daniel, except in those moments before I fell asleep, when I fantasized about weddings and children. Still, it was not anticipation that dominated my feelings for him. From the start, these feelings had been ones of serene happiness. It was as if I'd found something that I'd been looking for all my life; it was as if I'd arrived home.

Daniel was out fishing for the remainder of the month. I promised Jack and Kristy that I'd have an end of season party when I returned.

On a drizzly morning on the last day of September, Chief Charlie helped me to move my things over to Daniel's and arranged to pick me up in a few hours for my flight to Vancouver. I made some coffee and wandered around the house, which had once been a school portable. Then I went out to the beach and sat on the bench, looking out to the Passage. I thought about what I had accomplished that summer.

Using ethnography, I had enhanced knowledge around three sites, although answers around Xvnis remained a mystery. I had located numerous fish-processing sites and could make educated projections around where these sites could be found. Although mysteries remained unresolved, I had achieved my thesis goal on how to document wooden feature sites. This included ethnography, photography and archaeological documentation, all of which was carefully recorded on the forms we'd devised. Through these techniques, we'd found out that the eventual decomposition of the wooden features meant that these features could be preserved.

I stacked my books and files in a corner of the bedroom and set out my creams and some perfume on the counter in the bathroom, musing that I'd only used the perfume a few times in the last three months. I wrote down my Vancouver number and the number of my grandfather's house in Toronto.

Then I took a pinch of tobacco, spread it around the beach in front of the house and said a prayer, asking that I be welcome here. I was aware, in that moment, of the smells and sights and sounds of the Passage. There were seagulls and a raven, crying somewhere, and there was the smell of salty air. I felt a light breeze play about my hair and listened to the whispers in the tall cedars and the sound of the surf. And, then, it was time to go.

Chapter 28

Jake proudly met me at the terminal in Vancouver, ready to drive me to the North Shore. Had he grown? It looked as if he was going to be taller than the combined height of my parents, who were both tall. Like our mother, Jake was blond; from our father, he'd inherited blue eyes. But unlike Father, whose eyes were steely, Jake's eyes were full of humor and were very expressive.

I spent three days in North Vancouver, mostly visiting with Mom and Jake and then caught a flight to Toronto. For the first few hours in Toronto, I felt overwhelmed by the people, the buildings and the rush. But it was, after all, a familiar world, and these strange feelings quickly went away.

The next morning, a driver from my grandfather's firm, O'Donnell, Fitzgerald, Murphy and LaChapelle, picked me up and I spent the day with Richard Murphy going over financial details of Jake's and my inheritance. I'd known Richard since I was a little girl; in fact, he was a year younger than Michael, and the two were close friends when we were children. I inherited Richard as a friend, and in my late teens and early twenties, I was the one with common sense who seemed to be forever getting him out of scrapes. He had curtailed drinking beer and whatever else he did and ended up doing exactly what he said he would never do—become a lawyer. Over the years, we'd stayed up late and talked deep into the night and even traveled to Europe together. But there were never any romantic inclinations between us, and perhaps this was why we'd been friends for such a long time.

Richard was smart, and I think in the legal world, was already establishing himself as a forthcoming and relentless lawyer. After a couple of hours of going over financial details, Richard looked at me with frustration and said, "You've never been a financial guru, Laura, but you are barely listening to me."

"I'm sorry, Richard. I get the main thrust and know how much interest income I have, but I guess my mind is with that guy I was telling you about."

"Let's just not do this then and hope I am not robbing you blind," he smiled.

"You're not," I smiled back.

"So, interest rates are really high, you're in good shape—do you want the balance for the year, or reinvest some of it?"

"I think I should reinvest some of it. I earned a good wage this summer and didn't really spend much. On the other hand, I might want to put a skylight in my house." I paused and said, "How much to you think that will cost?"

"I don't have a clue," said Richard, who then burst out laughing.

"That's really professional, Richard," I snapped at him, but then followed it up with a grin.

We arranged to meet for dinner the following night. That evening Daniel called from the Passage. We talked for almost forty-five minutes; a record, said Daniel, because he didn't generally like to talk on the phone. The fishing was good, but he'd be glad when the season was over at the end of October. His plan for the winter was to spend it in bed with me. When I hung up, I realized that I was not only homesick for Daniel, but for the Passage.

The following day I went shopping. I was on a mission. I had a lot of fun picking out an outfit for Jenn and an outfit for each of Matt and Laney's children. Laney knew that I always brought the children gifts when I was away. She had made a comment that the kids needed durable clothes for school, so I made sure to get outfits for Jenn and Matt and Laney's children that were practical. I also bought gifts for Mom and Jake and a pair of simple diamond stud earrings for Nadine, whose birthday was the following month.

After lunch, I bought gifts for Chief Charlie, Rose, and Laney and then went to the restaurant where I was meeting Richard for dinner.

Dropping my parcels next to the chair, I told Richard I was exhausted.

"Is there anything left to buy in downtown Toronto?" he asked sardonically.

"Not much," I grinned.

"Well, you might be exhausted, but you look beautiful, Laura. In fact, over these past two days, I've noticed that you look better than you ever have. Being in love looks good on you."

We talked about Daniel and about the Passage. And as we usually did, we argued about politics and economics, and like he always did, Richard got the upper hand because he went into his calm, quiet lawyer stance. He hugged me tightly when we said our good-byes.

The day after I returned to Vancouver, I spent the afternoon with George Clements, who gave me some directions for my thesis, as well as a list of readings. I spent three days collecting books and photocopying articles at the university, glad that I'd already done a great deal of reading over the summer.

George was fascinated with Kristy's pictures and pronounced her to be one the best photographers that he'd come across. He said it was amazing that she had no prior training. He stated as a question: "Imagine what she could do if she did have some formal instruction?"

I told him I'd pass this information on to her and wondered if, with some encouragement, she could be convinced to formally explore her talent.

I found a lot of time to simply relax and visit with Mom and Jake and Joanna. As well, I embarked on a mission to eat non-stop, with my goal being to eat everything I'd missed over the summer. I ate salads, all manner of ethnic foods, pizza, exotic desserts and lots of beef and chicken. Often, I would get this food to go and gorge while I watched a video.

I also completed my shopping spree in Vancouver, buying clothes that I thought would be useful for the cold, rainy season that was coming up. I had thought a great deal about gifts for Jack and Kristy. I'd told Daniel that I wanted to get Jack a rifle. After careful consideration and quizzing me about how much I wanted to spend, Daniel had told me what kind of rifle to buy. I bought Jack a "30.06" caliber, Weatherby Mark V rifle. Without blinking an eye, the vendor had me fill out a few forms, and Jake and I walked out of the store with the rifle and a box of cartridges.

Kristy's present was easier: a Nikon camera with additional wide angle and zoom lenses, a tripod and a ton of film.

For Maggie, I bought a white down comforter, and this finished my shopping spree.

My house had been purchased with an advance in my inheritance, after careful consideration by Judge Murphy, Richard's father. The house was in Deep Cove, a suburb adjacent to North Vancouver. The main reason I'd bought it was because it was on the beach and had been built so that most of the living area faced the ocean. It occurred to me, being in that house, that Daniel's place would seem a lot smaller. I dismissed these thoughts.

I timed my departure to coincide with Daniel having a few days off. It was overcast as we approached the Passage; one minute we were in the clouds and the next we were descending towards the gravel landing strip. I could see Daniel's truck off to one side: this time he hadn't kept me waiting. When he walked towards me, I think I had a silly grin on my face. Gently putting his hand on my shoulder, he reached down and kissed me on the lips and whispered simply, "Laura."

On the drive back to his house we didn't talk much, and this time I sensed there was some awkwardness for both of us. At the house, he unloaded my things and I apologized for the heavy boxes of books. When we went inside, he asked if I wanted some coffee, or lunch, or anything. I smiled and replied, "I just want to make love with you and get rid of all this formality, or whatever it is."

He grinned and said, "Well yeah, sure. I can do that."

Later that evening, he sat in the chair next to the tub while I took a bath. I told him about my trip to Toronto and Vancouver. It was now mid-October and chilly out - the thought crossed my mind that perhaps winter baths wouldn't be as much fun as they'd been in the summer. Daniel talked about fishing, saying that in less than two weeks, they'd be done. He was looking forward to doing some carving—looking forward to exploring the ideas that came to him when he was out fishing.

The day after I returned to the Passage was a Sunday, and we went to Chief Charlie's for dinner. Jenn was overjoyed at the clothes I'd bought her, and I felt warm inside watching her parade the outfits for all to see.

"You're spoiling that girl, Laura," said Rose.

"Never mind," said Chief Charlie, "She'll get her hard times, just like the rest of us. Let her have her fun."

I gossiped with Laney and Rose, by now knowing enough people in the village that I could often keep up with who was together, who was apart, who had come back to the Reserve, who had left and who had gotten a job. The subject of jobs was always a big one, because there were so few. Laney whispered to me that Matt had told her that, since Daniel had gotten together with me, he was back to his old self and a "helluva a lot easier to get on with." I burst out laughing and Rose and Laney chuckled. Daniel eyed us suspiciously, aware somehow that we were talking about him.

Daniel left for fishing the next day, and I unpacked my things. He'd cleared off a big space on the bookshelf for my books, but there wasn't any room in the small bedroom closet for my clothes, so I left them in my suitcases against a wall in the bedroom. I spent part of the rest of the day visiting Nadine. I admired the decorating she was doing, which was turning Chris's "company" house into a home. She had her own study on the second floor, had ordered a desk and shelves from Sears and had brought her computer up from the Coast. The house was set some distance from the beach but was on the ocean side of the street, and from her study window, she had a good view of the Passage.

We drank coffee and then walked back to Daniel's. It was chilly and I was glad to be wearing a new, lined anorak that I'd bought in Vancouver. I admitted that I was envious of the space she had.

"You might have to work on getting used to that, Laura. It's going to be a challenge. Just keep talking. The one thing Chris has taught me is how important that is."

"How long do you think Chris is going to stay up here?" I asked her.

"I don't know. Maybe a long time. He likes it here. He has thousands of dollars in student loans, and I think he gets a break on his loans for working in a rural area. And he is best on the front lines. I think Chris really needs to feel like he's making a difference, and I think he has a huge sense of social responsibility. I guess I have a biased point of view, but I think he's gifted. Anyway, I'm content to stay here."

"Are you going to get married?" I teased her.

She grinned, but there was certainty in her voice when she answered simply, "Well, yeah, sure."

I couldn't think of what to do for the end of season party I'd promised Jack and Kristy. In the end, I settled for taking them to the

Hotel for dinner and then back to my place for Duncan Hines cake and ice cream.

Kristy ranted and raved about her gift and beamed when I told her what Dr. George Clements said about her photographs. She asked me if I really thought she could go to school. I emphatically replied that she could and said that I'd help her do some research on schools.

Jack's reaction to his gift took me by surprise. He sat, holding his rifle in his lap, while Kristy and I talked. Then he said simply, "Thank you, Laura"

There were tears in his eyes. I reached over and touched his arm and said, "You're welcome, Jack. You—you and Kristy and me—we were a good team.

"No, we weren't," said Kristy, "We were the best."

Chapter 29

The fishing season ended in the last week of October, and Daniel was home for the winter. We started the process of really getting to know each other. In the evenings we curled up on the couch, talking in front of a warm fire, and in the mornings, we lingered in the cozy bed.

One Thursday morning in early November, Brian MacCallum came to our door, and accepted the cup of coffee Daniel made for him. Blako, whose real name was Blake Fischer, had been found dead, stabbed outside of a bar in Nanaimo.

I was shaken by this news, not because I had any feelings of sadness for Blako, but because I had no feelings at all. Daniel talked this through with me. Blako had been inhuman to me, so why should I shed any tears about him being dead? It wasn't as if I was celebrating the death. This made sense to me, and after that conversation, I rarely ever thought about Blake Fischer again.

I learned small things about Daniel that endeared him to me: the way he expertly started a fire in the stove, the subtle looks of amusement that passed over his features, the way he would stand on the deck, looking out to the Passage. Sometimes, he would look mildly irritated, and I knew that it was because he felt crowded in that little house, and sometimes so did I.

I did my work at the kitchen table, writing a rough draft of my thesis in longhand. I formulated most of my ideas during the actual process of writing, and when I worked, I was very intense. Completely focused on my work, I frequently didn't bother to answer the phone, even though it was often Kristy or Nadine, wanting to go for lunch, or Maggie, telling me to come over with donuts and coffee. Sometimes when I was working, Daniel would make a pot of coffee and attempt a conversation but lost in my work, I didn't really register this…or anything, for that matter.

It began to irritate Daniel that it was he who had to put aside his carving and come out of his work room to answer the phone and that, when he would talk to me, I often wasn't really listening. When I was giving him my full attention, it was often to hint that I wanted to do some decorating, but he ignored this. Other differences soon became apparent.

Daniel was slow to form opinions, thought things through and had, I think, a patience that I simply didn't. I was sometimes quick to come to conclusions, and sometimes had a quick temper. Looking back, I see that some of these differences were ones of maturity. Daniel was seven years older than I, but they were crucial years. He also had the benefit of years of learning, that included many lessons about demeanor and the qualities of a chief that he had learned from Charlie. Daniel had far more life experience than I and self-contemplation seemed to be an ingrained trait in his thoughts and actions. I was much less self-contemplative. As well, I had been living alone for a while or with roommates who shared the same concern for concentration and pressure to meet course deadlines. I carried this jealousy of my time into my life with Daniel. We had in common the fact that we were both essentially romantics and shared a strong sense of humor. Both of us were also very strong willed.

One rainy afternoon, the phone rang, and Daniel asked me in a sharp voice, one that I'd never heard before, to answer it. I did. It was Matt and Daniel talked to him for a while and hung up. Angry at being ordered to answer the phone, I said, "Daniel, sometimes when I'm working. I don't answer the phone. I'm just concentrating really hard and don't want to talk to anyone."

"Laura, that's not fair. Sometimes the phone is for you, and this isn't the city. Sometimes when the phone rings, it's because there's an emergency."

"And what am I supposed to do about it?" was my retort.

Exasperated, he said, "You know, I don't think you're thinking about this. I don't even think you're listening."

I looked at him angrily, put on my jacket and walked out the door. I stomped all the way up to the Reservoir.

While I got angry quickly, I didn't stay angry. After half an hour looking out at the peaceful lake, I tried to make sense of the interchange. There were problems between Daniel and me. As for the phone, Daniel was right; I was acting like an idiot.

We nearly fell over each other apologizing for our first major disagreement. In the end, we agreed to take turns answering the phone, unless I didn't hear it, in which case Daniel would nicely remind me.

I had told Richard when I was in Toronto that my relationship with Daniel was like a Harlequin romance. So much for Harlequin romances because in those first few months, Daniel and I almost didn't make it. He was proud and perhaps a bit awed by my university education but began to resent the fact that I was often lost in thought, even in the evenings. His subtle resistance to my hints that I would like to decorate made me feel as if his home was not my home. He insisted on doing the shopping and paying for all the groceries, and while I understood that his identity as a man was tied to him being the provider, I thought this was incredibly antiquated. Daniel also did all the cooking, and while I wasn't a great cook, there were several meals that I was good at making. He resisted my suggestions that I cook sometimes.

We also had a strange arrangement for doing laundry. A woman in the village did Daniel's laundry, but when I'd sent mine along, I'd received back a load of pink clothes because she'd washed my red t-shirt with everything else. I told Daniel I was going to order a washer and dryer from Sears.

"Where are you going to put it?" he asked me.

So, Daniel's laundry went to a woman in the village, and when I had nothing left to wear, I went to the Hotel and did my laundry at the laundromat there. I had some miserable times there, mostly because I was usually seething with resentment.

It was with Nadine that I discussed my resentments. She listened patiently and, at the end of each discussion, told me that I had to talk to Daniel about the way I felt and to let him have his say, as well. I did try to talk about my feelings with Daniel, but my attempts fizzled. I was also reluctant to be direct because I was afraid that if I asked for change, Daniel would not only resist, but would end our relationship. And whatever our differences, I was deeply in love with him and was terrified at the thought of losing him.

I was also feeling some degree of discomfort that stemmed from the rift that went back to the death of Allie Owens. People in the village had formed sides. I'd heard of several fights at the bar, which stemmed from the incident. From the first day that I'd arrived at the Passage, I'd been overwhelmed by the friendliness of the people. Now, some of these same people averted their eyes when I passed. I assumed that they were on the other side of the faction than the Hunts. There was one girl who was always very rude to me. She worked in the Co-Op, and when I went through her till, she was sarcastic and surly. If both tills were open, I simply went to the other one. One rainy afternoon, I went into the Co-Op to buy some tampons and had no choice but to go through her till. As she rang in my purchase, she remarked in a loud, sarcastic vice, "I guess you're not pregnant yet, eh?"

My response was quick. I leaned over until my face was right next to hers and said, "Fuck you," then stomped out of the store, without the tampons.

Daniel was not sympathetic, saying, "That kind of talk only fuels the fire, Laura."

"Is this the protection and support that I, your concubine, get from the Hunt family?" I asked sarcastically. Then I put my coat back on and headed up to the Reservoir.

The fall, like the summer, had been unusually warm, a warmth which lasted right through until the end of October. Then the days grew shorter and shorter, and at the end of November, the winter rains began. It rained and rained and rained. One day, it snowed, and I remember feeling almost lightheaded with this change. It would take me a while to get the tempo of the seasons. The December rains were broken up by snow and several clear days. Not until April would the rain let up, although it steadily became warmer, with more and more clear days. Meanwhile, winter was potlatch season; I was looking forward to a potlatch being put on by Gordon, Chief Charlie's brother-in-law, when a memorial pole for the Raven would be raised to commemorate the one-year death of his father.

It was not to be. The day before the potlatch, I developed some combination of cold and flu and could barely get out of bed. Daniel filled me in on the details, but I was so sick that it did not really infiltrate my understanding. He did come home with a very beautiful original artwork by a well-known Pacific Northwest Coast Indigenous artist. I admired it, but Daniel was uncharacteristically circumspect. "It's a show of status, which is fine, but means I have to give Gordon something of equal value at my potlatch, if I want to hold my head up around here."

"What are you going to give him?"

"I don't have a clue. Charlie will think of something."

Daniel and I still had good days, and, sometimes, I'd catch him looking at me with a look of love in his eyes. I would admire his work, and he'd talk about the symbolic meanings of the carvings.

But our differences were creating anxiety for both of us. It was the bathtub that would cause these differences to come to a head. Our bathtub talks had ended. It was very chilly out now, and I no longer took delight in having a bath out in the cold. Once, I'd slipped on the deck rushing to get from the bath to the house. Daniel put a mat down after that, but it was still slippery.

The second time I slipped was just as I was entering the house. The only damage I could feel was a sore elbow; I got up, and then Daniel was there helping me.

His voice was raised in anger…or maybe fear, and he said, "How many times do I have to tell you not to run?"

I'd never seen Daniel really angry. My instant response was "Why don't you just go to hell?"

I could tell by the look on his face that he was even angrier, but I shuffled past him and went to the bedroom and got dressed, planning on going to the Hotel café to nurse my wounds. He was sitting on the couch, next to the fire, and didn't look up as I headed for the door. But he tersely said, "If you walk out that door Laura, you'd better think twice about coming back."

I paused in putting on my coat and then took it off again. My anger was gone, replaced by a strange feeling of resignation. Walking over to the couch, I said, "What do you mean? Do you mean this is it for us? If I walk out the door, I can just keep on walking, and that's it?"

He looked miserable and said, "I didn't think it was going to be like this, Laura. I can't live like this."

"You can't live like this? Well if you can't live like this Daniel, then maybe I should leave this home. God knows it's never been mine anyway."

I could see the pain in his eyes, but I had more to say. "Home is where there is some part of yourself. What part of me is here? All this." I gestured with my hand around the room. "All this is you. I thought we were going to be partners, but I'm just some kind of guest that has stayed too long. I haven't even unpacked my suitcases, Daniel."

"What can I do?" he asked in a bare whisper.

"You could start by letting me do a few things around here."

"But Laura, if you want a fancy home, that's not…"

I interrupted him. "Did I ask for a designer home? Daniel, I lived in a mansion for half of my life, and it was a prison to me. This house, with your love and some pieces of me—that's all I want."

"What kind of pieces do you want?"

"I'd like to cook sometimes; I'm not the greatest, but I'm tired of wild game and salmon. Couldn't I make salads and some other stuff? Couldn't you try to get a taste for some of the things I like?"

He nodded and I continued. "I'd like some new flooring and furniture. Some paint. Some curtains. Something I can put my clothes in. Some kitchen stuff and some of my pictures on the wall. A washer and dryer, but there's nowhere to put them, and that will have to wait. Daniel, all I'm asking is what any girl in the village would ask for. And I can pay for it."

My remark about what any girl in the village would want hit home more than anything I could have said.

Daniel looked down at me because I was still standing, and he said, "I'll pay for it."

He said this with such finality that I didn't argue. Then I sat down and said softly, "I've had my say. It's your turn now. What can I do?"

"Please don't run away when we don't agree on things. And maybe after you finish your work for the day, you could try to stop thinking about it. Or at least tell me what you're thinking. I just want you to listen to me sometimes, to really listen. And, Laura, please don't swear at me."

I was in his arms then, exhausted and shaking, thinking how close we'd come to ending our relationship.

Chapter 30

I started to try and confine my writing to the morning and, after lunch, would locate the books, articles and page numbers that I needed to reference my work. This latter task was boring and tedious and broke up the intensity of the way in which I was working, but I was much happier.

Daniel's senses were closer to the surface than mine, and when he carved, he was always aware of the sound of the ocean, of the wind and of the birds. I got into the habit of making coffee in the afternoon and taking our cups into his workroom. On those occasions we would talk. I became fascinated with his explanations of the processes that led to a finished piece of work. The design, he said, was already in the thin pieces of gold and silver, and he had to lift that design out of it. He needed to be aware of the elements in order to be open to discovering the design. I began to realize that Daniel had a deeply spiritual side.

I spent hours planning the decoration of his house. Jenn, whom I'd neglected because I'd been so obsessed in my work, was very happy that I was in the moment again. She often came over after school, and we discussed the merits of linoleum, rugs and furniture in the Sears catalogue. Because shipping furniture from anywhere else was a huge logistical endeavor, I was pretty much restricted to what was in the catalogue, at least as far as large items went. But the selection and quality were pretty good.

Jenn and I had a lot of fun writing down the measurements of various items of furniture and then using coffee mugs to delineate exactly how these might fit in the house. Daniel, who otherwise offered little comment on my interior decorating ideas, was hugely amused and even laughed outright when Jenn and I would move the "furniture" around.

Nadine was also an enthusiastic participant in my new venture. Both she and Chris often came over for dinner, and Daniel and I went over there. I cooked when they came to our house, and Nadine and I shared ideas about putting together meals from the limited meat and produce at the Band Store.

In planning the decoration of Daniel's house, I realized that I had no idea what kind of savings he had. One rainy morning when I was working, the phone rang. At some level I realized that it was Daniel's turn to answer.

"It's for you, Laura; it's someone named O'Donnell, Fitzgerald, and someone."

"It's my law firm."

I got up and took the phone, and a pleasant female voice said, "Miss Fitzgerald? Please hold for Mr. Richard Murphy."

In a moment, Richard was on the line. "Richard, how's it going now that you can't even dial a number?"

"Hey sweetums. It's my exemplary work. I won two big cases this month. The upside is I get more office privileges." He laughed.

"Well, then, I take my insult back. Congratulations."

We chatted for a minute. Then Richard asked me how my Harlequin romance was coming along.

"Heaven, now."

"What happened before heaven?"

"Adjustments."

"You mean he's in the room and you can't talk?"

"Exactly."

"I guess I can get the details when I see you. Have you decided for sure what you want to do with your interest?'

"I want the money to be there if I need it, so don't invest it... please."

"Alright. I'll deposit it for you. And, I must tell you, I am coming to Vancouver at the end of January. So, we can get together then?"

"Yes," I replied happily.

"Okay, sweetums. Love you and take care."

"Love you too," I said and hung up.

I returned to my work. Sometime later, Daniel came into the kitchen and made a pot of coffee. When it was ready, he handed me a cup. I took it, absently setting it down on the table.

"Laura?"

"Mmm?" I replied.

"You love someone named Richard?"

I put my pencil down and smiled. "Yes, very much."

Daniel raised his eyebrows. "His name is Richard Murphy, and he's my lawyer…and…" I paused to give my statement emphasis. "I've known him since I was 8 years old. Maybe younger."

Daniel looked baffled. I told him about my life-long friendship with Richard, who was still a friend, but who also administered my grandfather's estate. "Daniel," I said softly. We need to talk about money. Can we talk about that?"

"Sure," he replied.

When we were both sitting at the kitchen table, I searched for the appropriate words. "Daniel, why do you think that you should pay for everything?"

"Guess I never thought about it. Maybe because it's the way Charlie has always done it; maybe it's the traditional way. And, Laura, I guess I need to prove that I can take care of you."

"I think we need to share how much money we have, and I think I need to ask you to let me spend some of my money. That's the way people do it today. It's part of the partnership, and it's awkward for me because I don't know how much to spend to get the things I want for around here. If I could pay for it, it would just be more comfortable for me."

"Well, what if things don't work out? What's going to happen to all that stuff?" He looked genuinely worried.

"I can't think like that. We had a hard time for a while. And now we're both working to make things better. And they *are* better. I'm going with the idea that things are going to work out…and let's say they don't. Why would I be upset about losing some furniture?"

I paused, searching for my words again. "You've earned the money that you have. I get most of mine handed to me. If I'd earned the money, I'd probably feel a lot differently."

He nodded. I continued. "The other thing, Daniel, is that you and Charlie have been spending hours planning your potlatch. I don't want to take away from the money you need for that."

"Well, yeah, sure, that'll cost a lot of money."

Taking a breath, I asked, "How much money do you have?"

It was a considerable amount. I was impressed that Daniel had saved so much in the seven years since Matt and he had bought the seiner, although I didn't know how much of that had come from his work at carving.

"Do you want to know how much I have?"

"I'm not sure."

I told him anyway: about the principal and the yearly interest on my grandfather's estate that I got every year. This interest was enough to pay for university...and then some, and I'd worked most summers since I'd started school.

"The thing is, Daniel, I'd feel a lot better if I had some financial input into the household. I mean, as long as you're in charge, it's kind of like you're in control, and that makes me feel uncomfortable."

"Well, what do you want to do?"

Excited, I said, "Let me buy the furniture and stuff for the house. Then I don't have to worry about taking away from your potlatch money. And maybe we could open a joint checking account and put an equal amount of money in it every month for groceries and bills and stuff."

Daniel considered this. Finally, he said, "It's okay for you to pay for groceries, unless I happen to be at the store. But, I mean, would you expect me to pay for bills and furniture at your place down there in North Vancouver?"

"I guess not."

"Well then, let me pay for your redecorations here. To tell the truth, I'm looking forward to having some new things around here. And when we go down to the Coast, you can pay for the household bills, and I'll pay for the groceries."

It was a compromise that both of us were comfortable with. But the reason that I always remembered this conversation was because I saw how very important it was to talk.

Perhaps because I was happier, I started to adjust to the winter rains and, on the odd clear day, walked up to the Reservoir and sometimes to the cemetery at Old Town. At least once a week, rain or no rain, I went to Maggie's. Our talks were now a mixture of her past, of the past of the Heiltsuk and the goings-on of the present. I became an expert at feeding her the multiple strands of cedar as she wove her baskets.

Sometimes in the evenings, Daniel and I would go for a walk. On those evenings when I couldn't seem to let go of my work, I'd tell Daniel what I was thinking about. He remarked that I had so many streams of thought running through my head that it was no wonder that I was "lost in space." By discussing my ideas out loud with him, we were communicating, and he often offered helpful insights. Our talks would also lead to his sharing the challenges he faced in his work, as well as the rewards. He had an obligation to finish pieces that had been commissioned. It was double what it had been a few years ago. I asked him if he'd ever considered doing carving full-time.

"No, I won't ever do that. I love fishing, Laura. I can't say exactly why. Being out on the ocean, maybe. The physical work. It kind of clears my mind. Maybe it makes me a better carver."

Daniel and I agreed that we'd stay at the Passage until January, when I would hopefully be finished the rough draft of my thesis. Then we'd go to my place until the herring season started in mid-March.

I was a bit disappointed about missing Christmas with Mom and Jake, but when Daniel suggested that I go there alone for the holidays, I told him that my place was with him and that maybe we could spend the following Christmas with my family.

I did, however, decide to fly down to Vancouver for a few days before Christmas to visit Mom and Jake and to do some Christmas shopping. On an impulse, I invited Jenn to come with me. Her excitement over the upcoming trip was overwhelming. She came by every day after school and asked me a thousand questions about Vancouver.

"It's not that much different from Chilliwack, hon, except for the skyscrapers."

"Will we see them?"

"Sure. We'll go shopping right there downtown in the middle of them."

One day, she came over, looking dejected and said, "I don't have a proper suitcase."

"That's okay, Jenn. I have several that I brought my stuff up in, and you can use one of those."

Daniel, who'd been working in the other room, came out. "Jenny, if I hear one more word about all the things that you're worried about for this trip, I'm going to go crazy."

Jenn, who was in no way intimidated by Daniel, quickly replied,

"Well, that's easy for you to say now, isn't it? Because haven't you been to Vancouver lots of times when you had that girlfriend down there, eh Uncle Daniel?"

I raised my eyebrows. "Is this something I want to know about?"

There was humor in Daniel's eyes, but he replied with a simple, "No." Then he continued. "You women are driving me crazy. I think I'll go to the Hotel for coffee."

"Can I come and get an ice cream?" asked Jenn. "Pleasse, Uncle Daniel?"

"Can I come as well?" I asked. "I want a hamburger."

Daniel nodded. "Well, yeah, sure."

At the restaurant, the lady who served us was on the Dodd side of the village faction. She was fine with Daniel and Jenn but took my order while mumbling something under her breath, and she slammed my hamburger down when it was ready.

I sighed and started to eat.

"What was that all about?" asked Daniel.

"I don't know for sure, but I assume she's on the Dodd side of the Lyle Dodd faction," I replied.

"Well, yeah, she would be," he said.

"She's rude to me and Nadine when we come in here. I just ignore it like you said I should." There was some hurt in my voice.

"I didn't know it was that bad."

"Well, maybe you weren't listening to me. How come she's not rude to you?"

"I don't know. Maybe because I'm a man. Maybe she thinks I have a stronger position than you do."

"How's the Lyle Dodd rift going?" Jenn asked conversationally.

I assumed she must have overheard the adult conversation on this topic. It must not be playing out at the school, however, because she hadn't mentioned that.

Daniel and I grinned, but he looked at her. "It's not to talk about right now, Jenny."

The tone of his voice stopped her from pursuing the topic further. Instead, her little girl curiosity switched to questions about Daniel and me.

"Grandpa told me that lots of Heiltsuk people don't get married in a church because they don't believe in it, but that they are really just as married as anyone else. Are you guys married like that?" she asked.

"More or less." Daniel smiled.

"In my culture, Jenn," I said, but I was looking at Daniel. "That would be the Irish culture, marriage in a church is a very important tradition."

Jenn was oblivious to the interchange between Daniel and me and continued on with her concerns. "Well, when can I start calling you, 'Aunty Laura'? I mean, especially if we're going to be in Vancouver. Someone might think you stole me if we're not related."

Daniel and I burst out laughing. Jenn regarded us with chagrin.

I put my arm around her. "You can start calling me Aunty Laura right this minute, honey."

Chapter 31

Because I was seeing everything through Jenn's eyes, downtown Vancouver was a magical place. Fascinated by all the "fancy people," she held my hand in a tight grip, as we strolled down Georgia Street. In the children's department at Eaton's and the Bay, she completely forgot about me, as she darted from rack to rack. The same happened in the toy department, where we went to get gifts for Matt and Laney's children. I told her sternly that she had to stay close to me.

Later, when I would think back to this time, I guessed she'd said, "Look at this, Aunty Laura" about a hundred times.

Chief Charlie had given Jenn fifty dollars to spend in Vancouver and had sternly told me not to spend my own money. He was not a rich man, and this was a lot of money, but I ignored his directive and happily paid for many of her gifts, as well as for several outfits for her. She whispered to me that maybe Grandpa would be mad, but I told her that it was a strong Irish tradition to give money and presents to one's nieces. And this was the truth.

I couldn't resist spending one of the four nights we were in the Lower Mainland at the Hotel Vancouver. The streets were filled with Christmas lights and it was very beautiful in the evenings. I ordered room service, and we ate on a table overlooking the busy traffic, businesspeople, and shoppers below. Then we went to the poolroom. Jenn was in awe of the pool and Jacuzzi, and we stayed in the poolroom until I was so wrinkled, I couldn't stand it.

My mother made an early Christmas dinner on the 23rd and invited the whole family. Joanna, my dear friend, was also invited. She had continued her research in Borneo until just a few weeks before and we had so much to catch up on. I visited with her and with my cousins until late into the night. Everyone said they were eating and drinking too much and carried on anyway. My mother, with her impeccable manners and grace, made Jenn feel very welcome, and Jake went out of his way to give her attention.

Aside from shopping and eating in restaurants, Jenn was very impressed with my house. I tucked her into the guest room each night, carefully folding down cotton sheets and the down comforter from her perfect face. She would rattle on and on about the day and then quickly fall asleep. Looking at her, I thought that I would very much like to have a daughter like her, that maybe, someday, Daniel and I could have a daughter like her.

One night, after Jenn was sleeping, I wandered around the house, trying to picture how Daniel would view my home. I realized his awareness of his surroundings was not dependent on furniture or en-suite bathrooms. He would be aware of the atmosphere and of a good place to do his work.

I turned the light on in my study, which was on the second floor of the house. Looking around, I focused on the large windows that over-looked Deep Cove. There were three additional rooms upstairs: my bed-room, the guest bedroom and an empty bedroom. The study is where Daniel should do his work, I thought. Here, he could feel the outside environment that was so important to him when he worked, and that I was oblivious to.

The following day, I got Jake and one of his friends to move the furniture from the study into the empty bedroom.

We returned to the Passage on Christmas Eve morning. Loading everything up, Daniel remarked that we must have pretty much bought out the whole city. On the drive to the village, Jenn talked non-stop. There were the skyscrapers, the Hotel Vancouver, my beautiful house, my wonderful relations and so on.

"And did Aunty Laura spend her entire fortune?" asked Daniel. I knew he was teasing me.

"Well, maybe not all of it. She gave me a lot though. You know, for presents and clothes. It's an Irish tradition, Uncle Daniel," she chirped.

"I'm sure it is. You better be sure and tell Grandpa about it being a serious Irish tradition and all."

"Am I going to hear about Chief Charlie's disapproval via you later on?" I asked Daniel.

"Maybe. Maybe not." But he was smiling.

We spent Christmas Eve at Chief Charlie's, visiting with many guests and relatives. I spent a lot of time talking with Maggie and gave her some herbal remedies for arthritis that my mother had put together. The next day was Christmas Day, when Laney and I, along with Edith and one of her daughters, would help Rose with the traditional Christmas dinner. I was tired, and Daniel and I left early.

When we were about to leave, Chief Charlie said that he'd been meaning to tell me for some time that, as I was now a member of the family, I should call him simply, 'Charlie.' I was warmed by this public acceptance into the family and thanked him. "Thank you, Chief Charlie" was my response.

This was met with hoots and laughter. Smiling, I said, "I mean, thank you, Charlie."

Daniel and I opened our presents the following morning. Laney and I had talked over what to get Matt and Daniel for Christmas. She told me their pants, jackets and "so on" for fishing were completely worn-out, so I'd bought new sets at a specialty store in Vancouver.

Daniel handed me a shoe box that was wrapped from pages of the *Vancouver Sun*. Inside, were some beautifully crafted, drop gold earrings, that he had delicately carved with raven motifs. There were also several folded-over pieces of paper from the Sears catalogue. On these were pictures of a sink, a washer and a dryer, and a sketched picture of the tub that was on the porch. I looked at him, puzzled. He smiled. "That's part of my gift: a washer, dryer, and I think they call it a vanity. I would also like to just move the tub from the porch and put a shower head on it."

"But there's no room for these, Daniel."

"There will be. I'm going to put an addition off the bathroom and fit those in there…and build some closet space too."

I felt tears welling up in my eyes. He came over and hugged me. "You're supposed to be happy when you get presents."

"It's not that, Daniel. It's not the actual presents. It's that you're giving me so many pieces of your home."

He looked at me for a bit and said, "You're different than any woman I've ever met, Laura. And I love you."

Nadine came over halfway through Christmas morning with a conspiratorial look on her face. I raised my eyebrows in a question, and she shyly extended her left hand. On the third finger was a shiny, solitaire diamond. I gave an exclamation of happiness and hugged her tightly. Over coffee, she discussed Chris' and her plans for their marriage.

"I'd like you to be my bridesmaid, Laura. I just want one. It's going to be very simple. Just my family and Chris and a few friends. We're going to get married in the afternoon and then fly to Hawaii for ten days in February. You and Daniel will be on the Coast then?"

"Yes. And, of course I'll be your bridesmaid."

"It's pretty soon, I know," she said. "But, we're both sure. And we want children, lots of children. And I want to get started on that. When we get back from Hawaii, I'll start to slowly go off my medication and then try to get pregnant right away. We've done some research. Usually the pregnancy overrides the illness after the first trimester."

Even though it was going to be a small wedding, Nadine and I excitedly talked about the details.

I told Daniel that I could wait for the renovations until fishing season started, but he said that he wanted to get it done and that he and Matt were going to start on it right after Boxing Day.

While Daniel and Matt worked outside, Nadine, Jenn and I painted inside. It was a rare, clear day, late in the afternoon, with the last of the sunlight fading, and we'd almost completed the painting before evening. Jenn was putting some finishing touches around the balcony door. Suddenly, a huge black raven hit the glass door with enormous force and then crashed down onto the deck. All of us were startled, but Jenn screamed, dropped her paintbrush and started to cry.

I tried to comfort her, but her sobs only grew worse. Daniel came in just then, and it was to him that she ran, throwing her arms around his waist. He gently stroked her hair and whispered, "Shh Jenny," until the sobbing slowed.

"Now listen, honey," he said softly. "You've seen lots of hurt and dead birds. This one just hit the window and scared you is all."

"No, Uncle Daniel, I saw it coming. It was like that bird was wanting to talk to me," she sobbed.

For some reason, a shiver went up my spine. Daniel didn't discount what Jenn had said but told her, "I guess maybe that bird did want to talk to you, Jenny. Maybe that raven saw how beautiful you are, and you know how a raven loves beautiful things. So, it wanted to talk to you and just forgot that there was a window between you."

"Yes," whispered Jenn, still tightly gripping Daniel. In a minute or so, her breathing calmed, and she said she wanted to look at that raven. All of us went out to the deck and saw that the beautiful bird had a smashed head and a broken wing. It was dead.

"Uncle Daniel, can you bury that bird?"

"Sure, honey, but first, I'm going to take you home," he answered quietly.

When he returned, I sensed that Daniel was agitated. It was obvious that the event with the raven had affected him in some way. I asked him about it, and he started to say something but then shook his head; I knew he didn't want talk about it.

I had only a few days to admire my new home before we left for the Lower Mainland. I think that Daniel had some misgivings about going, but if he did, he kept these to himself.

I was very anxious to make him feel that he was a part of my home and asked him if he wanted to get anything to put in the rooms or to add anything. He smiled and said, "Well, this is a beautiful home, Laura. It's very comfortable; it feels like a home. And, anyway, those pieces you talk about; they are right here, inside of me, and I brought them along." He paused for a few seconds and added, "Although after that big speech, I have to tell you: I'm going to like working in that room with all those windows. And, no—a skylight won't be necessary."

I started the job of transferring my thesis onto a word processor, and Daniel continued with his carving. I had considered paying someone to type up my draft, but I was editing as I went through it, so there was no need for that. Still, it was tedious to sit in front of the screen all day, and I was happy to stop working by late afternoon. After a few days, Daniel asked me when I was going to get my hot tub going. It was located on the deck, facing the ocean. I'd never used it.

"I haven't ever used it, Daniel. Maybe because I'm gone a lot in the field; I just never got around to it. Do you want me to get it going?"

"Yeah, I'd like that Laura. It would be kind of like having a sweat, you know." Daniel often went for sweats with Charlie and other men in the village to a location "unknown" to me.

"Tomorrow I'll call someone and have them come out and get it going."

"Don't you have a manual? I could probably get it going myself."

"Sure, I can find it. But it might need some repairs. It's been sitting there for a long time."

Daniel spent the following day making the hot tub operational. He checked for leaks and cracks and pronounced it to be sound. Then he went out and got some chemicals, and by that evening, he had it going.

Having Daniel there made me appreciate the hot tub, and, with this added feature, we settled into a routine. I cooked dinner more often and even experimented with new recipes. In the evenings, we drank ice-cold Pepsi, while sitting in the hot tub. Often, before our hot tubs, we took long walks through the quiet suburbs of Deep Cove. On the weekends, we went on what I called "mall crawling," at Park Royal in West Vancouver. I was amazed to find that Daniel was like a kid, as he strolled through stores, entranced with all the merchandise. It was a new side; I took a lot of happiness from him carefully picking out shoes and even taking care with socks and underwear.

Daniel would often find trivial excuses for running errands because he really enjoyed driving my old Ford Bronco. He also sometimes attended AA meetings, saying there was a time when there were meetings at the Passage but that they'd fizzled out.

I met Joanna for lunch several times, and she came out for dinner and to spend the night when she could. I had asked for her opinion of Daniel with a simple raise of my eyebrows after she'd met him. I had thought we were alone.

"What's not to like?" She smiled. "He's smart, he works hard, he's in love with you and, as a bonus, he's good-looking."

At that exact moment, Daniel came into the kitchen. I knew he'd overheard, but he good-naturedly ignored our laughing and poured himself a cup of coffee.

We also frequently went to my mother's for dinner. From their first meeting, she liked Daniel very much. She saw in him the same things that I did. And she saw that I was very happy.

Having Daniel around in no way inhibited Jake from his usual after-dinner news commentary. Soon, Daniel began to ask Jake questions. In the resulting interchanges, I saw a new side of Daniel. Since starting on this archaeological project, I read the newspapers sporadically, but he read them regularly, and he also frequently listened to the CBC. Daniel was very much in tune with what was happening in Canada and in the rest of the world. Jokingly, he challenged Jake on some of his political discourses. This led to laughter and outrageously funny arguments between the two of them.

Soon, my brother began to look up to Daniel and to seek his opinions, not just about political matters but about affairs of the heart. His girlfriend had broken up with him, and he was devastated. I overheard him talking to Daniel about this one day, when I was coming down the hall to the kitchen.

"She said she loved me, and then a week later she's going out with a hotshot football player from West Van High," my brother said, in a dejected voice.

"Just 'cause she ditched you doesn't mean there's something wrong with you. Maybe there's something wrong with her. I mean, how real can she be if she loves you one week and ditches you the next? Let her go. Find a new girlfriend. Ask her best friend out."

They both laughed at this, and I came into the kitchen, pretending I hadn't heard a word.

Jake would often come over in the evenings, bringing junk food and videos. Both he and Daniel loved crazy, slapstick movies and teenage horror flicks. They invited me to watch these. I simply rolled my eyes and went to my study to do some more word processing. But it warmed my heart to hear the commentary and laughter coming from the living room.

One evening, when Daniel was reading the paper at the kitchen table and I was cleaning up the dinner dishes, he said, "In the newspaper, it says your father's going to be here this weekend to host a fundraising dinner."

"Yahoo for him," I replied.

"What about Jake?"

"Jake spent a couple of weeks with Father every summer until he was thirteen. All my father ever did was either criticize or ignore him. Sometimes, he hit him. The last time Mom had to practically put him kicking and screaming onto the plane And that was the end of that." There was a fair degree of bitterness in my voice, and Daniel nodded his concern.

"Maybe someday you might want to make peace with him," he said gently.

"Daniel, he's a destroyer of people. He destroyed Michael, and he nearly destroyed my mother and me. He's evil. I'll make peace with him when I dance on his grave."

"He didn't even 'nearly destroy' you, Laura. He made you strong."

I didn't understand then, as Daniel did, that adversity could lead to strength. I shook my head and said flippantly, "I'll send him a thank-you card."

But as it turned out, my father's visit to Vancouver would have an impact on us.

Daniel and I celebrated the completion of the first draft of my thesis by going out to dinner. After that, Jake came over with one movie for him and Daniel and one for me. I said that I'd watch their movie, if they'd watch mine. Much to my surprise, I enjoyed Jake's pick for the evening. We had a hot tub and were getting ready to start the second movie, when the doorbell rang. Jake answered the door. He immediately called to me.

I was stunned to see my father standing at the door. He wore an East Coast type of woolen coat over a tuxedo. His hair was thinning, and his complexion was pasty. He looked old I thought. With him, was his onetime girlfriend and now wife.

"Father," I said formally. "How are you?"

"I heard you had someone serious in your life. I thought that I would meet him."

"Daniel?" I called.

He came to the front door entrance and looked at me and at Father, with no expression on his face.

"This is Daniel Hunt. Daniel, I would like you to meet my father, Stephen Fitzgerald."

My father did not offer a hand. Adjusting the collar of his overcoat, he asked, "Are you planning on marrying this person?"

"If he'll have me," I answered softly.

"I thought I would give this picture as a gift to celebrate your union." he said coldly.

I had noticed he was holding a large picture of some sort in his hand. He leaned down and set it against the wall of the entranceway. Then he straightened and, looking at us speculatively, said, "I wonder what your what your grandfather would say?"

His wife was clearly uncomfortable, but she glanced at me with the disdain I clearly remembered from when I was 10 years old. After all these years, my father still reached out to hurt me. But in the process of growing up, I rejected his opinion and I did so now.

"I think you'd better go," I said.

"Go ahead and marry this man, but…" He paused, then shrugging again and turning said, "you won't be part of this family."

I tensed up; my voice rose by at least one octave: "Father, I belong to two families now, and you aren't part of either of them. You never have been."

He adjusted his coat again, gave a look of disdain and left.

Jake was more upset by the encounter than I was. I assured him that, while I'd been angry, I wasn't now, since I didn't "give a shit" what Father thought. Daniel reassured Jake that he didn't take what Father had said personally.

"But it wasn't fair what he said to Laura," my brother protested.

"Well, yeah, that's true. But, in case you hadn't noticed, your sister's strong with the comebacks," Daniel said, in a matter-of-fact tone.

"Yeah, she is," Jake agreed, and, then, looking at what appeared to be a picture by the door, asked, "What's that?"

"I didn't really get a look at it," I said and then went to get it and propped it up on the kitchen counter with my hands.

"My God," I whispered.

It was a photo portrait of me, taken when I was seventeen. The portrait was black and white, but the photographer had added color to parts of my outfit and to my eyes, cheeks and mouth. I was sitting on a piece of black velvet on the floor, with one hand resting on the velvet and the other draped casually over my left leg, pulled up to my chest. I clearly remembered the outfit. It was a narrow, strapped, green velvet top, with a mid-calf black nylon skirt. I'd worn it for the classical dance segment of my audition to the New York school I'd attended. The audition had been held in Toronto and my father had been in town that weekend. In a rare show of interest, he'd attended the audition and, afterwards, had insisted that the portrait be done. My eyes looked happy;

there was the barest hint of a smile because I knew that I'd done well in the audition. I'd never seen the portrait and had no idea that Father had even kept it…or where he'd kept it.

Jake said it was a beautiful picture, and I told him and Daniel the story behind it. I told them that I'd wondered, at the time, why Father had had the portrait done. I didn't comment on why he'd given it to me now. I knew his motives had been to hurt and reject me.

The photograph was a glimpse of the past and led to many questions by my brother. Questions about Michael and about Grandpa. I knew that both Mother and I had avoided discussing with Jake what life was like before we left Father. He took a keen interest in my recounting of Michael's escapades and the circumstances of his death. I told him about the day I'd found Father with the woman who was now his wife. He was old enough, I thought. Daniel simply listened, offering me reassurance with his eyes when I looked at him. We talked until well past midnight.

Chapter 32

Richard arrived a just before Valentine's Day. I met him downtown. We had had too much to drink, so I left my truck parked at his hotel and took a cab home. The minute I walked in the front door, I felt silly and apologized to Daniel for this.

He looked at me with a combination of humor and puzzlement. "Laura, I don't care if you drink...I mean, of course, unless you actually develop a problem. For me, I get sad and depressed when I drink. Sometimes, I get violent. Let's hope you never have to see that. Now go to bed, sweetheart. Tomorrow, you'll feel sick."

In the morning, I was nauseous, and my head hurt. I heard the phone ring, but its ring barely registered. It was 9 a.m. Daniel came in, gently shook me and, with a trace of humor, said, "Your lawyer is on the phone."

I picked up the phone alongside the bed, and Richard and I remonstrated about how awful we felt, although I admitted I didn't feel as bad as he did, as I didn't have meetings all day. I asked if he could come over to my place for dinner and—could he bring my truck?

Richard finished up his meetings and arrived late in the afternoon. We ordered Chinese food and ate in the living room. Jake showed up, got a coke and comfortably settled in. The conversation turned to politics and the way that Aboriginal issues were unfolding. The lawyer side of Richard was very soft spoken; it was interesting to see him and Daniel exchange views on various events. Their main topic of conversation was the direction that the Canadian government was taking in relation to various court rulings. Richard discussed the implications of the Supreme Court ruling in the Calder Case. It was ruled that the Nisga'a people of the Northern Coast of BC had existing Aboriginal title. Daniel and he also talked about their ideas on the route that the Nisga'a, Gitxsan and Wet'suweten treaty negotiations would take. I kept quiet because I didn't know much about these issues. When Richard asked me why I wasn't talking, I told him my area of expertise was the past. For once, Jake also simply listened, but it was obvious he was taking a lively interest in the conversation.

I did enter the discussion on the Indian Act and the way in which the repatriation of the Canadian Constitution would affect the Act.

The Indian Act, passed in 1876, essentially makes status Indigenous people wards of the government. The Department of Indian Affairs, who administers the Act, determines who has status and who does not. Indigenous people have been told whether they are qualified to live on reserves. Government officials, not parents, dictate where children will go to school. For a long time, First Nations people were not even allowed to leave a Reserve, unless a travel permit was issued to them by an Indian Agent.

The Indian Act dictates the lives of First Nation Canadians from the time of birth until the time of death. A person of Indigenous descent cannot necessarily have their death wishes carried out because wills are probated by the Department of Indian Affairs.

The Indian Act also determines the forms of government that bands can have, and this is based on the Euro-Canadian model, a form of government that is often directly opposed to traditional forms of government.

People who have grown up within the culture of a band can be denied status, and women who marry non-Native men lose their status. Status Indians were denied the right to vote until 1949, provincially, and 1960, federally.

Throughout its history, the Canadian government has tried to enfranchise Aboriginal people, offering land and other incentives in return for giving up Indian status. The reason for this is simple: the old goal of assimilation into the dominant society and the hope that the Indian culture, and therefore the Indian, will disappear. Very few Indigenous people are willing to give up their status because, although this means that they live under an incredibly intrusive regime; it also means that they maintain their identity as an Indigenous person.

Daniel, Richard and I talked about how a challenge to the rules for status would work under the new Charter of Rights and Freedoms.

It seemed certain that women would be able to maintain their status if they married non-Natives because of the discrimination in the clauses of the Charter.

I was more familiar with the topic of the Indian Act and the not-yet passed Charter, and my opinions were passionate. At one point, Richard rebuked me. "Laura, if you keep getting all worked up, you can't make your point."

I looked to Daniel for support, but he only smiled and said, "Well, that's true."

By the end of the evening, Richard and Daniel were clearly comfortable with each other. This left a glow in my heart; they were the two adult men I loved most in the world.

It was late when Daniel drove Richard back to his hotel. When he returned, he said he was glad he'd met Richard and that he no longer felt jealous of him.

"You were jealous of Richard?"

"Well, maybe…a bit. I mean, I know you said you were friends, but meeting him makes me understand it's true, and, also, I can see how close the two of you are, and I'm pretty sure he'd always be there for you."

Perhaps it was the nature of the day's conversation that led to the dream. It started like it always had:

In the dream, I know that Michael is going to die, but I can prevent this if only I can get to his school in time to tell him not to go waterskiing.

The dream starts with me frantically begging my father's driver to take me up Island. He doesn't appear to understand me. In desperation, I get on a city bus and go around and around the city of Victoria, until I realize the bus will not go up Island. Finally, I find a taxi driver who speeds to Michael's school. I run from the cab to the dock, just as Michael is pulling away. I scream at him to stop, but he doesn't understand me and happily waves. Continuing to scream, I watch as he speeds away far out on the lake. I watch him go down. I am quiet then, tears streaming down my face, knowing that he is dying.

That's where the dream ends. And that's where I wake up… usually…

But this time, just as Michael was about to go down, I felt a hand in mine. It was a dry, strong, man's hand. Looking up, I saw Franz Boas. He squeezed my hand and, looked at me gravely, and turned around to face the hill above the lake. I turned with him, and, there, where the school was supposed to be, was a concentration camp.

A huge crowd that I knew was mostly composed of Jewish people was being herded into an ominous gray building. Looking more closely, I saw that there were also many Indigenous people, some whose faces were unfamiliar, others whom I recognized. The Jewish people were dressed in the 1940s' style of dress. The Indigenous people were dressed in all manner of clothing, from traditional clothing, to that of the late 1800s, to the present. On the other side of the building, no Jewish people were coming out. Some Indigenous people did. But they weren't the same as the ones who had entered. They were slumped and twisted, and even, from far away, I could see that their faces wore no expression; there was no life in their eyes.

I watched this scene in horror, and then Daniel and Jenn and Kristy came into view. They're being herded into the building. I tried to break free of Franz Boas' hand, but I was just a little girl and he wouldn't let me go. I woke up, drenched with sweat and gasping for breath, holding my hand to my throat, trying to get enough air. Daniel woke up. I collapsed into his arms.

It was still night. Daniel made some tea and brought it over, sitting down beside me on the living room couch. I told him about the dream, then about other dreams I'd had. I told him about all of them: about my brother's death and about the dreams of Franz Boas. I asked what he'd thought they meant.

"That dream about your brother, maybe that's just a feeling of helplessness in not being able to stop his death."

"What about Franz Boas?"

"Well, that's interesting, Laura. Usually, when a spirit appears in a dream, it's to reveal itself as a guardian."

"Have you had dreams like that?"

"I have dreamed of the Whale, of the Orca—in a way that is different than my other dreams."

I contemplated this, and after a while Daniel said softly, "Come on, let's go to bed."

"Daniel, I want to sit up for a bit. I need to think for a while. You go ahead; I'll come to bed later."

"All right, sweetheart," he said gently. "Wake me if you need to."

What should have been the golden years of Franz Boas were marred by tragedy. In 1924, his daughter died of polio. A year later, his son was killed in a car accident. His beloved wife, Marie, was hit by a car and died in 1929.

Despite these personal tragedies, Franz Boas forged on as a champion of human rights. He spoke loudly and clearly against Nazi policies and against the discrimination of Blacks and Native American Indians. Even though he had been discriminated against in his own country, Boas would always have a deep connection and love for Germany. This would have made what happened there an impossible betrayal. Perhaps it was a blessing that he died in 1942, before the nature and enormity of Hitler's Final Solution for the Jewish people was known.

I reflected on the dream of the concentration camp. Then I whispered softly to the empty room: "Franz Boas, I don't know what you want from me. Please, just tell me, or release me from these dreams."

It would be a long time before I would dream of Franz Boas again.

Daniel had asked me what I wanted for Valentine's Day. I told him that it wasn't a big Irish tradition, and we could have dinner and 'stuff.' Daniel had just grinned at this.

I got him a card and some chocolates, and the evening after Richard left, I made a salad for dinner, while Daniel barbecued some steaks. After days of gray skies and cold, it was finally clear and balmy out. I gave him the chocolates, knowing he wasn't particularly fond of sweets. Smiling, I said, "I have to tell you that these are my favorite kind."

He laughed and reached into a jeans pocket and brought out a little box. I took the box but was afraid to open it. The question I was anticipating nevertheless surprised me.

"Will you marry me?" he asked softly.

Instead of answering, I started to cry and buried my head in his chest. After a while, he said, "Maybe you could answer the question, Laura?"

"Yes. I mean, yes, I can answer the question. The answer is 'yes.'"

He took my shoulders and stepped back. Taking the ring from its bed in the box, he put it on my finger. Then he kissed me. Pretty soon, I was beaming. We sat in the living room, and I admired the stunning ring. It was gold, with a simple setting of three equally sized diamonds.

"Daniel?" I hesitated, "Is this truly what you want?"

He paused. Then, as if searching for words, he answered, "Well, I guess it's more what you want, sweetheart. In these last months, when I think about you, you're already my wife. But you respect my traditions, and I guess I should respect yours. I know a wedding is important to you."

"Why the three diamonds, Daniel?"

"One for your world, one for mine and one for ours," he answered softly.

Chapter 33

I wanted to go to Mom's right after dinner to announce the news, and Daniel went along with this good-naturedly, although Jake already knew about it.

"How does Jake know about it?"

"I had to ask permission, and I wasn't going to ask your father, so I asked Jake."

"And of course, he said yes."

"Yeah, but I had to bargain for you." Daniel smiled.

"What?!"

"Told me he'd only give me his permission if I gave him a job fishing this summer."

"But Jake doesn't need a job," I said.

"Maybe not, but he needs experience being a man, Laura."

Jake hadn't said a word, so it was a surprise to my mother. Although, smiling, she said she'd been thinking that was the direction we were heading. I got Daniel to phone Charlie, whom I still thought of as Chief Charlie. Daniel and I talked to Charlie and Rose, and then Jenn came on the phone and said, "I knew it! I just knew it," followed by a quick, "Can I be your flower girl?"

"Of course, you can, honey," I told the excited little girl. "I wouldn't even think of asking anyone else."

Charlie was planning on being in the Lower Mainland on Band business in a few weeks and would be spending a few days with us. Daniel got back on the phone and talked about the details of his visit.

After the phone conversations were finished, Mom and I started to talk about dresses and colors and flowers, while Jake and Daniel drifted off to watch TV.

I met with George at the end of the week. He said, overall, I'd done an excellent job but some editing and changes were necessary. We spent the greater part of a day going over each chapter of my thesis. There were a few weak areas, which required clarification and more referencing. Some of the sections needed to be condensed and some, to be expanded on. We set a tentative date for my thesis defense, for May. Many people in the department would be away, but I told him I didn't need an audience and that I wanted to get it finished.

Nadine flew down a week before her wedding, and I helped her, her mother and her sister with the details. The entire event was to take place in a small banquet room in a hotel 'downtown,' as Nadine called it, and 'Overtown,' as I called it. I had decided that my wedding gift for Nadine would be some clothes for Hawaii, and we had a lot of fun shopping. I added a new anorak to the gift. Nadine's was getting worn-out; she'd need one when she got back to the Passage.

Nadine was very happy about my engagement. Her observation was that for a while it had really seemed to her as if the two of us were leading parallel lives. She had regained the easygoing manner and that carefree way that she had about her. We were now able to talk about the night of Allie's death and the events that followed. Even as we were preparing to be 'Passage wives,' we agreed that an advantage to living in the city was anonymity. We also agreed that the village rift over Allie's death was often difficult to know how to cope with.

Nadine's wedding was short, simple and beautiful. Tears ran freely down my face when they said their vows. Daniel told me I'd better wash the mascara off my face because I was going to ruin the pictures.

A few days after Nadine and Chris's wedding, Charlie spent two nights with us. He enjoyed my house very much, and knowing that he was wondering, I simply told him that my grandfather left it to me.

Mom invited Charlie over for dinner on the second night he was with us. Within an hour, she'd learned more about his job and the way a Band Council was run than I'd learned in the last eight months.

Charlie and Mother's conversation turned to the wedding.

"When do you plan to have the wedding?" Charlie asked, turning to Daniel.

"Haven't decided yet," Daniel answered.

"Well, maybe you should get married at that big potlatch, when you take your titles."

"Sure," Daniel agreed.

"That's not when I want to get married," I said firmly.

"Why not?" Daniel asked, turning to me.

"Because it is too far off, and I don't want my wedding day to get mixed up with your rise to royal status."

This remark elicited laughter from Charlie and Daniel and led to a long explanation by Chief Charlie on the traditions surrounding his titles being passed on to Daniel.

My mother picked up the subject of a date again. "When would you like to get married, Laura?"

"I think we should get married this July. It can be a slow month for fishing. And, anyway, a chief should have a wife before he becomes a chief. Maggie said that."

"Well, yeah, sure, but they should, usually, also have children," said Charlie.

"Maybe we can have one by then." I replied.

"July works fine for me," said Mom.

"Does July work for you, Daniel?" asked Jake, mimicking my mother's voice.

Daniel shrugged his shoulders, and the two of them burst out laughing.

Charlie ignored them and said, simply, "It works okay for me too. Daniel, is this going to be costly?"

"Well, now, that doesn't matter," I said. "My family will pay for everything. Mother would be insulted if you even suggested paying for anything. It's an Irish tradition. The bride's family pays for everything. Charlie, I respect your traditions, but this is one of my traditions that I have to keep if I expect to hold my head up down here in Vancouver."

"Laura is absolutely right about that, Charlie," said my mother in a firm voice.

When we were undressing for bed, Daniel said that although he knew I could lie like a trooper, he had no idea my mother could too. "It's an Irish tradition," I shot back at him.

In less than two weeks, we would be heading back to the Passage. Daniel worked long hours to complete his carving, and I worked on my thesis and consulted over the phone and twice in person with George. Going for long walks by myself, I thought that Daniel and I could achieve a nice balance in our lives between the Passage and the

Lower Mainland. I felt happy and secure in my love for him. Not only did I have these feelings, but I was grateful for what I had and found myself thanking some unknown power for the blessings in my life. But gratitude is no guarantee against fortune, or misfortune.

One morning when we were working, the phone rang. It was Daniel's turn to pick it up; working in my study, I ignored it. A few moments later, he came into the room. His face carried a lack of expression, which told me that there was something terribly wrong. "Jenny's been in an accident. She's being airlifted down here. Charlie's coming with her. We need to go to the hospital—Overtown."

"What happened to her?"

"He didn't say. Just that it's pretty bad."

We were quiet on the drive over. In the Emergency Room, we held hands, waiting for Jenn and Charlie. It had taken us a long time to reach Vancouver General Hospital because of the rush-hour traffic; we only had to wait about half an hour for Jenn to come in. The only reason we even knew she had arrived was that Charlie came out looking for us.

He didn't say anything, just that they were checking her now. I wanted to ask him what had happened, but Daniel didn't do so, so I stayed quiet. A short while later, a doctor came out and said, "Mr. Hunt?"

All three of us stood up; he addressed his remarks to all of us.

"I'm Dr. Lee. I'll be the Chief Surgeon operating on Jenny. When the vehicle struck her, she instinctively put her arm up to protect her head, and her arm is badly broken. But that isn't going to be a problem. Our biggest concern is that she has significant internal injuries. We're preparing her for surgery right now. The good news is that she does not appear to have any head injuries."

"Will she live?" whispered Charlie.

The surgeon hesitated and then said simply, "I don't know."

Charlie sank back down into the chair, his face unreadable. I could only see his tension by the way his hands gripped the steel arms of the waiting room chair. Daniel's face was also unreadable.

There are times when the only comfort one can offer is silence. I tried to be useful by getting food and coffee. The silence was broken when Chief Charlie said, in a voice that was as non-committal as if he had been describing the weather, "It was Lyle Dodd." He then told us what had happened.

"Rose sent Jenn down to the store to pick up some bread and

said she could get an ice cream there at the Hotel as well. Dodd was coming up from off the wharf with a load of something he'd picked up. He hit her when she was crossing the street, on her way back from the Hotel. Threw her up into the air and then onto the side of the road. And then he just kept on going. Sergeant MacCallum came to the hospital and told me this. Said Dodd had been drinking."

"Did he hit her on purpose?" I asked.

"I don't know," answered Charlie.

Several hours passed before the surgeon came out. His face was tired and drawn. We stood up.

"She made it through the surgery, but there was a lot of internal damage," said Dr. Lee. She's in pretty bad shape. The next seventy-two hours will be critical."

"Can we see her?" I asked.

"Yes, one of you can stay with her overnight, and the others can see her for a minute. She should be in the Intensive Care Unit soon. I'll get the nurse to come for you."

Shortly after, we were escorted through a labyrinth of corridors to Intensive Care.

Jenn looked so tiny and vulnerable in the bed. Her face had a pallor that sent warning signs to my heart. There were tubes everywhere, and she was hooked up to a myriad of machines. Except for her casted arm and one bruise on the side of her head, there was nothing visible to indicate the extent of her injuries.

Daniel and I offered what comfort we could to Charlie, as he settled down in a chair next to Jenn's bed. We stayed as long as they let us, and I tucked my phone number into Charlie's shirt pocket. We told him we'd be back early in the morning.

On the way home, we didn't talk because there wasn't anything to say. Still, even though the surgeon had said that she was in bad shape, I think we assumed that she'd be all right. We were exhausted and went straight to bed. I was woken sometime around dawn by the phone ringing. I was scrambling to remember if it was Daniel's or my turn to pick it up. Then I heard Daniel's voice, and I came awake. He slowly hung up the receiver. His face was blank.

"Daniel?" I asked.

"That was Charlie. Jenny died a few minutes ago. They did everything they could, but she died."

Chapter 34

Although I had just been told that Jenn was dead, I did not react. I searched for some emotion but found none. It did seem as if the world had tilted in some strange, surreal way, and I felt separated from myself.

Daniel, his voice sounding heavy and weary, said that he would go and pay his respects to Jenny and get Charlie from the hospital. No, I would not go. I wanted to remember Jenn alive. I asked Daniel if Rose would come down, and he said, "She'll see her soon enough."

When Daniel left, I called my mother, still wondering why I wasn't crying. She told me they would need to eat, and I should come over to help her. She said she would pick me up in twenty minutes. Daniel called my mother's a couple of hours later and said they'd be coming over to North Vancouver. Maybe he and Charlie could go to my place before dinner to clean up. I said I'd meet them there.

When they arrived, I asked Charlie if he needed to rest for a while. He seemed a bit dazed and went to lie down in the guest room. Daniel went out and sat on the deck and stared out to the sea. He didn't seem to want to talk, and I let him be.

My mother served a roast beef meal, although everyone just picked at the food. At the beginning of the meal, Charlie's posture was one of defeat, but my mother picked up the strands of the conversation they'd had just a few days before. With her gentle questioning, he began to sit taller in his chair. Through my haze, I saw how deep my mother, Ann Fitzgerald's, beauty went.

Sometime during the night, I woke up to the sound of muffled sobs coming from the guest room. Some instinct told me that I could offer Charlie some comfort. I got out of bed. Daniel gently gripped my arm and whispered, "Let him be."

"No," I replied.

I knocked gently on the door and went in. Charlie was sitting on the edge of the bed, slumped forward, with his head in his hands. I sat next to him on the bed and, reaching over, placed my hand over his.

He was saying Jenn's name over and over again, as well as a name that I didn't recognize. Later, Daniel told me that this was the name of his son who had drowned. After a while, measured, deep breaths replaced the sobbing. I remained silent. There was, really, nothing to say. He was gripping my hand tightly. "That's a beautiful picture of you, Laura."

I followed his gaze to the picture my father had brought. Not sure of what to do with it, I had put it in the guest room, where it was leaning against the wall.

"Thank you, Charlie. The truth is, I don't want it and don't know what to do with it."

"Well, I don't know why that is. It's a great accomplishment to be a dancer. Maybe you should give that picture to me, and I can show people that my daughter is a dancer. Then, later, if you want, you can have it back."

"I would be honored to give it to you, Charlie."

We were both silent for a while, and then, as if it had come from somewhere else, a thought made its way to my voice. "I'd like to get Jenn's casket, and you know, her clothes. The thing is, I think I know what she would like. I'd like to do that, if you'll let me."

"Well sure, Laura. Jenny would like that."

Jennifer Hunt was buried in Old Town, in Waglisla, on a Thursday afternoon in March, in a small white coffin that I'd picked out in a funeral home in North Vancouver. The day after I had volunteered to get the casket and clothes, I told my mother that I was terrified to do it.

"Shh," she said. "I'll come with you. But you can't fall apart, Laura, at least not yet. They are going to need food, a calm home to be in and comfort. Right now, you need to be strong."

I told the undertaker that it would be an open casket and that Jenn should look nice, and then I went shopping to find her funeral clothes. My mother helped me, and we picked out a frilly white dress, with long, loose sleeves that would hide her broken arm. We found a wide pink ribbon to fit around the waist of the dress because pink was Jenn's favorite color.

Daniel spoke for Jenn. He and Chief Charlie had written the eulogy together. The Dodd faction no longer had any moral position, but Charlie had decided it was time for a healing to take place. I don't know what part of the eulogy Daniel wrote and what part Charlie wrote, but when he spoke, Daniel captured in words a true picture of the artless and delightful little girl that had been lost. When he had finished paying tribute to Jenn, he said a few words that were obviously related to the rift and then said, simply, that it was over.

Because I was part of the family, I stood at the front of the church, while groups of people came forward to pay their respects to Jenn and to the family. And after all my fears, seeing her dead was not frightening. I thought she looked like a flower girl.

Being part of the family also meant that I stayed at the reception until almost the last person had left. When I saw that I could finally go, I walked home alone. When I got there, I sat on the deck, looked out to the Passage, and remembered the day that Jenn and I had danced along the edge of the surf. Suddenly, I was overcome with rage, and, going down to the fire pit, I kicked the stones about, until I had made a mess of it. Exhausted, I sat on the bench next to the fire pit and finally, finally, began to cry.

Daniel came home then, sat next to and held me tightly. He never did comment on the fire pit or my ruined shoes or the ashes on my dress. After a while, I told Daniel I needed to sleep; he said that he did too. He undid the zipper on my black dress. I didn't bother to put my nightgown on but fell asleep in my underwear. My last thought was that the rift in the village was over and that it had begun and ended in a death.

Chapter 35

Lyle Dodd was charged with impaired driving and vehicular manslaughter. He said that he'd known that he'd hit someone but had gotten scared and had kept on driving. He didn't know it was Jenny Hunt whom he'd hit. Dodd was imprisoned in the Lower Mainland and would be sentenced in the fall.

Daniel left for the March herring runs and came home, like all the fishermen did, when he could. Before he left, we set up a desk, along with my computer, next to the window in his workroom. I tried to work on my thesis but found myself staring out at the Passage, thinking about Jenn. I went over and over the times we had gone swimming at the Reservoir, our Christmas vacation, our dance on the beach and the countless times we visited and went for ice cream. I had never told her how much I treasured her, how much I loved her. When she was alive, I hadn't even thought about it.

Staring out the window, I would catch myself picking on the cuticle of my thumb, a habit that I'd believe had been broken. And at night, lying alone in bed, the rhythm of the foghorn worked its way into my memories of Jenn.

Finally, I just stopped working on my thesis, realizing that I would miss the May deadline and not caring. George Clements was very sympathetic and said I could do it in the fall, after he was back from the field.

Nadine and I had coffee almost every day. She was more balanced than I and only worked four hours a day because after that, she said, the results of her work were "nonsense."

She had started jogging every morning to get in shape for when she would start coming off her medication in May. Nadine thought problems with sleeping would be her biggest hurdle. She planned on using physical exercise to tire her out. She invited me to go jogging, but I declined, saying it wasn't my thing.

"But walking is," she said, smiling. And so, usually every other day, we walked up to Maggie's, to Old Town, or to the Reservoir. Because Nadine was so polite and easygoing, Maggie liked her instantly. Not only that, but Nadine was fascinated by the art of making baskets, and soon Maggie acquired her as an apprentice. Sometimes we talked about Native heritage and stories, but mostly the three of us just gossiped. We talked with Maggie about how nice it was that the village rift was over. Nadine and I noticed that people who had looked away now nodded at us and said, "Mmph." The girls in the Café and at the Band Store were no longer rude.

Sometimes, Nadine, Maggie and I spoke about my wedding. Maggie also told me that the status of the Hunt family had gone way up since Daniel had said the rift was over. It was a statement of healing and brought relief to the village. "After that big potlatch, I guess the Whale Clan will be Number One again; it's been quite a few years."

Traditionally in the Passage, a death is marked by a year of mourning. This is a time when the family is given the love and support of the community to go through the process of grief. They are free to give up any community responsibilities, if they choose to. Charlie, Rose, Daniel and I discussed whether to continue with the wedding in July. I knew that Rose and Charlie were taking Jenn's death very hard, as was I, but of course it was far worse for them.

Daniel and Charlie consulted with Maggie, who repeated the conversation to me. "She was a child, Laura, not, in our culture, a fully-formed person. It would be no disrespect to her that you have your wedding. And we must keep on with living. The wedding will be good for Charlie and Rose."

Maggie paused after this statement, chuckled and said, "For all I know, I might be dead myself next year and I want to go to that wedding."

One evening, when Daniel was home and we were over at Chris and Nadine's for dinner, Daniel suggested that we take his boat out if we wanted to explore or visit the springs.

I looked at him in mock surprise and said, "You trust me with your boat?"

He grinned and replied, "Not really. But I trust Nadine. Maybe she can teach you how to handle that boat."

After that, Nadine and I often used Daniel's boat to go the springs and other places where we would sit on a beach, or on rock outcroppings or on a bluff and eat lunch we'd bought at the Hotel.

One day, when we were eating lunch at the springs, I asked Nadine how she could reconcile herself to God when Allie died. She knew that I was really talking about Jenn.

"At first, I didn't. I was just angry at God. I asked myself how everything that happened could be God's will. I guess that's where the concept of free will comes in. Not everything that happens can be God's desire because then we wouldn't have free will."

She paused, taking a moment to find her words. "Or, maybe everything that happens is God's will. Maybe it doesn't matter. When I started to get over that first horrible grief after Allie died, I remembered something my father told me a long time ago. It's that our lives and other lives, and everything that is in the world, is like this big tapestry, and all I can see is one tiny square. If I could see the big picture, then I'd understand why things happen and how God weaves good from the bad things that happen." Nadine paused again, then said, "If you're looking for God, Laura, you have to look inside your heart."

"Why don't you go to church?" I asked.

"Well, I like that new United Church minister, and maybe I will go to some services, but the God of my understanding is much too large to fit into a church," she replied.

I felt a kind of shiver through my body. "That's the strangest thing, Nadine. My grandfather said those exact same words to me when I was a little girl."

"Well," she said, grinning. "I guess he was a wise man."

During dinner one evening, I asked Daniel what his concept of the Creator was. He continued to eat; I could see that he was searching for an answer to my question. "The Creator made all things and gave spirits to all things, to the trees, to the ocean, to every rock and animal and person. Human beings are the caretakers. It is expected that we treat all these things with reverence and respect. So, for example, if I don't thank the salmon for offering themselves up to my nets, then I'll be punished, and the salmon will go away."

Later that evening, tears came to my eyes, and I asked him why the Creator would allow Jenn to die. He moved closer to me on the couch and touched my hair and said that maybe there were evil spirits in the world, and maybe one of them had had a grip on Lyle Dodd. He went on to say that, usually, the Creator lets things happen to teach us a lesson. And, sometimes, maybe God wants beautiful spirits to be close by. I knew that he was thinking of the day that a raven had smashed into our window.

I noticed that Daniel did not distinguish between the terms, 'God' and 'Creator.'

Nadine and I went down to the Coast in May; we spent two nights in North Vancouver. Along with my mother, we pored over bridal and bridesmaid dresses and then ordered these from a shop in the city. The maid of honor was Laney, and the bridesmaids were Nadine, Joanna, Kristy and my cousin, Rachel. I thought the pictures of the dresses looked like the dresses of faeries. Nadine remarked how Jenn would have approved of the styles and colors. She asked me about a flower girl. I paused, searching for words. "I'll have one in the wings." In all, though, the planning of my wedding had taken my thoughts off Jenn and brought me some peace.

I told Rose and Maggie that I would find dresses for them in Vancouver. Rose had not argued with me, simply saying that she would like a dress she could wear at both weddings and funerals. A very nice saleslady showed me a navy-blue dress, with a small pocket on the right breast that Rose could put a handkerchief in for weddings and remove for funerals. The same lady put together a gray suit and blouse for Maggie.

I knew there would be questions about the absence of my father and told Daniel that I was dreading these questions. "What should I say? That there's a rift, that he's prejudiced?"

"I'll talk to Charlie and Rose, Laura."

I don't know exactly what he said, and I guess I didn't want to know. I was just grateful that Charlie, and not even Maggie, made any mention of my father.

One early evening, at the beginning of June, Daniel and I were snuggled on the bench by the fire pit, warming to the heat of the fire.

"Laura?" Daniel voiced my name as a question.

"Mmm?"

"You know, we haven't really talked about what our plans are for after we're married."

"I thought we had. You know, I want children. I want..." my voice trailed off.

Daniel never did finish sentences for me. He always let me struggle for the right words.

"I want a family. I know that you'll be a good father, and that, together, we'd make a good team for all those kids I want."

He took my hand and, smiling, said, "You mean they can come to me to be saved when you lose your temper."

I laughed and then, in a more serious voice, said, "I guess all parents face challenges, Daniel. What I know is—we'll both want and love those kids. And isn't that what's most important?"

"Sure it is. How are you going to be with me away fishing so much?"

"I don't know, Daniel. I guess I'll cope."

There was silence for a long time; then he said, "What about your career? Will you maybe start to think that you're missing out on that?"

"I've already thought about it. Yes, I think there might come a time when I want to continue with my studies. But having children and continuing with my studies don't have to be mutually exclusive. I could do my course work in the city and write up here. Anyway, it's not a pressing need right now."

"But if you do continue, you'll need to go the city."

"I suppose, but an academic semester is short, and we've already decided that we'll spend the winters at our house in the city." I stressed the *our.* "But," I continued. "I don't want to live there full-time. And it isn't just because of you, Daniel. I like living here, especially now that the rift ended. I want our children to be part of both of our worlds.

"What about the Irish culture?"

"Well, in a lot of ways, that's a convenient myth, isn't it, Daniel?"

"No, it isn't, Laura. You have a culture of your own. How are you going to teach our children that?"

"I think they'll just pick that up from me and from my family. I think our children will be accepted in both our worlds, as long as we set the example."

He changed the topic back to the possibility of my future studies. "Would you do a PhD on the Heiltsuk?"

"I don't think so. And I'm not going to work on the land claims process, although Charlie keeps hinting at it."

"Why?" asked Daniel. I could see he was surprised.

"Because I want to be removed from the politics in the village. I don't want to be in the center of any rifts. And the other thing is that I've come to realize that my frustrations come from the fact that in Archaeology, the past is often so distant that all you really get is just a whisper of culture."

Daniel had been listening carefully but then changed the subject abruptly, saying he'd better hurry because he had to go to an AA meeting.

"I thought you told me that AA fizzled out on the Reserve."

"Well it did, but Chris has been sending people down to Vancouver for treatment, and some of us got together and decided to try and get it going again."

I took Jack and Kristy out for lunch the next day. There was no work for either of them, and both were on unemployment insurance. As the result of Kristy's nagging, Jack had cut his hair and had gotten new glasses that were more flattering. He was also filling out. I thought that he was a late bloomer and was growing into some good looks.

Kristy, whom I thought had been moody the last few times I'd seen her, was back to her bubbly self.

"I'm going to a treatment center in Victoria at the end of this week," she said shyly. "It's for almost a month, and then I'll be home in time for your wedding."

"I didn't know it was that bad for you, Kristy. I'm glad that you're going," I told her.

"Dr. Sutherland told me about alcoholism being a disease. That it wasn't my fault that I have it, but it's my responsibility to deal with it. I haven't had a drink in a week. Last night I went to an Alcoholics Anonymous meeting."

"Did you see Daniel there?"

There was a pause in the conversation. Then Kristy smiled and said, "Well, I'm not allowed to say. That's why it's called Alcoholics *Anonymous*."

We laughed at Kristy's emphasis.

After lunch, our conversation turned to the possible satellite dish planned for the village. The Band Council was trying to decide whether to allow a satellite dish that would bring cable TV to the homes in the Passage. Opinions were so strongly divided that a new rift had appeared in the village.

"What do you think about cable TV?" Kristy asked.

I answered with, "What I think is this: I don't want to be on *any*one's side. If someone wants to bring it up, I say we should have it. If they don't want it, I say we shouldn't."

Kristy and I laughed at this statement, but for some reason, Jack found it hilarious and laughed even louder.

Chapter 36

I suppose that because of what happened so soon afterwards, the details of my wedding day have lost some clarity in my mind. I had hired a professional photographer, but it was Kristy's black and white pictures that make up the treasured memories of that day. To me, the events and people in these pictures are forever in the present.

There is Jake in a black tuxedo, so tall and handsome, his blonde hair trimmed neatly. Mom and I bullied him into getting it cut. He is grinning. There is Joanna, Nadine and I in our breezy, fairy dresses, sitting with our heads together on the couch at Daniel's, sharing some delightful secret. With the Passage as a backdrop, there is Maggie, sitting in a chair on the deck. I am standing behind her, with my hand on her shoulder, and on either side of me are Rose and Mother. At the kitchen table, there is Laney, adjusting the ribbons in my cousin Rachel's, hair; they are laughing.

At some point, I took the camera from Kristy and got her to pose on the deck. I wasn't much of photographer, compared to her, but the photo somehow turned out just right. She has a half-smile, and her dark eyes are full of a deeper beauty than I'd ever seen, certainly deeper than when I'd met her only a year before.

At the reception, there is Daniel and I, sitting at the head table, looking at each other in a way that leaves little doubt that we are both friends and lovers. There is Jack, looking directly into the camera. His head is tilted, and he is smiling.

There is Nadine, dancing with Richard, and they are laughing, as if they have known each other for years. And there is Charlie, dancing with his grandchildren, the youngest one just barely able to walk.

I noticed that Kristy took quite a few pictures of Richard, and at the reception, she spent a lot of time talking and dancing with him.

Later, I teased her, and she just laughed and said that he was the best guy to talk to at the wedding.

If most of the day was a blur, one moment was crystal-clear. I was so nervous when Jake walked me down the aisle of the United Church that when I got to where Daniel was standing, my hands were shaking badly. Daniel immediately took both of my hands in his and held them tightly. My anxiety slipped away, and when we said our vows, our voices were clear and strong.

By the time we got home, we were exhausted. "Laura," said Daniel. "If you want, we can consummate this marriage tomorrow."

"Not a chance, Daniel," I answered firmly. "I've got a frilly piece of nonsense to wear, and I'm right in the point of my cycle where I could get…well, not to put too fine a point on it, but pregnant tonight."

"All right then, sweetheart. I'll get out of this rig, and you put on that." He searched for the words: "That frilly thing."

When I came into the bedroom, Daniel said, "Well, now, that's a piece of work."

Daniel went fishing just a few days after the wedding. We would have our honeymoon later in the year in January. With no prompting from me, Richard suggested a week in Mexico, as a wedding present, and Daniel thought that was a great idea—telling Richard and me that maybe after six months of marriage, we'd need to get away.

Jake stayed after the wedding and was hired on as a hand on the *Caelum*. I ordered a cot from Sears and set it up for him in Daniel's workroom. It was very lively around our house when Daniel and Jake came in from fishing, and I was very happy to have my husband and my brother around to share the long summer evenings.

I settled into a routine of working on my thesis, which I was able to do now, although I still often thought of Jenn. On Sundays, I went to Charlie and Rose's for dinner. Often, I would also wander up to their place late in the afternoon and end up staying for dinner. If I hadn't acquired a burning desire for Native fare, I had come to like it well enough.

Sometimes, Laney and her kids were at Rose and Charlie's, and they'd watch the kids, while Laney and I went for lunch at the Hotel. Sometimes we'd stay behind, and Charlie and Rose would go for lunch.

Nadine and I continued with our walks and boat excursions and our visits to Maggie's. Nadine was two months into the four-month period over which she was gradually coming off her medication. So far, she said, she didn't notice any difference in the way she felt, and that this was a good thing. She took a keen interest in Maggie's baskets and was learning from Maggie how to weave. She was exceptionally good at it. I think Maggie was grateful to have an apprentice.

One day, when Nadine and I were walking to Old Town, taking along Matt's and Laney's two oldest children with us, I whispered to her that my period was one day overdue. She grabbed my arm with a great deal of excitement and exclaimed, "Oh, my God! Let's get a home pregnancy test. Do those tests work that soon?"

"I don't know, and anyway, Nadine, think about that. Is there anyone in the village who wouldn't go on to speculate if I picked up one of those at the Band Store?"

"I know what to do," said Nadine. "I'll ask Chris if, in a hypothetical situation, a person could get a pregnancy result when their period was, say, two days overdue...although," she added, "I'll have to make sure to tell him the hypothetical person isn't me, so he won't flip."

Later that evening, Nadine phoned and said that Chris had told her that the hypothetical person should probably wait until their period was overdue for two weeks, especially if the hypothetical person had just gone through something very stressful, such as a wedding, for example.

We laughed and laughed on the phone. I felt giddy inside.

My period was never late, and I was certain that I was pregnant, but when the result was positive, I was so happy I almost felt silly. I was also, of course, anxious to tell Daniel the news.

Jake and Daniel came in about a week later, and, sending Jake to the store on some trivial excuse, I told Daniel. I searched his eyes for a response and found only an impenetrable look.

"Daniel?" I was almost frantic.

"Well, that's a big responsibility, Laura. I hope it's not too soon for us."

But then his eyes lit up, and he grinned. "I guess that frilly thing worked."

Neither Jake nor Daniel treated my pregnancy with kid gloves, although they both mentioned I was eating more. Still, Daniel said he would find the absences more difficult because he worried about me being on my own in case anything should happen. I reassured him that I'd be fine.

The summer was almost over. In less than two weeks, it would be time for Jake to return to North Vancouver. Daniel was right. I noticed that Jake's self-confidence and maturity had grown over the summer… and that he now swore a lot. I asked him about this, seeing as Daniel rarely swore.

"Well, maybe not here," said Jake. "But you should hear him out there."

I looked quizzically at my husband, who I now realized had multiple personalities. He simply grinned and continued to chew on his toothpick.

Soon, it was the end of September and time for my annual trip to Toronto. I was looking forward to it and envisioned buying maternity clothes, although I didn't need them yet. I planned on spending a few days in Vancouver after the trip out east. It was overcast, as it usually was, when I left the Passage. I had no forebodings—only a feeling of looking forward to the next few days.

I spent my first full day in Toronto shopping, then met Richard for dinner. I arrived at the restaurant a few minutes ahead of him and sipped on a brandy glass of ice water. When Richard arrived and sat down, he accidentally knocked my glass of water over. It was the oddest moment, as if everything happened in slow motion. I saw the water spilling across the table, the glass rolling to edge of the table and Richard and I trying to catch it. Just before it smashed to the floor, I saw a piece of light reflecting off the glass. I thought a lot about this image later.

The moment passed, and Richard regaled me with the characteristics of the lawyers in the 'hot-shot,' big New York law firm he'd been dealing with. He also asked me a lot of questions about Kristy Mack and seemed a bit despondent at the fact that she was only twenty-one. Still, I could see the wheels were turning. I didn't say anything about their age difference or how they might manage to have a date. Who was I to judge? After dinner, we went to the bar in the hotel, and I drank a soft drink, while Richard sipped on a scotch. By 10, I was fast asleep.

The next morning promised to be a warm autumn day. In a hammock, on my grandfather's back porch, I lay in a haze of half-sleep. The oak trees were just changing color, and white cotton curtains edged with lace moved rhythmically in and out through the open kitchen window. I drifted off into a half-sleep, and my mind surveyed possible names for our baby.

I woke, feeling serene and still half-asleep, stretched, went into the kitchen, made coffee and returned to the porch. Not even the sound of the front doorbell ringing disturbed my musings; I walked through the house, still carrying my coffee, and looked out the living room window where Richard's car was parked in the driveway.

I opened the door. Richard was standing there, and from the look on his face, I knew that something was wrong. Adrenaline sharply brought me back to the here and now. My automatic response was, "Who is it?"

"It's Daniel—his boat has gone down in a place called Hecate Strait."

The coffee slipped from my hand, and the almond colored liquid moved downwards in slow motion circular waves. Shards of ceramic smashed across the floor. I moved sideways, until my shoulders and back were against the wall and slowly sank to the floor.

Richard knelt next to me. "The Coast Guard is searching for them. He's smart. Laura; he's strong."

"Please, God. Please, God. No."

"We can be on a 4:30 flight for Vancouver, stay the night there and catch a morning flight to the Passage. I have reserved the tickets for us. I talked to your mom, and her and Jake are already on the way there."

We drove through the quiet streets of Etobicoke to the airport. Richard asked me where Hecate Strait was. I told him that Hecate was the head witch in Shakespeare's play, Macbeth. Realizing this didn't make sense, I tried to tell him where it was, and he said quietly, "Never mind. It doesn't matter."

Even in times as these, there is social pressure to talk, but Richard and I had been friends for such a long time and through so many circumstances that I could remain simply silent. I guessed that they had called him, not wanting me to be alone to receive the news.

I was numb on the flight to Vancouver and sat next silently next to Richard. I did not cry. At the hotel in Vancouver, where we'd booked a suite, I stared at the ceiling, getting up sometimes to look through the windows. I did not sleep.

In the Passage, everyone knows who everyone else is, and events both minor and large, as well as good news and bad, rarely unfold in secret. On the morning flight to the Passage, the pilots knew, and the few boarding passengers knew. And I didn't want to talk about it, and they knew that too. And their eyes looked the other way, and so did mine.

Chapter 37

I drifted into a half-sleep on that trip to the Passage. My mind wandered and these musings were not linear When I fully woke up, it was mild turbulence as we descended into the Passage. I carried with me an odd feeling of detachment. Still, I was moved by the landscape. It was a clear, sunny day, and the mountains, and the forests and the ocean came alive. The islands of the West Coast Canadian Archipelago lay scattered across the sea, and I could see the browns and greens in the clear horizon.

Chief Charlie, my mother and Jake met us at the airstrip. The Coast Guard had found all the members of the *Aldebaran* in a life raft, blown some distance from where the boat had gone down. There was no word yet on the *Caelum* or on the *Regulus*.

The next days passed in a blur. Each day was clear and sunny. I slept next to my mother every night, grateful for her comforting presence, although if sleep came to me, I wasn't aware of it. Jake slept in his cot in the workroom and Richard stayed at the Hotel. Deep circles formed under my eyes. My mother cooked, and Charlie came over often. At other times, we went to his house. Laney looked as bad as I did. Richard had taken some time off, and I was grateful. Jake, Nadine, Richard, Kristy and I often played cards at the kitchen table. I went on long walks. Nadine offered to come, but I preferred to be alone. I walked out to Maggie's and held the cedar strands so tightly that she finally told me to just stop and sit.

Each time I returned, I hoped that I would hear that the men had been found. The Coast Guard had located the free-floating radio transmitter of the *Caelum*, along with a bunch of debris, but no sign of survivors.

The telephone became the most powerful instrument in the

house. Each time it rang, I held my breath to see if it was news that they had been found. But it was only people asking if there was any news.

On the evening of the third day, the Coast Guard called off the search and issued a news release saying that the crews of the seine boats *Caelum*, out of Waglisla, and the *Regulus*, out of Prince Rupert, were missing, and the crew presumed drowned.

I received the news of the drowning without tears and simply said I was going for a walk. I don't know why, but I headed towards the cemetery. I was maybe half crazy along that path to Old Town. Bits and pieces of words played through my head. I thought about Charlie and Rose's grief. They had not just lost a granddaughter and a nephew, but the cairn of the culture that they were fighting to hold on to.

I knelt on the ground in front of Jenn's tombstone, which had arrived just a few weeks before. It was too large for her, I thought: a big, black granite affair, with a picture of her that was taken at school last year. I wondered if Charlie would want a tombstone like that for Daniel; then I sat down on Jenn's grave and started to cry—deep, wracking sobs that left me exhausted, while the words, "Daniel is gone," played over and over inside my head, until I voiced them.

I had tried desperately to talk to God over the last few days. Standing up, I said, "God, thank you for the child. Please, let it be a girl because it will be easier for me to bring up a girl by myself."

As I stood up alongside Jenn's grave, the wind played through the trees, and I could smell the rich fragrance of cedar and the salty air. I knelt down again, leaned my head against Jenn's tombstone and whispered out loud, "Franz Boas, I need my husband. Whatever grace is given you, please give to me."

I heard a raven then, although maybe it had been chattering all along, and I made my way home.

No one noticed me when I first walked through the door. They were all too excited and were smiling. I don't know why the obvious reason for this was not apparent to me.

"What's going on?" I asked.

Charlie and Jake walked over to me, and Charlie said, "They found them, Laura. All of them—the crew of the *Caelum* and the *Regulus*. They are all alive, and only with some minor injuries."

The world started to go black. Jake caught me before I hit the floor.

No one could ever really figure out why the Coast Guard had missed them. It was someone sailing who'd found them: an American from San Francisco, who'd caught on that they were signaling from the shore of the outer island that they had drifted to.

They had only minor injuries. Daniel had a one-inch gash along his forehead that was beyond stitching.

After I'd fainted, Chris had me brought to the hospital. There, he gave me something to sleep. "Will it be bad for the baby?" I asked Chris. "No, it will be fine, and anyway maybe the baby needs some sleep too." I slept and slept and slept. During one of those times when I woke, there was Daniel, and I thought my heart would burst, but all I could do was reach out for his hand.

I started to cry, then, and apologized. "I'm sorry, Daniel. It's just that I nearly lost my mind."

"Well, you know. You, crying, people will talk, and they're already talking."

I knew that Daniel was pretty much indifferent to village gossip. I asked what they were saying.

"Well, they're saying that Daniel Hunt's boat went down, but it was his wife that ended up in the hospital, and maybe something has happened to the baby. But I know that isn't true because Chris told me that our baby is just fine."

And then he was grinning. And it was that smile. And I laughed and reached out again for his hand.

Epilogue

T*he* Caelum *was resurrected, and although they missed the summer and fall fishing season, the new boat was ready for the following spring. The construction of a high school was started, and soon the children came home to Waglisla.*

There has been some small movement forward for the Indigenous peoples of Canada. In 1982, the Canadian Constitution was repatriated, and existing Aboriginal and treaty rights were recognized. Amendments to the Indian Act in 1985 gave more power to bands over membership, removed the power of the government to automatically take away status and stopped discrimination against women who married non-Aboriginal men.

Indigenous Canadians are speaking out about the horror and reality of residential schools. The United Church and the government of Canada have made public apologies, but some denominations are scrambling to deny allegations. The outcry is becoming a surging tide that cannot be denied.

This summer, in 1990, the words 'Oka' and 'Kanehsatke' hang like a pall, and a hope, over the Passage. The generations of the past have maintained their identity as people of the First Nations through passive resistance. This may change. Many believe that if there is no progress, there will be revolution. Despite this, Daniel and I still believe that our children will be able to move easily in two worlds.

Richard was finally successful in wooing Kristy; they have two children. Kristy is now a photographer of considerable renown. They live in Toronto. Jake is continuing his talents of the past by studying Constitutional Law at the University of Victoria. Nadine, who kept her maiden name, is now Dr. Nadine Sinclair, and she works part-time for Environment Canada, studying the populations of various species. Jack is com-

pleting a master's degree in Physics and hopes to do a PhD on dating ar-
chaeological sites.

Nadine, Laney and I, and Kristy, when she comes home in the
summer, often walk with our children to Old Town. We tell them stories
about the people who are buried there. Along the way, we pick wildflow-
ers to remember the souls of Jenny Hunt and Allie Owens and others who
have died since.

And then, last night, for the first time in years, I dreamed of Franz
Boas. I saw myself in a hospital bed, holding Daniel's hand and the pool
cleared, and I was staring into the crystal-clear water of the springs at
Xvnis. I looked up at Franz Boas and we stood up and he smiled and
nodded to me and tucked my right hand under his arm. We walked down
the path that leads to the beach. The tide was high, and it was dark; the
mountains were etched in black against the brilliant sky.

We sat together along the shore on a weathered piece of driftwood.
It was a rare, warm, late fall night, with a gentle breeze coming in from
the Inlet. In the distance, I heard people laughing and talking along the
boardwalk in front of Xvnis.

Franz Boas said, "The people are speaking of land and of com-
pensation. They are speaking of self-determination."

"Yes," I reply.

"I am glad that they are asking because it means they believe they
are worth asking for things." He paused, and then said, "I hope they ask
for a lot."

"What will happen? I ask.

"If two cultures can meet as equals, then all things are possible."

We sat companionably and after a while, his voice broke the si-
lence. "It is time for you to use your gift."

"But what gift do I have?"

"The gift of moving freely in two worlds," he said softly.

I searched my mind, and then asked, "But what should I do?"

"The answer will come to you." He brought his hand up to his
head and said, "Listen here." Then he took my hand and put it over his
heart and said, "Listen here." He paused. "Do you remember what Wikash
said, that someday the Raven and the white God would meet as equals,
here at Xvnis?"

"Yes," I whispered.

"Maybe that time is coming. Look up and close your eyes and see

through the eyes of the Raven."

And for a few seconds, I flew with the Raven. As the Raven flew upward, I saw the islands of the archipelago, a dark emerald necklace spread across the sea. The Raven flew higher still, through the stars and into daylight, and I saw that we were heading towards the sun and I was filled with joy.

The Raven released me back to myself, and I found myself again alongside Franz Boas, my hand under his arm, listening to the waves fall gently on the shore.

I felt happy and serene; then, from deep inside, some fear rose to the surface.

"I am afraid," I whispered.

He took my hand and said, "The grace that is given me, I give to you."

And then he stood up, nodded to me and walked off along the beach, and was embraced by the sweet autumn night.

I slept in late the next morning. When I got up, I went into the kitchen. On the way there, I passed the laundry room where our youngest child was fumbling with the doorknob. Daniel was there at the table, reading the newspaper. I kissed the small white scar on his forehead, like I had done a thousand times before. My hand lingered on his shoulder, and I said, "I noticed April is in the laundry room, trying to get out. For sure, she is thinking about heading to the beach, and the tides up, with the wind whipping up the surf."

"Yeah, I know. That kid is more curious than a flock of ravens. I guess it's time to let her find out how dangerous that surf is. Guess I'll be getting my jeans wet." He got up and kissed the top of my head and headed down to the beach with April.

I poured myself a cup of coffee, went into my study and turned on the computer. I gazed out to the Passage for a minute, watching Daniel trail our youngest child in her dangerous explorations. Then I turned back to the computer screen, took a sip of coffee, and began to write. The first sentence that I wrote was, "I spoke to Franz Boas in a dream last night."

Acknowledgements

I could not have completed this novel without the kind support and patience of many individuals. My husband, Jim, supported me through the many hours and days, where I was mentally and physically absent. My sister, Barb, read an early draft of the novel and offered advice that much improved the writing and made the story more believable. The late Professor Philp M. Hobler was an enormous support at a time when I was floundering in my studies, and he set me on the journey to Waglisla. I would like to thank the people of Waglisla, who offered me friendship and advice on the project that became the inspiration for this novel. Finally, and with much gratitude, I thank my editor, Sharon Lax, who encouraged me, was patient, and offered invaluable insights.

Lightning Source UK Ltd.
Milton Keynes UK
UKHW010152151220
375229UK00002B/214